Bloodsong

**Other Simon & Schuster books
by Melvin Burgess**

Bloodtide
Sara's Face

**More Simon Pulse books
to challenge your imagination**

The Uglies trilogy
by Scott Westerfeld

Tithe and *Valiant*
by Holly Black

The Immortals series
by Tamora Pierce

The Farsala trilogy
by Hilari Bell

Tripping to Somewhere
by Kristopher Reisz

The Fallen series
by Tom Sniegoski

Bloodsong
MELVIN BURGESS

Simon Pulse
New York London Toronto Sydney

SIMON PULSE

An imprint of Simon & Schuster Children's Publishing Division

1230 Avenue of the Americas, New York, NY 10020

Copyright © 2005 by Melvin Burgess

Originally published in Great Britain in 2005 by Andersen Press, Ltd.

Published by arrangement with Andersen Press, Ltd.

All rights reserved, including the right of reproduction in whole or in part in any form.

SIMON PULSE and colophon are registered trademarks of Simon & Schuster, Inc.

Designed by Mike Rosamilia

The text of this book was set in Times.

Manufactured in the United States of America

First Simon Pulse edition August 2007

2 4 6 8 10 9 7 5 3 1

Library of Congress Control Number 2007920430

ISBN-13: 978-1-4169-3616-9

ISBN-10: 1-4169-3616-5

For Mary, Queen of Publicists

Bloodsong

1

sigurd

Regin said, "It's time." He smacked his lips. An old guy like him, it's all he can talk about. Adventure! And all the time there he is scowling away like it was a problem with the carburetor.

"A monster, Sigurd. A real live en. It's perfect." He licked his face like it was dipped in gravy.

"I'm too young," I said.

"Too young!" he scoffed.

"I'm fifteen. Just a boy."

"Some boy. Sigurd! What about it?" Regin crossed his arms and flopped down. He's a skinny old pig, Regin, but not stiff like most of them. He has a long bendy neck like a dog, so he can lie flat on the ground and lift his head up in the air and stare straight at you.

"I'm not going to do anything marvelous, Sig," he told me. "I just want to be around watching you do it." He tipped his head to one side and smiled. "What's up? Scared of it?" he teased.

"You won't get me into any of your crazy plans like that," I said.

For a practical person, Regin's very romantic. He crosses every "t" and checks everything twice and makes sure you have enough spare pants packed, but really he's living in fairyland. Killing dragons! I've got an adventure in mind, don't doubt me. I'm a Volson. It's what we do. But slaying dragons? Come on!

Look around you, what do you see? Not much, you might think. It's a beautiful place here—sand dunes, sea, the river winding its way down. Alf's a good ruler. My father Sigmund knew what he was doing when he sent my mother and me here when the war broke out.

Sigmund was a great man. He made friends out of enemies, peace out of war. He healed this country. That's what good government does.

Then the foreign planes came and nuked London flat, and my father and all his plans and organization with it—vaporized the lot. Even the foundations of the buildings in central London melted, they say. No one lives there anymore. Even the dust has blown away. There are trees charred with the heat of the blast as far away as Slough, but the Volson principles are still alive here in Wales. There're children playing and people going about their business, all at peace with one another—at least until the next little tyrant wants this stretch of beach and a few slaves, or until some foreign power decides we're getting above ourselves.

I want everywhere to be like this. That's my adventure. I want to put this land back together. I want the kids to grow up knowing that their kids are going to have more than they had, not less. Glory? Stuff that. War is the only dragon I want to fight.

"It'll make your name," said Regin. "They've been trying to finish Fafnir off for years. He's the real thing. It's your chance! You can show everyone what you're made of."

"There's no such thing as monsters, just people gone wrong," I said. It's an old pigman proverb, but in this case it's true—Fafnir really was a man gone wrong. He'd changed a lot, but you can always tell where a creature began. He'd grown enormous, given himself all sorts of wired-up senses— infrared, sonar, radar. He was about the most technologically advanced organism on earth, but he'd been a man once.

It makes you think. Who'd want to do that to themselves?

You know the story. The dragon on Hampstead Heath? Everyone thought it was nonsense until the first dodgy-looking photos began to circulate. That's when Regin went off to investigate. He's a clever old pig, Regin. He came back with proper evidence.

"Grrru. Must be ten meters long," Regin croaked. "Armor-coated. Some sort of liquid crystal. Look."

He dug in his pocket and pulled out—well. It looked like a limp jewel, that's the best I can do to describe Fafnir's scale. It was flat, three-lobed; it glinted and shone like a gem. Colours shot out from somewhere inside it as he draped it lightly over his fingers. Later I discovered it did that even in the dark. Maybe it was still alive.

"Diamond won't scratch it, bullets won't pierce it, but it's as flexible as skin."

"Wow." That set me off. I wanted to go straight down to the beach and try to shoot holes in it, but Regin wouldn't have it.

"Nah, nah!" he said. "I need to run some tests on it." He took the scale back and waved it in the air. It was like tissue paper. If you threw it up in the air it floated down like a leaf. You could roll it up like leather. That was some piece of engineering.

"This is the secret of beating him," he snorted. "Once I find out how to get through his skin, I can make a weapon that'll kill him."

I laughed at him, but I felt a thrill go through me despite myself. "It sounds like a lot of danger for not much gain to me," I said.

"It's not just the glory. It'd be a good deed, Sig! He terrorizes the whole area."

I shrugged. "There's a lot of suffering nearer home. Why start with him?"

Regin stood up. He shook himself. "He's got the bullion," he said, and he cocked his head at me with a little smile.

I looked up at him. I wasn't smiling now. "You know that?"

"Sure as I can be."

"We better get going then."

A nation needs gold. How do you build roads? With gold. How do you build schools and hospitals? With gold. How do you feed and clothe people? How do you get them the good things of life? How do you raise an army? Fight disease? How do you make a people grow? Gold, gold, and more gold. That bomb didn't just destroy the centers of business and government. It destroyed our gold reserves as well. We've been living like beggars every since.

Some people say the gold just melted away to nothing, vaporized. Another story is that my father's first son, Styr, came back to take it away before the bomb fell. All I know is this: A nation needs gold. Sigmund spent a lifetime raising the wealth to make this country hold together. If Regin was right, I could get it back overnight.

The gold. That's the beginning of everything.

Regin got to work straight away, but it wasn't going to be easy. Fafnir was cutting-edge stuff. He'd been using viral-recoding—using viruses to carry DNA into the cells to change you from the inside. Easy as catching a cold, much superior to the old womb-tanks. A lot of people didn't like it at first—you might remember the fuss in the papers. Viruses mean disease, and people found it hard to accept they could be used for our benefit. But it's clever stuff. You can just get on with your normal life while the changes take place. Very superior. What's more, with recoding you never had to stop. You could change day by day. As time went by Fafnir was only going to get bigger and deadlier and harder to kill. A lot of people had already tried and failed to work him out—but they weren't Regin. If anyone could do it, it was him.

First problem: That scale was more or less indestructible. We couldn't dissolve it or burn it, we couldn't file it or scrape it or chip it. It had no reactions. Regin couldn't get so much as a molecule off it. If you couldn't get a sample, how could you run tests? On he went, poor old Regin—genetics, physics, chemistry, reason—nothing could get to grips with it. It drove him mad because—well, as he kept saying, if it didn't react with anything, it couldn't be there. You wouldn't be able to see it because light would go straight through it, you wouldn't be able to touch it, because it wouldn't react with your skin or flesh. It wouldn't even make a noise. But the scale did all those things. Nothing reacted to it—but there it was. Impossible!

Now, where did something like that come from?

You know those old stories about the lift shaft in the old Galaxy building, where my grandfather used to have his headquarters? Nothing could scratch it or dent it, it never even got dirty because nothing would stick to it. It was still glittering like it was brand-new when it was a hundred years old. That disappeared after the bomb, too—so maybe it wasn't indestructible after all. What if Fafnir got his hands on that? Nothing else I ever heard of was as tough as that scale.

Regin's theory was that it was some sort of crystalline structure, diamond most like, but bound together in another way.

"Like what?" I said.

"Like the breath of a fish. Or the sound of a cat walking, or the roots of the mountain," he grunted, and then started laughing down his snout to himself, "Grun grun grun!"

"Really? Really, Regin? Are you joking?" Godpower! Regin says this world is full of objects we can never see or hear. He says the gods walk about among us all the time, but we can never know it because we can't react with them—only they can react with us. That's how they guide lives and affect us in ways we can never tell. He says there are many universes, all packed up together in exactly the same place as this one. Someone—some god—had made this scale move across from one universe to another. It was a god-object.

"Can Fafnir only be killed by a god? Is that what you're telling me?" I said.

Regin looked at me over his specs. "No. I'm saying he can only be killed with something from another world. Now what might that be? And didn't I tell you? This is made for you." He nodded. "It's time to find out."

I felt a thrill go through me then. He was right: This was mine. He must have known the whole time. What was the only thing that ever cut into the Galaxy lift shaft? What else could cut a hole in Fafnir's hide but my father's knife? What was left of it, that is.

The knife was given to my father by Odin himself. On the day my aunt was married to King Conor, he appeared and plunged it into the lift shaft and only my father was able to take it out again. Everybody knows that story, and the story of the terrible war that followed. But not so many people know the story of how the knife came to be destroyed.

It was the dawn of the final war. My father was confident that morning, according my mother, Hiordis. The population was loyal, we were well armed, he was a brilliant general. There had been many wars before in his long reign and he'd won them all. There was no reason to suppose this one was going to be any different until Odin showed up.

He appeared in their bedroom—don't ask why, it's not the sort of place you'd associate with him. My mother was sitting up in bed watching my father do his exercises. I tease her about that. She looks down her nose at me and lowers her great eyelids and purrs slightly—she has some lion in her, my mother—and she says nothing, but I think maybe she liked to sit there in bed watching the king limber up. She was younger than him by what? Eighty or ninety years? Oh, kings can live a long time without getting old. He used the tanks for that. In another ten years he would have ruled for a century.

Then Odin opens the door and walks right in. A smell of carrion came in with him. My mother pulled the covers up to her face. He walked right up to my father and held out his hand.

And my father's face just crumpled. That's how my mother described it; he crumpled. Suddenly he looked all his one hundred and twenty years. He knew at once that the god wanted his knife back. It meant the end.

He was never too keen on the gods, old Sigmund. Mother says that whenever the subject came up, he used to hold his finger to the side of his nose and say that there were a few questions needed answering before he was going to have any dealings with that bunch of crooks. He only had one prayer. "Have the grace to leave us to our own affairs. Amen!"

You can't blame him. A god who loves warfare and death and calls it poetry? What's that about? A god who steals secrets from the dead? Whose side was he on? Not the living, that's for sure. So, instead of quietly handing it over, Sigmund snatched the knife from the table where it lay close at hand and stabbed him instead. That was my father. He tried to murder God! And you know what? I think the god loved him for it.

That knife had cut diamond and tungsten for him as if they had been bananas. Odin turned away, but sure enough, it grazed his neck and left a long red scratch. Calmly Odin took it out of his hand. He didn't seem angry at what had happened; he just smiled. Then he rubbed the knife between his hands. A fine gray dust fell to the floor—all that was left of the indestructible symbol of Volson power.

"See you later," said Odin, and he turned on his heel and walked toward the door.

But Father wasn't done yet. Naked as he was, he ran after

Odin, grabbed him by the shoulders, heaved—and flung him to the ground.

"I told you," he hissed. "Stay out of our affairs!"

"I *am* your affairs," growled the god. He stood up, pushed Sigmund to one side, and left the room. By the time Father got up and opened the door, the corridor was already empty.

He told Hiordis that at least he had met his god naked, just as a man should.

That same day, Sigmund sent Hiordis, still pregnant with me, out to stay with Alf on the far coast of South Wales. The next day, they dropped the bomb on London. Puff! All gone. Hiordis says they picked up radar traces of planes, high up in the stratosphere. We thought they'd just come to keep an eye on things, same as usual. But we were getting too powerful, and this time, they came to squash us.

Hiordis and Alf didn't want to give it to me at first. I was too young, I could wait a few years, Fafnir would still be there when I was older. Blah blah blah, wait wait wait. They had a point—I'd made it myself to Regin. Okay, okay—I want to go and fight the worst monster you ever heard of because my mother says I shouldn't—so maybe I'm young and stupid. Well, maybe you have to be young and stupid to do a thing like this. To fight a dragon! As soon as she started, I felt the strength inside me, I felt the certainty. I was ready.

"You're not at your full strength," complained Alf.

"It's my time," I told him. And in the end I got my way. Neither of them could refuse me anything. People can't. I don't know why, no one ever says no to me. So I'd better be bloody right, hadn't I?

My mother went to fetch the dust. When she gave it to me my life began. I was stepping onto a road that stretched from now to my death. There were no diversions, no way back. I'd started up, and nothing could ever turn me off till I was dead and gone. I could feel the weight of years gone and the weight of the years to come passing through that moment. Destiny was there, and not just mine, either. I am the destiny of this whole nation.

You think I'm arrogant; I'm not. I was made for this—literally. My father designed me for it. Every gene in my body was picked for just this purpose. My mother brought me up for it, the gods shaped me as the keystone for this time and place. It's no credit to me. I have less choice than anyone. I'm more a machine than a human being. Sometimes I wonder if I'm even human.

Hiordis kept the dust in a small wooden box, inside another box, inside another box. Originally it was in a single steel box. My mother only realized what was going on when she looked into it one day and it seemed to her that the dust had grown. She got quite excited about it at the time, she told me, until she realized what was going on. As the dust moved, it was wearing away at the steel, and it was gradually getting mixed up with steel filings. That's why she kept it in wood after that—it was easier to tell apart. Once, it wore right through a box, and when she picked it up it spilled out all over the floor—it took her ages to clean it all up. So she kept it in several boxes to keep it safe.

I opened the box—and there it was, waiting for me. It was like sand—well, it was sand, in a sense. Some sand. I took a pinch of it between my fingers and rubbed it on the buckle of my belt. It was like scrubbing an apple with a wire brush, the buckle just rubbed away. Then I rubbed a pinch on my tooth;

nothing. And if I wasn't sure before, I was then. It was with me as it was with my father. The dust could cut anything—but not me. It was tuned in to me. It was *mine*.

"Godworld!" said Regin, and I just smiled.

I think Regin could've spent the rest of his life experimenting with that dust, but I didn't have time for that. All I was bothered about was what sort of weapon to make it into, and how to use it.

We spent hours trying to work out what the best means of attack was. We watched the few scraps of film there were of Fafnir, read everything anyone had ever written about him. What his habits were, what he ate, what he did, everything. And you know what? No one knew hardly anything. No one had even seen him eat. He did everything in private. About the only piece of what you might call personal detail there was about Fafnir was this: He liked to swim. There was a pool on the Heath not far from his citadel, and once or twice a week he'd come down to swim. There was a great path made where he crawled. It got like a mudslide when it was wet.

It wasn't much, but it was enough. This was our plan. We'd dig a hole in that track where I could hide myself, cover me over with some sort of lid, then mud, and then smooth it down so there was no disturbance. When Fafnir passed over me, that would be my chance.

"What do you think?"

Regin squinted at me. We were sitting in his lab by the window. There was that acrid laboratory smell, but outside the rain was pelting down in gray sheets and you could smell the wet earth and the cool air.

"It might work," he said.

Then I had a nasty thought. "What if he's wired for X-ray?" I said. "He'll spot me lying there under the ground."

Regin thought about it. "There's a hundred skeletons buried in the earth. Men he's killed. You'll just be one more. Infrared would be more of a danger, but anyway, we can find something to mask you. And how about this? We can dig up one of the skeletons and replace it with you, so that he won't notice you even if he can remember what lies under the ground."

I liked that! The worm would think one of his own dead had risen up to take him on. And Odin would like it. God of the dead, god of killing, god of poetry. It'd be a plan that'd suit him well.

But we still had the problem of what weapon to use. That wasn't as obvious as it seemed, either. On the end of an armor-piercing shell? What if we missed? What if the explosion blew the dust off the end before it penetrated? It wouldn't even break Fafnir's skin if that happened—the blast would get flung downward and I'd get it.

How about bullets?

We tried it out—a titanium bullet with a layer of dust on the surface. It got through the scale all right, but then it was spent. It fell out the other side like a slug coming through a lettuce leaf. So then we tried making a titanium bullet with dust mixed in right the way through it. Better. It came whacking out the other end, but—I didn't like it. There wasn't that much dust, we'd only be able to make a handful of them. The risk of missing was too high.

We must have been through every type of firearm there was before the answer suddenly dawned on me.

It was ridiculous really. Regin thought it was hilarious.

"Obvious!" he said. "So simple! Why didn't I think of that before?"

With this weapon I could carve a hole in the monster two or three meters long, from his heart to his arse. I could have his guts on the floor next to him before he knew what was going on. The beauty of it was, I'd use his own strength and weight as he passed above me to rip him open. All I had to do was stick it up out of the pit as he went overhead and his own momentum would do the rest. Fantastic. Fafnir was about the most advanced piece of technology on the planet and we were going to kill him—with a sword!

We both laughed like maniacs, but you know what? Inside me my heart was fizzing. To kill a dragon like that, hand to hand! Oh, man! This was going to be the boldest thing you ever heard!

2

the sword

So Odin's knife became a sword. Regin forged it from a steel alloy, stretching and folding the metal over and over like a ribbon to make it strong and flexible. As he hammered and folded, he dusted in the remains of Odin's knife wrapped up in microscopic packets of Sigurd's own DNA, treated to stand the heat. The DNA held the dust secure, the metal alloy held the DNA secure. The result was a slim, elegant, flexible blade that could cut through any known substance—except for the flesh of its owner.

But it had one small flaw. As he was working the bellows, a blowfly landed on Regin's forehead and stung him on his eyelid. With a yelp, the old pigman dropped the bellows to swat it off and wipe away the blood—only for a second, but in that second the heat lessened. Afterward, he examined the blade closely and could see nothing, but he knew there was a chance of a hidden flaw deep inside the metal, halfway along. Regin had done his work well and nothing on this earth could melt the metal now that it was mixed with the dust, so he said nothing of it to Sigurd. He could only hope that the damage was small and that the blade was still strong enough to do its work.

When he handed the sword over to Sigurd, Regin felt as if he was offering a prayer. The boy was so bright and perfect, at the beginning of everything. He was handing the golden child the future—not just his own future, but the future of his whole people. He was certain that Sigurd was capable of performing any task asked of him.

Sigurd gripped the handle and the weapon gripped his hand back just as it had gripped his father's hand over a hundred years before. It was more than his; it was a part of him.

The boy's first concern was simple. Turning to the wall beside him, he pushed the point lightly against the brickwork. The sword slid easily in with a slight, grainy hiss.

From his pocket, Regin plucked a small handful of fleece that he had plucked off the barbed wire during a walk the day before, and let it fall on the edge of the blade as Sigurd held it out. The wool fell through the air and across the blade, and without even changing speed, fell in two neat halves toward the ground under its own weight. Nothing could stand in the way of that blade but Sigurd himself. He tested that too, trying to slice through his hand and arm. Soon he had Regin striking him with some force, but the blade just slipped off, fell to the ground point first, and stuck in the rock like something from a fairy tale.

They made preparations to leave.

Journeys in an age with no roads were adventures in themselves. Sigmund had built roads, but on that day fifteen years before when his regime was atomized, the building and repair programs had stopped. All along the way there were ganglords, outlaws, men who would be king, men who would eat, robbers, refugees, and a frightened population to contend with.

There were many among the pigmen who did not expect Sigurd to come back. Letting a fifteen-year-old child do a job small armies had failed at—it was absurd! Hiordis herself was terrified for him, but she was unable to stop him. Sigurd was a prodigy. His father had planned him with science, prayer, and love, and no one, not even his own mother, was ever able to deny him. But now that the time had come, Sigurd himself was uncertain. On that last night of his boyhood when he went to see his mother, he was pale and unhappy. Hiordis thought her boy was sad to be leaving her, but when she took him in her arms, he began to tremble and cry.

He was always open, ready to share his worries and fears, but she had not seen him so distressed since he was little. "What is it?" she asked him. Sigurd shook his head, but when she pressed his face into her tawny neck he whispered,

"I'm scared, I'm so scared."

Hiordis's heart cracked. She squeezed him tight and stroked his head. "There," she murmured; but the words "Don't go" failed in her throat. It could be that he was going to his death, right now, at the beginning of his life. She wept, but her instinct that he was made for this was even stronger than her mother's love.

"It'll be all right, you know it will," she said at last. It was the best she could do.

There was a long pause, and then he nodded his head. He was Sigurd, son of the great king and the hope of the future. He had been so independent, so sure of himself all his life, and often Hiordis had found this hard; she wanted to mother

her boy. But when at last he came to her as a child, she sent him on his way. The mother had no words of comfort to offer her son. It was always this way with Sigurd—so vulnerable, so easily hurt, so bravely on his way to a destiny no one had a say in, not even himself. She never knew whether or not she'd let him down that day.

In the morning, he was dry eyed. Good-byes had already been said. There was only time for one more embrace before he was mounted and gone with Regin into the early morning mist.

3
the journey east

Their journey took them down the south coast of Wales and east along the route followed two hundred years before by the old M4 motorway. The meadows of wild flowers that had covered these ways when Sigmund was young had given way first to birch trees breaking up the tarmac, then to sycamores and oaks. A track had been preserved in the center for a long time, but as the tarmac beneath became broken up by roots, it became too rutted to work. Sigmund had rebuilt a decent metalled road alongside the strip of woodland where the motorway once was, but now even that had fallen into disrepair and the road was on the move again. Those with carts and on foot had to toil through the mud. Sigurd and Regin were mounted, able to cut across the meadows and run through the woods.

Along the way they had to pass through five separate administrations, varying from loose coalitions of towns and villages who had banded together for their own security, to corporate organizations, would-be nations, and ganglords. Food was scarce, wealth scarcer, and traveling across country was a fraught business. Alf's little kingdom in the far west was too far away to trouble any of the bigger players, but the whole country knew that Sigmund had designed a son to rule after him. He was a Volson, a rallying point for anyone interested in either war or peace. Many people would follow him, but many others wanted him dead. The two travelers needed to be well armed and well mounted, too.

Mounted? A king's son in this age of science? But car or horse—what's the difference? Some pump blood, some pump oil; some run on oats, some run on fuel. Some did both. There wasn't a stretch of road in England longer than a few miles that could take a car or truck these days. It was tractors or 4x4s if you wanted to drive, but they were for the rich and wealth attracts attention. Horses were the usual way of traveling distances—they could be easily bred, they were cheap to run. The better ones had improvements—alloy frames, carbon-fiber muscle systems, and so on. The advantage of beasts like this for people like Sigurd and Regin, wealthy, traveling alone, was that you could be driving a racing car and a tank combined, but it looked no different from an old nag.

Regin was riding something of this sort—a beast that had so many improvements to its skeletal, muscle, nervous, and other systems that not much more than the central nervous and hormonal systems remained of the organic base. Sigurd was mounted on something of another order: a real, live cyborg.

He had been given to Alf long ago by Sigmund, and Alf in turn had given it to Sigmund's son. He was called Slipper, a name Sigurd had given him when he was only four years old. No one alive had the skills to build something like him. Two systems in Slipper worked together, side by side or on their own. If the flesh was destroyed, the machine took over; if the machine broke down, the beast took over. In either case, the damaged parts were regrown, regenerated, fixed, or replaced. He grazed on grass, flesh, or scrap, one just as well as the other, self-repairing, self-regulating, self-building. He was the only one of his kind left, one of three made at the height of the old king's reign. Technology was not enough to make these creatures. Odin himself was said to have had a hand in their brewing.

The name Slipper had come about like this: Hiordis liked to tell stories to her boy, and the ones he loved best were the old myths, hero tales. One of his favorites was the story of Perseus and the Gorgon Medusa. Alf's folk didn't wear shoes, they liked the feel of the earth and mud under their trotters and between their toes, so Hiordis always made her son wash his feet and wear slippers in the house. Since he had no idea about any other footwear, she had explained the winged sandals worn by Perseus as slippers. So, when he saw the horse running across the beach, Sigurd had said that he went as fast as a flying slipper. Slipper it was from that day on.

In secret storage compartments inside the horses, Sigurd and Regin carried a great deal of sophisticated hardware. Regin was after other treasure than bullion—it was technology he was after. Fafnir had raided near and far, beyond the sea, perhaps even beyond the ocean. Genetic technology had never been loosed into the population anywhere else except Britain and that, with the proximity of the godworld, made it a place foreign powers wanted kept down. But in terms of straight technology, Britain was a backwater, a third-world dumping ground for cheap, outdated goods. Regin was greedy for imported science. Companies like the Destiny Corporation and the Norn Group in particular made products he wanted, devices for use in the science of government that manipulated mood and mind. It was rumoured that Fafnir had captured machines such as Fear, Greed, and Awe, which could stimulate and manipulate the feelings they were named after. And was it true, as old Sigmund used to speculate, that some of the African superpowers had other, even more sophisticated machines? Did Odin really exist? Jesus? Could the Destiny Corporation generate godhead?

And then, there was Andvari's ring. A small, solid-state device, disguised as a gold finger ring, it was rumored that Fafnir had stolen it on a raid to one of the Asian superpowers, but he had not known what it was he was stealing, or how it worked. Rings of this kind were inventions with a more practical turn than those that generated emotions and godhead. They were made to set the future to work on your account. They were destiny machines, controlling the chaos of chance events into luck, either good or bad. The kings and presidents of Nigeria, China, and South Africa were said to wear similar rings on their fingers, generating a field to turn chance events in their favor. But Andvari's ring was the opposite. It turned chance against you. Within its field of influence, nothing could work out well in the end.

In other words, the ring was a curse.

Yoking the future to your wishes—that was a prize worth dying for in Regin's eyes. This ring, if it existed, had to be destroyed; it was here only to make the years to come as sour as the ones that had passed, a funnel to channel destiny down to the darkness. It closed doors, crushed hopes, ended. But before he destroyed it, Regin wanted to understand it, to unravel how it was made. His hope was that he could learn how to make one that served good fortune, and make luck favor the home market.

But Regin said nothing of this to Sigurd. He was worried that the boy would think that the ring was too dangerous, and demand that it be destroyed before he had found out how it worked.

Sigurd himself carried a small arsenal of weaponry hidden in Slipper's hold. He wasn't only going to cut the dragon open, he was going to blow it to pieces, as well. Odin alone knew how difficult such a monster would be to kill—and to keep dead. Resurrection was no longer an impossible science.

That's how Sigurd began his first adventure—in disguise, on a horse that wasn't a horse, with a saddlebag full of science and a sword forged with grit from the godworld. There were secrets kept from him. And burning in his heart, a hope that he could, with the strength of his bare hands and his love for the world, turn darkness into light, bad luck into good, and sorrow into gladness.

So he set off with his mentor to win the finance he needed to drive hope through the heart of a riven land.

As they traveled east, the land changed. Outside Alf's territory there were more signs of conflict—hungry people, injured people, ruined buildings, poisoned fields, and war hospitals. There were whole slave villages, the populations ill fed, ill kept, ill used. And what for? The owners could have used their people well and not gone without themselves. But they considered that they were doing these people a favor in the first place just letting them live on the land. They could have brewed some witless halfman machine that would work day and night for a century on sunshine and cabbage and never complain. Sentience was a luxury in the workforce.

Farther east the settlements grew fewer, the inhabitants less and less human—from dogmen to dog, from pigmen to pig. They were closing in on the poisoned heart of the country. Hedgerows and trees shrank and darkened, the roadsides and wastelands were full of strange looking plants. They began to see signs of halfman misfits—broken monsters begging for help in the hedges or roaring on the road; flocks of strange birds soaring above them, calling out promises and offering bribes, trying to strike deals if they'd just follow them to their roost. There was only one end to those promises. Then, as they got closer still, big creatures began to disappear and were replaced by little things— rats with odd faces, giant insects, and crippled reptiles. The gene pool close to London had been scrambled. Just as armies long ago used to sow the fields around a conquered city with salt to prevent people ever coming back and growing crops, so the new conquerors made sure that nothing that bred here would ever again come out straight. They had scattered chemicals that twisted the codes of life out of shape.

Now the plants began to die. Sigurd watched the trees wither as each day advanced, their leaves becoming yellow and spotted, their bark cracked. The rubble and ruins of the old city accumulated, but where a day behind them it had been green with brambles and bindweed, now the vegetation was yellowing and ill. The brambles thinned, grew weedy and malformed, then disappeared. The rubble became covered in a layer of moss—beautiful, and as still as a ghost. Eventually, even that disappeared.

The dragon was a horror, but this man-made devastation made it clearer than ever to Sigurd that Fafnir was only a little thing. You can kill a dragon, but a sick society was a monster with a million heads. If you kill one, there are a hundred more ready with the same thoughts and ambitions ready to take its place. Humanity, he thought—that's a monster you can never kill; and it would be inhuman even to try.

By the time they came within the remains of the old city walls from the days when man and halfman were at each other's throats, there was nothing. It was a desert of broken brick and glazed sand. Occasionally they saw some scrawny lizardy thing scurrying among the rocks, the odd cockroach or beetle, a few twisted lichens and tough little plants, but that was it.

Regin seemed to be unaffected by the horrors of the broken landscape. He was getting excited by the treasures ahead of them. He wondered what new powers they would win for themselves in the dragon's hoard.

"Power, what good will that do us?" asked Sigurd, disgusted by what he had seen of power in this place.

Regin was amazed at the boy's attitude. "Isn't it good to be strong?" he asked.

"You start off being more than human, but you end up being less. Look at Fafnir. They say he was a man once," said Sigurd.

"That'll never happen to you," said Regin with conviction. But Sigurd was unconvinced. How strange, Regin thought, that even Sigurd, who had been given all the gifts, still found something in himself to find fault with—his own strength.

4
despair

Sigurd was right. Every tyrant loses some of their humanity along the way, but none ever carried it so far as Fafnir. His dominion was over rock and gold, he did his best to destroy any thinking creature that came near him, and to this end he had transformed himself into a weapon of war. It would take a taxonomist to deduce his humanity, but only fifty years ago he had walked on two legs. His miraculous skin, as Sigurd guessed, originated from the lift shaft in the Galaxy Tower; yes, Fafnir knew all about the Volsons and Sigmund's knife. If he'd known its remains still existed he would have been out on the Welsh coast long ago to deal with Sigurd, Hiordis, Alf, and anyone else who might have access to it. As it was, he believed that no living creature had the means to pierce him. Fafnir had his own plans for the nation—to own it. But he was in no hurry. He had time on his hands. The monster considered himself immortal.

Even so he possessed countless defensive mechanisms. As Regin had speculated, he had radar, infrared, and magnetic imaging built into his nervous system, and he could wire himself into various security systems set up around his citadel while he slept. Organic security utilized plants or even animals to pick up vibrations and transmit information back to him. Fafnir might have been better to live in a forest, where so many living things could have protected him, but he liked the desolation of London. Here, there was no traffic, no ambiguity. The only people who came here, came for him.

Fafnir was clever, but for every trick there's another trick. As a technician, Regin was Fafnir's match. Invisibility and silence were arts well known to him. The monster slept undisturbed as they closed in.

At the Heath, the landscape degraded even further. They were near the epicenter of the blast; the subrock here had melted. A grotesque vitreous surface glinted around them, stuck in the form it had taken fifteen years ago when the intolerable heat of the bomb had blossomed in the sky. This was once the heart of the country. It was hard to imagine anyone living here ever again.

Like ants across the broken land, they began the ascent up to Hampstead Heath. Here began signs of Fafnir's occupation. He'd raised earthworks, dug trenches, laid coils of razor wire in glittering loops stretching from horizon to horizon. They wandered in and out of minefields, trying to avoid the sensors posted everywhere. Sigurd thought, How scared he must be! How mad and miserable, to live his life hoarding his gold all alone.

As dusk began to fall, they found the most extraordinary sight of all. They turned a ridge of glassy waste and rubble, and there, hidden in a dip in the land, was the skeleton of a vast creature. It must have been eight meters long. The bones were iridescent, tinged with the colors of alloy and carbon polymers. Scattered among them were wires, fibers, and other devices, some organic, others manufactured, some both. The huge bones seemed to have sunk into the rock beneath it with their weight, and yet when Sigurd picked one up, he almost fell back. It was as light as a feather.

"Polymers. Clever. So that's how something so vast can fly," remarked Regin.

"Fafnir," whispered Sigurd. A ray of hope sprang in him. Was the monster already dead?

But Regin shook his head. "Fafnir as he once was, or could be," he said. "He's cloned himself at some point."

"Cloned? What for?"

"Any number of reasons. Perhaps he found alterations that necessitated going back to an earlier version of himself. He'll have stored genetic material and other blueprints from various stages of his development, to be on the safe side."

"But wouldn't he need to store his own mind and his memories to do that? Is that possible?"

"There are stories." Regin grunted and shrugged. "Fafnir has been abroad."

For the first time, Sigurd had a failure of hope. Fafnir was impossibly, hopelessly dangerous. A scientist, a wizard, a monster; a tank, a gunship . . . was there anything he wasn't? What chance had he got to kill such a thing with just a sword, however sharp? He began to pick among the bones as if he could find some clues to help him out of the dilemma, but he could see no way out.

By now the light was fading. Tomorrow they would set their trap, ready to spring it the next morning when Fafnir went down to the water to bathe. The site with the skeleton was hidden in a dip. It was as good a place as any to make their camp. Sigurd would rather have slept anywhere else, but he was ashamed of his steadily growing fear and said nothing.

As they made camp, the fear began to rise up in him. He fought it, but it was unstoppable. By the time their little shelter for the night was ready, he felt like weeping with it. Regin had warned him that Fafnir would have Fear, Terror, and other devices working for him. He told his old mentor that he was feeling uncomfortable, and Regin turned up his blockers, but it made no difference.

The fearful vortex in his stomach did not stop him from falling asleep, but as he slept a cliff of terror continued to grow inside him. In the dark of the night he woke up from a dreadful dream, retching with fear, wet through with his own urine, in the realization that he was utterly unprepared to deal with this. He had been designed, conceived, and brought up to be a hero, but alone in the night the truth came to him. He'd had such a soft life playing in the breakers on the sandy beaches of South Wales, while everyone around him promised him that the world would fall at his feet as soon as he lifted his arm. Now, in this awful landscape, armed only with a sword, facing a foe that armies ran from, Sigurd realized what a fool's mission he was on. The world was huge and ancient and wicked; he was helpless and young. What hope did he have? He had been fooling himself. Worse, he had been fooled. Why had his friends and family let him believe such lies?

Sigurd opened his eyes and looked up into the bright, inhuman sky. He had been set up to fail. His father had intended him to inherit power, not win it from nothing. He was going to let everyone down and die here, soaked in his own piss. In a few hours he would face the dragon. He could taste death, his death, in his mouth now.

Unable to stay still any longer he sat up suddenly. Next to him, Regin stirred.

"What?" he whispered.

Sigurd turned to stare at him. "I can't do it," he whispered.

"What?" Regin could not decipher the words. They were half choked. Even if he had heard them, Regin, like everyone else, assumed the boy was destined to win. They would have made no sense to him.

Sigurd paused. "I need a pee," he said.

"Be careful to stay in range," said Regin.

Sigurd nodded, got out of his bag, and picked his way through the tall bones of Fafnir's other self. He wandered around distractedly, trying to think what on earth he could do to escape this dreadful death, when there was a noise behind him. Thinking that it was the dragon come for him already, he turned with a scream—but it was only Regin. Sigurd's voice had alarmed him. He came closer and peered into his face.

"Sigurd?" he said. Sigurd looked back and tried to smile and to tell him that it was all right, but what came out instead were tears.

regin

What could I say? I loved him, but I had my orders. Alf's not a bad man, ambitious in the nicest way. He only wants to be a good stepfather, the one who brought up the great king and set him on his way. He'd never betray Sigurd. No one ever could! We loved him too much.

He's just a child. I have children myself, five of them, but I don't see that much of them. Their mother said I work too hard for family life, but Sigurd's been like a son to me. All I wanted to do was take him in my arms and say, Sssh, I understand. It's your choice—'course you can go home! But I didn't. We were all so convinced about his greatness. Even his mother never told him not to do dangerous things. We all thought he was some sort of big hero and it turns out he's just a nice kid who's good at games. Here he was taking on the biggest shit in the world because we expected him to and now he was realizing what I was realizing too: It was out of his league.

But he couldn't be allowed to betray himself. I couldn't have that.

So I sat him down and gave him a talking to. Pep talk. How brave he was, how Odin loved him, how he was destined for greatness. The sword that only he could use, all that. And all the way through he was nodding away. Fine, okay, he understood, but he couldn't do it anyhow. He was too scared. He'd failed before he ever got there, that's all there was to it.

Sigurd, see, I said, those dark thoughts you have—they're not real. Fafnir has some strange things hidden away up here. Men have killed themselves from fear just because they wandered too close to the Heath before now. He owns the secret to control men's thoughts. I had devices at work to counter that, but Sigurd wasn't proving as strong as we'd hoped. He was proving to be a sensitive little duck. Not much use in a hero, eh? What would it be like for him away from my instruments, lying in a pit under the earth waiting for the dragon to come? Others had lain in wait for Fafnir before and not one of them was still alive by the time he came. Some ran; some died of fear, some were suicides. What chance did he have? Our wonderful golden boy! He wasn't even going to get near enough to smell his breath.

Not that I told him that. I said, "So it ain't your fault, my dear. It's not real, all this fear. It's generated. It's those devices Fafnir has that make you feel so weak and frightened, that's all."

He looked at me and shook his head, but I was getting angry by this time. This was bigger than him. He had no right! What other chance did we have? What if someone else got hold of all that weaponry, all that wealth? He had to try! What was his life worth after all? You could rule the heart of every man alive with what Fafnir had in that black citadel of his, for good or for bad. We're the good. We should have it. Anyone can see that.

He wept and wept. All snot and tears and pissy pants. I put my arms around him despite all the mess and he cuddled into me—just like when he was little. And I didn't say, Yes, m'dear, we've asked too much, you're far too young. Let's go home and have another look in a year or two. I didn't say, Well, of course, actually Fafnir is technically almost impossible to kill. I just said, It'll be better in the morning, like it was a bad dream or a spot of exam nerves. I don't know why I didn't just pack up our bags and go home. I suppose, the thing is, somewhere inside me, I believed along with all the other idiots that he was the one. Funny thing. I just can't bear the idea that he's no better than me. He has to be better than all of us.

He broke my heart that night. Such a little fool! I don't think he knows what a lie is. All the time I was urging him into the jaws of death for the sake of humanity, but actually it was all for me. I wanted him to win for me. Yes, I wanted the products of the Destiny Corporation and the Norn Group technology. I wanted Andvari's ring; but it wasn't just that. I wanted to believe in him. I'm a cynical old pig, I've broken my snout on hard facts too often to believe in much anymore, but I still want to think that a pure heart can defeat all the wickedness in this world. So I was pitiless, even though it broke my heart to do it.

You know what scares me most? That I'll betray him. Someone's going to do it sooner or later. What if it was me? All the time I was holding him and comforting him I was thinking, Don't let it be me. Please don't let it be me!

I got him back to his sleeping bag in the end. I doubt if he slept, I only got a few hours myself. Then came the dawn and the beginning of a long day. I was busy setting up my surveillance and blocking gear and so on. He just lay in his bag like a corpse, didn't speak, didn't move—didn't run away, either, mind. I was angry at him for letting me work alone—he could have helped.

Yes, such a long day. It seemed to go on forever, but it came and went anyhow, and then it was time.

I said, "It's time." He didn't move, just lay there staring at space. God knows what he was thinking. I didn't know whether to be furious or relieved. It'd be the death of all my ambitions— no ring, no nothing—and how would I explain that back in Wales? No one would understand. At least I wouldn't have his death on my conscience, I suppose. I sat down next to him. Didn't nag him, it was too late for that. I just sat there and waited.

After an hour I said, "It's time, Sigurd. It's past time. You going?"

He got to his feet and wiped his mouth. He looked out into the darkness and then back at me.

"Wish me luck!" he said.

"Good luck? You don't need it!"

"I'm going to die tonight," whispered Sigurd. He pulled a face—I don't know what emotion it expressed—and before I could say another word, he ran out into the night.

6

sigurd

I was running across bent over double to the remains of a low stone wall, going so fast I was toppling forward. I was dead already, there was nothing to lose. I flung myself facedown in the dirt. I retched again, pure bile. Shit! The fear's supposed to stop once you get going. I pulled my face out of the mess and looked back. Regin was out of sight already, hidden safe away.

I felt so *betrayed*. Everyone had led me to this. That's why I couldn't say no, that's why I couldn't run away. It wasn't me doing this—it was them. My father, my stepfather, my friends, Regin, my own mother. They were sending me to die and I was going along with it. Coward, I said to myself. Coward! I did what they said because I lacked the courage to do anything else.

I got up and started to crawl along, keeping down under the cover of the wall. At the end of the wall I was sick again. I looked at it hanging out of my mouth in strands and I thought, I'm still here. I didn't mean I was still alive. I meant, I was still myself. Dead or alive, this was my fate. The time and place and manner of my death—these things are fixed. All I have of my own is how I face it. And this is how—on my hands and knees with green vomit hanging out of my mouth, scared shitless.

"Today is a good day to die," I whispered to myself. I was almost tempted to walk the rest of the way just for the style of it. But you've got to try. That's right, isn't it? You've got to try. Stupid! Even then I was hoping to survive.

I got to my feet and ran down the muddy slope that led to the lake. There was Fafnir's track—a muddy rut, two meters wide, with the mud squidged up at the sides where his weight had crushed the earth. Gods! He was just so vast. This was where he slid on his way down to the pool to swim. I'd seen the film of it. It was poor quality film, shot from a mile away, but you could still see how he went down there like a kid on a slide, rolling and twisting in the mud until he hit the water like a ship being launched. This time he was going to disembowel himself on the way down.

Not. He'd dig me out of the ground like a badger digs up baby rabbits.

We'd already picked a place where a skeleton was buried so that the monster's X-ray eyes wouldn't see anything amiss. I pulled off my backpack, unbuckled the spade from the straps, and got digging.

It was a joke. Heroes and dragons! Fafnir was the most advanced piece of military hardware on the planet. What did I have? A sword. I was so dead.

Actually, I had a few other things. A Dranby-Cocke machine gun with five hundred rounds and a shotgun with explosive shells. It might as well have been a slingshot. I needed a fleet of helicopter gunships and a nuclear warhead to see this bastard off. Still—you gotta try. As I dug, I thought to myself, okay, if I have to die, I'm going to die as if my life depended on it. Does that make sense? This digging in the cold clay, the vomit, the piss, the fear and loneliness. It was *mine*. This was *my* death. It was all I had and I wasn't going to miss out on one drop of bile. I had no choice. It was life. It was shit life, but it was all I had.

Out there in the brightness of the security lights I was like a black fly on a white plate. I was relying on Regin's bag of tricks. He reckoned he could use Quiet Technology to hide me from Fafnir's security system on the small area from where he was hidden to where I was digging. It was backbreaking work. Fafnir's weight had crushed the mud into a dense clay; I had to lever out every spadeful. Every second I expected him to appear, but either Regin had done his work well or the dragon was asleep, or playing with me, or something. Gradually I scraped away a grave for myself, over a meter deep and just long enough for me to lie down in. It wasn't done yet, though. I had to camouflage it. I had some short ribs of invisible plastic with me—I don't mean invisible to the eye, I mean invisible to X-ray and so on—and some latex sheet in my pack. I laid the ribs over the hole and rubbed the latex in the mud before I stretched it over the pit and smoothed it over.

I wished Regin was there. I didn't want to die alone. But this was my place, that was his. I had to die; he had to watch.

I'd come this far, though.

I was just about ready to push my pack in and follow it down when I heard a sound. I looked up and there was an old man standing by the side of the track watching me.

My heart leapt. Fafnir? Could it be him? Could he shape-change? No one ever said so. So what was this old bloke doing here, standing watching me like I was a workman digging a hole in the road?

"What are you doing?" I said, getting to my feet. Then I thought, A spy! I felt at my belt for my knife.

The old man took no notice. He simply pointed down at the trench. "Haven't you thought what will happen when Fafnir's blood pours out into the trench and his body slumps down on top of it? What will happen then, Sigurd? How will you escape?"

I was about to grab him, but he flashed me a warning look. "Listen to what I say, boy," he snapped. I stopped. There was something about him. I was finding it difficult to think.

I glanced up the slope to where the dragon would come. I had to hide! But the old man had a point. I scowled, not knowing what to make of him.

"You'll drown in his blood." He pointed down. "Dig a channel out to the side, like the blood gully on a knife. The blood will run off and you'll have a way out."

"But I have no more latex. He'll see!"

I was in a panic already, but the old man shook his head. "Dig the channel here, where the mud slopes up. It'll be hidden from him when he comes down the track from his citadel . . . at least until it's too late."

He had a point. But I was suspicious. "How do you know so much about Fafnir?"

The old man smiled and glanced up at me. He was wearing a wide-brimmed trilby and a herringbone coat, dripping with the rain. He had a short gray beard and only one eye.

"Sigurd, my love. You were wishing you weren't alone. I'm here now. Do as I say."

I frowned at him, trying to work it out. What on earth was this—in the middle of this destroyed land with the dragon only half a mile away, and this old guy turns up in his herringbone coat like it was the high street in some little country town talking about blood gullies and reading my mind? But what he said made sense. I thought that maybe he was keeping me occupied until Fafnir got here, but I did what he said anyway. I was so tired, but I picked up the shovel and started to lever more clods of rock-hard clay out of the ground. He stood there with his hands behind his back and watched.

"But don't try to avoid his blood. If you bathe in the blood of Fafnir, you'll take its qualities. No weapon will ever harm you then, Sigurd."

"You know too much," I said; and as soon as I'd said it, I realized—my god! Who knows too much? Who has only one eye? It was Odin, the Allfather. Odin! He'd come here in person to help me.

How can I describe that feeling? Odin was with me! It didn't mean I was going to live—not with him by me. Odin is the god of violent death. Maybe he'd come to take me with him—not that I needed any help to die here on the Heath, waiting to face the dragon. But—the god was with me. He had come to be with me.

My first thought was to bend my knee to him. But then I thought of my father, who had never accepted his fate but fought against it. I remembered the story of how he wrestled the god to the ground on the last night of his life. That's something, to wrestle with god! I always thought that was the most glorious thing I ever heard of. And—I don't know why, maybe because I'd already decided I was going to die, I'd lost everything already—but I suddenly threw down the spade, leapt over the trench that lay between us, and grabbed hold of him. I had the god in my hands! I twisted him round, forced him down. He grunted in surprise and I saw his face flush with anger. He was strong, but I was stronger, and I felt him yield to me. Then I had him, he was down in the mud and . . .

And then I was holding his coat in my hand and the man was gone. I thought to myself, What a fool! Fighting the gods! But maybe no worse than fighting a dragon.

"Thanks!" I called out into the rain. "Thanks, old man!" Why I should thank him after trying to fight him I don't know. He was my god—my destiny. Everything that I felt that day was of Odin—the fear and the poetry of fear, and the blood lust and the embracing of death. I loved him almost like a lover. But although I had to accept, I didn't have to go quietly, and I don't think he held it against me, although I made him slip in the mud and lose his coat.

Then I bent my back again to the task he had set me. I dug a gully leading down, hidden by a ridge of mud, and then I was ready. I offered up a prayer—my father's prayer. "And have the grace to leave us to our own affairs. Amen!" Then I slid down under the earth, into the grace of the grave. I pulled the latex over the gap where I came in, got out my rations, my water, and my weapons, and began the wait.

7

1st death

Regin had told Sigurd that the dragon would come to bathe at the pool that night, or maybe the next, but he was wrong. Fafnir changed his habits from week to week, day to day, even from hour to hour, so that there could be no predicting him. As luck had it, he didn't come that night, nor the night after, nor the night after that. Sigurd had only a handful of dried fruit and a bottle of water with him and that was soon finished. In the total darkness underground, in growing fear, with his food and water all gone, the boy very soon lost all sense of time and reason. No light or sound crept into his little prison. The smell of the cold clay filled his nostrils and then seeped into his whole body until he felt he was a part of it.

Hours passed and he was already unsure of the day. By the end of the first night, Sigurd was so unhinged with fear and darkness that his dreams had become as real as the cold earth he lay in. In his mind the dragon came a dozen times; in his mind he died a dozen times and still he lay there and suffered, stiffening like a corpse.

In the shit and the piss and the cold mud underground, in the darkness that his mind populated with phantoms—surely none of them worse than the reality waiting for him above—Sigurd at last seemed to awake; someone, something, was approaching. He knew it wasn't Fafnir, the tread was too light. It was the old man. He stood quietly above Sigurd for a minute or two before he began to work. He had come to heap more mud up on the latex, smoothing it down, sealing Sigurd even more firmly into his tomb. Grateful for something to listen to, Sigurd lay still and said nothing while the old man worked. It was a long job; Odin seemed to want to be sure that not even the air could get in or out of the little tomb underground. As the clay heaped up above him, the latex skin sank closer and closer to his face, and Sigurd lay still and listened until the work above his head was done, and the figure retreated.

Then came the bad air. The heaving of the chest, the tearing pain and desperation. Was this another nightmare? The blackness entering beyond his eyes and into his soul; the body begging for fresh air. But there was none. The god had sealed the tomb against that. Still Sigurd waited, faithful to his fate. Now his limbs began to twitch and shudder, his hands involuntarily to snatch and claw at the covering above him— but it was too late now, the weight was too great, the clay too densely packed, the fiber sheet too strong for him to make any impact at all. At last, with the air all gone and his struggles exhausted, Sigurd ceased to breathe and began to turn blue.

Of that time, what can we say? The grave is the most private place. What words are heard? Who visits us, apart from the worm? It is said that there are secrets only the dead can understand and that the Allfather knows how to make them speak. Perhaps that's why Odin murdered his favorite underground. But after death, came the divine. Odin opened the gully he had told Sigurd to dig, entered into the grave, and lay there with him. What passed between them? Don't dare ask! This is death; it is beyond the understanding of the living. For us there is only silence to hear. Odin came; that is enough. Whether it was to question or to whisper his own secrets to the dead boy, we shall never know. But there he breathed new life into him. Odin, the god who turns soldiers into priests, poets and angels, blew death away, reversed decay, and turned the bitterness of fear and pain into joy—the joy of life, the joy of living. Sigurd would never fear death again.

After the god left him, Sigurd lay very still, not even breathing; he didn't need to. He lay for another day in utter stillness until at last he felt the ground shaking around him and he knew that the dragon was coming. Then he lifted his head, drew in air, bared his teeth at the unseen sky above his head, and prepared to die again in a torrent of blood.

It was a simple plan, and like so much that is simple, it had to be done well. Sigurd was to plunge the sword up through the clay at exactly the right moment. Fafnir was traveling fast; too soon and the monster would see the sword and fling himself aside. Too late and he would miss the vital organs. In his dark cell underground, all Sigurd had to go on was the shaking of the ground around him.

Fafnir was sliding like an otter on a mud slide by the water's edge. In the fifteen years that he had ruled Hampstead Heath and all that remained of London around it, this was his only sport—to slide out of his citadel on his belly and plunge headfirst into the water below. To Sigurd, it sounded like a train rushing toward him—every second he thought the monster was over him, but still the noise grew, still he held back waiting for the perfect moment. Odin would tell him when, he thought. Then suddenly the latex ballooned down above him. For a split second the thought was in his mind: Hold back, lie low, you can still live. Then he lunged upward with the blade with all his strength, up through the latex and the mud, up through the impossible, impassable skin and deep into the bowels of Fafnir.

The sword was wrenched violently along in the direction the dragon was traveling, and Sigurd was crumpled violently up against the end of the chamber with such force that the steel of the sword cracked. Stunned, Sigurd hung on for a moment longer while the dragon, forcing his claws deep into the clay to stop his flight, continued down the slope and the sword carried on with its deadly work. Then, as it hit the pelvic bone, the blade snapped. There was a terrifying scream above him like a bomb falling, and a torrent of blood and guts came tumbling down into the trench, covering Sigurd's eyes and filling his mouth. Stuffing the stub of the sword into his belt, he began fighting his way upward, toward air and life.

He burst out of the ground in a rush of blood like a baby coming into the world for the first time. Fafnir had stopped himself just short of the water and lay there right by him, writhing on the ground on his side, swinging his great tail from side to side and scooping his arms in front of him in a desperate effort to force his spilled guts back into his body cavity. There was a three-meter wound in his belly, from his sternum to his tail. He saw Sigurd rise out of the ground and swung at him with a groan, but the boy danced to one side. In the same movement he pulled the machine gun from his back and fired, a hundred rounds in three seconds, raking up and down directly into the wound. Fafnir roared in pain and flailed. Inside the great wound he had cut, Sigurd could see his diaphragm moving as his lungs worked and the pulsing beat above where the great heart did its work. There was a deep gash in his sternum where the blade had first struck; exactly right.

The boy dropped the machine gun, pulled the shotgun off his back, walked right up to the monster, thrust the double barrels in under the breastbone and up until he felt them press against the beating muscle inside. Then he gave it both barrels.

"Got you, you fucker! Now die!" he screamed, and jumped back to watch. The wound throbbed violently as the shells exploded. Fafnir screamed and clawed at him but Sigurd was dashed to one side as a fountain of blood burst over him. The dragon groaned again and rolled back onto his front, reaching out with his great clawed hand in a last effort to recapture his spilled insides. He took a deep sigh, which Sigurd was certain would be his last, rolled over so that the wound was buried in the mud, and settled his great and beautiful head upon the bloody ground. But his yellow eye was still half open, and he fixed Sigurd in his stare. There was a long, still moment. Then the dragon spoke.

"A child, a beautiful child," he whispered. "Who are you?"

"Sigurd Volson, son of Sigmund."

Fafnir, who had closed his eye in pain, opened it again to stare at his killer. Sigurd frowned back. He was thinking—I blew your heart to shreds! Why aren't you dead? What's happening?

The dragon coughed and snarled. "Brother!" he hissed.

"No brother of mine!"

"This is the kind of hero you are. I'm Styr. Do you know me, boy?"

"They call you Fafnir."

"They know nothing."

Styr! Could it be true? Sigmund's first son who had run off after killing his aunt and clone-brother. Had he spent all these years turning himself into this?

Sigurd was shaken, but he didn't show it. "If you ever were my brother, you gave it away long ago. What sort of a man turns himself into this?"

"I was invulnerable!" boasted Styr. "I ruled. Lord of London!"

Sigurd laughed. "Ruled over what?" he demanded. "Burnt brick and gold? Some king. Some kingdom."

Fafnir groaned again. His eye fluttered. But he wasn't dead yet. "All those treasures brought me no joy, and no joy will they bring you either, Sigurd. You'll end like me, don't doubt it."

Sigurd laughed. "If I was immortal like the gods, then maybe I'd fear death. But we all have to die, Fafnir. Why should I fear what can't be changed?"

All the time the dragon was lying there with his clammy eye fixed on Sigurd, watching closely. And all the time Sigurd was getting more and more anxious and confused. What was going on? He'd destroyed the monster's heart! What more did he have to do to? And why was the creature talking to him? What was going to happen next?

Fafnir—Styr—was keeping his arms wrapped over the wound, which he pressed closely into the mud beneath him. What was he doing—just holding on to life? But with no heart . . . ? As the dragon had passed over him, it had twisted to one side in an effort to escape the blade, and so the wound twisted up his side toward the pelvis. Sigurd suddenly took two rapid steps to the side, bent down to look, and managed to catch sight of the end of the wound, by the monster's tail, before he rolled on his belly to hide it. He looked into it and saw . . .

. . . flesh knitting together; blood sucking its way back up, the tubes of his insides reuniting, muscle knotting and pushing back into place, bone forming splinters that reached out to bone, forcing themselves together, knitting, stitching, joining. Styr was healing himself before Sigurd's very eyes.

There was a brief frozen moment; Sigurd knew; Fafnir knew Sigurd knew. They stared into each other's eyes.

"You thought you were watching my death," hissed the dragon. "But you were watching your own."

And then he lunged.

There was to be no escape. You can catch the dragon unawares, but you cannot fight him. Sigurd had a few rounds left in the machine gun, but what good could they do, when so many had already failed? The monster was already partly healed. Wounded as he was, he was a hundred times faster and stronger than Sigurd—better armed already, and getting better by the second. There was only one place to go. Sigurd did not run, but dived forward. He hit the ground behind the striking claw, right before Fafnir's belly, rolled forward, and plunged headfirst back into the blood-filled trench. He dived down through the hot, thick blood and then up again, under the dragon. Here was the slit the sword had cut in the mud. Above it—skin. Frantically he pushed his way through the blood and abandoned guts—more skin! Bubbles escaped from his nose and mouth as he desperately hung on to his air. Lungs bursting, he groped farther along—and there! Right up at the end he found a gap; his hand plunged straight through into the hot, wet insides of his brother Styr. He pushed his hands into the lips of the wound and hauled himself right up inside the monster.

There in the pulsing dark, Sigurd fought his way up, pushing aside the dark coils of intestines, hacking as he went, gagging on spilled food, blood, and bile. He pulled himself forward, up to the tight ball of the stomach, chopped that open, felt the atrocious sting of acids, and still fought on, up past the diaphragm and into the ballooning lungs. Here he sucked in more precious air—then up again, up and up, deeper and deeper into the body of the dragon. Above him something pulsed and beat, pulsed and beat, pulsed and beat.

"Two hearts! The bastard has two hearts!" Dropping the sword to move faster, Sigurd pushed his way forward, toward the pulse of life and seized it in his two hands.

Fafnir hauled himself upright, howling in pain, clawing at his own chest, hacking and fighting to tear himself open. At last he got a claw into the place where Sigurd had entered him, and, ripping upward, split himself open for a second time along the new scar from his belly right up to his rib cage. He was screaming like a boiler ready to explode as he sawed through the plate of his own sternum, which stitched itself back together even as he fought to open it. Now the dragon began to pull himself apart, heaving on his own skeleton, forcing himself open in a last desperate attempt to save his life. He gave a huge final tug; there was a loud crack as his ribs stretched backward like bloody wings. He looked down into his center just in time to see Sigurd reach up to the football of the huge heart, wrap his hands around it, and with a terrific tug wrench it from its bearings with his bare hands. As his light died, Styr reached in to pluck out his tormentor, but the life was gone before his claws touched him, and with a great spout of blood from the torn vessels, Fafnir the terrible fell and died.

8

regin

I didn't run down straight away. Fafnir was dead all right, but I still didn't trust him. Resurrection, even that might be possible, why not? After all that action everything had gone very still. The wind was blowing quite hard but there were no leaves or trees to sway. There were no birds flying over. And no Sigurd.

Come on, kid—you've done it, don't die now! I thought. When he fell, Fafnir went down like an avalanche and Sigurd was underneath him. I stood waiting for a long time, maybe fifteen minutes thinking, My god, what have I witnessed? Because it was truly impossible. At every second you knew Sigurd was going to die, but somehow he'd pulled it off.

I kept bending to the scope, and there was nothing, no movement. I still couldn't believe that it had actually happened. There were flies gathering on the monster's eye but even they could be a trap. I was sure Sigurd had died too, and, god help me, I thought, Two birds with one stone. Because . . . well. He was such a good person, it could never work. This is politics—he was bound to mess things up. I felt that there was nothing to worry about for him anymore because the worst had already happened.

Then there was a small movement at the side. Love him! That dragon was a truck made of meat and there was this little piggy squeezing out from under him. Yes! And I forgot all my caution and I just shouted, "Oh, I love you, Sigurd, I do, I really do," and without thinking I ran down on all fours to meet him, grunting and snorting like something off the farm.

Impossible! A boy against a thing like that! That's our Sigs, he can do anything! About halfway down I suddenly worried that maybe that small movement was something else—maybe Fafnir was escaping from his own corpse? Well, you don't know what they can do these days, do you? I stopped and looked again but it was Sigs all right, red with blood from head to foot, trying to drag himself out from under all those tons of dead meat. It made me weep to see him, that little thing, that baby. How could we have let him? How could we? We're just a bunch of shits, the whole lot of us.

I thought he was dying when I got close up, covered in gore like that and babbling away about a lot of things that made no sense. The dragon was his brother, he said. He said he'd died under the ground, that he knew how to live without breath, that no weapon could ever harm him, that he knew the secrets Odin won from the dead, because he'd died himself. He said he'd become less than human now. Mad as you like. I kept saying, "Now stop that, shut up, will you!" I was scared he was injured, you see, and he was yelling so loud I thought he'd push out what blood was still left in him. I had to hack him out with an ax in the end, he was stuck so hard. I was certain that there'd be only half of him left to pull out, I could hardly bear to look when I finally got him free. But he was all there. No wounds, no broken bones, nothing. All the blood was Fafnir's.

It was like another miracle—not a scratch on him! I was weeping with excitement. He was shaking like a leaf and still ranting about this old man who'd slept with him underground.

"Look," I said—he was scaring me with his mad talk, he needed to calm down. "I had the whole site plugged. There was no one else there. I'd have known. No old man, nothing, just you lying in the ground." I paused a moment. It's true that I'd lost track of him for a time—some failure of the equipment, it'd scared the life out of me at the time because I thought Fafnir was on to us. He might have been dead out there for a while so far as I knew, I couldn't find his heat or heartbeat or anything. But there was no one else. I was sure of that.

"You were hallucinating, Sigurd. Three days in the dark, hardly any food and water. Straightforward sensory deprivation, that's all it is."

Sigurd waved me away. "There're things even you can't measure, Regin," he gasped.

"Secrets of the dead, right?" I joked. I just wanted to try and bring him back to his senses. He glared at me.

"You don't know what you can't know," he panted.

"Well, I can't see inside your head, if that's what you mean," I told him. "But believe me, Sigurd, there was no living thing there but you and the dragon."

"Who's talking about the living?" he snarled. He leaned across and gripped my arm. "Regin, it was Odin. Odin came to me. Don't tell me you couldn't pick him up?" He laughed again. I thought, Look at you, always so sure of yourself. All he ever wants is the best for everyone, I know that, but this certainty he has of himself, it's indecent. If you want to see a god, getting buried alive in fear of your life is as good a way to do it as any, I suppose, but he didn't have to believe it. Just because it was him it happened to! Obviously he'd had some sort of experience down there, but being Sigurd, nothing on earth was going to convince him it wasn't real.

But then—killing Fafnir was more than human. How else could he have done it unless he had the gods with him? I felt a chill go through me. If it was true he was Odin's now and he knew things the rest of us could never understand.

"Odin has chosen me," he said. He was lying flat on his back in the mud and gore, and I was leaning over him, with one hand on his shoulder. He wasn't focused on me, he was staring up with his blood-covered eyes at the sky. What a sight, staring up through that mask of blood, with his mad eyes. I shivered and looked up over my shoulder, thinking I might see the god there myself but there were only the clouds and the sky above me.

I thought, He has everything—everything! Power, wealth, strength, youth—and the gods love him into the bargain.

"What did he tell you then, this underground god?" I asked, sarcastically. Sigurd looked at me, an unknowable look. I couldn't meet his glance.

"I don't know," he whispered. He looked so sad for a moment. Then, before I could stop him—he was as quick as an adder—he snatched a steel knife from his belt and stabbed himself violently in the stomach.

"No!" I screamed. I made a grab for the knife, too late, but he just laughed.

"He told me, Regin, no weapon would ever harm me where the dragon's blood had touched me." He lifted up his shirt. As I say, he was covered in blood, but then he took my hand and thrust it onto his stomach—like Jesus putting Thomas's hand in the wound. But with Sigurd, there was no wound.

"There," he whispered. His eyes lit on my face and he smiled, as if he recognized me for the first time.

The hair stood up all over my body; I felt myself grunt and cringe back. I flattened down my ears, I shook my head. He smiled at me.

"You believe in the godworld right up until the moment you see it. Why's that, Regin?" He pushed me away, got to his feet, and started to make his way down to the lake. I watched him for a minute. I was scared of him now. I used to dangle him on my knee and help him with his homework. Now he was unknowable. I ran after him and started going on about genetics and technology and normal explanations for things, but he waved his hand at me, and I had nothing more to say.

Well, it shook up me up at the time, I admit it—but I'm a scientist. I look for a rational explanation first. Fafnir was state of the art, see. All those onboard modifications were done using virus recoding. The point is, the viruses would still be active inside the body. That's one of the things that makes virus work so dodgy. If you can catch it yourself, other people can too. There've been escapes before. You get these weird epidemics where a change gets loose in the general population. Of course it's usually bigger boobs or more muscles, some silly rich kid trying to look more attractive. That's right—tit-job virus, big-muscle disease. The papers have a field day. It's usually babies and old people that get it, of course. Grotesque. So far none of the military viral hardware has escaped, but it's only a matter of time, if you ask me. Like now, for instance. Sigurd had literally swum in the dragon's blood. He'd be bound to have ingested some. He was contaminated—infected with Fafnir. He already had the skin. Once he washed off some of the blood you could see it shimmering, just like Fafnir's had. Who knows what else he'd caught? Fafnir's mind? He'd have recoded that, too, see? You can get rid of things mentally, too. There are a lot of things a tyrant might not like—mercy, pity, love. It was said that Sigmund's sister Signy eliminated love from herself, once it started getting in the way.

Fafnir had been human once. Sigurd still was. But for how long? The chances were pretty good that he was going to turn into a monster too.

He got into the water where Fafnir used to bathe, and when he took his clothes off, I saw something. It was a little leaf, an aspen, I think. I don't know how it got there, there were no trees for miles. It must have blown in on the wind. Somehow it'd got in under his shirt, trapped between his skin and the fabric. In that one spot, that one little place in the shape of a small leaf, the blood hadn't touched him.

I followed him into the water. I couldn't help thinking that if I shot him in the back there and then I might be saving the world from a great deal of trouble—but I couldn't do that. I loved him. We all loved him. That was how he worked. I walked into the pond after him and tapped him on the back.

"There was a leaf trapped under your shirt," I told him. "There's no blood on you on that spot."

Sigurd looked at me over his shoulder. I couldn't read his expression. "Prick me," he said.

I had a badge on my coat—I've had it for years, one of my children gave it to me ages ago. Now I took it off and gently pressed it into the flesh between his shoulder blades. A drop of blood sprang out. I dipped my finger in and showed him.

To my surprise, Sigurd was delighted. "Prick me and I bleed!" he crowed. "So there's one place left where I'm still myself. How about that? Even Odin never gets everywhere!" He put his hands on his knees and laughed weakly. "You'd better keep my secret, Regin," he said. Then with another little smile, he ducked under the water and began to wash.

I thought, Do you have to be so pleased about *everything*?

Regin left the boy to clean himself up and went back to where Fafnir lay. He could feel the heat from the huge body meters away, but it was cooling rapidly. Going behind the corpse, out of sight of Sigurd, Regin took off his clothes, got down into the trench where Sigurd had hidden, and bathed in the blood himself. Carefully he ran his fingers all over his body, making sure that there was no part of him that was not covered. He took care to open his eyes and mouth under the blood, so that as much of him as possible would be touched with immunity. He even swallowed the blood.

A little later, as he climbed up, he was shocked to see Sigurd standing by the side of the body waiting for him with a curious little smile on his face.

"You want to be indestructible too, Regin?" he asked.

Under his dark covering of blood, Regin blushed. "Don't think badly of me, Sigurd," he said. "Why should you be the only one to benefit? I have enemies too."

Sigurd nodded. "I don't think badly of you, why should I? Here." He took his knife out of his belt and handed it to the pigman, who pressed it against his arm, tentatively at first, but then hard. He drew no blood; the skin was not even creased.

Regin looked up and smiled. "The virus was still alive. I thought it might have died as the blood cooled."

Sigurd nodded at Fafnir, who lay so hugely and grotesquely dead before them. "Look at us," he said, "stealing everything from him! What does that make us? More human or less?" And he laughed.

The boy turned and walked off. As he watched him go, Regin thought to himself, That may be, Sigurd. But I made sure every inch of me was covered with the dragon's blood. I can kill you; but you can never kill me.

But it never occurred to Regin, that if by bathing in Fafnir's blood Sigurd was contaminated, so was he, too, now.

9

sigurd

Listen: I died down there. It wasn't sleep. The air turned bad.
I died and then the old man came and talked to me. Questions
and answers. But what they were, I can't think. You can't
know it. My body remembers, though. My body knows death.
It knows how to go there and back.

Then when I had to fight, there was nothing left to be scared
about.

After I found Regin bathing in the blood, I left him to it and
walked off. I was horrified. He didn't understand what he was
doing to himself. When I looked back he was already making
his way over to the door of the citadel, a great black rock as big
as a hill, that looked as if it'd crashed out of the sky and stuck
in the earth where it landed. He looked like a fly standing next
to it.

But I had other business. There were such thoughts in my
mind!

How could I have died and still be here? Was there more
than one of me? Was I still there? Was I—was my corpse—still
underneath the body?

I know it's mad. But it's not me that's mad, it's what

happened. I got a spade and started digging out the pit where I had hidden. I heard Regin calling to me from the rock, but I took no notice; I wanted to see if I was still under there. I dug and dug, and the blood kept on filling up the trench. I heard Regin shout again.

"What are you looking for? Sigurd, do you know something you haven't told me?" But I couldn't say. Dying is a secret thing. We who come back have nothing to say you'd understand.

I had to dig another channel to carry away the blood—the first one was blocked with body debris. Suddenly, with a final spadeful, it all flushed out and I could get on my knees and peer under the dragon.

I wasn't there.

I was so relieved! So relieved. I remember kneeling there on the ground, half weeping, half crying, "Thank you! Thank you!" over and over again. I don't know why, it just seemed to be such a terrible, terrible thing that there could be more than one of me. I still wasn't satisfied, though. I started getting scared then that I'd died inside him. Regin must have thought I was mad. But I *knew* I was dead—or had been. How could that be? I began hacking away, chopping the carcass to pieces—his belly, his chest, up to his neck, his hearts. I was so certain my body was in there somewhere, I had to see it. But there was nothing. If it was ever there, Odin must have carried it off. By the time I'd finished, Fafnir was disembowelled, dismembered, reduced to butchery. I stood back panting, looking at it, and I thought, I am mad. I must be careful now or I'll never come back.

I started to feel myself all over. Was it still me? Was that scar still there that I got when I was young, only five or six, when I fell in the long grass on my hands and landed on glass? There it was, a pale, twisted crescent on the thumb muscle. And that small dent in my eyebrow that I got when I was drunk one day and ran into a concrete lintel that had just been put up—there it was.

Same body. But I was different. My skin had begun to shimmer like Fafnir's had. I'd died and come back to life. I'd killed the dragon; I'd never be the same again. As I stood there, I felt this: that these were things that had been done to me. I wonder if it was the same for all the heroes in history. It isn't us doing these things. We have no choice. It's the gods, it's the people—it's you; the sheer weight of your belief in us makes us act the way we do. I felt it so strongly. None of it was anything to do with me at all.

Now I had nothing left. Everything had been taken away from me—my fate, my thoughts, my feelings, my whole life, stolen from within. The god was some kind of parasite. But at the same time, nothing had changed. All I had was the same as I had before I died: how I face my fate. My courage isn't mine, my leadership isn't mine—even my thoughts are not my own. I'm a puppet. But I do have this—my heart.

Then it came to me—the thing that makes me myself. It hit me like a blow, but I knew it was true. I could feel it all around me. Love. That's what I have, that alone is mine and mine alone. The heap of butchered meat and chopped-up guts that was all that was left of Fafnir steamed beside me, the hugest death you could imagine, but good would come of this. I made up my mind that *this* was why I'm here, *this* is what I want in my life—not to rule and govern and win, not to unite the country and build peace—that was my fate, that would happen anyway. For myself, all I want is to love—love for everyone, alive or dead, treacherous or faithful, with their daggers in my back or their hands in mine, with their hearts open or closed, for me or against me. Even if I had to kill them—and I knew I would have to kill a great many people—I would do it with my heart full of love for them, because that was all I had. I am so full of love, I want only this—to be able to give it freely, abundantly away.

It's the only thing you can learn from death—the value of life.

the treasure

Sigurd slept through the night and into the next day, but Regin lay awake, his mind in turmoil. Inside the sheer black rock of the citadel everything he had dreamed about was waiting. Dawn was not yet lighting the sky when he was up again, trying to find the way in.

A slow but steady rain had fallen through the night, turning the site into a mire of clay. Regin had to squelch his way through sticky mud, sliding and tripping over the clay-slicked rock to get there. It was exhausting just moving about. He was tempted to wake Sigurd at once—they had to work fast. As soon as it was known that the dragon was dead, everyone would be there for a share of the spoils. But he let the boy sleep on. He wanted to investigate the treasures of Fafnir's hoard on his own.

There's more than one sort of treasure. As he approached the steel doors set in a vast crown of rock, Regin's mind was full of measurements and ways of measuring, of subatomic chemistry, of genetic change, self-cloning, cell-destructive blasts, and the creation and manipulation of emotion and destiny through space and time. Regin was a scientist and an engineer. What he wanted were tools. Tools to change and be changed. Tools to make or break power. Perhaps even Andvari's ring itself. Good luck, Regin! With such a machine, anything was possible. Despite its reputation as a curse, a device to turn things out wrong, he had begun to believe that if he could understand it he could make something he could use, a device with which even a skinny old pigman such as himself could become another Sigurd. Not beautiful, not young perhaps, but with the strange gift of loving, of being loved, and of always being the right person in the right place at the right time.

Everyone has their own ambitions. Regin had always wanted to be the one who knows, an enabler—to put the world at the fingertips of other men. But as he approached the sheer black face of manufactured rock that Fafnir had chosen for his front door, he was aware of the stirrings of another desire inside him. If he had the means to carry out other men's ambitions, why should those ambitions not be his, too?

Regin scowled and shook his head. He knew what this was: Fafnir's defenses were still operating, filling his mind with dangerous thoughts. This was not him. But Regin had never before been near so much power. For a few hours, alone here with Fafnir's treasures, he would be the most powerful man in the world.

Getting into the stronghold was not likely to be easy. To every lock there is a key, of course; but like all the best keys, this one only worked for one person. If you were Fafnir, it opened. If you weren't, it didn't. Such keys were based on an individual genetic code, scrambled up, say, in the skin of the thumb, and they were notoriously difficult to replicate. Regin had to transcribe Fafnir's genetic code, find how much of it was used in the key, then work out how the code had been scrambled and ciphered. This was something he had anticipated. He had a small dedicated computer to analyze the monster's tissue. Of course Fafnir would have laid false trails in his chromosomes, blind alleys in the code, repeated loops, all sorts of tricks. Regin had confidence in his device, however. He had set it up overnight and fully expected to find the code waiting for him.

But the machine had frozen. Fafnir had doubled his double helix, and then doubled that, and then doubled that and so on many times. The cell nucleus was enlarged to take these countless multiples of genetic material. There were devices that could handle that amount of data, but Regin's handy portable was not one of them. It would take the machine literally years to get the code in order, let alone break the cipher.

They had to find another way in.

Regin was flummoxed. He had such faith in his machines and now, suddenly, he had no answers up his sleeve and so little time. To lose the prize now after coming so far—so much farther than anyone else! He couldn't let some croaking, uneducated halfman king come marching in and steal it. He wandered off to try and marshal his thoughts, but the task was impossible. The code was as impermeable as the black face of the citadel. For hours he wandered in the mud, trying to work out what to do, but he could think of nothing. At last, cold, covered in black mud from head to foot, and in near despair, he went to wake Sigurd and announce that their efforts had been in vain. But Sigurd was already up. He looked surprised. What was the problem? He had already been inside the citadel. Now he was having some breakfast. Did Regin want some, or would he prefer to go and have a recce first?

Regin was astonished. "How?" he asked.

Sigurd smiled and touched the broken stub of his sword. "Have you forgotten?" he asked. "I cut my way in. It was like cake."

Regin shook his head. How had he forgotten? Of course, Fafnir had devices to scramble the mind, he wasn't thinking clearly, that must be it. He looked resentfully at Sigurd. It was so easy for him! Everything was waiting to be given to him.

"What's the matter, Regin, are you angry with me?" asked the boy.

Regin shook his head, but he was full of dark thoughts as he followed on up the hill to Fafnir's front door.

It stank; that was the first impression. It was rotten food, BO, and stale urine. Fafnir was a military marvel, but at home he was just a derelict old man who never washed, pissed in the corner, and ate out of tins that he never threw out. The squalor was unbelievable. Fafnir did not live alone, after all. Down the passages came a thick buzzing. The dragon shared his home with a million flies.

Along the corridors and in the chambers to the sides were pallets stacked with tins of beer, baked beans, sardines, cans of stew or ham that he had raided—enough to keep a small army going for years. There were vitamin supplements, as well, but nothing fresh. Fafnir was no gourmet. When he emptied a tin he threw it in a corner for the flies to find. The rubbish was strewn everywhere, the maggots crawling blindly in the tins and pupating in the cracks of the walls and floors. There was a sleeping chamber—Fafnir still had some human habits—with a vast heap of blankets and mattresses stinking of sweat and the long unwashed. Along the walls, heaps of pornography. Fafnir had changed himself so much that he was useless for any sexual act, except those committed on himself. His life had narrowed down to just one thing: ownership. But he owned a very great deal.

Regin and Sigurd wandered off down the long corridors, baldly lit with neon light that never went off. Many chambers were behind locked doors—some behind twin doors, with an airlock between them, with small viewing windows installed. Sigurd wrinkled his nose and peered into the various chambers. Gold? No. Chamber after chamber was filled with gray cases, some small, some large. There were monitor screens, loud speakers in some cases. The gray cases hummed, whirred, and clicked. Regin grunted with excitement. Time and time again he made Sigurd cut a way in through the doors. Treasure! Who knows what these things could do! Half of them he couldn't even begin to guess at—they just stood there and hummed, or gave off a gentle heat or a chill. He examined each one and checked the codes against a small book that listed what each one did before he turned them off, one after the other. Yes! They were all here. Dark. Bright. Excite. Delight. He knew those: crowd manipulation technology. These machines bore the name of the Norn Group. Treasure indeed! As he suspected, Fafnir had got his hands on the very latest technology. Threat. Fear. Murder. Better and better! Murder technology!

Some of the machines—Delight, for example—were not turned on, but there was a great deal of fear and confusion being generated in Fafnir's house. Often, when he flicked a switch to off, a pressure inside him seemed to lift. Even in his excitement, Regin breathed a sigh of relief. The resentment that had been slowly growing inside him receded. Good thing they had gotten here quickly! You could end up committing any sort of crime even against those you loved with devices like this at work.

The chambers went on and on. Regin examined each one, listed its contents, and then had to go scurrying off after Sigurd to beg for another hole to crawl through, like a child, he thought crossly, pestering its parent. It was only right at the end, last of all, that he found the real treasure, the newest technology, hidden away in the deepest part of the caves—the tall, green machines of the Destiny Corporation. Loki. Jesus. Tyr. Odin. Destiny technology. Was this heaven? Had he found the homes of the gods or did these devices just mimic? And what happened when you turned them off?

Despite himself, Regin paused before he looked for the switches. What if he was switching off God himself? Regin had no idea what purpose these things served.

"I'm in awe," realized Regin. Of course! The generation of the numinous. Well—it must be more than that, surely. The machines sat silently in their place, no lights, no heat, nothing to give him any clues. When he looked for the power source, there was nothing. Fafnir had never activated them—unless they were solid state? That could well be, but either way, there was nothing Regin could do now. Superstitiously, he was glad of it.

But one treasure remained elusive: Andvari's ring. Such a small thing, it could be anywhere. More likely, it simply did not exist.

• • •

While Regin ran about trying to catalog his cave of wonders, Sigurd was searching for the gold. He felt a cur for doing it. There was all this fascinating stuff on all sides, machines alive in more ways than one—there was flesh and blood inside those cases as well as circuitry—and here he was plodding up and down looking for dead metal. But what a wonder gold is, too. Each of these devices had their purpose, but wealth is the beginning of everything, the alchemy that can create all the works of man. Everything in these chambers could be bought. And Sigurd had no need for machines to manipulate the crowd, or generate awe, or love, or fill people with delight. He was such a device himself, tuned perfectly to his times.

The citadel was huge—it had to be, to take Fafnir's bulk—but there were not so many chambers as he had thought at first sight. It took him little over an hour to examine them all, and he found no gold. He thought that perhaps the monster had spent it—but what use has a thief for money? In fact, it was the gold that Fafnir loved most of all, and he had taken care to hide it carefully. It was bricked up in a small chamber right at the back of one of the longest rooms—four small pallets of gold bars. Scattered all around were other precious things—Fafnir loved anything of value. Jewelry and treasures looted over the years from state apartments, government buildings, royal palaces, and museums were jumbled about, stuffed into cardboard boxes, or just dumped in fistfuls on the floor. And here, as elsewhere in Fafnir's citadel, not all was as it seemed. The most dangerous things are often in disguise.

Looking around, Sigurd could see any number of gorgeous and curious objects, but his eye was caught by a small ring, unremarkable to look at. Perhaps it was the proportions that caught his attention, or the looped design engraved inside and out, or simply that the other things there were too ostentatious to actually wear. He put it on his finger, and wondered where it had come from before he went to find Regin. It was time to load up and leave.

11
betrayal

For the rest of that day and all through the next, Sigurd and Regin worked packing away their loot—one the gold, the other technology. Inside the horses there were spacious holds where they could pack away a ton or more of gold apiece, but there was not going to be room for everything. Sigurd wanted to be sure that all the gold was taken, but Regin wanted the machinery to have priority. He had radioed back to Alf; help was on its way and most of the machines would have to wait until then, but Regin wanted to make sure that the most precious and advanced items were safe.

Sigurd was unhappy about machines designed to control and destroy people. Regin was amused at first.

"You're just such a machine yourself!" he teased. But it was more serious than that and a real argument developed. Regin pointed out that with these machines, they could win back any gold they lost and win tons more besides. Maybe, replied Sigurd, but at what a cost: people's freedom of thought. Maybe even their souls, he added, glancing sideways at the still, quiet machines labeled JESUS, ALLAH, and ODIN. But look at gold as a machine—what a device that was! It could buy anything within the wits of man or halfman and leave everyone it touched more able, not less. It was the gold that would do people good, not some artificial generator of delight or fear.

They agreed to postpone the argument until they saw how much space the gold took. Sigurd loaded the gold into Slipper while Regin chose the most important items of machinery to put inside his beast. But Sigurd was young and strong, while Regin was old and weak. He needed help with his cargo and soon he had to stop and sit outside the cave watching Sigurd go about his work, raging in his heart.

Sigurd could not understand his old mentor. This wasn't the Regin who had once only wanted to help Sigurd achieve his plans and share his aims. He thought it was selfish to put these strange devices before the gold that could buy the nation peace and prosperity, mundane though those things were.

Or am I being selfish? he thought. Gold was the source of so many conflicts—was he falling into that trap too, fooling himself into thinking that his wealth was good for all? As he worked, he turned it over in his head. He felt uncomfortable under Regin's angry eye, but he could not like these machines. He had no need for them; all they represented was threat. It was no longer a question of giving up gold—he was going to manage to stow it all away inside Slipper; but by the time the light was failing he had begun to believe that the machines were evil, thieves of life, and that it would be best simply to destroy them all.

That night, Regin talked excitedly of the devices they had captured and how they could help a leader conquer and rule. Sigurd listened carefully, frowning as the old pigman stuttered with enthusiasm. The treasure Fafnir had! With this device, for instance, Sigurd could wipe out a city, and yet leave everything intact—the machines, the buildings, even the plants that grew between the paving stones and the insects that crawled among them would be unharmed; but every mammal would be destroyed. Clever! No enemies, but all their wealth . . .

"But what use would that weapon be, Regin?" Sigurd wanted to know.

Regin wiped the sweat off his face and laughed. What use? Who knew what his enemies might be prepared to do? An army could invade a town and massacre the inhabitants—what then? Or they might capture an industrial complex. What would Sigurd do then, blow up the lot? But seeing the boy's look of bewilderment, he backtracked. Well, maybe it would be useful as a threat against greater powers, a terrorist weapon, perhaps, something to scare them off if they threatened to invade. Of course the weapon had to be real for it to be a threat, but that didn't mean you had to use it.

But Regin soon lost his caution again as his enthusiasm took over. Look at this device—it could make the people happy! Look at this one—it could make his enemies fear. This one could disable machinery, this one scrambled genes. This one affected memory. But Sigurd was appalled. To him, these weapons were not treasures, they were a curse. He wanted to lead people, not manipulate them. Look at Fafnir, Lord of London. What was London when no one lived there? But Regin laughed at him for being naive, and talked about the wonders of knowledge, the realities of power.

"If you don't use them, someone else will," he said. "Leadership goes to the one with the best weaponry. You know that. If you don't have this stuff, you don't rule."

"We defeated Fafnir with a sword."

"But what a sword!" said Regin. "Without that, you would have been helpless."

Sigurd was stung—as if the sword had done the killing itself. Regin was amused. It was true, wasn't it? he taunted. Without the sword, no death. Fafnir would still be here.

"You're drunk, Regin," said Sigurd quietly. The old pigman had forgotten what Sigurd had gone through—waiting in the pit, struggling through the guts of the monster to reach his second heart. Who else could have done that?

Regin had drunk nothing, but he laughed again, just to taunt the boy. His thoughts whirled forward without him. How small Sigurd looked sitting next to him. It was the sword that had killed Fafnir, not Sigurd. And who had made that sword? Given a little more time he could have designed the sword to be used by anyone—himself, for instance. He could have killed the monster alone, if he had chosen. Of course it was more sensible to get someone else to take the risks. He, Regin, had knowledge. Sigurd was expendable; he was not.

And he alone knew the one place on Sigurd's body where he might be killed if he ever needed to do such a thing.

But then, as his mind flew to these dangerous places, the reality of his thinking came to him. What was he doing, thinking such terrible thoughts, as if all his values and principles and way of life had suddenly dropped off him like old clothes? As if a skinny old pig like him could ever have done what Sigurd had done. Flustered, overcome with emotion, he jumped up and ran over to hug Sigurd. He was affected by the air, he was in shock . . . something.

"See, Sig, I'm not fit even to help you," he gasped.

"I could never have done it without you, Regin," said Sigurd. But he had made up his mind now—seeing Regin change so drastically had finally convinced him. "But look what these machines have done to you. We have to destroy them."

Regin drew back. Was that it? But he had turned them off—at least, he had turned off the ones he knew how to turn off. Perhaps it was true—yes, yes, it could be like that. Some device of Fafnir's was working on him. In shock at how far he had been brought—even to dream of murder!—he did not argue his case; but he could not agree. In the morning they would talk again, his head would be clearer.

Later, when they lay down to sleep, he ran his mind over and over and over all the devices. Fear, Hatred, Murder—they had all been turned off, it couldn't be that. The Destiny technology? The god machines? They had never been turned on in the first place. Fafnir had obviously not learned how to use them.

Unable to sleep, he got up and went around the citadel, from room to room, checking. Nothing seemed to be operating. Could it be possible, then, that these thoughts were not generated at all, but were his own? Was there a truth in it? Regin sat with his back to the wall and his head in his hands and thought until his head hurt. Sigurd was a fine person, none better. He was a hero, a fighter. But a ruler? Someone so naive, so young, so hopelessly idealistic—what chance would he stand in the slippery, backstabbing world of politics? You needed an old head, a wise head, and cunning mind for that. It was possible that someone else—Alf, perhaps, or maybe Regin himself—would serve the people and the nation better by seizing power for themselves before Sigurd had a chance to lose it to some easy friend, out to use him and steal his power.

In the morning, Sigurd was more certain than ever that his instincts were right. What had all this technology to do with his vision? Destruction and control—what sort of power was that? Where were the schools, the hospitals? Where was the hope? True, it might be that one of the devices hidden in the citadel might generate hope, but what use was even hope if it was not based on the realities of life? One thing he was sure Regin was right about: If he didn't use these things, someone else would. There were a dozen kings and ganglords who would be emperor and wouldn't hesitate to use them if they had them. So it was possible to treat the people like caged dogs and fill them with hope? How the tyrants would love that! It was exactly the kind of thing Sigurd had pledged himself to fight.

He rose early and began work at once, laying down the wires that would set off a series of explosive charges. Once that was done, he would unload Regin's horse; everything would be destroyed—everything. The work was well under way when Regin woke and wandered across to see what he was up to. When he realized, he went mad. He tried to pull authority—he was old, the boy was young. Alf had not given him permission to do this—he was still king, the lord of them both. Sigurd was unmoved. He had won his right, he had killed the dragon. Nothing of the monster's hoard would be left to take but the gold, and that was his.

Regin became so incensed, he seized Sigurd's arm and tried to fling him to one side. The boy gently released himself and insisted; this was going to be. Regin was under the influence of something evil among all this crazy weaponry, he needed to calm down. When it was done he would feel better and understand.

"No! Everything is turned off. This is me, Sigurd. What you're doing—it's like burning the books, tearing down the museums, the libraries. You can't do this!" screamed Regin, beside himself. But Sigurd placidly put the older man to one side and went about his business.

All these wonders were going to be destroyed in front of his eyes, and Regin was helpless to stop it. He left the citadel and raged about outside, skidding and falling in the mud, beating the rocks with his fists in his frustration. His mind was in its darkest hour, and that's how he went to his death, that kind man—trapped at his lowest, unable to think, hysterical with rage. Who can say what he remembered or had forgotten at the last moment? He had loved many things and many people in his life, but none more so than Sigurd, yet now it seemed to him that the boy had turned into a tyrant, a monster who was capable of anything. He became implacable. He alone had the knowledge to do this, it was his duty. He was ten feet away as he raised his rifle and took sight to the aspen, leaf-size point, where Sigurd was still mortal.

Regin was no marksman, he had to get so close to be sure. What warned Sigurd? A sound? A birdcall, some said—a blackbird that had strayed inside the citadel after maggots, calling alarm from the rubbish stinking in heaps along the corridors. Sigurd's hearing and sense of smell had already become more acute as a result of bathing in Fafnir's blood. Perhaps he caught the scent of murder as he crouched over his wires. He turned anyway and saw the gun. He was already out of harm's way—the bullet was fired that very second as Regin saw him move, and the aspen leaf was already out of sight—but he was not used to his immunity and instinct took over. He drew the stub of the sword from his belt and flung it. It glittered in the light, twisting and turning in the air for only a fraction of a second before it struck Regin in the chest.

Every day for the rest of his life Sigurd asked himself if he could have avoided that action, but the decision to strike back when death threatened was made long ago, when he was three or four and through all his other years, when he was trained to bypass any thoughts that might delay his hand. And perhaps Andvari's ring on his finger helped to push him in that split second to an act he would forever regret.

Sigurd rose and walked across to where Regin lay, his life's blood pumping out of him on the rock floor. Regin had forgotten that Sigurd had the means to pierce him, as he had Fafnir. He gasped, met the boy's eyes, tried to speak but could not, and died.

Standing there over the body, Sigurd's world began to fall apart around him, like sections of land falling into the sea. Nothing he believed in was real. All his assumptions were wrong. He had been betrayed by someone he loved, and, it seemed to him, had reacted by betraying back. He had not needed to kill Regin. He could have protected him from this—restrained him, kept him safe until he'd blown this evil place to kingdom come. Then Regin would have come to his senses and understood.

Overwhelmed by the ordeal of the past few days, Sigurd for a second in his mind slipped out of the darkness of the present into the bright past he had loved so much. Before him was the sea of the Welsh coast, the dunes, the beach, his friends playing, voices calling, seagulls. His friend and tutor lay on the ground playing dead in a childhood game, as he'd done many times before. Sigurd leaned forward and shook his shoulder.

"Regin? This was a game we were playing. Wake up, Regin. Take me home. I want to go home now."

But Regin never moved. Kneeling by his side, Sigurd laid his head in his hands and began to weep, there in the shattered vales of Hampstead Heath, where only sorrow ever lived.

12

destruction

Sigurd rises from the floor by the side of his murdered friend and glances over his shoulder into the cavern at the ranks of weaponry and machines—Fear, Delight, Conflict, Bliss; Odin, Jesus, Allah. He has them all. He killed the dragon and won the prize. He is favored by the chief of all the gods. He has died and resurrected. His is the highest star.

And he has killed a brother and a dear friend. Is he turning into a god, or simply losing his humanity?

Outside, a small bird comes to stand on a rock near the cavern's mouth, opens its mouth, and puts out a song. Sigurd listens, astonished in this terrible moment by the sheer beauty of it—and astonished at his own ability to be moved by it, now of all times. A blackbird, a small common thing, but it makes Sigurd's heart so full that tears spring to his eyes. The small things. The wind in the grass, birdsong, his mother's kiss, every living thing. It would burst your heart open if you didn't keep your eyes closed sometimes.

He fills himself with a great breath of air. The vaults stink, but the wind is blowing sweeter scents over the burned rock and poisoned waters of Hampstead. There is a world beyond the bombsite. There is birdsong and the smell of grass and the scent of another person's skin. So full of love is Sigurd, and so full of death, too, that he hardly knows who he is anymore. He is fifteen years old, and he has been broken and put together again in a way no one ever should be.

Outside, the blackbird flips its wings and flies away. Sigurd wipes away his tears. All he wants to do is lie down and sleep until life ends. What does it matter? The gods will have their way. But what else is there to do but carry on as full of love as if your life was your own and what you did mattered? It is an act of faith. So Sigurd stands up and gets on with the work that Regin interrupted. But as he turns back to his wires and detonators, he realizes that there is an easier solution. All he has to do is plant a homing device and then fire a missile from a few miles away. The missile would fly through the hole in Fafnir's front door like a letter through the letter box. The whole place would go off like a bomb.

Outside it had begun to rain again; Fafnir's corpse with that impossible skin glistened like a huge, dead jewel. Beyond it—the world. Birdsong and sun and sea and the millions of living things. Sigurd thought to himself—that had to be enough for anyone. To rule and conquer and make the world a safe place was a big job, a job for generations. He was no longer sure of himself after what had just happened. It was enough just to be alive.

It was only left to say good-bye to Regin.

Sigurd could not conceive that Regin could love him any less than he loved Regin. Betrayal was not in his nature and he did not understand it in others. In his mind, it would always be he who was the murderer. He lifted the body and carried him into the citadel, leading Slipper behind him. He laid the body down on top of the machine labeled DELIGHT. The old custom of burning the dead with things that were precious to them had come back with the old gods, and Sigurd planned a funeral pyre for Regin of a kind no one had ever seen before.

He kissed his old friend, straightened out his limbs. His horse with its belly full of horror would stay there. Then he went to destroy the den of destruction.

He rode Slipper hard for fifteen minutes. He had no idea how all that stuff would go up, but he wanted to be miles away when it went. Already he was surrounded by bushes and grass and a few small trees. The spring sunshine was brightening the leaves, he could smell the sap rising. From this place, where life had a hold, he would put an end to many deaths.

He dismounted, set up his missile, tracked and recorded the place where he wanted it to go—and launched.

The missile leapt into the air and wove an uncertain path as it nosed along the radio signal to its own destruction. As it got higher, it found a clear signal and headed straight off. Two minutes later there was a heavy crump and a shock in the air as it passed through the door and exploded inside. Sigurd lifted his binoculars to watch, but before the smoke could rise high enough for him to see it, there was another, bigger explosion; the ground shuddered under his feet and a thick cloud of black smoke and blue and orange flames rushed skyward. Then, another bang, and another, and another—and then to Sigurd's horror the horizon itself began to rise. He dropped the binoculars; this event was too big to see magnified. A great wall of ground had lifted up high above the trees and was rolling toward him. Something so violent had exploded underground that the bedrock itself was behaving like liquid. A tsunami of solid rock was rushing toward him.

Sigurd leapt aboard Slipper. Everything around him was shaking. The trees were falling over, the rocks shuddering, the ground quaking and cracking even though the event was still kilometers distant. The cyber-horse leapt forward as if it was putting a soul it did not have at Sigurd's service. Behind them the wall of rock had begun to glow with heat. Mountainous though it was, it was traveling as fast as flight and had already begun to break, leaning forward like a giant hand.

Sigurd cried out; Slipper redoubled his efforts, bounding sure-footedly across the quivering ground. As he rode, the horse was seeking: Where was safe in this tumultuous landscape? Radar, sonar, infrared, every means of looking was available to him, but he could see nothing. From his shoulder a small missile fired. In seconds it was hovering below the clouds, checking out the lie of the land. Where? Where?

Behind them the tidal wave of magma broke, toppled, and fell. It struck earth and washed forward. A splatter of it fell on Sigurd's back and he screamed in pain. A rain of red hot rocks and burning earth began to fall around them. Now they were in danger of being crushed under the avalanche. Even Slipper could not outrun the debris, but at last he spotted a place it could not reach. A fiery crack was opening up before them. Without a pause, Slipper charged straight down into it.

It was an evil-looking place, a maw of fire and black smoke. The billowing fug was lit by huge flames, thrashing and beating in violent winds. Sigurd choked and screamed as the flames swept over him, but Slipper charged onward down the tunnel, which shook and rattled like a copper pipe as the ground above it compressed. Behind them, it began to collapse, closing down like a swallowing throat. In between the smoke and fires, Sigurd could see twisted machinery, abandoned cranes and trucks, vents and pipes leaking fumes and polluted fluids. There was fire everywhere. What was this place? Hel? Did they have industry in Hel? There was fire everywhere. It seemed as if even the metal and rock around him were ablaze.

Ahead of him now as well as behind was only fire. Sigurd looked backward—surely anywhere would be safer than in this underground catastrophe! But behind him the sea of rubble and glowing rock was melting after them. He leaned forward and whispered encouragement in Slipper's ear, and the beast leapt forward directly into the burning gas. Sigurd screamed as the fire beat around his head and neck and set his clothes ablaze, turned his hair and the top layer of his skin into ash; Slipper screamed as his coat and skin caught fire. Forward they charged, through the heat, onward and deeper until they left the earthquake behind them in the upper layers of the earth's mantle, and entered the deep underground where an ancient city still torturously attempted to function.

This was Crayley.

Long ago, before the government had withdrawn from the community, this had been the home of industry—a city of machines hidden underground. For almost a century it had provided for the nation, manufacturing electrical goods, weaponry, cars and trains, kitchenware, building materials, medicines—whatever it was asked for. With the age of genetic design it had been modified, but it soon became outdated and inefficient. Too expensive to close down, it had simply been abandoned. And so it remained, hundreds of years later, a huge industrial complex rusting and grinding away to no end. Deserted, lame, degenerating, isolated from its purpose, the city nursed a bitter heart. Its software maintained it, mended, replaced, expanded; its primitive nerve and muscle technology bred and evolved, but it could not change or redesign itself in any fundamental way. It stuck to its old ways, growing bitter over the centuries, resenting its creators and lamenting its fate. Inch by inch it mined its way through the deep layers of the earth, looking for new resources, new ores and fuels, sometimes sending an arm up to make use of ancient earthfill, or even up to the surface if it needed air. Automated vehicles trundled along the rock roads, oil and waste pipes ruptured and rusted; colonies of bacteria blossomed along the damp, warm passages, and strange creatures roamed in little packs, components of nerve and muscle that had separated off and become alive. Up near the surface, fires blazed, fed on leaking reservoirs of methane, tars, and hydrogen captured from water. Into this ancient, malevolent machine, down its only remaining airway, Sigurd now rode away from the terrors of Fafnir's hoard, through fire and acid into a man-made Hel.

For a long time all he could hear was the beating of flames in his ears, the rapid drumbeat of Slipper's hooves ringing out on the floor, and the sound of his own moaning as the fires scorched him. Everything dead, the top layers of his skin, his hair, his fingernails and toenails, had now been burnt away; Fafnir's blood only protected what was alive. Between his shoulder blades, in the shape of an aspen leaf, a great blister formed, boiled, and burst. Between his thighs, Slipper was ablaze, his skin falling off him in rags, then his flesh, then his nerves, then his organs; but the machine in him remained. Black with carbonized flesh and bone, his titanium skeleton tore on like a living thing.

After a time Sigurd fainted and Slipper paused, unsure of what to do or where to go. Already half of his systems were down; he was having trouble analyzing the environment. He needed to get Sigurd to safety—but which way did safety lie? Then in front of him appeared an impossible sight: a tiny reddish-brown bird, whizzing through the flames. The bird was not burning. It was so small and moved so fast it appeared to flick from place to place, to disappear, and then reappear. It perched suddenly on the horse's nose. Slipper snorted. The little thing turned to look at him and then suddenly flew off straight ahead—and the horse jumped after her. The wren could have changed direction on a penny piece if she had to, but she set him no such task, flying only a meter from the end of his nose. If she turned too quickly, she reappeared when he paused, squeaking as if amused by the great beast's weakness.

So the horse and wren passed through the fire, one ablaze, the other unharmed, through the passages and ducts, through vents and across ancient factory floors glowing with heat where great machines pounded relentlessly and pointlessly on as they had done for centuries, stamping out dies that would never be used, bending and cracking under the heat. Blind robots tested and analyzed, ran to and fro, carrying out their endless repairs.

Sigurd remained unconscious as Slipper at last cantered out of the fire, both of them glowing cherry red with heat. A few minutes later, when the air was cool enough not to burn flesh, they stopped in a clearing, red with rust, green with verdigris. At last the great horse collapsed. Sigurd, burned naked, and every cell of him alive, rolled on the ground and opened his eyes. In front of him was a young woman looking down at him, dressed in an amazing collection of rags and skins, holding a stick with a hook on the end of it in her hand. Behind her was a rough gibbet of scaffolding from which the body of a man hung, one eye shut and one open in a permanent wink. Sigurd glanced behind him in terror, unaware that he was safe now. The flames were behind him.

"Quick! There's no time!" he yelled. He tried to jump up but he was too weak and just scrabbled bizarrely like a dying rabbit as his legs gave way repeatedly underneath him.

"There's plenty of time here," the girl replied. Sigurd stared at her from the ground, and at the permanently winking man behind her, and slid back into a dead faint.

13
the girl

Bryony had waited a long time for this visitor—all her life. She was seventeen and the future was a monster that terrorized her every day, but it was her hope and her promise that one day she would be free. The promise had been made to her mother by the dead man long ago, when he was still alive and Bryony in the womb. Sigurd was the only person who had ever come to her from the world above. He lay there, naked and beautiful, something from myth, a unicorn, an angel from Heaven, the word made flesh. He was a dream come true.

It was hard to believe when all you had ever known was this cramped world of fire and passages that there was another world as huge as the one her mother used to talk about, with oceans and sky and fresh air and millions of people. People! She couldn't imagine it, but she had to believe, because what was the point otherwise? Although she had been born and bred down here and the routines of survival in Crayley were all she'd ever known, Bryony knew very well that this was no life for a human being. Every single day she burned for freedom, but it scared her. How would she cope with it when it finally came? What if she couldn't bear it? What if she had actually become a part of this terrible place?

She was strong—stronger than her mother for instance, who had spent months in black depressions living down here. She was gone now—Bryony had never been able to find out what happened to her. She might have been taken by the creatures who shared this Hel with them, or by the city itself; but she would not have been surprised if her mother had taken her own life. She had lived in the upper world, the real world as she called it. It was all she ever talked about—how beautiful it was, how big it was, how open and cool, how full of life. Throughout Bryony's childhood this other world was the basis for all her stories and games. It was a litany she still repeated. Birds, mice, trees, sun, sky, moon, cats and dogs, rainfall, snow, the sea. Weather! The wind. Clouds, huge mists in the sky that looked like cotton wool. She had made her mother tell her everything and tried to picture it in her mind, but it was impossible. Toast. Butter. Marmalade. Cows. Houses. Roast potatoes. Her mind was so full of pictures, all of them wrong. Her mother had told her so. Only a god could picture the truth of a single blade of grass; but when she saw one for herself, her mother told her, it would be like coming home.

Promises could go wrong, she knew that, too. It was another thing her mother had taught her, before she had disappeared. Her mother used to live on a farm on the outskirts of a small town. A town was a collection of houses where lots of people lived. Her father was a traveler who had put up at a nearby hotel. He was very rich and handsome in those days, despite having only one eye. He had stayed on for weeks, wooing her.

They became lovers. He had taken a room in the farmhouse to be near her. Every night they crept out of their windows and made love in the barn, surrounded by the animals. She was so much in love, she had never hesitated when he suggested they run away together. He was so passionate, so romantic! They would run away to a place where no one would ever find them. He would stay with her forever. That was a promise, and he kept it to the letter, but see how it had ended up. No one had ever found them, and here he still was, even after she had gone. It's just that he never told her he was taking her to Hel, and that he would be dead within a month of their arrival.

Not so handsome now, hanging upside down by one leg, with his face swollen and black and his arms and free leg hanging awkwardly awry and his clothes the wrong way, like a parody of an acrobat or dancer, caught in a movement he could never finish. The maggots came and went as he rejuvenated himself, but never enough to come back to life. She hoped he would one day, though. Why didn't he just dissolve away to nothing like dead things usually did, if he didn't want his body back one day?

Bryony came to see him every day. She talked to him, and although he never replied, Bryony believed he could still see, hear, think, and feel. His expression changed. Today he was wearing a smile.

Bryony laid down her hook, which she used for scratching through the waste heaps for anything useful, and went to crouch by the side of the unconscious boy. He was amazing. The fire had burned him more naked than anyone else had ever been. She ran her hands gingerly across his long, straight limbs and shouted, "Ouch!" He was far too hot to touch. Bryony jumped about waving her hands in the air for a minute. Then she stopped and glared at him. Would she never be able to touch him? In a panic she sat down on her haunches and blew on his fingers until at last she could put one in her mouth and cool it down. She sighed happily. To have and never to hold— that would be unbearable.

Bryony glanced over to the gibbet, where the dead man had stopped turning slowly on his heel and was staring right at them. Taking a strip of cloth from her pocket, she bound up his eye. She suspected that Odin sometimes looked through that eye, and she wanted her first moments with another person to be private. Then she sat down and waited quietly until the boy had cooled down and began to run her hands all over his body. At the base of his back was a short extension to his spine, the remains of what might have turned into a lion's tail, a legacy of his mother's line. She pressed her hand against this curiously, before sliding her hand down to the bottom of her own back where she had a similar shape.

At last she stood up, her hands on her hips, and looked him all over. "Beautiful," she decided. She smiled with anticipation. He was hers.

She bent and lifted him up in one smooth, easy movement. She stood, feeling his lovely weight. He was still hot enough to burn her gently, although she padded her arms with cloth. She was going to take him home. As she walked she called out, "Jenny!" A tiny bird, the same brown-red wren that had guided Slipper there, flew suddenly out of a tangle of twisted metal nearby and landed next to her ear. The bird perched there for a second. Bryony felt the sharp little feet digging into her skin, but whether from fear, or anger, or jealousy, or simply excitement, she had no idea. She opened her mouth; the wren flew inside and perched there, peeping to and fro for a second, until Bryony pursed her lips and blew her out. They played this game on and off all the way home, until Jenny got tired and went to sit in her pocket for the rest of the journey.

He was too hot! As I walked home I wondered if he was a thing that lived in the fire and now he was dying of the cold, but I hadn't the heart to put him back in. He was no use to me there. I was so relieved when he got cool and he was still alive.

He was red from head to toe. No hair, no eyelashes or eyebrows, no hair on his body at all. No secrets. From head to toe, bare and beautiful. He came through the fire to me. Nothing ever came through the fire before, except Jenny Wren, and so I knew he was a god, or of the gods, or touched by god. He had no fingerprints—the fire had burned those away, too. He'd been through some terrible ordeal, but I had no idea what it was except I could see he'd come out of it brand new—brand new for me, like a baby.

My heart filled up. I thought, I love him! He's not spoken a word and I love him. But what do I know? No one can guess how little I know or how much I feel.

I laid him down on my bed. I didn't even think of my mother's bed, but then I realized where I'd put him and I remembered that he wasn't a baby, he was a man, and I was embarrassed. Mother always told me Odin would send me a lovely man when I was old enough, but she also told me I mustn't throw myself at him when he came. I put some water to his lips and he sipped it. He started mumbling and muttering again. His eyes were closed, he was still asleep.

There was never any man there except my father and I would never touch him. I'd never seen a man, or a boy or anything male. Maybe it's such a small thing it's not worth the telling, or it's a private thing of a kind I shouldn't put down. But because I believe *everything* should be put down, every tiny detail in case it is forgotten—why else are we here?—I put it down now.

I'm trying to tell you it was just because I was curious, but anyway, I lifted the blanket and had a good look. My mother always called it a thing, but there was more than one, that's all. I thought, It's like a load of old giblets! What can he do with them, flap them at me? But an awful lot of old giblets. I giggled and dropped the blanket. Then I thought that maybe there was something wrong with him or it had been damaged and I was disappointed. I was angry, suddenly, and I stamped about a bit and shouted, but he called for water in his sleep and I told myself, He's just a baby after all, and I went to pour some more between his lips.

I sat by him and waited. He began to ramble. Words. Dreams. I listened carefully. Was it a prophecy? Tales of the outside? Dreams, or reality, how could I tell? What was it that Odin had sent through the fire—a lover or a baby, a friend or a brother? A patient, perhaps? I couldn't know, so for the time being I decided to watch over him like a mother—like my mother did when I was sick, covering him with blankets, touching his head to see if he was too hot or too cool. I gave him some soup, and soon he became quiet. I was tired. I lay down on the bed next to him and closed my eyes.

14

meeting

There was a girl bending over him with dark eyes. He felt scared of her and moved his head deeper into the pillow. She licked her lips; she had eye teeth like a cat's. No, thicker. Like a lion's. Like his.

"Are you from the outside?" she demanded.

"Where am I?"

"Hel." She laughed.

"Then I'm from the outside."

She stood up and clenched her fists. Her eyes shot from side to side, trying to find a question that would ask all the things she needed to know.

"Is it grassy outside?" she blurted.

"No," he answered, surprised.

She frowned. "Where is it, then? The grass, has it gone?"

"It's just farther away."

"Has it moved?"

"I don't understand."

She glared at him.

"There's lots of grass, it's just not near here because of the dragon."

"Dragons! So they're real?"

"This one was. Except he sort of . . . sort of made himself up."

"I see," said the girl, not seeing anything really. "Listen! There's a way out. You came here. You know the way!"

"I don't know."

"You're from outside. You got down. Tell me the way."

"I can't remember. I was unconscious."

"You can't remember? You can't *remember*? You idiot!"

Sigurd stared back up at her in fear. Tears sprang to his eyes. She looked curiously at him.

"What's the matter?" she asked.

"You're scaring me."

"Huh!" She snorted in derision. "You're frightened of questions! Who are you?"

Sigurd had to think about it. She was right; he was scared of questions. In fact he was scared of everything—her bright eyes, her sharp teeth, her questions. He tried to sit up, but his body was as exhausted as his mind and he fell back down. She put her hands on her hips and stared aggressively at him.

"I died. Then I killed the dragon," he said. "Then my teacher tried to kill me so I killed him, as well. I need to rest."

The girl stared down at him. "You *died*?" she asked. Well, why not? Her father had stopped just the other side of death, her mother had just disappeared. Perhaps people didn't die in the same way as animals did.

"What's it like?" she asked.

"What?"

"Dying."

"Hard."

She laughed at him, and he smiled back up at her. She nodded. "I'll look after you. And then we'll see."

"See what?"

"What you are. To me."

Sigurd sighed. More tests! He closed his eyes and went back to sleep. Looking down at him, the girl bit her lip. She'd made a bad impression. She was too excited. He wasn't a weakling at all. He'd killed a dragon; he'd died and returned to life. He was a wounded hero! She would nurse him, she would love him. She would love him with all her heart if only he would let her.

Bryony sighed and sat down in a chair by the bed, her eyes soaking up the form of the sleeping boy. He was everything to her already, all her hopes and ambitions, and she didn't even know him. Escape—perhaps! If not—love, a baby. At the very least someone to care for. Someone to talk to! Even that would transform her utterly. Just to talk to someone, just that could make her happy.

But that wasn't really true. She knew that. To be happy, Bryony needed everything—the whole world. Look at that pretty head of his! It was full of memories—the memories of outside! Yes, he'd seen a lot. She'd like to crack it open and eat them all up. Memories were holy. She only hoped she had enough time to make them all hers.

As she sat there, the little wren appeared suddenly on the edge of the bed. In her beak she held a small twig with a little cluster of pale white flowers on it. Bryony took it carefully in her hand, sniffed the flowers, sniffed the bark. She peeled a bit off, tasted it, and spat it out. She got up and put it in a jar of water on the windowsill by the boy's head.

"Thank you," she said, although it sometimes seemed to her that the bird was teasing her with these scraps of evidence of a wonderful world that she brought to her every few days. She put her hands behind her head and looked carefully at the flowers. She ought to be going out to find something for them to eat, but she was scared to leave him. He might be gone by the time she got back. He might be a dream! With this thought, Bryony got up and prowled a couple of times around the room anxiously. She resisted an urge to wake him up and make him speak.

On a whim, she got into the bed with him. She could keep guard over him there. Feeling her there, Sigurd moved, and murmured something and put his arms around her. Bryony was thrilled, thrilled! He was holding her! They were cuddling! Gently, so as not to disturb the magic, she put her arms around him and laughed softly to herself with pleasure. He snuggled his nose into her neck and sniffed her skin. It tickled. She had to hold her breath so as not to giggle.

Sigurd snuffled and turned half over toward her, cupped her breast in his hand. What? she thought. This already? Her mother had always said to her, "Not the first one, Bryony!" very sharply, because she was as keen to do that as she was keen to do everything else. Ridiculous! As if she could pick and choose.

She moved her hand and touched him down there. It was all soft and warm: Sigurd had not been thinking of sex, he was just cuddling up. She smiled and relaxed. This was lovely. Oh, yes, she liked cuddling! She rested her face gently on his, stroked the bare skin of his scalp, and after a time fell asleep in his arms.

15

bryony

When I awoke, he was still fast asleep. I bent over him and smelled his breath, then I sniffed his face, his neck, his scalp—I wanted to know him all over. He didn't move. I took the cover off him and looked at him. He was the most beautiful thing I had ever seen. I put my ear to his chest and listened to his heart—ba-boom, ba-boom, ba-boom. I listened to his head and his stomach. I pressed my ear to his things; they made no noise. I felt him all over. He was delicious.

I covered him up and lay there a bit, but I was so full of what was happening I couldn't keep still. I had to go outside to think. I took the twig Jenny had brought me and went out.

I'm always dreaming of things. What the sky's like, or the moon over water, or how about grass? My mother was a farmer's daughter, she was always talking about grass. Dried grass that smells sweet, cut grass that smells fresh, grass under your bare feet, grass hissing in the wind. And all the other things she told me, like rain and sunshine and sand and sea and dogs and . . . everything. The world. The wide world, she used to say.

Now things are coming true. The boy, the first promise. Him with all his precious memories. That's why I'm here, to honor memories, to worship them, to dedicate them to Odin. I'm his priest. Most people have so many memories they don't know what they're worth, so Odin gives me just a few. That's what my mother believed anyway. Since she disappeared, it's just me, so whenever anything happens, or whenever Jenny brings me something from outside, I honor it. I hope that one day there'll be a reward, a release. I want to be set free.

Perhaps the boy is my reward. If he can't get me out, I have to make sure he never leaves.

I have a memory of my own now. He is a boy. We slept together. I thought to myself, Maybe I won't dedicate that to Odin. Maybe that's just for me. Why should he have everything? He knows everything that has gone and everything that will be. Everything, down to the smallest cinder. Imagine that! Knowing everything. Why should he have this, as well?

I ran down the pipes and corridors to the dead man's place. The flames were high today. I could see them licking over the walls, out across the roofs, creeping along the floors. Some places burn all the time even though you can't see anything to burn. Fire that doesn't consume—that must be Odin's work. But it consumes you quickly enough if you go near it. Except for this boy. He had been burned only on the surface.

Another person here with me! You don't understand. How could you?

There he was, turning on his heel. My father, Odin. There was a trickle of blood coming out of his mouth. I took the flowers and put them in the glass jar under him. There were hundreds of other little bits and pieces there. He had old leaves turned brown in his buttonhole and a handful of sand scattered over him, and a bunch of flowers stuffed down his trouser pockets. All his. Gifts to me from Jenny from the outside world that I had given to him. Each day I come and tell him about my day, offer him my memories, but I said nothing about the boy. He was mine. Odin had given him to me—the only thing he had ever given back. He was mine and I wasn't going to share him ever, not with anyone. You understand? He was *mine*.

I went to the edge where the fire began and put my hand low to the ground, into the flames. Perhaps I had become like the boy—my hair would burn and the skin would shrivel off, but I would remain unharmed. I watched as the little downy hairs on the back of my hand burned and shriveled—but then the fire scorched me and I had to whip it out with a little yelp of pain. It hurt like Hel. I was jumping about waving it in the air and blowing on it to cool it down. I was furious! I turned to the dead man and shouted, "You won't ever trust me, then!" But he just hung there, spun slowly around on the rope on his ankle, and never gave a sign.

"How long, oh Lord, how long?" I asked him. It was a prayer that my mother taught me. I think maybe he smiled slightly but as usual he never said a word.

16

love in the machine

Sigurd recovered slowly. Physically there wasn't much wrong with him—his burns weren't even skin deep. But he was exhausted in body, spirit, and mind.

In a couple of days his red shine was gone and in a few more a soft fuzz began to cover his whole body. It was as if the fire had burned away a human layer of him and the lion in his genes was showing through. He began to grow a soft, short covering of tawny fur. Where his skin showed through it glowed and shimmered like the dragon's, and never again did he have finger or toe prints. Within a week, he was golden. His hair grew down his neck and across his shoulders, flecked with silver and chocolate brown.

He recovered in a dream, in which the past and present lost their boundaries. He spoke with his mother, or Alf, or Regin, he played with his childhood friends and made love with the girls who grew up with him among the dunes. He spoke with Bryony, inspected the little gifts that she showed him—a tiny cream-colored shell, the broken lock from a bracelet, the petal from a daffodil, a blade of grass, things small enough for a wren to carry in her beak. She often didn't know what they were and she was thrilled when he gave them a name.

As he emerged from his convalescence, Sigurd suffered nightmares, in which he endured death after death, but had lost the ability to die. Odin had shown him death; was he showing him eternity now? If so, Sigurd knew what he feared the most. Every pleasure finally becomes a torment, and the gods, like kings, go mad at the end. All he wanted was to be human, with its little span of years and its frustrations and unfulfilled yearnings. He knew that the world was more lovely by far than any heaven. Eternity disgusted him. The immortals cannot love. They never age, they never change, they aren't really alive at all. The thought that he was turning into one of them so terrified him that he awoke from his dreams, screaming at the top of his lungs to be sure that Odin heard his rejection.

Bryony ran through from the kitchen to his call. She touched his face. His eyes snapped open and he stared up at her.

"Hush, hush—it's all right. There's nothing here," she murmured. Sigurd suddenly reached up and flung his arms around her. She was like him—human. He understood now why Odin interfered and fouled things up. He was jealous. All gods are. Their lives, so diluted by endless time, are worthless; they have nothing.

"Unchanging, invisible," he muttered to himself, then he laughed. Eternity was a frozen moment in which nothing ever happened. Every second he lived as a man was worth more than all their countless centuries. Bryony believed that memories were holy—she was right. The gods were parasites on the lives of the living. The truest way to worship them was to forget them forever.

Sigurd took the girl in his hands and held her face so that he could see her better. Another human being—the most precious thing imaginable. She was beautiful, full of life, living and growing, knowing, remembering, rushing along with him now in the arms of the present. She was so much more than anything you could possibly make up. Lovingly, Sigurd traced his fingers around her face, exploring her eyes, her ears, the contours of her jaw. He ran his fingers through her hair and watched her watching him. No one had ever touched her like that before. He seemed to be sharing the sensations in her skin.

Encouraged, Bryony put her hand to his face and did the same back, exploring all the shapes of his face.

"This is just for us," he said. "Not for Odin—this is for us." Bryony nodded, yes, yes! She knew exactly what he meant.

"He has too much already," she said. "He can't ever know what it's really like, anyway."

There on the bed, they explored each other from head to foot, stroking, smelling, tasting, listening, soaking up every sensation, filling every sense—in between the toes, the tips of the fingers, behind the ears, eyes, mouth, nose—yes, every part. What nicer parts to kiss, but those that feel the nicest? It was all delicious.

Bryony frowned at his penis, nodding its head at her. "I know what this is for," she said, holding it in her hand.

Sigurd leaned forward and touched her underneath. "And I know what this is for," he replied. They laughed, reached out to each other, and became lovers.

Every day they made love and talked—about gods, about dreams, about hope, about life. They shared their histories in whispers. Within a week, when Sigurd was well enough to get out of bed, they had already fallen in love.

They were the only thinking creatures in their world. There was no society, no crowds, no parks where they could mingle with other people—just the warm metal under their feet, the beating flames, the grinding of worn metal parts. There was the smell of hot metal and oil, of chemicals and protein soups, boiled fur and rusty blood. Sigurd had the memory of a rich life, and all she knew was this. She had no way to measure him, no memories or experience of other boys and girls, or men and women, but she wanted to give all she had, her entire self, body, mind, spirit, and soul, to this experience here and now. There were never two people more prepared to fall in love, more suited to fall in love, more willing to carry it through to the end.

And love, which we can all have, which is common as grass, truly does conquer all. Prisoners fall in love with guards, torturers with their victims, racists with other races. There's no corner of Hel you can't find people in love; but it doesn't always make you whole again. There are wounds of the mind that never heal. What is the future for these two—the boy so young, designed for greatness, so easily loved and loving? And the girl, so greedy for life? Look at the two of them, amazed at this sudden secret between them. Love is a secret society, a community of two. Only you know, only you understand, only you can see. It's sex and talk and discovery; everything one learns about the other, they learn about themselves, as well. It's a revelation. But after that? Maybe Bryony was bound to fall in love with the first boy she ever met—she'd been on her own so long, you couldn't blame her. Maybe Sigurd, after what he'd suffered, was bound to fall in love with whoever happened to be there. But maybe, just maybe they are made for each other, two people only complete in their togetherness. For now at least, in their secret place, they believe that this is forever. They are visionaries. There is no one more loyal than Sigurd, except for Bryony herself.

And in a room half a mile away, a dead man swings by his heel and half smiles with his cold lips. If Odin wants this, surely it can work?

And if he doesn't, what then?

the search
through crayley

It is six months later. Sigurd and Bryony are preparing Slipper
for a journey. It's time to go back to the world.

They hadn't missed it so far, not even Bryony, who felt at
first that she couldn't wait another day, another hour to reach
the fresh air now that the means of her deliverance was with
her. She'd had to wait while Sigurd recovered, and by the time
he was better, neither of them wanted anything but each other.
The world above, that festival of everything—that'd still be
there tomorrow and the next day and the day after that. There
was so much here already to know in their world of two.

But love is a story, the same as everything else, it moves on
and changes. They'd explored Bryony's world. They'd
crawled through the ducts and vents, run together in the great
machine halls, scooped creamy liquids from the protein vats,
hunted the packs of creatures whose ancestors had been
trapped here when the factory city had been closed down.
She'd shown him the high voltage creeping around the cables
in the refrigeration units, the great drilling machines and blue
fire burning up the rock face where Crayley was opening up
new areas underground and slowly colonizing them, the crystal

rooms, the chemical units, the pigment units that endlessly, uselessly made every color under the sun, the vehicle factory where antiquated engines were manufactured, discarded, and then reclaimed over and over to be made again into exactly the same things.

All the time during those first few months, Sigurd had been keeping an eye out for a possible escape route. Bryony had pointed out the possibilities—that tunnel leads into a mess of tangled machinery, you can't get through; that duct leads to fire, that door never opened; behind that wall of steel it sounds hollow. Sigurd took the stub of his sword and carved a hole in the walls, or through the stone or a duct or pipe, but every way they opened up led nowhere. Time passed. It was love in a dungeon. Gradually the search had become more earnest.

Sigurd himself could have ridden through the flames with Slipper, but he would have had to go alone; Bryony did not have dragon's skin. If their story was to grow, it had to move out of the factory and into the world. They had to find a way out.

The search was not only in the visible. They used sonar, magnetic resonance, wave and particle analysis, and other processes to explore areas they couldn't see. Slipper was the secret; his senses could pass through walls, go around corners, explore heat, density, and structure.

The cyber-horse had been left where he collapsed, near the dead man on the gibbet where the fire ended. When Bryony returned a few days later, the horse was gone and she'd assumed that the city had cleaned him away and recycled him. He'd been missing for a week before he returned, looking like a terror with his organics already beginning to regrow. He'd taken himself off to find the materials he needed to repair and regenerate himself, grazing in the steel forests and silicone meadows of the factory city, feeding from the protein vats and chemical works, hunting down the living things that hid in the tubes and pipes. He looked demonic, part metal skeleton and other inorganic components, part cyber-form, with titanium and plastics wedded to flesh. Over the next few months he'd grown back entirely, and he looked again like the Slipper Sigurd had known when he raced around the beaches and sand dunes of South Wales.

They'd worked their way slowly through the galleries, checking every few meters for hidden passages. If they found one, they painstakingly plotted it for size and for heat. The equipment was good, but not perfect; the results needed to be analyzed carefully. Often what seemed to be a passage turned out after several scans to be only a gap. Many ways that started out broad and wide turned narrow and disappeared, or branched endlessly and endlessly again. To have followed them all would take a thousand years, so they just stuck to the biggest ones, the ones that could take Slipper, as well. Every day, another hundred yards or so. Then, while they analyzed the results, Slipper hunted for them, or collected food and brought it back. If they found anything that looked promising, the next day they went to investigate. With the sword stub Sigurd cut his way through cables and metal work, rock face, concrete, ceramic or any other kind of material, to expose the likely hopes and follow them through. Some ways led on for a mile or more, coiling through abandoned scrapyards or galleries of solid rock, but they all ended the same way—in fire, hot enough to melt metal. They were in a little bubble of air surrounded by Hel.

All around Bryony's circumscribed little world they went. They found nothing. Then they went around again, and then again, obsessive with the panic of the trapped, until the dreadful urge to escape became weary and they found each other again.

And now they are still where they had started. Two lovers trapped—not a healthy situation for any love affair. They both look well. Sigurd has grown taller. It troubles him; he is still scared of becoming a monster himself. With his gifts and additions, he is already more than human; it's such a small step to become less than human next. Bryony, too, looks well. Her skin is better, her hair is better, she stands differently. She is more confident. She is loved and in love; how else could it be?

And what's this? Has she put on weight? Certainly around the stomach—but it's obvious. The way these two are together it would be a miracle if she wasn't pregnant. Another six months and there'll be three of them down there. The beginnings perhaps of an underground community? But that will not be; they will not allow it. This family is for the world.

And on her finger, a ring. Is she married? There are no priests here, unless you count the dead man, her father, and neither of them wants anything to do with him even if he was willing to speak the rites. Even Bryony has stopped visiting him. The little flowers and buds that Jenny Wren brings her she keeps for herself these days, and uses them to decorate the bedroom she and Sigurd share. He is the past, he is over. He is death: they are life.

But she has a ring anyway. A curious ring, strangely carved, a gift from Sigurd's own finger. This is her love token. She plays with it, feels it on her finger, and smiles. It reminds her of all the good things she has. A pretty, golden thing. Neither of them has any idea of the curse it carries.

Having found no way out, they have come up with another plan: Fafnir's skin. If Bryony were wrapped in that, she could survive the blaze as well. If! If it had survived the holocaust when Fafnir's arsenal went up. If it's not buried under a million tons of rubble, or blown into space, or captured and taken away as a souvenir by some prince or ganglord.

If if if. But it's a chance. And to get it, Sigurd must leave.

"What if you can't come back?" she asks. They are standing holding each other, face to face, body to body. He wants to have her, she wants to have him—it just happens whenever they touch. But they have been trying to escape for so long and now at last they are both scared.

"Why should that happen? I have the sword. I have my skin. I can survive."

"But what if? Perhaps. What then?"

"Then we'd be apart," he says.

They look carefully at each other.

"It could come to that," she says.

"It'd be better for me to stay here, then."

"No. You can't. You'll go mad. I'll go mad."

"This is terrible. This is so terrible." Sigurd turns and walks away, rubbing his face. He is the golden one! Things fall into his hand. Why was this so wrong?

"There's always been a way for me in my life, things happen. I was made for things to work."

"This is just you and me, Sig. Maybe no one built you and me into the way things are."

He looks at her. She looks at him. She holds her stomach. "You could wait for the baby to be born?"

"Yes."

"You can't. You're impatient. And I'm impatient too."

"If I wait for the baby, I'll have to wait again after it's born. It'll be helpless—you'll be helpless, maybe. You'll need me here."

"Not for long."

He smiled, no, she wouldn't be helpless, not for long. "But you know what I mean."

Bryony thought, bit her thumb, tried to see a way that was safer than this terrible separation, but couldn't.

"Then go now," she said. "You'll be back in time for the birth. You'll be back in time to take me up and our baby will be born in the real world."

Sigurd nodded, but said, "One more week. Give us another week, maybe two. That won't hurt. A holiday. Time to say good-bye."

Bryony didn't like it—they were both boiling with frustration already. But because she didn't want to lose him, because she thought that maybe this would be the last time she ever saw him, she agreed. Two more weeks. A holiday. Then the separation.

18

mother

So they had their holiday, but it was a desultory thing. The world was calling them. The search had become obsessive and that didn't stop now just because they wanted it to. They tried to take their time, go swimming, go hunting, make love, but the real business, the next thing, the escape, wouldn't leave them alone. Impatient, irritable with themselves and each other, they spent more time apart than they ever had before. Bryony spent hours poring over the maps and charts and scan results they had taken, pinned up in long rows on the walls of a deserted hangar, while Sigurd wandered about the galleries and shop floors, searching for clues. Either could have found one; it happened to be Bryony.

"Look at this." They were standing in the hangar. Three of the walls were covered with printed sheets of various scans. The entire reachable interior of Crayley was covered.

Sigurd looked. The scans she was showing him were of an area right on the edge of their world.

"I can't see anything."

"Here, and here." She showed him with her finger—small inconsistencies in the rock.

"That could be anything—denser rock, ores. Anyway, it's on the other side of the fire."

"And over here." She led him on to a set of scans for the area to the right of the first. "The same pattern, do you see? The same shade, the same order. And in between—can you see?" Very faint, hardly visible, another set of marks.

"It's too faint."

"If it was darker, what would you say it was?"

Sigurd looked closely. "Well, if it was darker it might be pipework. But . . ." He shrugged. The marks could mean anything.

"Bit of a coincidence, though. Regular markings like these, all pale, I know, but it's all regular. And then these marks where it's cooler."

"There's a lot of coincidences," pointed out Sigurd.

"But this bit just looks—it looks like it might look if someone was hiding something. It looks like it might be in disguise."

"Who has anything to hide down here?"

"I don't know. But there's a lot I don't know. It could be."

"It could be."

"It might be."

Sigurd grinned at her. "It's something. It's something to do if nothing else."

"And you never know."

"But the fire?"

"There's not much of it. I'll go in Slipper's hold. We could get through that much fire. It's doable."

"Then let's do it."

• • •

The area Bryony had found was in a long, high, wide corridor, sided by sheer rock. The rock was warm to the touch. A number of different pipes and ducts ran into it high up.

Bryony was right. Those pipes had to lead somewhere. Something lay beyond.

They gathered together some machinery, a drilling rig, and some scaffolding—there was plenty of that sort of thing in Crayley—and did some investigation before they went any farther. They used the scaffolding to reach the pipes and scanned them in detail. They carried air, water, and nutrients. The pipes carried on into the rock; it was their pale markings that Bryony had noticed, looking so much like natural variations in the rock. They didn't double back at any time, but carried straight in and disappeared. What for? What needed feeding on the other side of rock and heat, with no way in or out?

They set up the drill rig to gouge its way into the rock face and a conveyor to carry the resulting rubble away. Straight away they noticed something strange about the rock. It was artificial. As Bryony had suggested, this area was in camouflage.

The rig bored its way in, driving a tunnel two meters wide into the rock face. Almost at once there was a disturbance in the corridor behind them—a stream of rumbling machines heading for them: reclaim-bots. Crayley was coming to put a stop to this. It was a moment of fear as the ugly machines trundled forward, but one of triumph, too. They were onto something. For the first time, the city was showing its hand. Crayley was scared.

That initial attack was frightening, but not deadly. The bots were clumsy efforts, no match for anything as advanced as

Sigurd and Slipper, and they held the drill head easily. It was when the rig finally broke through and the last layer of rock crumbled away that the real defenses became apparent. Suddenly the rig was torn to pieces; it seemed to dissolve in front of their eyes. Then out of the tunnel came a blast, a rocket-rush of burning fuel so hot the air turned red. Through this heat came another army—terrible creatures of steel and polysilicone, able to resist any temperature, and armed front and back, above and below with all the weaponry Crayley could design. These weren't adapted reclaimers—they were designed to kill. Even before they drew near, they began their attack, firing a rain of hot steel, rounds fired at the rate of dozens a second. Coils of razor wire were hurled forward. Pushing Bryony to one side, Sigurd took the force of them to protect her.

Without needing instruction, Slipper dropped his hatch and Bryony jumped inside. Her human skin was no match for this game. Sigurd jumped on the horse's back, the horse crouched down low, bending his legs so that his belly brushed the ground, and ran forward into the narrow tunnel in a strange, swaying crouch, straight into the faces of the killing machines and the blast of burning fuel. The heat was tremendous. Sigurd screamed; Slipper screamed. Sigurd felt the hair bloom on his head, saw the tawny hair on his arm turn to ash, and his skin flush crimson with flame. Slipper was ablaze under him, but without pausing the cyber-horse plowed forward, crushing the enemy beneath his titanium frame, pulping them under his belly, tearing them to pieces with his kicking hooves and tearing teeth, spraying them with ammunition, while Sigurd hacked and chopped like a machine himself. Inch by inch they pushed forward until at last they burst out into the open. The heat multiplied. For a second boy and horse spiraled in confusion, screaming in pain. Then the cyber-horse reared up and bounded forward, scanning as he went, on to where the heat lessened.

It didn't take long to reach the place he had charted, but here again was another wall. No time or chance to fetch another rig. Sigurd dismounted, drew the stub of his sword, and carved his way in, while Slipper held the space behind him against the following army of deathbots. The wall was five meters thick; it took him an hour to carve through that. Out to the other side and there they found the cool air again—a place designed for living things. But what living thing was it that Crayley kept so secret and so safe?

Slipper opened his hatch and Bryony jumped out to join in the fight. The bots had had their fun—now it was time for the living and the half alive, cyborgs with mutated weaponry, soldier bots that lived and breathed. Other monsters—beasts of incredible shape and size, flesh bolted, welded metal to bone, bone to resin, resin to flesh, came forward to attack them. Dismounting, Sigurd left Slipper to fight his way forward while he and Bryony kept to the rear. Together, shoulder to shoulder, the two lovers hacked and chopped at the ranks of soulless things, fighting their way forward at a snail's pace down a narrowing tunnel and toward a steel door. They reached it and cut it open only to find another passage leading to another door. Behind that, another and then another and then another. Only when they burst through the fourth and final door did the chaos and slaughter stop.

It was as if they had pressed the off switch. The cyborgs

stopped hacking and crouched down quietly; the machines whirred dully and rested, their commands ceased. The lovers had won the battle. Ancient and half alive as the city was, it was cunning and heartless in a way nothing born could ever be. The years had only increased its cunning, determination, and intelligence, but there was no point in fighting anymore, the secret had been reached. Crayley had no choice but to wait and watch.

They were in a small room carved out of raw rock. In front of them was a tank and in the tank was a gray-haired woman, catheterized for her bodily functions. Her head was covered with wires and tubing, running to a bank of machinery lining one wall. There was the quiet hum of electrical activity. The woman's eyes were shut. She did not seem to be aware of anything. Bryony walked up to her. She put her hands on the glass above the woman's face and half turned to Sigurd.

"My mother," she said.

Sigurd came to stand by her and put an arm around her. Gently Bryony rapped the glass above the woman's face. There was no response. "Mother," she called. But the old woman did not move, could not move, couldn't see or hear her. Bryony banged the glass hard, so hard the woman rocked softly in the liquid, like a sea creature in the tide. But her eyes remained shut.

Gently Sigurd took her arm.

"I've been dying," said a voice. Startled, they looked around. The voice came from loudspeakers set in amongst the equipment all around them. It was not possible to place it.

"I've been dying for a hundred years."

"The city," said Sigurd. "It's Crayley. It's here."

"They cut off my fuel. I made fuel from cultures. They cut off my air. I made air from rock. I drove tubes to the surface to breathe. I have been alone a long time, and I can only last so long. I use things up. I need to redesign myself to use new resources. I need more power, more organization. I need imagination. If it wasn't for her, I would be dead. If it wasn't for her, Bryony, you would be dead. All this, the shop floors, the machines, the bots, the programming and organization, it all begins here. Your mother is running this . . . she is running *me*. She's a part of me now. If you cut her off, we will all die."

Sigurd looked at Bryony. "Do we believe it? Why should we?"

Bryony scowled. "I haven't noticed many changes since you—did this to her."

"She's old. Her brain is already fixed, I can only adapt her so far. She keeps things running, no more."

"Why didn't you take me?"

"You're too fast, too quick, too clever. I had to make do . . . I had to use what I could. For a long time, I've used what I could."

Sigurd walked over to the banks of machinery where the voice came from. "And why shouldn't I stick my sword in your circuits right now? You had no right!"

"I have a right to live, the same as everyone else. Why should I die for you? And if I die, Bryony dies. And you, too, Sigurd. We are two miles underground here. When I explode, how will your skin help you then? I am your home. You are me, and we are her. She is the mother of us all now."

Behind them, Slipper had begun to graze on the orgo-mechanisms. They made no attempt to evade him, didn't even groan or moan as he bit into them. Their purpose did not require them to have pain. The cool air, the dull light, the sound of Slipper munching away at the creatures on the threshold, the old woman lying puffy with liquid in the tank, the eerie voice explaining it all to them—all these things gave the place an air of unreality, as if they were in a strange dream, and in the morning it would all be forgotten.

Bryony looked down at her mother through the glass. Was it true, what the city said? It was using her mother, that much was obvious. The city could not live forever in isolation here deep underground, that much had to be true too. But the rest of it? Would everything collapse if they took her out?

"Can she hear me?"

"No."

"Can she hear what you're saying?"

"No. She will never regain consciousness. That was in the way."

Bryony turned to Sigurd. "If we free her, will she be all right?"

"No," said Crayley.

Sigurd shook his head. "I can't tell," he said. "It depends on what Crayley has disabled. She might not be able to breathe on her own. . . ."

"She can't," said Crayley.

"Or she could bleed through the connections."

"She will."

"Shut up!" screamed Bryony. "Why should we believe anything you say?" She put her hands to her face. She couldn't bear to see her mother like this, expressionless, puffy with years of immersion in liquid, naked. She was a modest woman, she had never liked to be seen naked. Bryony took off her coat and draped it over the tank.

"We need to think," she said. "I don't know what to do."

It was an impossible situation. If they tried to rescue the old woman, they'd kill her. It would take an expert to get her out—many of those wires went deep into her brain. It would certainly be to the city's advantage to disable the parts of her it did not need—consciousness, voluntary muscle control, anything that might disrupt her use as a component. As for the threat that it depended on her—why else had it protected her so well from them? Crayley had thrown everything at them in an effort to keep this place a secret. It needed her, that was for sure.

But did they?

In frustration, Sigurd walked up to a bank of computing equipment and drew his sword, but the machine mocked him.

"Kill me and you kill yourself. Harm me and you harm the one you love. What else do you have up your sleeve?"

"A deal," said Sigurd. Perhaps they could bargain with it. "Let us out. We want a way to the surface."

"Not possible."

"Why?"

"I am buried! You buried me. I am damaged—you damaged me. When you blew Fafnir's weapons to pieces, you blew half a mile of bedrock into the sky. It's heaped on top of us. I had a passage up there to the air—I could get that at least—but now it's closed, thanks to you."

"Drill up, then."

"I am," hissed the machine. "It's going to take months more. A year. Wait a year. Then you can leave."

Sigurd and Bryony talked, thought, plotted—but they could

come up with no plan to outwit the city. The old woman lay impassive in her living death. A vegetable; could she be made human again? Who knew? For now, they had no choice but to believe Crayley.

So they left, promising to be back. The city knew now that they could get back—they had gained that much at least. As they left the chamber, the city called after them, "She's taking care of you. She still loves you, Bryony. She's still your mother." It lifted the fire, parted the hordes of creatures and machines it had used to keep them out: it was pleased to see them go.

It was Sigurd's first defeat. But the battle wasn't over yet.

Back in the safety of their house, Bryony turned to him grimly. "It wants my baby. You have to go. You have to get out of here before the baby comes."

"Through half a mile of rock! It said—"

"It's lying. It wants my baby! Don't you see? That's why I'm here. It's why you're here. Crayley planned it all. It wants our baby for a brain."

The human brain has seven billion connections. A baby's brain could be wired as it grew. What a processor! What couldn't Crayley do with one of those?

19

parting

The baby was their future, their treasure, their love. Nothing could be allowed to harm the baby. They began preparations for Sigurd's journey back to the surface at once, planning which way he should go, how the city would try to stop him, how he could fight back. Sigurd was expendable now as far as Crayley was concerned—what if it tried to cover him in an avalanche? What if it let him escape and then closed the doors? Every possibility was discussed in hushed whispers long into the night, both fearful that the city was eavesdropping on their plans.

At last they fell quickly asleep, exhausted. Sigurd slept on, but Bryony awoke after only a few hours. She got up quietly. There was a shrill peep, and from out of a crevice somewhere on the wall, Jenny Wren suddenly appeared. A second later she was on her shoulder, nibbling Bryony's ear with her bill. Bryony put a finger up and stroked her tiny head. Then the bird was gone, hidden in her clothes.

Close in her mind Bryony could feel the darkness waiting. Sadness, anger, frustration, rage. This was going to cripple her. She'd had so little, she'd gained so much, and so much more was promised. Love. A baby. The world! It was all in her hand and now it was going to be snatched away. She was certain of it. She was a little piece in a big game. The baby was not for her, the world above was not for her. But one thing she did have, one thing was truly hers: Sigurd. Her love for him and his love for her, that was real. No one could ever take it away from her. But she was going to send him away anyway.

Bryony was certain that once he'd gone, she'd never see him again. If Crayley couldn't kill him it would certainly never let him back. Her only ray of hope was that it wouldn't let him leave at all—that it would keep him down here with her, breeding stock for brains to keep the underground city supplied with quality processors. That was a hope? A breeding program for the machine?

The hope was a no-hope, it could not be allowed to happen. Sigurd had to have a life even if she couldn't. He had to go, she had to send him away and stand here alone. At least she wouldn't lose the love they'd had for each other. That could never become part of the machine, another component to keep things running smoothly, something to be manipulated and used. It would remain theirs, a holy memory, hers and his, at the center of her life.

When he had gone, the depression would come; but she would recover. She would have her baby and fight to save it and lose; then more depression, and waiting, waiting, hoping, hoping. How could she bear to wait and hope, when she knew that the waiting would last forever? How would the hours pass, the weeks and the years? What would she do with all that time? How could she live when she had no future?

Bryony paced the floor silently. She had to do something—

she had to do something now, or she'd never have the strength to let him go. She dressed quietly and walked alone through the hot corridors to the clearing in the rubble, close to the flames, where the dead man still hung.

Odin, her father. What good had he ever done her? Here he was as always, freshly dead at the moment. She bent to look closely into his face. He wasn't handsome and young like Sigurd was. His face was deeply lined, squat and heavy. He had a good deal of the animal in him, although there was no trace of halfman characteristics. His nose was crooked and flat as if it had been squashed. He had high cheek bones. There was dried mucus around his eyes where the flies gathered and spittle dribbling down past his upside-down nose into his eyes.

"You big shit," she whispered. But for all she knew, Odin was a fly caught in the passage of time as much as she was.

She put her face close to his. He didn't smell bad today— just the clammy, heavy smell of cooling flesh. She tried to feel if there was any breath on her face—sometimes she thought it might be so—but today there was nothing. She pressed her cheek against his. It was cold and wet. She jerked away, disgusted.

"Change this for me," she whispered. "Make it different. Stop the fire, give us a way out. Give us a *chance*, Father."

Dead men don't speak. She drew back. Odin swayed slightly. Something moved in the corner of his eye, a slight dull glint. It overflowed and crept out of the corner, down into his eyebrows and hair. A tear, a dead tear from a dead god.

Bryony stood up. What use were his tears to her? She had enough of her own. She looked around her feet at all the offerings she had given him—the little leaves and dried-up flowers, the twigs, the twists of paper and scraps of cloth, the buds and butterfly wings, the dried insect skeletons and the little bones of mice and voles that Jenny had brought her over the years. She kicked her foot lightly over them.

"I gave you everything," she said. "And you gave me nothing back." As she said it, she thought she hadn't given him everything after all. Not Sigurd. But then Odin already had him. Odin had everything. Odin had enough.

She took her knife out of her belt and cut the god down. He fell with a heavy thud on the raw stone floor among the litter at her feet. Then she went to scavenge around in the empty storage units close by. She soon found what she was looking for—an old trolley, an attachment the robots used for ferrying spare parts and items for repair around the factory floor. When she pushed it back to Odin's clearing, Sigurd was waiting for her.

"I thought you'd be here." She shrugged but held him tight when he came up to her.

"Last day," she said.

"I'll be back."

"If anyone can, you can," she told him.

Together, they heaved Odin up onto the trolley and heaped over him all the gifts Bryony had given him. They stuffed them in his pockets, piled them on his chest and thighs, until he was covered with all the things a wren could carry to show what the world was like. Jenny perched on top of the dead man's chest, piping, flying between him and Bryony, sometimes even carrying a leaf or twig as if she was helping to make a nest.

When it was done, they wheeled him to the edge of the fire. Bryony kissed him on the cheek, and then pushed him, trolley and all, into the flames. The pieces of dried vegetation and paper flared up at once, then his hair, then his clothes. He began to smoke. With a section of pipe, Sigurd pushed him farther into the fire where it was hotter and he began to blaze, his skin shriveling, his flesh hissing. The flames soon covered him. He seemed to move a little, to twist and writhe.

"Just the fire moving him," said Bryony. They watched until the burning body was nothing but a denser patch of fire before they left and began to walk back. They were filled with an exhilaration at having destroyed Odin, even though they didn't really believe that it was the end of the god. Exhilaration, and a sense of privacy, too, as if he had been watching them all the time from his hidden place inside death. They were on their own now. They felt like children left alone in a house for the first time.

They walked around by the edge of the fire for a while, throwing bits and pieces into the flames and watching them burn. It was hot so close to the flames. They kissed. Sigurd pulled Bryony's clothes down her back, and then his. They piled the clothes on the ground underneath them, and made love to each other, very softly and tenderly. Then they fell asleep, warmed by the fire, in each other's arms.

Before he left, Sigurd put in his pocket two small items—a small stainless steel nut and the bolt to fit it. Jenny could survive the flames, they knew that. She would come to him and he would send her back with a message. If she had the nut in her beak, then the skin was there and he would be quick; if it was the bolt, he would have to go searching. Either way, he promised he would be back, with or without the skin, in time to see their baby born. Nothing this earth had could stop him.

Bryony nodded. He would do his best to be quick; she would do her best to wait. They kissed one more time. Then Sigurd jumped up onto Slipper and ran at a gallop for the great pipe that had led him down in the first place.

"Love!" he shouted through the flames as they closed in around him.

"Love," she shouted back. He glanced once more over his shoulder, then the flames beating against the metal around him roared in his ears, the terrible pain of burning enveloped his senses, and the sight and sound of her was gone.

20

the surface

Riding into the fire wasn't easy, especially since Sigurd had done it only a few days before. The pain was terrifyingly real. There was the acrid stink of burnt meat as the new flesh forming on Slipper's alloy bones burned, the screaming of the horse under him. He drew breath; the fire penetrated his throat and his spittle began to boil on his tongue.

"All this for love," thought Sigurd deep inside, behind the pain. But he was unharmed. Knowing that his living flesh could only be burned on that one spot between his shoulder blades where the blood had not touched, he padded the place with fireproof rags.

Acid winds on fire in bright green, yellow, and blue raged around his head. They rode on, dodging and diving between passages, down vents gushing fumes and flames, through rooms filled with explosions in blazing colors. Slipper dashed to and fro, up and down, scanning ahead to avoid perils.

As they got closer to the surface, the way got harder. The vast explosion caused by the destruction of Fafnir's arsenal had crushed the top levels of Crayley; flattened pipework and rooms full of rubble blocked the way. But the city had lied when it said it was far from the surface. Fire and smoke showed them the way, whisking and rushing through narrow passages and flues under pressure. Slipper followed them, rushed forward, launched a missile of his own to unblock stone-fall and crushed machinery. He had a dozen senses more than us, but even so there were many false turns as he found his route. At last they were under a final lid of rock and crushed debris. Slipper loosed one more rocket to blast through the last few meters of wreckage, leapt forward into the heart of the explosion—and they were suddenly out in the open, in the bright light of a drizzly spring day, leaving a wreckage of wet rocks, shattered earth, and mud behind them.

The bawling of the city stopped suddenly as the rocks fell back into the crater. Slipper, burned to his metal bones once more, collapsed on his side and laid his head down to rest after the trauma.

The quiet of day filled Sigurd's ears.

He could feel his whole body drinking it up, just soaking it in. All that goodness. Rain is magic, he'd forgotten. Cool, beautiful water falling from the sky, like a blessing. He got to his knees in a muddy puddle, dipped in his hand, and tried to splash his face, but he was still too hot and the water vaporized at his touch. So he just took in a huge lungful of the beautiful cool air and let it out in a long stream. It formed a plume of steam, like a dragon.

The smells! Wet rock, wet earth, green plants. He picked up a tuft of moss and sniffed it. It smelled of earth and life— it was like nothing you could ever imagine. He thought to himself, Isn't the world a million times better than anything you could make up? What single god could ever think of all this? We could only know a fraction of all the gods that exist.

There must be legions of them for every living thing.

And Bryony was away from this. Every second she spent down there was like murder. What was the point if she wasn't here too? Suddenly Sigurd felt more alone than he ever had, and burst into tears. He felt as if he had traveled to another world and back.

A little later, somewhere not far off, I heard dogs barking. If they were halfmen, I could get some clothes off them. I got up and moved on. Maybe they even knew something about Fafnir's skin.

I wandered about for a while trying to find the source of the noise, but in among the canyons and scattered boulders, it was difficult to trace. The ground had been torn to pieces, rocks lying about broken and smashed in fields of clay and debris. Sounds seemed to come first from one place, then another, then it stopped altogether. I was trying to work out landmarks but everything was so jumbled about it all looked the same. It was a huge, rough garden someone had just built but life was already returning. There were little seedlings creeping out of cracks everywhere, clumps of moss and little ferns shooting up. Everything was young. It was as if the whole place had been just made. It made me smile. It was another thing I could show Bryony. You can't begin to imagine how much I was looking forward to getting her up here. Just to hold her hand and show her this wrecked place would be like showering her with presents. Look! Here are the mosses, here's the sky, this is rain. It's all yours!

And then I thought, But the skin could be anywhere. It could be buried under a billion tons of rubble. Anywhere!

I speeded up even though I could have run as fast as light and it would get me no nearer to Fafnir's skin if it was buried under this lot. Then I turned a corner and I heard the noise again—yip-yip-yip, and a barrage of squealing and enraged grunting.

"Get im get im get im! Graaah! Heee ha ha ho ho. Faaaark!" Now I was close, it sounded like mainly piggy squealing, although there was something barky about it too. I rounded a corner and came across this bizarre scene. There was a crowd of halfmen—well, half beasts, really. They had long bodies, high in the shoulders like a hyena, or an ape on all fours. There was a bit of human there, but not much; they had low brain boxes, and long snouts. Pig-dog people, but a lot more pig than dog and not much people. I like pigs—I grew up with them— but they can be bastards, really brutal when they get a temper on them. They'll eat anything and do anything—a big mean pig is the last thing you want to get cornered by. This lot were hunting in a pack like dogs—really dangerous. They were huge too—about three meters long, one and a half at the shoulder and their heads were maybe a quarter of their entire length, full of ugly yellow tusks, big as chair legs.

They stank of shite, stale meat, BO, and pork, and they were making an earsplitting racket, squealing and shouting and grunting and snorting and barking—unbelievable. You'd have thought there were about three hundred of them from at least four different species, rather than just fifteen from one.

They'd gathered on the slope of a huge slab of rock maybe thirty meters long and perched right on the top of it, about fifteen meters off the ground, there was dinner. Dinner was a long skinny dog—a sort of cross between a monkey, a man, and a dog, really. He was tall and thin, with long arms and legs and big hands and black and white sheepdog hair falling forward on his face. He had a fairly human face, jaws stuck out a bit, plenty of teeth, and a high brain box: a true halfman.

The pig-dogs had him right where they wanted him. They weren't hunting anymore, they were just having fun. The rock he was on was steep but not that difficult to climb and the halfman was unarmed. They were just taking their time, lolling about shouting abuse up at their prisoner. "Hey, man! Gonna eat your leg!" That sort of thing. They would, too. Their heads were as big as a small table and they had jaw bones like road diggers. They could take your leg off at the thigh with one bite.

The halfman was in a hopeless situation. He was crouching down holding on to the rock with both hands, glancing behind him as if he was scared he'd fall off. Whenever he did, the pig-dogs broke out in a new fit of squealing and jeering to make him look back at them.

"Come on down, the water's great!" one of them yelled, and they all started rolling around on the floor and grunting and laughing like a bunch of comedians.

We all have to eat, but the dogman had a high head. We high heads need to stick together. The other lot didn't look as if they knew much except where the next meal was coming from.

On the other hand, if I got in their way, I might be seconds.

I was thinking, Well, but what could I do anyway? There were so many of them. I ought to be creeping quietly out of the way—but then it was taken out of my hands. They spotted me. Not as dumb as they looked, see; they had a few lookouts posted. I turned round and there was one right behind me grinning like a bastard.

"Yeah! Goin sumwhere, eh? Naaaaah!" it said. It gave a high-pitched squeal and the others were on their feet at once, giving me the once-over with those piggy eyes. One of them let out a whoop—it must have been like meals on legs for them—and they came running to see who could have first taste.

I had no weapons except for the stub of the sword. I was stark bollock naked, I didn't even have my hair, for god's sake. They were big guys, full of teeth and hunger in their big mouths—and the sheer size of them! Their shoulders were up around my chest. There's nothing more dangerous than something with just enough brain to think and not enough to care. They were going to go through me like dicing carrots.

I turned to make a run for it, but there was the lookout grinning in my face. Shit! Slipper'd wandered off, gone to get some fodder or something. He'd come, he was coming now, but that was already too late. The pack could run faster than I could fall off a cliff. I turned, conscious of my vulnerable back, and by that time they were already only four or five meters off. The lookout was behind me, crouched, ready to leap on me, his jaws wide open. They'd kept their tongues still all that way, but now they were ready for the kill, they broke into jeering and shouting. "You dead, man-face—eat him, eat him, eat the fucker."

The lookout jumped. I lifted up the sword—it was all I had. I struck out at his face and caught him on the nose and I split that bugger from snout to ring in one blow as he went over my head. The sword stub wasn't big enough to go right through his back, but it had gouged a rut in him a foot deep right along. He hit the ground behind me with a heavy flap, spilled out all over the ground, coughed, and died.

There was a sudden silence. No one could believe it, not even me. The pig-dog lay there on the ground spouting blood and guts. And suddenly, suddenly, I thought, Hang on. I'm the Dragon Man. Cut me, do I bleed? Strike me, do I cry? No, I don't.

Those boys were *dead*.

I kicked the dead pig's snout and spat on him. I stretched out a hand in welcome. "Come on, boys," I said. "Come and get it."

There was another second of silence. Then they charged.

They were all over me before I could move—bang! Jaws on my arms and legs, one on my face. I just stood there and howled. It was agony! I might not bleed but they could crush me to a pulp inside my own skin. I thought, What am I doing? Fifteen-plus giant killer pig-dogs against one little me? I must have been mad. I tried to move, but I was held in two dozen vices, and they were crushing the life out of me.

Then one of them, who had the whole of my head in his jaws, started scrabbling with his legs up my back, trying to tear the insides out of me, and one of his claws caught the spot where the aspen leaf had fallen. It was *sore*.

So I started to fight back. And you know what? It was easy. It was so easy, it was ridiculous. I sliced, sheared, poked, and stabbed, and the next thing I knew, I was standing chest high in body parts. Slipper had turned up in the middle of it but he hardly even bothered to join in. By the time I stopped he was already off grazing on the bodies. The few that weren't dead were crawling off whimpering and moaning, limbs off, spilling blood and guts behind them. One of them had his jaw sheered off at the base of his skull. It was that quick.

In a fit of disgust I ran after the ones still alive and killed them quick. It wasn't bloodlust, it was pity. Better than letting them die slowly. Then—well, then I began to shake. I felt sick. What had happened? Where did I get that strength from? I was good at war games, I knew that, but this was something else. It was something new.

And it was *unnecessary*. I'd always wanted to be humane— you understand? It's part of being a man that you show mercy. War is a last resort and I hadn't had to do this. Half of them had been trying to get away once it became clear how unfair the fight was. It wasn't self defense, I'd done it because I could— because it was easy.

It was proof I'd taken more from Fafnir than just his skin. I was turning into something else.

I made myself a promise right there and then never to kill unless I had to. I was too strong. I was stuff from the stories, but these were real lives. This time it was pig-dogs, no one was going to miss them, they probably had to die anyway if the country was ever going to get back to normal. But next time it might be people. You should have seen the mess—so easy, so quick! I never wanted to do anything like that again.

There was a noise behind me, a little clatter of stones; it was doggy, coming down from his rock. He looked a bit sheepish—he was trying to sneak off, I guess. He stood a little way off—not too near—shivering and rubbing his hands together. He was a good-looking piece of work. You know how it is with dogmen sometimes, they look all snout. This guy had a nice smile.

"Thanks," he said, and he gestured around at the mess I'd made.

"Bit over the top," I croaked.

He raised his eyebrows and looked surprised. It made me smile, he looked so put out. I think he was putting it on. "Don't worry 'bout it. Them pig-dogs—yow! We're better off without em."

I didn't know what to say. We stood looking at the slaughter. "Short work," he said in a bit.

"I didn't expect . . . ," I began. Doggy started nodding eagerly, agreeing with whatever I said before I even said it. I found I had tears trickling down my face. He peered at them in confusion.

"What's the matter?" he asked incredulously. "You're not crying for them, are you? You saved my life. Don't feel sorry for *them*."

I shook my head. He had me all wrong, I wasn't that human. Stupid! I was crying for myself. Every time something like this happens something dies inside me. I was thinking, I'm fifteen years old. I shouldn't be doing this. I should still be at home with my mum. Then I felt cross with myself. I was sorry for *myself*? What was that about, in the middle of all this death? But doggy felt sorry for me too.

"You okay?" he asked. I nodded. It was no time for grief. I had things to do.

"Let's talk," I said. I saw him looking down at me—then I remembered, I had no clothes. "Sorry," I said, but he just smiled at me.

"I don't mind," he said, grinning. "Rather nice actually. Mmm." Then he came up to me and put his arm through mine. "You need a drink," he said. "C'mon—let's get out of here, before the piggy friends come along, huh?"

"No, listen—I'm looking for something. The dragon's skin.

You know of it? Heard any stories. I need to get it."

"Oh?" He looked closely at me. "Are you Volson?"

"How can you tell?"

"Call it intuition."

"I need the skin. Do you know anything? Heard anything?"

"Ah," he said. "Fafnir's skin. Rrrr. That wouldn't be something easy to take. You better come along with me."

"You know where it is?" I grabbed his arm in my excitement, and he had to ease my hand, I was squeezing so hard.

"Yeah, I know where it is. We can be friends."

Yes! The way things just unfold for me! I felt a thrill of fear go through me, because things shouldn't be that easy. Love or war, it all just falls into my hand. I knew then that saying goodbye to the god wasn't such an easy thing. Odin was still working for me, or through me—who knows which? Things weren't going to stop happening. Nothing could stop me now.

hogni

What d'ya make of him? Gor-geous. Two meters tall, easy. Muscles—not the lumpy sort, either—long, lean ones. My favorites. Very excited. And bright pink all over. And stark naked! Oh, dear! Have I forgotten something? Is it Christmas? Is it my birthday today?

On the other hand, he chopped up those pig-dogs like a butcher making mince. He was covered in blood from head to foot, smiling down at me, that big sword end in his hand.

I didn't know which way to turn. And then he started crying! Bless! And then when he found out I knew something about the skin, he started beaming all over his face and chatting away—blab, blab, blab—like a big kid who'd just found out where his mum was. Sweet. But, wowser! I wanted to put him over my shoulder and pat him better. Rrrra! Yes. All brotherly: not.

Well, woof, woof, woof. You know what they say about me: a lot of leering lightly worn—I mean, learning. I knew who this was. Who else? Volson! The cyber-horse just confirmed it. Fucking terror! It was enormous—half tank, half skeleton, eyes like televisions. It strolls up in the middle of the fight and starts eating the dead bodies! Ugh. Who else has one of those for a pet? Horrified!

A Volson. We thought they were all finished. Sigurd was supposed to have died after he killed the dragon. So what do you do about one of them? Better to have him on your side than not on your side; but then how can he be on our side if he wants to be king? What would Gunar have to say about that, eh? Roowf! Not happy at all.

So I ponced over to him, very charming, and linked arms and led him off. Get him to talk, see what he was up to, gerrowf? He had some spare clothes tucked away in that monster horse he had with him, which was a shame, really. No, it was just as well—you can imagine what he was doing to me. Ruf, ruf, ruf. I thought to myself, Oooh, *this* is a good job, I could see plenty of advantages in being *his* personal minder. Pity he was in the way. So open and trusting, it made you want to look after him. Really—just charming. Full of the joys. Oooh, look at the weather, he says, isn't it a lovely day? Look at the rocks, what a lovely view. Well, it was pissing with rain and the scenery was just crap. Possibly a bit unstable, I'd have to admit. Mad rage, weeping, then full of the joys all in the space of ten minutes. Bit dodgy. Although you knew you could trust him, funnily enough. You could read him like a book.

But—in the way. Undeniably in the way. Certainly he needed to be removed. Tragic, really. The good die young. I just hoped I'd have time to take advantage of him in the meantime—in the nicest possible way, of course!

22

plots

Sigurd was certain he'd discovered a key ally. He'd saved Hogni's life and now all the dogman wanted to do was to help him. Most importantly, he knew something about the dragon's skin. According to Hogni it had been picked up by the Niberlins, old allies of Sigmund who shared his vision of unification and peace and ruled a large part of the Midlands. This was excellent news. Hogni apparently had trading links with them.

Sigurd wanted to run there as fast as possible on Slipper's back, but Hogni refused to get up on him.

"He looks like *Death*," he said. "You know. In *person*."

So the two of them walked along, leaving the horse to graze on the slaughtered animals behind them. He could catch up later. It was a chance, Hogni said, for them to get to know each other and make their plans.

The dogman kept his arm firmly linked through Sigurd's as they walked, swapping stories about each other, sharing histories. Hogni came from a large family who ran a chain of restaurants and food shops farther north. He was a bit of a wild sheepdog, as he put it. Didn't want to join in the retail trade.

He was always running off on his own on odd little adventures that never came to anything. He'd come down to the Heath to investigate stories about scattered bits of treasure from the dragon's hoard that were supposed to be lying around the shattered landscape, just on the off chance that he could pick up a bit of free wealth.

"I'm a scavenger," he told him. "You better watch out."

But it was lies. Hogni was loyal and affectionate, he liked Sigurd, and he felt deeply in his debt. But he came from a family with other interests. He was one of the Niberlins himself.

The Niberlins had been rulers since Sigmund's early days. Things had changed a lot since then, and the Niberlins, like everyone else, had had to arm themselves and defend their borders. As result, most of the wealth they generated went into defense, but they had done their best to keep the vision going. Their people still had schools and hospitals, roads, a stable economy, a decent justice system. Like Sigurd and Sigmund before him, they knew that the only way for the country to have peace was to unite and the only way to unite in the current climate was to go to war. The Volsons and the Niberlins were natural allies, but the Niberlins knew themselves to be the best remaining hope for the nation.

It made sense. What was Sigurd, after all? A boy from the far west, an unknown, with no experience in government. Their credentials were far better.

Hogni was right. Sigurd was truly in the way—an unknown, a wild card, someone the people might rally around without knowing what they were getting themselves into. If he would join them, so much the better. But how likely was that? And it was late, so late in the day. War was coming, everyone understood that. The Niberlins had been slowly drawing up their plans, as had their enemies. Only a fool would suddenly transfer all the political hopes of England into the hands of this unknown boy, whoever his father was.

As they chatted and joked, Hogni extracted a great deal of information. He soon knew that Sigurd planned to return to his home in the west, raise the seeds of a national army there, and fight to unite the country.

"Alf hasn't much of an army, I've heard," Hogni pointed out.

Sigurd laughed. "Things happen for me," he said. "Look! I've met you already, you know where the skin is. You see?"

Hogni saw; but meeting him wasn't necessarily the good fortune Sigurd thought.

Sigurd did not tell his new friend everything, though. Not about Bryony, for example. He had been on his own with her for so long and he did not want to break the society of two just yet. And he did not tell him that he had the gold. He let Hogni believe that the treasure had gone up with the rest of Fafnir's hoard.

The two of them walked until they were emerging from the area of devastation. Both were tired, so they made camp early, hidden away among some rocks thrown out by the blast, surrounded by birch trees. Neither had anything to eat, and Hogni went off to scavenge. By the time he came back with a dead squirrel he had knocked out of a tree with a stone, Sigurd was already fast asleep.

Hogni walked over to the sleeping boy and looked down closely at his face.

"Far too good," he said to himself. He considered killing him there and then—he'd seen what Sigurd could do. But he had no stomach for it. He needed more than his own authority for such a deed. He made his way a little farther off, well out of earshot, and took a small two-way radio out of his bag.

There were four surviving Niberlins—Gunar, the eldest, Hogni himself, their sister, Gudrun, the baby of the family, a late arrival and only eighteen years old, and their mother, Grimhild. The old king had died in an assassination attempt ten years before, from which Grimhild had only just survived. She had been a powerful woman, Grimhild, a witch, and a scientist—the two often went together these days—and she had her secrets still. Hogni was telling the truth when he said he was a wild card—he spent much of the time away from home, leaving the government of the land to Gunar. Gunar—Gunar-who-would-be-king, as Hogni called him when he wanted to tease—was a meticulous man in all his work, carefully drawing up the legislation, filling in the loopholes. They had all been trained in the work of government since they could walk and between them they managed the best-run lands remaining in the country.

Hogni told them what had happened and who he had met. The family owed Sigurd something now—the life of a brother. They were reluctant to act against him, but the stakes were very big. The death of Fafnir had sparked off a whole new series of wars, the country was in chaos, and the Niberlins were in the final stages of drawing up their war plans. There was another powerful family, the Portlands, to the south and west with whom they held an uneasy truce; it would not last much longer. The Niberlins intended to strike first.

Personal loyalty was one thing—and the Niberlins, like many dog people, held that in very high esteem—but this was war. It was lives by the million, it was the future. Sometimes there was no space even for loyalty.

Hogni returned to sleep a short while later. He lay down and sighed. In the morning he would contact Gunar again and see what had been decided. He had done his best for the boy, tried to play him up to his brother and sister. But it was very late in the day. He knew what his instructions would be.

It was a little before dawn when Sigurd awoke. He lay for a moment, staring out at the brightening sky before he remembered where he was. Outside! And Bryony wasn't with him. There hadn't been a minute since he had left that she wasn't in his mind, and he was awakening now from dreams of her.

Something light and sharp scratched gently at his ear. It was Jenny Wren. He sat up and held out his hand for her to sit on. The little bird piped and bent her neck for his finger. How long had she been here? Maybe she had sat in Bryony's hand only a few hours before.

Sorrowfully he had to give the little bird the bolt he had taken from Crayley as a symbol of waiting. He wrapped a piece of grass around it, and hoped she would see it as a symbol of hope. Then he sat and stroked the little bird with his fingertip. Such a slight thing to hold the thread between them! But Jenny was special, that much was clear. She was informed by some god—Loki, most like, the one who tricked fate. If so, who was he tricking this time? Sigurd and Bryony? Was he about to twist the love he was sustaining? Or was Odin the butt of this joke? If so, thought Sigurd, humanity could only gain.

Without warning, the wren flew off and Sigurd settled back down to sleep.

Less than fifteen minutes later, Jenny was awaking Bryony in exactly the same way—standing on her temple and gently pecking her ear. She was separated from Sigurd by less than half a kilometer.

There was no day or night underground; it was not the normal time for Bryony to sleep, but after Sigurd left, her heart had collapsed inside her. She was back where she'd started, facing a lifetime in solitary. Her misery had already become so deep, she felt that was poisoning her own baby. But Jenny was quick and full of life on her pillow—it was difficult to resist. With a little smile, Bryony put out her finger and Jenny jumped up, her tiny feet pricking her finger.

In her beak was a bolt. Delay.

Bryony's heart sank, but around the bolt was a little weave of fresh grass. Hope, then. Is that what it meant? Bryony felt inside herself for something, anything—the tiniest blossom of pleasure. But there was nothing there. She flicked the wren away and lay back on her bed. There was nothing to get up for. Not yet.

23

the monkey's paw

The next day, Sigurd and Hogni continued on their way toward the Niberlin capital. They were still on foot. Sigurd had sent Slipper to follow them along in hiding, following Hogni's advice that they should go incognito; the cyber-horse was unmistakable until he had grown back his hide. It had been hard to resist the urge to fly like the wind straight to the Niberlins, but Hogni urged caution and Sigurd's own common sense agreed. It would do him no good tearing in and making demands. He had to make alliances, strike deals. There was more at stake than just the skin. The Niberlins had an army and all the makings of a state intact, and Hogni was sure Sigurd could get an audience with Gunar and Gudrun, the rulers. The second brother he did not mention.

Toward the end of the day, Sigurd and Hogni arrived at Milton. The network of roads that surrounded the old office town had turned the place into a market center—all roads led there. Hogni grew quiet as they drew near. Sigurd suspected that something was troubling his new friend, but he could not know what it was. Hogni said he was tired and did not want to talk. Perhaps later, after a few drinks.

Sigurd had an urge for luxury—a deep hot bath, a deep warm bed. There was an expensive hotel just back from the main street. Sigurd had the wealth of nations but it was tucked away inside Slipper, so he borrowed the money off Hogni. Hogni himself did not care to be pampered just yet, he said; he had some business at a bar not far off. He made arrangements with Sigurd to meet up there to eat and have a few drinks in three hours' time.

"We need to get drunk together," he told him. "You're not friends with someone until you've got drunk together."

They parted in a busy street. The boy put his arms around him and kissed him. He smiled, nodded, turned, and left.

"Too good, too trusting, too honest. He wouldn't have lasted long, anyway," thought Hogni as he watched him weave his way through the crowds. But he felt that it was himself he was plotting against. No one could betray Sigurd without betraying themselves first.

The Monkey's Paw was one of a chain of bars and eateries owned by the Portlands, the oldest halfman family in the country, able to trace their line all the way back to the laboratories at Portland Down where the original experiments were made. Entrepreneurial, ruthless, innovative, and greedy, the line had made a living ever since, first as pets, then as citizens, and finally as the owners of large areas of real estate, franchise eateries, media, entertainment, and clothing businesses. They made vast amounts of money through these interests, but that was just poop compared to their primary concern, politics.

The family had lived for years in Ragnor, the glittering city where government and big business had retreated centuries before when ganglaw made their daily lives impossible elsewhere. The head of the family, old Bill Portland, had escaped ahead of Sigmund's conquering armies, and taken with him the complete genetic archives of New World, the company formed by the remains of the government to control its most valuable asset. As a result the Portlands had copyrights on the codes for half the species on the planet.

The family had taken full advantage of owning the most comprehensive genetic archives in the world. Most of the thousands of organisms that had become extinct over the past few hundred years had their genome preserved in code on New World files, as well as an ever-expanding list of those still current. Anyone wanting to brew up creatures for any reason, military, industrial, or retail, had to come to the Portlands for the basic ingredients. The archives of New World amounted to the biggest recipe book in the world.

Old Bill took the view that if there had to be anything as inconvenient as government, it ought to be him. Businessmen get rich, but rulers get richest. He had many advantages—his own ancient cunning and experience, an organization stable over several centuries, and, above all, that New World archive. The past is a big place and Bill had it right there at his fingertips. He could pick and choose from the genome of over a million species, from mammoth to microbe, whilst simultaneously cross-referencing an equally vast archive of inorganic materials and systems to synthesize the final result into whatever he desired.

For the past five years or more, the Portlands had been using this technology to build an army—the day would come. They already effectively occupied a stretch of land from Gloucester to mid Wales and as far south as London. Bill was big enough to call his protection rackets taxation these days. In the meantime, the family did not neglect their commercial interests, which stretched far beyond their own territory. Some years previously, the Portlands had made a commercial bid to take over Niberlin lands by buying up hospitals, schools, social service franchises, utilities, and so on over a period of years until they owned almost everything paid for out of taxes. Bill was confident of victory, but Hogni's father had simply waited until he had spent a large part of his fortune, nationalized everything overnight, and then sold it off to the highest bidders the very next morning while the Portlands were almost penniless. The group protested violently, but there was nothing they could do. It put them back years; Bill was furious. It fortified his conviction that government was too powerful for anyone but himself.

Such flash points apart, relations between the Portlands and the Niberlins were tense, but had not yet fully broken down. Hogni enjoyed drinking at the Portland bars, chatting with the customers, and perhaps picking up one of the younger family members to take home for the night. One day, as he and they all knew, he would become an enemy to his drinking friends and lovers overnight, but in the meantime it served everyone's interest to have some sort of contact and Hogni could come and go unharmed.

It was a Tuesday evening and the bar at the Monkey's Paw wasn't busy when Hogni came in to fix things up. The managers, Eve and Elijah Portland, recognized him as both a family enemy and a personal friend. They'd had good times with Hogni. They called him over for a drink, which he was happy to accept.

"Woof, woof and down the hatch. Mmmm. Lovely. So, sweeties, what's on the menu? I have a friend with me tonight."

Elijah and Eve rolled their eyes at each other. Hogni nearly always had a friend with him. If he didn't, he usually did by the end of the evening.

"Wha! Nice boy?" said Elijah.

"Depends on your point of view, really," said Hogni.

"Na—hahaha! He won't be by the time you're finished with him," chortled Eve.

"Something s-s-sexy? Oysters? Does he like seafood?" asked Elijah.

"Oh, no, not that sort of friend. Didn't you get my message? This one is business."

He eyed them significantly, but he wasn't surprised that they didn't know what he was on about. Gunar and Gudrun would certainly have been in touch with the top brass about this and it wasn't the sort of thing Old Bill liked to entrust to lowly bar managers. Eve nodded over Hogni's shoulder. He looked round and saw a senior Portland sitting surrounded by a group of heavily built monkey-men; Portlands again, but bred for size, strength, and obedience rather than anything you could call brain. They were gorillas in every sense of the word.

Hogni sighed; he hated dealing with the seniors. He downed his drink, asked for another, and went over to sort it out. Loathsome! He hated himself for this. But what else could he do?

The gorillas moved over to make room for him, and Hogni squeezed himself in opposite the neatly suited monkey, who shook his hand with distaste, announced that Hogni could just call him Portland—"Can it be Bill himself?" wondered Hogni—and asked what the Volson was like.

"Big bloke. Very strong. Very *ambitious*," emphasized Hogni. "He took out about twenty of those pig-dog things— know them?" Portland glanced over at one of his aides, who looked seriously impressed, nodding and hooting softly.

"What, eh?" said Portland. "Tikit tik tik. And what's he doing alive?"

"Oh, really—I can't deal with him on my own. Why do you think I got in touch with you? This boy needs an army to take him out. Anyhow, he saved my life. I owe him a favor."

"Er? You owe him a favor? This it? You bringing him here for a favor?"

Hogni shrugged. "Politics." He downed his drink. "Family," he emphasized.

"Don wanna get his hands dirty," observed one of the gorillas. Hogni ignored him.

"No one wants another Volson messing up the waters," he said briefly. "We want him out of the way too. My people are miles away; this is your territory. Well? Do you think you can handle it?"

Bill ignored the question, and his gorillas began to pant and rattle their knuckles under the table. You didn't ask a senior Portland questions like that. Hogni began to feel uncomfortable. He almost wished he had Sigurd with him; he wasn't safe himself. Quickly he went on to an inventory of Sigurd. His skin was something special, it was going to take an awful lot of firepower to get through it. "Really strong," he said. Words didn't do justice to what he'd seen Sigurd do to those pig-dogs. He was fairly confident this was not something he could explain to the Portlands or anyone else who hadn't seen it, but he had to try.

"Weapons?"

Hogni licked his lips. "He has a broken sword," he said.

Portland looked a him incredulously. "That it?"

"He may have more stacked away in the horse," said Hogni. He told them a little about Slipper. Portland nodded.

"Ik ik ik. We know the model. We can deal with the horse. Okay, son. When you meeting up with him?"

"An hour," replied Hogni, feeling sick. "Watch him, though—he's a bit of a berserker."

"E e e e e. Ha! He can be as berserk as he likes after a few drinks of what we have ere," said Elijah, who had come across to serve drinks. The monkeys started hooting, swearing, and laughing.

The Volson boy was bad business. Thinking him dead, a great many rulers hadn't bothered to stop, or had even encouraged, the lionization and hero worship of the young boy. People can dream, can't they? But a living hero isn't anywhere near as predictable as the dead variety, and now that he'd turned up, a lot of people in positions of power were very anxious to get him back where he belonged—in the ground.

Too good to be true, thought Hogni. And therefore, he had to cease to be true as soon as possible.

By the time Sigurd arrived, the bar had livened up quite a bit. Over three-quarters of the drinkers were Portlands.

"Lot of monkeys in here," said Sigurd to Hogni as he joined him at the table. Hogni smiled and nodded. Sigurd leaned close.

"It'll be okay, don't worry," he said softly.

Hogni started. "What? Nothing to go wrong, is there?" he stuttered. How much did Sigurd know?

Sigurd smiled at him. "Nothing I know of," he replied. "You don't look happy, that's all." He banged the table with his hands and laughed. He knew something was going on, but not what. Hogni was his friend. He loved him; therefore, nothing bad could happen. "Now we can get drunk."

He sat down next to Hogni, ordered beer and chasers, and they began to drink.

It was an evil hour. Sigurd broke Hogni's heart that night. His talk was all of friendship and hope and the power of good, making the world a better place for everyone to live in. Hogni was from an ancient ruling family and a lot of his intrinsic optimism had evaporated but Sigurd raised his spirits, made him believe again that anything was possible. He was about to snuff his own hopes out.

Sigurd was not a big drinker, and Hogni was doing his best to set him up time and time again with beer and chasers—small glasses of pale green liquid. There was, Hogni reflected, maybe enough drug in those to kill the boy with an overdose as it was.

Sigurd swiftly became blurred and began to droop heavily over the table. Slow enough to murder already, Hogni thought. He could see the Portlands watching closely. Hogni ordered another round. Sigurd shook his head. Hogni almost had to throw this one down his throat for him. Arms crossed, Sigurd slumped. Hogni called his name. Sigurd raised his head sluggishly and smiled blearily at his friend, then put his head back down. His breath had begun to rattle in his throat.

A group of Portland gorillas sauntered over from behind the

bar cradling automatic weapons in their arms.

Hogni put his hand out and shook Sigurd by the head. "Just going to the toilet," he said. Sigurd didn't move.

Hogni walked a few steps toward the toilets, then broke into a run. They were going to gun Sigurd down right here in the middle of the bar—a public show. He could see Eve and Elijah chattering their teeth and cursing as they got out of the way. Hogni burst out of the bar and into the street. He wanted to be well out of the way once the shooting started. He wouldn't put it past the Portlands to try to take him out at the same time just for the hell of it.

He wasn't twenty meters away when the firing began, a brief rattle and then a violent thunder of gunfire. They sure were making sure. Hogni felt like bursting into tears. He turned round to see if he was being pursued. It felt inevitable that he was; he deserved it. But there was no one on his tail.

The gunfire started up again. Almost against his own will, Hogni crept back toward the building. As he advanced the noise reached a terrible crescendo, then shouting started. A couple of Portlands suddenly shot through the door and beat it off down the road.

Hogni got to the window and looked in.

Sigurd was lying on his back on the ground in the middle of a hail of bullets. The floorboards were dissolving into sawdust around him and Hogni could see his skin dimpling under their impact. Dimpling? thought Hogni. *Dimpling?* But it was true. The bullets were bouncing right off him. Sigurd had his hands over his face to keep them out of his eyes. Whenever there was a pause he tried to get up, but then they started again and he went back down. All around him the Portlands were shouting orders. It seemed to Hogni that they were just firing now to keep him down. What on earth were they going to do once they ran out of ammunition and he got to his feet?

Hogni was panting in fear and excitement. They're trapped, he thought. Sigurd was on his back, in their sights, at their mercy—and they were trapped.

The Portlands were beginning to run out of ammunition. Every few seconds someone would fling down his weapon and make a run for it, making the remaining monkey-men even more edgy. A few of the leaders were running around the edges, ordering more ammo, more men, more everything.

Hogni clung to the window, still panting with excitement. It was impossible! Sigurd was like nothing you could ever imagine.

Behind the bar, the office door burst open and Elijah and Eve came in hauling a large mortar between them. Someone else was standing behind them with a flame thrower. Elijah sank to one knee, aimed—"No!" yelled Hogni, because this was surely the end—and fired. Sigurd exploded. Immediately the other monkey ran in and began to flame the remains that lay scattered among burning tables, chairs and floorboards.

Out of the inferno a shape could be seem. Two arms, two legs, staggering drunkenly about. Then there was a yell from the fire. A chair came hurling out of the flames at an impossible velocity. It struck the flame thrower operator on the chest and smashed him into the wall, killing him instantly.

There was another yell. Sigurd was angry.

The burning figure leapt out of the fire and landed directly on Elijah. There was an audible snap as Sigurd broke his neck with a twist of his wrist. The flames were burning out now and

Sigurd was now as Hogni had first seen him, stark naked; but this time his body glowed with the heat. Hogni had never seen anything so beautiful in all his life.

"This keeps happening!" yelled Sigurd in fury.

He struck out sideways at Eve and knocked her five meters onto the bar, where she broke. Then he grabbed a gun from the floor and began to fire rounds from the hip. By now the Portlands were in full retreat.

"Run, shitshitshitshit, run, run!" they were yelling. They poured out of the windows and doors. Hogni could even see some of them erupting through the roof and upstairs windows, in a total panic.

"Yes! Yes!" yelled Hogni. Sigurd had done it again— impossible, wonderful, beautiful! He yelled and whooped for joy as the raging figure stormed through the bar on a murderous rampage. Then suddenly Sigurd stopped, turned his head, and looked through the window straight at Hogni. Hogni froze; he had forgotten in the excitement that he was the one who had set this up. He paled, staggered backward. But Sigurd was coming. He jumped over the scattered, blazing furniture and was right now coming through the window to get him.

Hogni made no attempt to run. He could never get away, and even if he could, he deserved whatever was coming to him. Sigurd was in a rage, and just as he had never seen such beauty, so Hogni had never seen such rage in a person before. He knew that it could be held back by nothing in this world.

Sigurd descended in a rain of shattered glass and towered above him. Involuntarily Hogni sank to his knees.

"I betrayed you," he begged, and he burst into tears.

Sigurd smiled, put out a hand, and lifted him effortlessly to his feet. "You're my friend," he said. "I will always forgive you. Don't you understand that?"

Hogni stared up at him in amazement.

"I love you," said Sigurd. "And there's nothing on earth you can do to stop that." He reached forward to kiss him and Hogni screamed suddenly in pain from the heat of the scalding man.

24

hogni

A crowd was beginning to gather. Someone plucked up the courage to ask, "Are you the Volson boy?"

Sigurd nodded. "I'm Sigurd."

"And I'm Hogni Niberlin," said Hogni, admitting his family name at last. Sigurd laughed, but didn't seem surprised.

"Did you know?" asked Hogni.

"You were someone important. Why else did we meet?"

As they stood in the street, the sound of hooves thudded rapidly along the road; Slipper was on his way. The Portlands were nowhere to be seen, but the crowd was getting bigger by the second and Sigurd was worried that they might attack again while he was surrounded by so many people. As the horse rode up, he swung himself up on his back, put out an arm, and pulled Hogni up behind him. He was still hot enough for Hogni to cry out at his touch.

"You've seen me now," Sigurd told the crowd. "I killed Fafnir. I took his skin, his gold, and his strength. We're to make this nation one again, like it was in my father's day. Remember me!" He pressed his heels lightly into the horse's flanks, and they fled the town.

• • •

As they rode on, Sigurd cooled down enough for Hogni to put his arms around him and hold on tight. The boy had such smooth skin, burned clean so many times already. Underneath, the hard muscles moved like liquid. Hogni felt comforted and safe, like a cat lying on a warm stove at home. What would happen next? It was out of his hands, so far out of his hands that he hardly cared anymore.

He rested his head on the boy's back and felt something against his cheek; something hot and wet—a patch of raw, burned flesh. Hogni pressed it gently with his fingers.

Sigurd winced and glanced over his shoulder at Hogni. "A leaf got stuck between my clothes and Fafnir's blood couldn't reach the skin there. It's the only place where I can be killed."

He smiled wryly, and then looked forward, searching for a place to spend the night. Behind him, Hogni gently put his hand on the place. Yes, a leaf shape. He felt Sigurd wince. Yes, it was tender. Yes, Sigurd could be killed here.

Hogni put his hand down to his side where he carried a knife. Inside his jacket was a small handgun, he couldn't use that, Sigurd would feel him take it out. But the knife . . . ? If he wanted, the lad was his to take, his to have, his to kill. Perhaps no one else in the world had the knowledge. But Hogni did not reach for his knife. He put his arms back around Sigurd's waist, leaned his face against the warm back, and let the tears come again. There was no uncertainty. Who could doubt such love? Hogni was won over to the last fiber in him. He leaned his head tenderly against Sigurd's back, and wept.

• • •

There was a moment back there, kneeling in front of him, when I was about to spill my life out for him—slit my throat and die at his feet for what I'd done. But he didn't want it. What about that? He didn't want my life or even my apologies. He just wanted *me*.

Impossible, beautiful, perfect boy.

Yep; I was in love. Again. Already! Rrrruf. After two days. What does that say about me? I mean! It happens *all* the time; but this time was different. Like—*really* in love. After what I did! After what *he* did. But it was unfair. It was unfair to me, I knew that at once, even though he was the one making all the sacrifices, because he had enough love in him to love the whole world and I barely had enough for one. I was his, body and soul. He loved me more than anyone else ever had or could, but at the same time, I felt that he loved the ground under his feet as much as me. Funny, but it didn't seem to matter. It was just unfair, that's all.

And you know what? Bumping up and down on the back of that horse—ruuuuuf! Well, what can I say? He was like a god, but, woof, woof!—he was flesh all right. I tried to ignore it, but . . . well. I was practically lying on top of him already, with that horse trotting along.

Grrr-ruf!

He dropped me off in a little town nearby to get him yet more clothes, and then we carried on out to find a place to stay. We'd decided to sleep out that night. And you know what was going through my mind. Yes, yes. Well, I had to ask. I'd never forgive myself. Can you imagine, years later over a beer or a glass of wine, and I asked if he'd have said yes and he would have and I'd never asked? So I had to really. I mean. I was so nervous, I hardly knew what to say. But I was determined I was going to have a go.

We found this lovely place. Well, it was a bit damp actually—I expect we could have found something better but I insisted because it was so romantic. It was this half-fallen-down old church. Someone had been adapting it to Thor and Freya, I think, one of that lot. It was all overgrown. *Very* fertile. Wildflowers everywhere. Creepers all over it. We had something to eat, settled down—and I made my move. I came over and asked if we could cuddle up. He turned over—there was just a sliver of a moon, enough to see his face, shining because he'd been burned—burned for me, I thought. Funny. I wasn't guilty. He'd forgiven me, you see? There was nothing to feel guilty about.

"I'm not cold, if that's what you think," I said.

"You can cuddle up, Hogni," he said. Yes! Oh, yes! So I lay down by him and put my arm over him and stroked him all over. He sighed and lay still. Then I reached round to you know where. He turned to look at me. "There's someone else, Hogni."

"I'm sure you have to fight them off."

"Someone I love."

I was surprised. But it didn't necessarily mean no, did it?

"But you could be mine if you wanted to, for just for one night."

Sigurd smiled. "Yes, I can be yours for one night," he said. And then we kissed. And then—we made love.

And in the morning—in the morning I was heartbroken. You fall for someone, you want them more than they want you, and of course it all ends in tears. In those two days he'd taken everything I had to give—forced it out of me, literally. I was drained dry—and I don't mean it like that, either. I thought, Now the pain starts. We never slept together again, I became more of a follower than a lover after that. But Sigurd and I, we loved each other until the end, one way or the other. Funny! So, yes, it was sad, but it in another way, you see, it had only just begun.

25

sigurd

Why did I do *that*? It happened spontaneously, but it was planned all along. By who? Not me! And Bryony underground waiting for me . . . I'd been unfaithful to her without a thought.

But it didn't feel wrong. He wanted it—he wanted me—so badly, I had no right to say no. I'd taken everything from him and I had to give him everything back, too, for that one night at least. In the morning, when I made it clear that it wouldn't happen again, he looked so heartbroken. But he was still pleased we'd done it.

"We had this time together at least," he said. It made me blush. As if I'd done him a favor!

I must have seemed like a god to Hogni. I don't like gods. Who are they? Do you think they have friends? Who do they talk to when things are getting them down? It must be very lonely in heaven. And then there's power—dragon power. Power is the real dragon. It eats away into your soul and turns your heart into stone. First it turns your friends into admirers, then to followers and servants, and finally into slaves. Hogni is mine now. He's bound to me by bonds of love as well as gratitude. I walked into his trap just so that I could fight like a demon, forgive him like a father, and love him like a girl. How can he resist me now? Yet I swear I never planned it. It's just how I am. My bones understand. I swear to you, I had no more choice in this than Hogni did.

He's a Niberlin. You see? Destiny, destiny. They are the seeds of the new nation. They have organization, a bureaucracy, government. The hardware—the tanks and guns, the industry, all those things you can build or buy, but the organization, the skills and experience—those you can't buy, and if you take them, you break them. They have to *give* them to me. They have to come behind me.

The Niberlin family is like a treasure chest and Hogni is my key. Why else did I come across him just as his life was in danger? When I won Hogni, I was on my way to winning the Niberlins; and when I have the Niberlins, I can begin the fight. It scares me sometimes. It can't be a good thing, can it, to have all roads, all actions, even the moving of the human heart calculated to lift me up and bear me forward? But there is a goodness in it too, because around me, the very best in people flowers. Hogni would give his life for me and although I tell you the truth when I say that I would give my life for him this second if I had to—well. I'm not easily killed and he is. It's a measure of how great his heart is that he will give *everything* he has. I may give more, but I have so much more to give. That is why the least of my followers will always be better than I can ever be.

But I also wonder if maybe I slept with him to become human again, in his eyes at least. Sex is so human, isn't it?

That night I wanted Hogni to show me that I was ordinary, too. He did show me, and I'll always be grateful for that. He'd seen me fighting a hundred enemies and winning, but in his arms I was just a boy, doing something I'd never done before.

fame

The sun illuminated the mist in a pearly sheen across the fields and woods as Sigurd and Hogni rode away from the small church where they had spent the night into a morning filled with the scents of water and wet leaves. Hogni sat behind Sigurd with his arms wrapped around his waist. He laid his head briefly on his back, taking care to avoid the weeping wound between his shoulder blades. Sigurd turned and kissed him. Then they set out on their way, Slipper placing his prosthetic hooves silently on the stones in between the puddles on the track. They headed northeast, toward the Niberlin lands. Soon Hogni would have to radio ahead and let his family know what was going on—but not yet. This beautiful morning was the last time he had Sigurd to himself. In a few hours politics would begin again.

On such a morning as this you could feel that the world stands still around you, but of course it never does. Beyond the mist, death was sharpening his tools. The Portlands had done their best to contain the fallout from the failed ambush at the Monkey's Paw. They had imposed a curfew and radio silence in Milton, put up roadblocks, tried to ring-fence the town; but word was already out. Runners and rumors, banned TV and telephone lines, carrier pigeons even, spread the news. There's always a way. Governments themselves are the worst blabbermouths of all. Already the world and his wife knew that the Niberlins had betrayed Sigurd, that the Portlands had ambushed him with opiates and small artillery, and that Sigurd had rescued Hogni and disappeared. The dragon killer, the son of the great king, the golden boy had returned from death, stronger and more beautiful than ever, wearing the dragon's skin as his own, blazing fire and with the strength to fight an armored division without a wound to show for it. You could shoot him, you could burn him, but you couldn't kill him. And he knew how to love. The Volsons were back.

Around the two riders the air began to warm up, the dew dried, the mist lifted, the day opened out before them. Hogni was thinking ahead, but Sigurd was oblivious. His mind was filling up with Bryony. He was looking around at the fields, the trees shadowy in the mist, the gathering light and warmth, the birdsong, all the sights, sounds, and smells of the advancing morning, thinking how joyful it would be when he introduced all this to her. The world! They would become drunk on it, the two of them. She was a traveler from another world, he would see it all anew through her eyes. It would be the first day of creation all over again.

And Hogni—the soldier prince with several hundred deaths to his name and a reputation for ruthlessness—sat behind him and wondered what on earth was going to happen next. And how was his family going to react to it? Sigurd was irresistible.

But he needs us, thought Hogni. He needs us more than we

need him. He needed their army, their bureaucracy, their government.

"Yes," said Sigurd, turning briefly round to face him. "I need you."

Hogni felt a thrill of fear and wonder go up his spine. Sigurd nodded at him and turned away. Hogni thought, Does he know everything? He blushed at that idea—a great many of his private thoughts were not for public consumption. He put his arms more tightly about the boy in front of him, but the gentle morning was over. Hogni felt awe rather than tenderness. Sigurd had died and come to life in the arms of Odin, the Allfather, the all-knowing. People were turning inside out before him. He was learning to see without eyes.

He's a god, thought Hogni. Or he's becoming one. But he said nothing.

About an hour later they arrived on the outskirts of the next small town. Hogni wanted to skirt around it.

"Why? This is the quickest way," replied Sigurd.

"There'll be people," began Hogni; but then shook his head. Was Sigurd truly unaware that word would have spread? He shrugged, giving up. "Crowds are what happens next," he said. "See? I can see into the future too."

Sigurd frowned at him, half smiling, not sure what his friend meant.

"Go on, then," said Hogni. "Maybe we can stop off for a drink."

"Good idea," said Sigurd. Hogni laughed. The dragon killer was going to stop off for a cup of tea.

And so began the public part of the story of Sigurd, right

there and then as they rode out of the mist past the first few houses. Everyone knew at once who it was—how could it possibly be anyone else? And as they ran to greet them they brought their cameras with them, and so we have the first images of Sigurd since his resurrection. Those first stills, that video footage—remember? It was like Jesus on the street. Everyone, even the tiniest children, who knew nothing of all this or what it meant, recognized somehow in those first poor images the beginnings of a new world. Where were you when you first saw them? We all remember. The great skeletal horse, skeins of blood vessels and pulsing muscles growing over his alloy bones and carbonic systems. On his back, clinging on like a child, Hogni, the forgiven one, looking so small, his white face unreadable as he stares into the lens, inviting you to interpret what it was like to be there so close behind the great man. And Sigurd himself, red as fire, as beautiful as a girl, as strong as a machine, smiling fondly down, as if he had no idea how great he was. We look into his face today and we wonder how much he knew of what was to come. His smile is kind but enigmatic. It may just be the bad quality of the footage, or perhaps there is simply too much there for us to read. Perhaps he already knew the fate of every single one of us.

Outside The Table and Chairs bar, Sigurd and Hogni came down from Slipper to eat, but had to get back up because the crowd was already too big. People fetched food for them to eat as they rode—sandwiches, pies, fruit, sweets, handed over heads to reach them. There was no scrum, no fan-fighting, no crowds squabbling about who had the honor of standing next to them, or touching their feet or the horse's sides, no one tearing at their clothes. The people were good-natured. They were watching the future smile at them.

Over the day as the news spread, the numbers grew from tens to hundreds, from hundreds to thousands. So quick! By the dawn of the next day, nearly a million people lined the route between them and the Niberlin capital, and numbers were still growing. People had walked through the night, now they were walking through the day. At first they simply wanted to see the arrival of the king, but when numbers like this are involved, things change. The strings of power loosen, the glue between leaders and the led begins to dissolve. Even the most brutal dictator cannot fight his entire people. The crowd understood that, and the rulers knew it too. At that moment, they had already been defeated. Of course they drew up their battle plans anyway.

Once people realized what was happening, they came in greater numbers than ever before. Every mile, every hundred meters, the crowd got thicker and Sigurd and Hogni's progress grew slower and slower. Sigurd stood up on the saddle and waved. How they roared back at him! Hogni was spotted and the crowd roared louder than ever. A Niberlin was with him! A truce, an alliance! Half the war was already won and not a shot fired!

Slipper slowed down to a steady trot, then to a walk, then stopped. Things needed organizing. Sigurd stood up on the horse's back and made a short speech. Times were changing. Already the dragon was dead. He was on his way to sign a truce with the Niberlins—who, as they could see, were already on his side. Hogni winced, waved, and was cheered hoarse. It was the first he'd heard about it. Sigurd beamed down at him, gleeful in his childish trick. And it would work—it *had* worked. They both knew it.

Meanwhile, he told the crowd, their enemies were gathering—did they think the Portlands would sit still for long? Did they think the Smiths to the west and the Winstons to the southeast were going to hand power over on a plate? Word must spread. Everyone must prepare. He needed to raise an army. He had the money, his father's gold was at the service of the people once again. It was time to rebuild.

An air-shaking cheer went up. Who would dare fight against him? Hogni wondered. Was it possible that Sigurd could take over the country just by marching into it? What would the little kings and tyrants of this age do if they didn't want Sigurd? Sack the people? Elect a new electorate? Shoot everyone?

Sigurd asked for volunteers. He chose men, women, and children to help clear his route forward, set them marching ahead of him, keeping the road open for Slipper to go forward at a few miles an hour—fast enough to get there, slow enough to let word spread and make his progress inevitable.

Off they set again. It was Sigurd's third day above ground. Already it was like another age.

There were enemies, too, hiding in the crowds. It was hardly to be heard at first, the first gunshot; but in a shocked, spreading silence, there was a further burst of noise and the scattering bullets ricocheting off Slipper, and from Sigurd's head. Hogni caught a bullet in his arm; there was the blood to be seen by all. Ten meters away in the crowd, a small group of local militia were spotted easing their way backward. They had been used to these people obeying their every word up till now, but now the crowd had new horizons. There was a roar of rage, a glimpse of scared white faces as the militiamen held up their hands and tried to bark orders. Then, the crowd closed in. The men were literally stamped to death. The bloodied uniforms were passed forward and raised like a flag in front of Slipper— a standard and a warning to any enemies.

Many people had seen the bullets bounce off Sigurd's head. So it was true: He was invulnerable. Victory was already theirs.

war without conflict

Ganglords and godfathers, kings and presidents, prime ministers, chieftains, head executives and chairmen of the board; everyone was scared. The people had found a new hope and hope means change. The boss never likes hope. He's always the first to go.

At the Niberlins' house, Democracy Palace, it was the same. President Gunar and his sister peered out of their windows at the hordes gathering in Democracy Square outside. Flowers were being heaped up at the gates, kids were screaming, but it wasn't just girls and boys. Volson fever had spread to the militia. Whole divisions were turning up and pledging themselves, their arms, and their artillery to the wonderful boy. Everyone knew the Volson principles: unity, freedom, peace. Sigurd stood for us, for you and me. He was freedom from tyrants and the ambitions of kings. He was good government— so devastating when it goes wrong, so dull you can barely see it when it's done well. To make it work everyone has to agree—and look! Here we all are agreeing, millions upon millions upon millions of us.

The crowd was like an ocean; it murmured, it roared. You

could float in it—but not if you were a Niberlin. They had been good rulers, it had been their pride. They were loved once but suddenly their fate was in the balance.

Peeping out from behind the curtain, Gunar and Gudrun felt like children watching something scary on the TV from behind the sofa. You don't dare watch it but you don't dare miss it. An ocean of faces, all of them ready to judge, all of them ready to act. They were safe in their millions, and their rulers were so suddenly all alone.

Gunar looked at his sister, who stood behind watching him carefully. Lying on a Windsor chair farther back in the room was a black and white sheepdog bitch watching them both intently, occasionally letting out a slight, nervous whine. Her head was only a little domed. This was Grimhild. Their mother—a dog? Yes, but it hadn't always been like this. Once she had been as halfman as any of them, a woman famous for her intelligence, but now her long jaws made speech impossible even if she was capable of it. You could only guess how much she could understand. What else could she do but sit on a chair and cry for them?

To one side stood Ida, big-boned Ida, in her floral print frock, watching the wallpaper with nothing to say. Grimhild's personal servant, she dotes silently on her mistress. She has no tongue. The two are rarely seen apart.

"He's only fifteen," hissed Gunar. "Knows n-nothing! Educated like a beach bum, silly hippy kid. Is he going to waltz in and take over everything we've w-worked for all these years?"

Gudrun shook her head. "People get impatient. It'll pass. He'll show himself up, they'll turn against him. We'll be here to pick up the pieces."

"What if the p-pieces are us?"

Gudrun rolled her eyes as if he was being a pain. "Poor old Gunar, whinge, whinge, whinge," she said. Gunar snorted in amusement.

"I only want to be king of everything," he joked. They smiled fondly at each other.

Gunar and Gudrun had fewer traces of the dog in them than their brother Hogni. Black and white hair brushed back, wide-apart eyes the color of dark honey, deep chests, just the trace of a muzzle—a bit of a tendency to whine or bark when they got excited. The family used to be proud of their human side and tended to hide their dogginess until the past ten years or so—Gunar put his slight stutter down to this suppression—but there was a game they'd had since childhood, and they played it now to amuse each other; hung out their tongues, which were suddenly revealed to be nearly a foot long, and panted like a pair of stupid old dogs.

"Hu hu hu hu hu," they went, and then burst out laughing. In her chair, Grimhild yapped disapprovingly.

"Bitch," said Gunar.

"Labrador," she accused him.

"Not a Labrador! If I'm a Lab, you're a p-poodle—an arse-sniffing poodle with bad hair." They smiled, trouble out of mind for a moment. Then Gunar looked back out of the window.

"Have we been wr-wrong all this time?" he asked.

"Wrong about what?"

"A-ba, about *us*. The family."

It was so important to Gunar—to all the family, but to him especially: to do the right thing. Power was a stewardship of the people's good and the land they lived in. The Niberlins' claim to power was the belief that they made the best stewards. So far this had been undisputed.

"Hogni thinks he's on the same side as us," said Gudrun.

"Hogni gets infatuated with every p-piece he meets. . . ."

"Sigurd was brought up by Alf, he's a good ruler."

"But we don't *know*. It's s-s-so late!"

Gudrun looked out of the window again. The crowd was everywhere. "There's nothing we can do about it," she said.

Gunar looked unhappily at her. What about doing the right thing? What was the right thing? It's not just you standing there trying to be honest and open for the sake of your own honor—millions of lives could be affected. Politicians sometimes have no right to be honest.

"There's nothing we *should* do about it," Gudrun corrected herself. "Until we know." She watched her brother anxiously. Gunar had been brought up to be king. Being king went hand in hand with doing what was right—with *being* right. Suddenly it was all being taken away from him. The people had changed their allegiance. He was deeply shaken.

"We don't know how it's going to work out," said Gudrun. "I think they'll turn on him as soon as they see what a child he is. But maybe not. Maybe it's our turn to be ruled now, Gunar. Look—all those people. If you want to stop him, you have to overrule them, and we don't have that right."

"And what if he r-r-ruins it?" said Gunar. He glanced at her. "We're the c-certainty in this world. This boy—what is he? No one knows."

"We tried to stop him," Gudrun pointed out. "Now we have to try and work with him—for now at least."

Gunar looked at his sister. "Thought it was g-going to be me," he said.

"Remember what Father used to say?"

"'Only the ruled have rights. We just do our duty.' I know."

Gudrun put her arms around him. Gunar was in a kind of shock. All his plans and ambitions were crumbling away to nothing. He'd thought power was planning, care, legislation. Now he saw for the first time what it really was: It was people, millions of them, wanting you, following you, believing in you. His armies would be like lost children in this crowd even if he cared to use them. These quick few hours had swallowed his ambitions whole and turned his honesty, his cleverness, his plots, and his ambitions to dust.

There was a heavy thud as Grimhild jumped down off her chair and came over to comfort her children. Ida's pale blue eyes turned to follow her mistress across the floor. With a whine, she lifted her muzzle up for Gunar to stroke. He rubbed her ears. "What would you say, Mother?" he said, and shrugged.

Gudrun laughed "Would be bad advice," she said. "She'd tell you to fight for what's yours. You know Mum—family always comes first."

The dog licked her lips, but had nothing to say. The days when Grimhild could give advice were long gone.

Down below, the crowds were still streaming in. They had been trying to stop the flood into the square for fear of people getting killed in the crush, but the soldiers they had sent in to guide the crowds had been pushed to one side. They'd had warnings announced all over the square about crowd safety and control, but no one seemed to be taking any notice.

"What are we going to do?" Gudrun asked.

Gunar smiled wryly. "W-welcome him with open arms, like the king he is."

Grimhild whined and pawed his leg. Gunar laughed and spread his hand over the scene before them. "Look! That's royalty. We're just in admin." He nodded. "Everything we've d-d . . . d-d-done has been preparing for this. Everything will be different from now on."

Gudrun nodded. Yes. Banners would be flown, the red carpet laid out. The story of how the family had tried to have Sigurd killed was already abroad. People needed to know that they were on the right side. Then they would see what this boy was made of.

"But we won't side with a tyrant no matter what the crowd wants," said Gunar, meeting her eye. She nodded. No tyranny. That was the most important thing.

They had thought the arrival would be in the late afternoon, but the crowd was still growing and Sigurd's progress was getting slower and slower. It would be the nighttime, then. Gunar and Gudrun had the square lit by floodlights, bright enough to film the meeting. They wanted all eyes to see them welcome Sigurd. A guard of honor was not possible—the crowd would not allow anyone with a rifle anywhere near him—but an area had been cordoned off by a barrier of soldiers, space for a small raised platform where the Niberlins could be seen standing shoulder to shoulder with him.

Sigurd's progress could be marked by the loudness of the cheering as he approached. The crowd was ecstatic. They knew their own power. Anything was possible this night.

Gudrun had ordered screens to be put up in public places all around the city and farther afield in town squares and village greens, in public buildings, pubs and inns and hotels, in the hope that people would gather there rather than descend on the capital. Even so, Democracy Square was packed so tightly that people began to be displaced as the cavalcade began to arrive. Troops, tanks, and other artillery moved in ahead of Sigurd. The noise swelled. Gunar and Gudrun became increasingly worried that things would come to a head before he even arrived. Fights were breaking out. If serious violence began between the Niberlin guard and the men Sigurd had picked up along the way, people could die in the thousands.

The uniforms of various defected militia mingled with the green of the Niberlins' as the front of Sigurd's cavalcade entered the square. But no Portlands; the monkeymen kept to their own. To their relief, Gunar and Gudrun saw that Sigurd had sent men ahead to usher people in and out at the edges of the square and make sure there were as few injuries as possible.

Then, at last, Sigurd himself came into view. The noise was so loud now, you could hardly think. As the advance guard drew up to the palace, they looked up at Gunar and Gudrun waiting at the window, and shook the bloody uniforms of militiamen who had tried to assassinate Sigurd. The uniforms had multiplied over the miles. It wasn't just cloth, either; body parts and bones were held overhead like trophies. One or two of them carried heads on sharpened sticks, high above the crowd. Make no mistake: This was an army of conquest.

It was a terrifying sight. Gunar and Gudrun, as they descended through a corridor of loyal soldiers five thick on their way to the platform, were as white as sheets. Had Sigurd sanctioned this waving of the dead at them? Was it a threat—or a promise?

Gunar thought suddenly, My god, he can't control this! There are millions here, millions! How could one man—one boy—control all this? What if he lifted a hand and no one stopped? What if he spoke and no one heard? A crowd this big, it was an animal. No one ordered such a beast around. Gunar looked across into the eager, open face of the boy riding toward him and knew for certain they were going to die there and then, he and Gudrun, and Sigurd, too. It was impossible to rule this! It was all he could do to breathe in the face of such raw power.

He turned round to look at his sister. Her face showed the same terror. No one could hold such a weight. They were about to die.

The great horse, all skeleton, sinew, raw muscle, and circuit boards, pranced close to the platform and shook his huge head. Sigurd stood up in the saddle and waved; the crowd cheered back. The noise, which seemed at every second to have reached an impossible peak, rose again. Gunar had to swallow to stop himself vomiting with fear. Now death was close. Behind the boy—just a boy!—sat Hogni, looking as scared as anyone else. He looked down at his brother and shrugged as if to say, What did you expect me to do about *this*?

Sigurd and Hogni dismounted and made their way up the steps toward Gunar and Gudrun. Sigurd stood for a moment, looking into Gunar's eyes, then turned to face the crowd. Together they stared out to the thousands of faces staring back—straight into the eye of the world. Again the noise increased in volume. Gunar flinched, and Gudrun turned in fright. Hogni turned away and was sick behind the podium. He straightened up, wiping his mouth, looking at Gunar with an expression of hopelessness.

Gunar leaned across to him. "What happens now?" he bellowed, but Hogni only shrugged.

Something had to happen. Gunar took Sigurd's hand in his and tried to raise it above their heads to show that they were allies, but Sigurd did not respond. He squeezed Gunar's hand back but did not let his arm move. Gunar was caught off balance and glanced at him. Tentatively he tugged at the boy's arm, but it was impossible. Sigurd's hand was a vice. The boy was as strong as ten. Gunar's eyes began to leak tears, although his face showed no expression. A powerful man, he was not used to being so utterly at another's command. Then Sigurd turned and looked at him, straight into his eyes.

At this time Sigurd had no idea what to do. He was waiting himself. But now it began.

When he looked into Gunar's eyes, he saw him as the gods see us—straight through to his soul. In a flash he knew everything about Gunar—his hopes and fears, his childhood dreams, his grown-up ambitions, his loves, his hates—everything. He knew that Gunar was desperate to love but was scared to; that he wanted to be open but could not trust, wished to give everything but could not let go. He saw that there was no better man in all the world—none more honest, none harder on himself, none more generous. But he could not reach out from himself. A good man, a fine man, but a flawed man.

When Gunar felt the vision on him everything else around him vanished—the crowd, his brother and sister, the state hanging in the balance, his own fate. All there was was the face of the boy and behind it the godhead watching him, taking all his secrets into itself, judging him, forgiving him, loving him.

There were no secrets from that gaze of Sigurd's. No one should ever look at you like that unless they had created you. Then Sigurd seemed to withdraw, taking all his secrets with him, and Gunar felt the world come back into focus. There in front of him was Sigurd's smiling face, full of love. Yes, yes, Gunar realized—he was loved. Sigurd loved him like no one else could ever love him; and he loved Sigurd back. He didn't understand what had just happened, but knew this: It was divine. He had been touched by god.

When he felt his love for Gunar overflow and fill the other man, Sigurd remembered the crowd. The moment had been not for him and Gunar alone; it had been for all. Not one out of all the hundreds of thousands who saw it had any idea of time passing, but during it the crowd had fallen utterly silent. In that gathering of over a million people, there was not so much as a cough to be heard. It was the same in a thousand village greens, town halls, and street sides throughout the country where people were watching the scene on video. A miracle had occurred, something holy: an exchange of pure love.

Gunar was trembling from head to foot. He was ready to sink to his knees, but before he could move, Sigurd did the most unexpected thing it was possible for him to do. He sank to *his* knees, he bowed his head and kissed Gunar's hand.

What did this mean? Gunar stood there, shaking his head, mouthing the words, "No, no . . ." It was wrong—all the wrong way round!

From his knees, Sigurd addressed the crowd.

"Did you think I came here to rule?" he asked. "I came to serve. I'm Gunar's because he is yours. My father had to build from nothing. We're luckier. We have the Niberlin country.

There is nothing here to change until the world is like this. Now go home, and prepare for war."

With that, he raised Gunar's hand in his above their heads and the crowd burst into a frenzy of cheers, an eruption of hope. Gunar understood then that everything the Niberlins had hoped to achieve in a hundred years, Sigurd was going to do in months, and all in his name. It was going to be all right. Everyone would get what they wanted—even him. He looked across to Gudrun, who beamed back at him. Sigurd was a combination they had never dreamed of—selflessness, charisma, pure love, pure power. He was irresistible.

Gudrun glanced at Sigurd and made a face at her brothers— phwooar! Tasty. Gunar and Hogni laughed. Yes, Sigurd was gorgeous. Making sure only they could see her, Gudrun clenched her fist and pouted in an expression of lust, and the three of them laughed again. Sigurd saw them laughing, and not knowing what they found funny, but seeing fun, laughed with them. The crowd at his feet began to laugh too. It was funny! What was funny? No one knew anymore, but the tension was released. Guess what? It was going to be all right! After all the suffering and hope and anger, it was funny. The laughter spread. A million people stood and roared for the sheer fun of it.

Above, a small black and white muzzle dropped out of sight from a window ledge. Grimhild sat on the floor and scratched her ear, relieved. Their skins were going to be spared. Sigurd was a nice young man. Power rested with him now, that much was clear. It was just a question of how she could best ally the family with his star.

28

sigurd

We went inside, it was just the four of us. These days, what do they mean? I was becoming impossible. It wasn't a real life anymore, I was changing all the time, like an insect. For a while out there I was scared that the sky would open and I would ascend to heaven and leave the whole lovely world behind me forever.

There was food on the table and Gudrun was telling me to sit down and eat. They were all looking at me like I was some sort of atomic weapon. We'd left the laughter outside. They were scared of me, but I just wanted to be friends with them, so I flung my arms around Gudrun and told her how lovely she was, and then I kissed Gunar and then Hogni . . . then we all started talking at once—god knows what about. I was getting kind of hysterical, babbling away. All those people! What did it all mean?

And what happened with Gunar? I saw him. I mean, I didn't see him; I saw his *soul*.

We were suddenly looking at each other, him and me. It was embarrassing. It was unfair, because I knew everything about him and he knew nothing about me.

"I'm just a kid," I said, and then I blushed because it was such a stupid thing to say.

"What do you remember?" he said, too quickly.

He had been more naked to me than it should be possible to be. I could remember *everything*. It was like his life had become mine. What could I say? Things happen in their time as they need to. Myself, I know nothing—less than nothing. I used to think I was going to be the king and it was him all the time!

Why him and not me? I wonder why.

I told Gunar I remembered nothing—just a shape, perhaps, a general feeling—the certainty that he was to be the king and I was to be the power behind him. The anointer. I had anointed him out there, that was his coronation. And now I wanted to be friends with him! I clapped my hands together and felt the warm flesh and I thought, This is the real thing! All that business with the soul and seeing with god's eye—stuff that. I want the wine, I want the flesh. Food on the table and friends to be with—what more is there? I was scared silly they wouldn't be friends with me, that I was already some sort of god or monster trapped in an eternity that no one could ever relate to. That's why I lied to Gunar about what I knew, that's why I kissed Gudrun and slapped hands with Hogni. I was terrified of godhead, of becoming without meaning. God has no point unless he dies. You see? Without death, life is worth nothing. Every child who dies has had more than any of them. Jesus, Allah, Odin, the Buddha, they live forever; they have entered Hel.

So I talked and laughed and ate the food and sipped the beer and touched them—I kept wanting to touch them—and I thought to myself, All this could be taken from me at any second! This is life. It is so precious.

And—Bryony! Every time I remembered her it was with a jolt. Life was moving so fast! The dragon skin!

"Do you have it?" I begged Gunar.

"We have it," he said. And I was so happy then, I cried. So happy. Nothing could stop me rescuing her now.

But I didn't tell them why I wanted the skin. There was time for that. Bryony was just for me.

It was a great evening. Gunar kept trying to get me to read military reports—the Portlands were on the move already, by all accounts. But I couldn't think just then—no sleep for two days, so much had happened. I'd been a schoolboy at home a few months ago, now look! Ridiculous! My life's ridiculous!

"Leave him alone, Gunar," ordered Gudrun. "He never stops," she told me. "He's the incredible working man." Gunar laughed at himself, and she slid her hand around my waist and smiled at me. And I thought . . . Ahhhh. Is that what she wants? She was lovely—but I'm afraid not. Bryony, Bryony was in my mind.

It was a lovely evening, but I was so tired. The world had changed in the last few hours. When I was so exhausted I just couldn't stand up anymore, Gudrun showed me to my room.

29

gudrun

I stood there in the doorway, half smiling. Smiling hopefully, to be precise. Rrrrr! Embarrassing! Will he, won't he, will he, won't he? Rough. I was almost ready to go, fuck it, and go in myself and say yes before he had a chance. But something held me back. When I opened my mouth, I almost expected myself to say, "Go on, then," meaning, Go on, ask me, I'll say yes. Maybe he was shy because I was Gudrun, a Niberlin, or because I was older than him or something.

"Good night," I said, and I waited again, even though it was pushing it a bit by that time. I was so sure he was going to say something . . . you know, It'd be better if you were in here, too, or, What about a good night kiss? or even, How about it then, honey pot? would have done me fine, I was so horny. But all he did was smile.

"Is the bed comfy?" I asked, and we both laughed out loud, I was being so obvious.

"It's lovely. I've been sleeping on rags for months." He lay down and sighed. "Good night, sweet dreams," he said, and he closed his eyes briefly, then opened them to watch me leave. Dismissed! Rrrr . . . I was glad of the half-light because I was blushing. I couldn't have been more obvious if I'd thrown my knickers at him. I closed the door and tiptoed back to the kitchen. Gunar and Hogni were still up.

"No luck?" said Hogni.

"Was it that obvious?" I asked. I was blushing again. They both roared with laughter.

"Bastards," I told them, and reached for more wine.

Gunar was finding it hilarious. "Think Hogni has a l-l-little secret to tell you."

"What? No!" I said, as I guessed what he was going to say.

Hogni grinned. "Sorry, sweetie," he said. "He bats for my team." And both of them hooted, as if it was some huge joke.

"Made a complete arse of myself, then," I said. I felt like a real prat. I'd misinterpreted him completely. He was lovely, and we got on like a house on fire—but he was just being friendly after all.

"Makes you a fag-hag," giggled Gunar. He was finding it hilarious, the fact that both of us were lusting after the same bloke. So did Hogni.

"Not only did he do it with me, but I don't even think he's gay," he said. "That makes me *loads* more attractive than you, sweetie."

"Makes you a slut," I told him.

"Means I'm a successful slut, while you're just a failed slut."

"But I'm the only one here with any se-se . . . oh, bugger . . . se-se-se . . ."

"Sexual integrity?" finished Hogni.

"Yes!"

So we both told him immediately that we might be sluts, but at least we weren't Mr. No-Shags, like him.

"Yes!" howled Gunar, who was prepared to laugh at just about anything when he got drunk. "Hogni's a sex machine and you're a love machine but I'm just a r-r-rejection machine." Then Gunar got up and started being me trying to chat to Sigurd at one end while Hogni was shagging him at the other, and I got fed up suddenly.

"I've had enough of this now. Can we stop now?" I said. "I have just actually been rejected." Obediently they both sat down. See, we tease one another to bits but they're nice guys, my brothers, they'd go to the ends of the world for me.

"You might have told me," I said to Hogni. "So are you going up there now?"

He didn't look so smug then. "It was a one-night stand."

"Ah-haa!"

"What do you mean, Ah-ha?"

"So you got him pissed."

"No."

"You're not actually sure he bats for your team, then? He might be a *floating* player."

"A fl-floater?" said Gunar. "That's appropriate."

"Fuck off," said Hogni. He looked at me. "I think there's someone else, actually," he said. "I think he's already in love."

And that made sense. I *know* he fancies me.

We didn't stay up much longer. Poor Hogni got all sad; turned out he was smitten. Which was a bit of an event actually, because he gets around, Hogni. We're all always on at him because we're terrified he's going to catch some awful cross-species virus. He's always getting his heart broken, but it's always temporary. Rrr. You know, a few days or a week, a month at the most, and then he's found a new boyfriend and he's as happy as—well—happy as a dog with a bone.

"Nah, it's g-g-gonna be just the same, you'll be back on the game by next Tuesday," said Gunar. But Hogni was really feeling this one. Gunar was in the middle of some joke and I saw Hogni's eyes just fill up. I put my arms around him.

"Is it a bad one?" I asked. He sat there with his arms crossed leaning on the table and nodded his head. Gunar had shut up, but I could see him over Hogni's shoulder, and you know what? His eyes had filled up as well. I'd forgotten with all the drinks and the talk and half expecting to end up in bed with Sigurd. You know: what Sigurd had done to him.

I nudged Hogni. "You're not the only one," I said. He looked across.

"Oh—poor Gunar. Yes; what was all that about?"

But all Gunar could do was shake his head. What had Sigurd done to him—in front of all those people, where everyone could see? It had made all those tens of thousands fall silent, but I don't think any one of us could have said what had actually happened.

Hogni said, "I think he might be some sort of god."

"Oh, he was that good, was he?" said Gunar.

"Well, tell us, what did he do to you, Gunar? What happened?"

Gunar shook his head and bit his lip and couldn't reply.

"But he's just a man—just a boy!" I exclaimed.

"Maybe that's how they start off," said Hogni.

We were all quiet then. We were all thinking about the boy asleep above us. What did he mean, why was he here?

What was he going to do next?

30

the mother of the house

This is Grimhild, mother of the house. It's the very pitch black of night and she's swishing smoothly down the dark corridors on a foldaway scooter. It's a good way to get about, she's been using them for years. Her perfect white hands, no bigger than a child's and covered with perfect white fur, hold tight on to the handle while her neat little doggy foot pushes away down below. She keeps the scooters folded up in cupboards scattered throughout the palace—there's always one on hand. Quick and quiet—just the job for an elderly lady moving to fat.

But in the black of night? Dark corridors? Why is there so little light down here? The Niberlins can afford generators and fuel. See there, as she drifts past a room where a small lamp glows—her eyes shine in the dark like a cat's. Grimhild has see-in-the-dark eyes. You'd expect it, looking at her. She stands upright, she has hands, but she's a dog through and through. Look at her mouth. Look at her tongue; there's no speech. Look at her skull—there are no frontal lobes, either. And Grimhild can smell—boy, can she smell! She can smell a chewy-bar, a thief, or a fortune from a hundred meters.

She needs no light.

What was the old king thinking of, marrying a creature like that? Of course these days, things are different, we understand that. If you can have a conversation with your dog it does wonders for the relationship. Things . . . well, they develop, put it like that. Grimhild has a decent pair of breasts—we forgot to mention them when we were listing her more human attributes—covered in that same flat white fur. Ideal for stroking. But still! Kings have to think ahead. The bloodline, succession. They spend a lot of time on this stuff. When one of your children is going to lead the nation one day, you take your breeding seriously. There are the womb-tanks, of course, cloning techniques and so on—but that basic genetic material is still important. What was he doing, breeding from a sheepdog? It makes no sense. It's not even good taste. He could have chosen a decent breed, an old English, or a spaniel of some kind, if he wanted to be traditional, or something grand—a wolfhound, or an Afghan even. Something with a bit of class.

But Grimhild wasn't always like this. You should have seen her when she was first married! Frontal lobes? She had them in her elbows. Looks? She had them in her brains. She's never been the same since the assassination. She lost everything— her husband, her looks, her brains, the lot. She barely got away with her life.

It's a story that's never been told. Grimhild and Ida were the only ones there, and they ain't talking. The assassins got in and out of the royal apartments without leaving a sign— shape-changers, most likely. The king was dead on the floor, Ida lay tied to a chair, the blood all down her front and her tongue on the table beside her. Grimhild lay whining on her husband's feet, faithful old bitch that she was. What had happened, who was it? Ida had never learned to read and write and resisted all attempts to teach her, and Grimhild— well, she was a sorceress and a shape-changer herself. Everyone was familiar with that black and white sheepdog bitch—she'd used the shape many times. They stroked her and cuddled her, fed her, talked to her and petted her. It was surely just a matter of time before she changed back. Maybe the shock, the terror . . . ? Or maybe the murderers had done more to her than met the eye. But the hours turned into days, the days to years, and Grimhild remained the same, resistant to either sorcery or medicine. Palace security was reviewed and renewed—too late for the king and his queen. Grimhild never got back to the way she was.

It's ironic really. When she had the equipment, she was such a talker. Couldn't shut up. Her husband was always telling her—"You talk too much, Grimhild," he used to say. "You'll give yourself away, one day." But not anymore. Her long jaws and loose tongue have silenced her forever.

What does she want, anyway, up so late? The whole palace is asleep. Is she nocturnal? She's certainly an insomniac, old Grimhild. She walks the day with bags under her eyes. If she went to bed early it would do her no good, she'd only lie there sighing and scratching and staring at her cushion, tormented by anxious thoughts. Better to be up and listen to the radio or read a book when no one is watching. Or making plans. Her children, who love her dearly, would be surprised to think she has any plans left. In fact she's full of them. She's made of them. They pulse through her blood and flow through her water, they come out of her eyes and her ears, anywhere but out of her mouth. Secrets, secrets, old Grimhild. But from your own children? What for? You're on the same side, after all. But people, sometimes even people you're very close to, have a habit of disagreeing. The fact is they don't know diddly-poo. Grimhild likes to be informed. Her motto: one step ahead.

There she goes, past the flock wallpaper that was put up to please some fussy foreign minister who designed it himself; past toilets one, two, and three, past dining rooms, under chandeliers and sprinklers, clickety-click, clickety-clack over endless tiles—carpet is quiet but hard work—past lifts and trophy rooms, past the clock collection that fills two halls and was her mother-in-law's obsession, past galleries with their displays of ancient artefacts depicting the ages of stone, bronze, iron, steam, petroleum, and electricity.

Over her shoulder is a bag with a small portable radio in it. If something interesting is on, she might pause and sit down on one of the many chairs and sofas lining the corridors, and have a listen. Why not? There's plenty of time. She'd have a book there too, but she doesn't like to be seen reading.

Oh dear! She likes the dark, she lets her children think she has the mental capacity of an aging sheepdog, never speaks, and, worst of all, she reads in secret. Bad signs. Yes, there is certainly more to Grimhild than meets the eye. Is there a sliver of fox in there, alongside the sheepdog? Could be. She can be sly enough, this one. What's she up to? What does she want? What's her *game*?

No secrets! There's nothing to know. It's my favorite time of day, that's all. Everyone fast asleep, the house so still. It's a time when you can see the soul most easily. You need a glass, say one meter tall. You fill it up with spring water and if you know the runes you can catch the shadow of the soul moving inside by moonlight. You can understand it by signs—its color, its shape, how it moves. A person's personality isn't always anything like their soul. Souls have their own business.

My mother showed me how. It's a trick, that's all—a party trick, like changing shape. Hide-and-seek. Nothing that means much.

Yes, secrets move out of their hidey-holes at this time of night. The local wildlife, my husband used to call them— foxes, witches, ghosts, the spirit-world; the gods. Up to no good, he used to say, but he wasn't above my using a little witchery when it suited him.

And then GRAAAA-GRA-GRA-GRA-GRAHHHHHN NNNN . . . . snoring! Gunar, my eldest. And he even stutters when he snores! It's enough to make you jump right out of your skin.

Poor boy. I have to live until I'm a hundred! My children need me, they don't know it, but they do. Flat on his back, head to one side, snoring like a pig. Just like his father. He used to drive me out of the bedroom with his noise. Not that Gunar has anyone to drive away. He complains that he's full of love and no one to give it to, but he's too fussy. Always picking faults. This one's too ordinary, this one's too fat, this one's quiet, this one's not mad enough. I've heard him say that. What sort of a thing is that, to want someone mad? "Only a bit mad," he says. What does he want, a goddess? A good-looking man, any girl'd be proud to have him—but he's too proud. Gunar-all-alone, Hogni calls him when he wants to tease.

At least he had the job—but not now. Oh, don't let that business of naming him king fool you, Sigurd's the one in charge. Sad, but you can't fight history; Sigurd has the following. Well, there's no shame in following the likes of him. I watched him, I saw his soul. It's true: He's almost a god. Perhaps he'll become one, with a little help. Everyone needs a bit of help. Yes. A pity. But if the Volsons are good enough for everyone else, they're good enough for us, too.

Grimhild, Grimhild! More secrets? And what ambition! You'd make your guest a god? Inside that flat skull of hers the language is rolling like the seas. She's thinking like a human—yes, and lying like one too. There's more layers to this one than an onion.

In the old days, before her accident, Grimhild used to creep in on her children late every night, until they compared notes and worked out what was going on. They started staying awake to try and catch her spying. Yes, they called it spying—looking over her own children? Spying! It was always the way. Children have no gratitude.

Tonight could be like old times, but although she pauses outside her boy's room to listen, she doesn't turn to go in.

Off she goes again, pushing on her little scooter. As she rounds the corner, at the far end of the corridor behind her, Ida appears, stolidly plodding on her way around the palace after her mistress. She likes to keep an eye on things in case she's needed. Wherever she goes, Grimhild knows that sooner or later, Ida will turn up behind her.

And clickety click, past more doors, more rooms, more paintings. She doesn't even pause at Hogni's door tonight, although she can't help being mildly irritated by the sound of his snores. Does he have to sound camp even in his sleep?

• • •

'Course, it's his own business, but does he have any right to deprive me of grandchildren? That's the thing. Ahh, my Hogni. Always the wrong thing in the wrong place. He can't help it! And then he gets into bed with Sigurd when it should have been Gudrun! Oh, it makes me want to give him a good slap! The best fish in the sea and he's gay! But Sigurd isn't gay—just curious, I reckon. And of course he's shy to get in with Gudrun after he's already been with her brother. Time'll sort it out. With a little help. Ha! And who will help, do you suppose? Oh, I need to live forever. My children! You can see how fine they are but they need me.

Anyone can see—the way they look at each other. They ought to be together. The Niberlins and the Volsons—what a team! Poor Gunar! Well, I knew all the time of course. Gunar has a gift for detail but he's a bureaucrat, not a politician. He has no nose for it. It's Gudrun that understands politics, if you ask me.

Mum's the word. It'll be Sigurd and Gudrun, king and queen. I can see it now.

Wheeeeee—and along the corridors, past the photos of Niberlins past and present: Grimhild and her Al shaking hands with Sigmund, old and gray, but still a vigorous man, in those days, before he was blown to smithereens.

Yes, she will support Sigmund's son. She'll help, even. Prod things along in the right direction. She'll take care of him. Accidents will happen, but Grimhild has her insurance policies.

And past more toilets one, two, and three, down another corridor, around a corner. Why, the boy's part of the family already. So much depends on him! What if he fell and broke his neck? He could fall under a bus tomorrow, damage his jewels, and leave no heir, fall in love with the wrong person, anything. Oh, no, no, no. But not to worry. Grimhild has the means of making it better before it even happens.

Outside his door. Yes, the old bitch has a favor to do for her new son tonight. It's no more than she's done for her own. But—what's this? He's not asleep? Grimhild didn't have him down for secrets. His soul is nothing like that—so straight and so clear, you can see straight through it. She's never seen anything like it. So what's he . . . oh.

Oh. That secret; the one we all have. So he's human after all. She'll have to come back later, that's all. Well, well. It's secrets in the dead of night. Mum's the word! She'll never tell a soul.

A disgruntled Grimhild made her way back on her scooter— not to bed, though. Long ago the old woman decided that sleep wasn't good enough for her. The right chemicals and hormones, speeded-up dreams—a lot of it can be dispensed with. Most doctors won't do it, the risks are too high. But some can doctor themselves. These days Grimhild only sleeps for any length of time when she needs her dreams to prophecy.

She was annoyed with Sigurd. He could have slept with her daughter if he'd chosen. Gudrun had made that clear enough. Instead he preferred to lie on his own between the sheets and do it himself. Well, boys will be boys—but good grief! It was unthinkable that that could be preferable to a night with her lovely daughter!

She has many talents, this old woman, and many secrets. She'd hidden herself away in that little dogsbody, her brain folded up and down her spine while she played pet to her own flesh and blood. But she was all there, just as she had been a decade or more ago on that terrible night, the night of the assassination. She and her crafts were all totally intact.

Expecting to find the boy in a deep sleep, she'd planned on taking a scrape from the inside of his mouth. Sigurd's DNA would be worth having a look at for curiosity's sake alone, but it was more important than that. The boy was too valuable an asset to risk, for mankind in general and to her family in particular. It was the least she could do. A little duplication could undo any serious harm. She already had several Gunars, Hognis, and Gudruns cloned, fit and ready to step into the shoes of the original if they needed to. It was only sensible.

Exactly. Grimhild kept spares.

The cloning was just science, it could only do so much— you can't clone a good upbringing! So the old woman made a trip once in a while around the palace to copy her children's minds, duplicate them and file them away—just in case. She spent many hours sitting down in her den under the palace with Ida, scanning their memories. Spying? Gunar, Gudrun, and Hogni had no idea what real spying was.

She's a hoarder, old Grimhild. It's only common sense. This night was to have been the first step in doing the same for Sigurd. It didn't take long with cloning techniques these days, she could have the first copies up and running within a few weeks. She was foiled this time because he was awake, but Grimhild knew how to wait.

She headed down to her private quarters underground, to inspect her treasures fondly—her replacement children, lying still in their tanks. Ah, so sweet. Sleeping so deeply, just like they used to when they were babies. So sweet, so still, so ready to come to life whenever she wanted them to. Soon it will be time to renew the clones again. You have to keep things up to date. Scars and wrinkles, memories and impressions. It was delicate, painstaking work. The originals had to be carefully scanned, the clones prepared, updated, and eventually replaced. Then there was the nasty business of destroying the out-of-date version. She left that to Ida. What sort of mother would she be if she could face that—destroying your own children, even it was only to help them live? Yes, you had to keep busy when your country needs your children and your children need you.

She could wait. The time would come. She would prepare a tank for Sigurd while she was down there this very night.

31

1st strike

A long day was followed by a short night. Sigurd had fallen asleep as soon as Gudrun left him. Wild elephants and factory hooters couldn't have woken him up, but a tiny scratch at his window did at once. The windows were closed, because of the noise from the crowd outside, but even asleep, Sigurd was waiting for Jenny Wren to come.

"Yes," he murmured, and slipped out of bed to let her in. She wouldn't come to him unless he was alone, and he hadn't seen her since that first night, when Hogni had gone off to radio back home and get his instructions. She had hidden in the ivy and watched him in secret while he slept in the church and made love with Hogni—there were no secrets from Jenny, but she never judged. She had kept on waiting with her gift from Bryony, and now she was as pleased to see him as he was to see her.

Joyfully she perched on his finger as he stroked her head and kissed her beak and made a fuss of her. Brave little bird— flying all this way through the fire to carry a message of love. Such a tiny link between two worlds.

Around the wren's slender foot was a small golden nut, a

tiny little thing from a delicate golden circuit that Bryony had slipped on like a ring. Sigurd took it and put it carefully in his pocket. Now for something to send back. But what? Outside the window, a clematis was climbing up around the frame. It was late spring and the plant was covered in pink, star-shaped flowers. He picked one and gave it to Jenny; the flower was as big as she was. Too big? She took it up in her beak and shook her feathers. She could do it! She flicked her wings—and fell straight to the floor. Laughing, Sigurd plucked a single petal from the flower and gave that to her instead. She stood on the carpet looking up at him with it in her beak, then flicked, and there she was on the windowsill, looking over her shoulder at him. He laughed again, she looked ridiculous with that huge petal in her bill—then she turned, flicked again, and was gone.

He thought how she would be with Bryony so soon—within hours perhaps. If only he could change his shape and fly like her through the tiniest holes. But shape-changing was not one of his gifts.

Sigurd lay back down. Thinking about Bryony led him to sexual thoughts, which was why he was busy when Grimhild came by. Then he fell back to sleep.

Gunar, as usual, was right. "Gunar is always right," Gudrun used to say, without any sarcasm, when she was only three years old. Sigurd's arrival in the region had turned the balance of power in favor of the Niberlins. War was on its way: Old Bill figured it might as well be now, before the Niberlins had time to organize.

There had been no troop movements—that would have been picked up on—but weapons were readied, barracks put on alert, strategy discussed, and, disguised as ordinary business activity, munitions and supplies put into place.

As every playground fighter knows, you go for the big bugger first. Bill had a few advantages yet. Ruthlessness was one, although he'd drawn back from attacking the crowds in the square the day before, if only because he needed people to do business with after he'd won. Your competitors are always wrong, but your customer is always right, as he often impressed on his workforce. The other advantage was surprise. Get in quick, go for the big bugger first, attack with extreme prejudice. He planned to open the war on several fronts at once and push forward rapidly. If he could establish a major advance in the first few hours, it could be decisive. His very first shot, the opening move, was directly on Democracy Palace. If he could kill Sigurd and the Niberlins in one raid, the war would be as good as won.

Grimhild had not yet reached her secret basement when the sirens started up. Air strike! Ten-minute alert. In a panic she turned and headed back to where her children slept. Had they heard? Her precious cargo. Oh, time is a cruel sea! Faster, Grimhild, faster! Then—oh no! The clones! What about them? If her children were killed, the clones could live on. She had replacements. Surely the clones were the most important?

Quick! No time to lose! She scooted the other way, caught in a dilemma: What is real? What is *right*? Poor Grimhild; maybe that accident had had more effect on her than she knew. The clones were every bit as precious to her as her actual children. She was unable to distinguish one from the other.

Faster, faster, Grimhild—you only have ten minutes. But look, she's turned round again! What is it now? The clones are below ground, much safer than her children, who are so vulnerable up there on the first floor. But another thought—the clones couldn't run away. Oh, help! She stopped, panting on her scooter in a frenzy of indecision.

And of course she didn't have ten minutes at all. The Portlands had stealth; the radar was late. Only two minutes after the siren went off, a missile crashed into the palace. It lifted one side of the roof half a meter into the air before it fell back down with a violent thud and burst into flames. It was one of those occasions that Grimhild cursed her dog's mouth. She'd had a good voice, deep and silky. "Hot smoke," her husband had called her. Now she couldn't even ring through and ask where the damage was or who had been hurt. Alarms were ringing furiously throughout the building. In a total panic, the old bitch abandoned her scooter and started bounding down the corridors on foot. Like a little nightmare she was, sometimes running upright on her little doggy legs, one black, one white, her child's arms and hairy elbows pumping furiously up and down, sometimes going on all fours with her bum high in the air, sometimes rolling forward in a series of somersaults in her efforts to go faster and overcome her awkward anatomy, suited to neither.

But there were no more missiles. Gunar had his defenses on high alert. It was a risky move on old Bill's part. The great powers in the east and Africa made sure that western Europe never had much of an air force, and the four planes Bill had sent on this mission represented a sizeable percentage of his air power. Only one missile got through and two of the planes were lost, but perhaps the gamble had still paid off. The missile had only tipped the private accommodation, but it knocked out several systems and badly damaged communications at a time when Bill was at his most dangerous.

Grimhild didn't need to run all the way. There was a heavy pounding behind her and Ida appeared, her mouth open in her flat face, her blue eyes alarmed that something might have happened to her beloved. She scooped the old bitch up in her arms and, pausing only to stroke her head and tousle her fur, carried on— she never has to be told—down to the underground incident room, where the family was to gather in such emergencies.

Once there, Ida put her down and went to lean against a wall, panting; she'd had a bad fright. Grimhild looked around—all well, thank god! Gunar, Hogni, Gudrun, not a scratch. Grimhild ran from one to the other, licking and stroking their faces and hands, whimpering, barking excitedly. But where was Sigurd?

He arrived a few minutes later, led there by a guard. There was blood and his skin was shining with a peculiarly fractured light. He had been closest to the blast. He'd actually heard the missile swooping in, had got out of bed, and was on his way to the window to see what it was when it struck. The blast had pushed his windows in, shattered them to shards and dust. It was these tiny fragments on his impenetrable skin that made him shine like crystal.

"I need a shower," he said, and had to fend Hogni off from an embrace, for fear of cutting his friend.

But something caught Gunar's eye. Not the light fracturing on Sigurd's skin, but the blood on his back. Blood meant humanity; humanity meant vulnerability.

He sent the guards out before he said anything. This was for family only. Then he asked his question.

"You're bleeding, Sigurd. How is that possible?"

Sigurd smiled and reached behind himself, to touch his vulnerable spot.

"There's one place that Fafnir's blood didn't touch, where a leaf was stuck on my back. I still have my own skin just there. Still human in one place, anyway," he joked. Gunar looked at him curiously and Grimhild growled right in her throat. That was something to know—and the boy was mad! Why give himself away like that? But Sigurd was pleased to share his secret with his new friends, it gave him pleasure.

"We're equal now—if only because we can all stab each other in the back," he said, and he laughed at the thought.

There was a shocked silence. It's a rare thing, a strange thing, when someone with such power shows their weakness—and so casually, as if it simply hadn't come up before. He trusted them so quickly, so completely, so foolishly. Sigurd glanced up at them in surprise—why were they staring at him? Old Grimhild broke the frozen moment by crossing the floor to her adopted son—that was how she thought of him already—and taking his hands in hers. Sigurd smiled, looking down at her. When the others gathered around him to touch him and inspect the place on his back, she left and went to the bathroom for tissues and cotton wool, and cleaned his wound with her own hands. Sigurd knelt patiently in front of her while she dabbed the blood off. Everyone watched quietly as she did him this service.

Then the guards reentered with the first news of the fronts opening up to the south, to the north, and to the west. The fighting was already raging. The Niberlins had been caught on the hop. Forgotten, Grimhild quietly left the room and scooted off, down to her own private quarters, the bloody tissues stuffed tightly under her arm. Behind her came a steady thud, thud, thud. Ida was on her tail.

She had Sigurd's genes. She would begin the procedure at once.

While Grimhild was gleefully running off with her bloody rags, Sigurd, with Gunar, Hogni, Gudrun, and various generals and aides, was collating the flood of information coming in, trying to work out responses and allocate resources to the fronts opening up all around them.

Old Bill had attacked to the south and west on a number of fronts, including one pushing through to Alf's kingdom. Alf was small fry but Bill had no intention of being caught between two enemies. There were other fronts to the north and the east from Portland allies. So far the Niberlins had had no reports of their own allies.

Sigurd listened to the reports with growing distress. As he looked at the map, he could already see patterns emerging, futures evolving. He would win this war; he knew that. There would be many deaths and a great deal of pain and destruction. The fight would not be long but it would require his full attention. It had already started. But—Bryony! It was no longer a question of just riding through. The Portlands held the land around London. There would be roadblocks, armed guards. Slipper would be instantly noticed. Sigurd was strong but he could not win an entire war on his own. This was bigger than him, bigger than love. He could not leave a war started in his name, not for love, not for hope, not for any reason.

"I'm too late," he thought. As he bent over the screen with

Gunar, watching the news flash through, he felt his heart turn cold inside him. Was this to be the cost? It didn't make sense. Destiny and desire had gone hand in hand for him so far, but suddenly his world was falling in two. What he wanted and what was were different. It made him feel sick, as if the ground was lurching under his feet.

Gunar pointed at some significant information. Sigurd nodded, but in his heart he was thinking, Bryony, Bryony Bryony! Was he going to lose her? And the baby, the unborn baby?

And there was more of course—his mother and Alf to the west, who were even now being overwhelmed by the Portland armies. Too late for them—he could only pray that they would escape. Was he to lose Bryony as well?

That could not be allowed to happen.

Sigurd nodded to himself. He couldn't move at the moment, but he still had time. Crayley wouldn't harm her until it could get her baby and that wasn't due for some months yet. But right now, this very second, he had to concentrate on winning a war.

He shook his head and turned his attention to the map. Inside his mind a web of thoughts began to unwrap themselves. He could see the strategy unfolding, not just now but into the future, too, as if the map was giving up its secrets to him, foretelling the shape of things to come. He knew exactly what he had to do.

He looked up. The others were staring at him.

"Can't you hear us, Sigurd?" said Gunar.

"Okay," said Sigurd. "This is what we have to do."

They listened, then began to argue. A lot of it seemed to make no sense. But how could he explain? It wasn't simply clever working out and intelligent guesses; it wasn't even that he knew what Bill would think and how he would react under certain circumstances. He simply knew the course of things. Reluctantly Gunar gave the orders Sigurd wanted. It went against what he could understand; but what else was Sigurd for?

So the fight began.

It was a desperate few hours—perhaps, in terms of heart's fear, the worst of the war. But the Niberlin armies were on the alert, the commanders well trained, able to take control and fight their own battles while HQ drew up the big picture. The first strike was at four; by half past Sigurd was issuing the first orders. By ten the following morning the situation had stabilized and they were moving on to the attack.

The long haul of the war was underway.

The following night, when it was possible to snatch a few hours' sleep, Sigurd lay in his bed, exhausted. Now he knew what war was. Behind the maps, men, women, and children were dying in their thousands. Soon it would be tens of thousands, and on it would go. Blood, pain, ruination, mutilation—what for? Was anything worth this price? Only one thing: peace. But it was a disgusting irony that you had to create the very opposite to win it.

Die for the future, or live for the present. So much to give up! So much lost forever.

Bryony! His beloved Bryony. And his unborn child.

"Casualties of war," he whispered.

Bryony was trapped below the bludgeoning holocaust, imprisoned but safe. The forces of war could not get near her. Crayley would see to that. She was safer down there than anywhere in the country, at least until the baby was born. But at what a cost! Solitary confinement in Hel. Even up here, even now when he was feeling the agony of a nation at war, he could imagine how it must be for her, trapped and alone. But there would be a way. If he had to burrow down with his bare hands, if he had to die a trillion deaths, he would bring his love to the surface.

Since I have to fight this war, he thought, I shall fight it hard. I'll crush this Portland army so that I can get to my Bryony sooner. Nothing will stop that. We will have our time when the war is over. She'll be safe for a few more months. I'll have her out of there when the war is over, or I'll die trying.

With this thought, that he was only postponing rescuing her, Sigurd turned over in his bed and went to sleep.

When the war is over. How many lovers have believed that?

And in the underground, Bryony waited for her Sigurd to come back for her. He had been gone under a week when the war broke out, but the gunfire and shellfire did not penetrate Crayley. She was expecting him every day, every hour almost. Sigurd had no way of communicating to her all that was happening to him—Hogni, the ambush at the Monkey's Paw, the gathering crowds, the breaking war. But when Jenny visited him the day after the attack on Democracy Palace, Sigurd had his message prepared. A piece of blue ribbon—a pale, sad blue, he thought—with tiny words written on it in black ink: WAR, DELAY and—HOPE.

Bryony wept. Hope? What about SOON—what about NOW? Hope! Hope was a lie. In a rage she beat herself against the wall, but then stopped suddenly and held her hands protectively over her stomach.

"Sorry, little one," she murmured. She could not allow herself to think like that. She was surrounded by her enemy—the walls, the floor, the roof, the fire, the very air. It was all Crayley. The machine was everywhere. But inside—inside was hope, inside was love. She had to hang on to that.

Bryony looked down at her little scrap of ribbon and thought how the last fingers to touch it had been Sigurd's. She had to wait, not for hours, not days, maybe not even for weeks.

She tried to think of all those millions of people living over her head, fighting one another, but in her world of one, she found it impossible. They had everything—why should they want to fight? War—such a definite thing. But hope, what was that? The color of the air, the wind in another country.

The baby growing inside her.

"He will do everything he can," she whispered. Yes, he would do whatever was possible. But for now she was on her own, fending for herself, looking after her child in an uncertain future.

Something tickled her arm—Jenny Wren, wiping her beak on Bryony's arm. She laughed and touched the little creature on the head. "Not all alone, then," she said. Jenny cocked her head and piped. Bryony sighed. More time to kill. How would she fill it? But she already knew the answer to that.

"Sabotage," she whispered. The city was weak. She would damage it. Pipelines, the old electrical nervous system, reservoirs. All it had were those creaky old bots. What sort of a creature was she, to sabotage her own home? But Crayley would never be home to her, even if she lived here all her life.

Bryony wagged her finger at the machinery piled up behind her. She smiled—she had a new hobby. She headed back to one of her huts to make her plans.

32

the old house

Then came a time when survival was all there was. It would break your heart and turn your stomach to see it—the village squares and alleyways heaped with bodies, the crushed buildings with the stink of rotting flesh hanging over them, and the flies crawling out of the fallen bricks. Murder and arson on such an industrial scale, and all for peace. How can peace ever win a war? Such bitter destruction can only ever leave a legacy of hate. What a foundation to build on!

At such times the gods show themselves. The destiny of individuals and nations all roll up into one. Rich pickings for the immortals. Mad gods shouting from under the ruined brickwork and twisted girders of fallen buildings, sane gods weeping with the dead at dawn, as the beautiful sun casts first light on scenes of sickening violence. Odin, he would be there of course, reaping the rich harvest of the dead, listening to choirs of the slaughtered, gathering secrets like a crow pecking out eyes, stacking up souls like brickwork. Was this all he wanted? The Allfather, to whom the future is as clear as the past. What can the powerful do in the end but add to their collections?

Andvari's ring sat prettily on Bryony's finger. Deep in the

underground, it was working out its debt of misfortune. But how? Is the war a misfortune? Such a terrible loss of life, but good can come if evil is defeated. Bryony's life is sour enough; perhaps its influence went no further than that.

In the first few days, the Niberlin losses were terrible, but the attack back was swift. Furiously old Bill Portland ordered a burnt earth policy in the hope of terrorizing the population into submission. The Portlands were better armed than the Niberlins. They had extensive foreign aid, not to mention that terrible halfman army, created from the best technology and the most extensive genetic library on earth. Soldier, weapon, and vehicle were no longer clear distinctions in their divisions. The preemptive strike had increased their natural advantage. Despite huge popular support, no one would have backed the Niberlins at this point.

Now Sigurd showed his true worth. Within hours of the first battle, Gunar, Hogni, and Gudrun had learned to leave strategic planning entirely to him. It was not always possible to work out why—he often didn't know himself—but his warfare was so surprising, impossible to predict, and so full of strange tricks that he often seemed to be more like a stage magician than a general. Several times he had the Portlands' armies fighting each other in the dark, or attacking their own towns, and even managed to divert shipments of arms from abroad into Niberlin hands. He seemed to understand what the Portlands were planning even before they did and danced round old Bill like a little bird between the feet of a rhino. Within two weeks he had forced the enemy back to his previous boundaries. A month later, old Bill was negotiating for a peaceful settlement. Without Sigurd, it could have gone on for years.

• • •

Summer was here, and the war was drawing to a close. Sigurd was now sixteen years old and he felt like a death machine. For weeks his brain had been churning out plan after plan after plan, most of which he didn't understand himself. He had only just begun to realize how much of him had been designed by his father Sigmund and reinvented by Odin. His genius did not require thought or consciousness; he produced strategy even when he slept. It scared him. Half designed, half divine—how much was left for himself to be human?

But now it was nearly over. For Sigurd as with the rest of the nation, it was not without losses—Hiordis and Alf had both died. He'd had no time to mourn them but now it was time to make the peace and there would be space for the living to count their dead.

It was June. He had been at the surface for two months. He was riding Slipper along a rutted track, off the main roads, on his way to the Old House, a country home of the Niberlins, to meet up with his allies and look over the proposals Bill Portland had put to them. They knew already they were going to reject them. No doubt he had many tricks left to play, but Bill held no more cards. It was just a question of whether they allowed him any conditions at all.

The Old House was set in large overgrown gardens, with an orchard, untidy flowerbeds, lawns, and terraces. There were numerous little outhouses and a stream that led into a small lake, half choked with lilies. Beyond were wooded river valleys and rough pastures on the hills above. Once an old livestock barn, the house had been originally converted nearly seventy years ago. Several generations of Niberlin children had spent their summers here, helping on the local farms with the harvest and the lambing, knocking up the pig swill, cutting down the thistles. It was the home of their fondest childhood memories.

The big central space under the roof had been kept as a kind of covered courtyard; the rest of it, the withy, the stables, various lean-tos and outbuildings, made up the rooms. There was a staircase up to a walkway around the main hall that led to the upper story and various attics and platforms high in the roof. The garden was tended by a single overworked gardener, who fought a losing battle against the rambling, weedy tumble of leaves and flowers they all loved. The old man wandered to and fro with his hoe and wheelbarrow, moving plants and clearing the weeds when something looked in danger of disappearing. The place was a haven for birds. There were swallows in the roof, barn owls in the attic, martins on the walls, birds in the air, birds on the grass, in the hedges and flowerbeds and the holes in the walls. The place was infested with them.

There was also heavy artillery hidden in the copse beyond the end of the garden, and missiles in a bunker under the edge of the hill in the bottom pasture. There was a network of underground passages, hiding places, tunnels and bunkers, a small hospital, storerooms, control rooms—everything that made up the muscles of power, wherever the powerful dwell. That rustic-looking farm that was their nearest neighbor on the other side of the beck was a barracks, housing a small but well armed and highly trained task force. In the nearby village, a battalion was stationed.

Grimhild lived here permanently since war had broken

out—her beloved children were scattered all over the country, running various operations. She watched the servants run the house and bit her tongue when they took liberties. It was the price she had to pay. She had her own work—secret things, kept out of sight. Now of all times it was important to keep copies of everything. Duplicates of duplicates; you never knew when they would be needed.

When Sigurd arrived, she greeted him fondly, running out on her odd little legs, taking him by the hand and jumping up at him in little starts. Sigurd picked her up and they embraced, soldier and sorceress, man and dog, neither quite what they seemed. Then she led him inside and watched as he ate a sandwich, wagging her plumed tail whenever he looked up at her, barking in reply when he spoke.

As he ate, Sigurd wondered—how much did Grimhild know, how much could she understand? It was something her children often talked about. The doctor who had first treated her after her accident told them she knew more than an ordinary dog, but he was being kind. Privately he suspected she couldn't recognize much more than sit and lie down. They had all come to share this view. For kindness's sake, Sigurd talked to her, since she wanted company and Gunar had told him that she liked it. He felt a bit of a fool at first, not knowing if he was talking to the air or not. Gudrun had once remarked that maybe she was better this way, a comment that puzzled him, but which he hadn't had time to probe further. Had they known just how aware she was they might have warned him that she was prone to crazy little plans and secrets, but she had hidden herself more deeply than anyone could have guessed and no one thought to forewarn him.

So he chatted on to Grimhild, talking for the sake of it. The journey over, fine. It was summer, the woods were full of birds—wasn't it lovely, what a day! Summer. Sunlight. Sigurd sighed, thinking of who was missing this fine bright day, with its blue skies and bright high clouds. And the war ending, and how life can now begin. In another week or so, Grimhild, he'll be taking off with the dragon skin. It was kept here, at the Old House, he was told, did she know if that was true?

Grimhild hung out her tongue to dry and panted lightly, cocking her head to one side in that bright, inquisitive way dogs have, but she didn't say a word or nod her head. Yes, he has someone to rescue, someone very dear to his heart—very dear. Isn't it wonderful, the war is almost over? Wonderful! Sigurd stood up and smiled, suddenly overcome with it. Now death stops and life begins. Yes!

"And Bryony will be with me!" he exclaimed, and he smiled down at the dog at his feet.

Sigurd pulled a face, frustrated that there was no one there to share his joy with. When the war had broken out, he felt bereft. Now it was time for the real adventure to begin—love.

Later, as he lay in the bath, there was that familiar tap at the window. Streaming water, Sigurd jumped up to let Jenny Wren in. It had been three days. He was scared that Bryony was in trouble.

He need not have feared. There was a scrap of her vest, cut neatly away. Lately she had been sending him these shreds of her underwear. Fondly Sigurd imagined her wandering around down there naked from the waist up. Yes . . .

No words—she didn't need words. What could she say? Waiting? What else could she do? Sigurd had his return gift ready—another piece of ribbon. On it, the words, PEACE, LOVE, and SOON. Yes, he could say that now—soon. He would be there soon. What on earth could stop him now?

The little bird sat on the edge of the bath while Sigurd petted her, stroking her soft back. But the wren never hung around for long. Already she was flickering her wings; now she was on the windowsill. She lived life at ten times human speed.

"Okay, okay already," said Sigurd. He reached over and tied the ribbon around the little bony leg. Jenny piped and was gone again, out of the window.

Sigurd sighed and leaned back in the bath. He was melting with exhaustion. He needed a night's sleep, but then: peace, soon. Yes, soon. Very soon. And love.

Then it was time for bed.

33

2nd death

Every one of us, they say, has infinite selves living out their lives in universes folded up together in such a way that one can never know the other. Here, in our particular little bag of reality, we have a single past and many possible futures, of which only one can ever be realized. If you turn left now, you can never turn right at that time ever again; turn right and you can never go left, everything will change forever. Some say that for those who live in the world where the old gods have risen up out of our souls and from rusted factories and cloned flesh, the future is as fixed as the past.

Could it have been different? Could Sigurd have seen the dangers the old woman presented—looked beyond her kind doggy face into the madness underneath? In other worlds, in other times, in another age of self determination and free will, any one of a thousand decisions he or his parents and guardians, friends and lovers made could have changed Grimhild's plans for this night. Or what if there was another kind of world altogether, with another kind of god less familiar to us, where the past can be changed by decision, just as we think the future can? How deep our lives would become then, if we could live their entirety backward and forward, over and over again, no two runs ever the same. Such a world is not familiar to us but we carry with us at least one set of the endless possible pasts. When she took the bloodstained bandage from Sigurd a month before, Grimhild was trying to ensure that come accident or murder, one version of Sigurd at least would always be with us.

See now, he sleeps. Oh, Sigurd—don't sleep now when the danger is greatest. Didn't you learn that the greatest danger always comes from home? Guns are obvious—it's love and kindness and goodwill and hope that hide things. Grimhild means well—do you doubt it? Or do you think goodwill is enough? Perhaps you do. Sleep on, then, as the old woman and her servant wheel you down the hallway and into the main barn. The house is empty tonight, the servants dismissed. Tomorrow Gudrun will be here, too late. Sleep as they take you across the lawn to the ruins of an old stone outhouse. It's a feature, a kind of folly, with rose and clematis scrambling over it, a bit of roof left up—big enough to shelter under from the rain; and enough to fit in a secret door. Sleep, Sigurd, as they carry you through the door and into Grimhild's secret place; sleep as they push you along to the laboratories where Grimhild keeps her experiments. You'd have thought that soldiers, servants, and the family themselves would have worked out that there was space unaccounted for down there— but why should they? The entire thing is folded away like Grimhild's brain, folded up and hidden—clever Grimhild!— inside a door. Magic objects are not what they seem.

Sleep on, Sigurd. You have no choice. Your good-night cocoa was drugged.

A fond old thing is Grimhild. Fond of her children, fond of insurance. When he was alive, Al Niberlin always used to complain about it—she spent a fortune on insurance, more than you could ever get back. Overcautious to the point of recklessness, he used to joke, but he knew that something didn't fit. It was greed, greed for control, greed to protect, fear of losing what she had. Like the dragon on his hoard, Grimhild watched over every trinket. In her case, her treasure was her family.

She and Ida roll the sleeping godling through the corridors to the treatment room. On the walls, her favorite expressions. When she was at school, they used to paint worthy sayings and exhortations on the walls. "Excellence is a habit," for example. "We lead by example," is another. Here, she has her own favorites up, things her mother used to say to her, sayings that she heard over the years that come to mind about her daily life.

She and Ida wheel Sigurd past the writing on the wall: HONESTY IS THE GOOD MAN'S BURDEN. True, Grimhild, very true. Worth knowing. A sense of humor perhaps behind those dark eyes? Grimhild can't smile and Ida never does. Perhaps she's heard the joke once too often. Dear old Ida. She has a face like a slab of stone, a good solid Lancashire face, as Grimhild used to say. The children always called her Ugly behind her broad back, she could scare them just by staring at them when they were small. But she has nice eyes, a pretty pair of blue that look forever surprised. Perhaps they are.

But what's this one, on the inside door of the treatment room? A PROVERB UNSAID IS WISDOM WASTED. What's all that about, Grimhild? Not much wisdom coming out of your mouth, is there? Well? Speak, tell us what you think! But no, nothing. Can't speak? Won't speak.

It's a penance, that's how she thinks of it, although it serves her purpose. The fact is Grimhild never could keep a secret. Things just slipped out of her brain onto her tongue and gone—whoops! She could wander around all day with her lips pressed together and then out it would come, plop, onto the floor, embarrassing everyone. It was a form of self-sabotage, she used to think. It didn't happen often, once in a few years, but when it did, it blew her away.

When she had her own shape, when she was a woman, she had affairs. Several. Not that she was ever promiscuous, but the king was busy a lot of the time, and, well—she had an eye for an attractive man. There was a bullish member of the bodyguard, strong as an ox, who used to make love to her like a rough sea; a wolfishly handsome member of a big business family, and an older man from the corporation, white-haired, slow but vigorous who spent the whole night moving over her body like a kind old friend.

But she let it slip—one, two, three times, regularly, every few years. Some silly clue fell out of her lips, giving away that she hadn't actually been where she said she was the previous night, or that she had actually met someone she'd sworn she never had. Silly mistakes, palpable lies, enough to lead her husband on to discover the truth. On the third occasion he'd had enough and swore to divorce her. He'd said that before but this time he meant it. And so he had to be . . . replaced? No, that was not the plan. Altered.

It was a simple thing in theory, she'd planned it for long enough, but it was the first time and it went wrong and he woke up in the middle of the transfer process. The point was to remove a memory—well, several memories to be precise, might as well make a few more adjustments while they were at it. But Al had come to, looked around, seen the versions of himself staring at him like huge pale prunes in their glass tanks. Sick with the drugs, he'd gone a bit crazy. Then, as he came round even more and realized it was actually not a nightmare but real, he'd become angry. Copies of him! Copies of his children! How dare she do this without his knowledge.

"It's not just them, Al. I've done me, too," insisted Grimhild. But Al was furious; there was no reasoning with him. He went mad, smashing up the tanks, destroying himself over and over again. Suddenly his hands were on her throat, his hot breath in her face, his eyes glaring, his face twisting. Of course it wasn't his fault—he wasn't all there, poor dear. Ida had saved the situation with an ax in the back of his head, and that was the end of him. It was awful. Grimhild was inconsolable; she hadn't planned on murder, merely a readjustment. Remove the memories of her infidelities, and they could get on with their lives as if nothing had happened. She hadn't even wanted to replace him with a clone, the original was good enough for her. Now he was gone, his memories out of date, his clones damaged beyond repair. What a mess!

She and Ida had saved the situation with a good old-fashioned lie. Assassination! The king dead, Grimhild attacked. They staged it all in her bedroom and waited for the morning and discovery. She had insisted on her own punishment—imprisonment in the shape of a dog. Her children assumed she had been trapped magically in mid-change, between dog and woman. But it served a purpose, this punishment. Now she had one secret too many. What if this stupidly slipped out? The dog's face takes care of that. Ida, bless her, was as helpful as ever and cut out her own tongue with a kitchen knife before Grimhild performed her last act in her own body, and tied her convincingly to a chair.

They lay Sigurd out next to the computers and begin to attach wires, coils, fibers and drips. The transfer of the mind is a delicate and tricky thing. Behind the smooth gray paneling where the blood-filled computers are housed are cloned brains; yes, what else can store so much information? As Crayley realized sometime ago, there is no substitute. Each one of these machines has to be individually grown. Those gray coils bathed in blood behind the machine are all grown from Sigurd's own cells. Fast work, Grimhild—only a few weeks and it's all ready. Science? Certainly—but there has to be a little sorcery in there, I think. The recipe's a secret? I won't tell, I promise—but neither will you. . . .

And what's this on the wall above him?

A BARGAIN YOU DON'T WANT IS A LUXURY YOU DON'T NEED. That's a bit thick, isn't it, Grimhild? When you have no less than five replacements for each of your children hanging around down here as well as the other five back at Democracy Palace? Just in case, you say? In case of what— serial murder of the same person?

And sleep, Sigurd, as Grimhild watches carefully over the dials. Already you are you and not you. Like Gunar, Hogni, and Gudrun, Grimhild has made five of you—see how closely she has taken you into her family. Your own faces look impassively on, the bright blood throbbing inside them, the empty brains registering nothing. Every cell of those brains is separate; not until the tails entwine will a single thought or feeling come. They are blank Sigurds, Sigurds from other worlds brought into this one, bottles waiting to be filled. What an army they would make! Each one with his invulnerable skin, each one made to lead. They could destroy the world, this lot.

What Grimhild is up to is possible nowhere else in the world. Scientists with technologies years ahead of ours who have been experimenting with personality transfer for generations would grind their teeth to hear about it. Look! The poor old woman is using a 1207/35 Matsina computer to try and hold an entire personality during transfer! She wouldn't be able to manage a newt with that equipment. And the carvings on the computer housings? What's that all about, it means nothing! But still the World Trade Organization has embargoes on England, for unfair competition.

Anything is possible if Odin wills it. But nothing turns out as it seems if Loki is involved.

One Sigurd from all these Sigurds, chosen at random; they're all the same. Out of its tank, it is laid next to the old one. Grimhild and Ida prepare to fire up the new and close down the old. Throughout it all, Sigurd sleeps on like a baby— the soldier, the lover, the golden boy. It's already too late. With wires and currents, chants and elixirs, he is poured across to his twin from another place. One Sigurd is emptied and another filled: one taken out of the world, one put in.

It doesn't take long. If you can fit a house into a door you can pass a man down a wire. Four hours, that's how long Sigurd took. And at the end of it the two men lie so much the same. The same bodies, the same scars even—Grimhild has great art. The same gifts and weaknesses, the same hopes and dreams. The same memories—well, most of them, anyway. Grimhild nods, content. The deed's been done.

But why? Why pour wine from one identical bottle into another? Sigurd never lost a leg or an eye, he could hear with both ears. He was as perfect as it was possible for anyone to be, ready for his time and place. What fault was there in this Sigurd, that she wanted him swapped? Surely not simply to move him from left to right for fun?

Now the two women go back to work. The Sigurds are unplugged, one with a universe inside him, the other empty, with only a few dregs of memory left swimming around his skull. Ida helps the old bitch upstairs with the new version, and then trundles the old out of the back door and along the path to the lake. It has been tightly bound. Around its feet, a great ring of steel locked with a key.

At the lakeside, Ida bends and looks into the face of the empty bottle and scowls. She doesn't like it. Grimhild should have emptied it right out. You can't kill an empty man, he's already dead, but this one still has . . . something left. Ida's not got the stomach for murder unless it's absolutely necessary. She doesn't like the suggestion of a smile on the drooling face, that faraway look, or the tears. There's a memory left in there, though god knows how such a cabbage as Sigurd is now could reach it.

Ida grunts: dregs. That's what Grimhild said. Dregs. She dumps the body in the boat and gets in after it and grabs the oars. The boat slides quietly out over the dark water.

But another has an interest here. The sliver of a moon reflecting on the water is cut by a dark spot moving rapidly toward the boat. It is the tiniest of breathing things, a bird.

Unusual for this time of night. Unusual too that it makes no noise, but lands in the bottom of the boat in the pitch dark and looks up into the face of the empty vessel. So small, Jenny Wren—but so full of intent. Without a squeak—Ida looks around but sees nothing—the wren flits up, stands briefly on Sigurd's nose. She pecks his cheek. A flick of that tiny tail. Standing on his face, she stares carefully into the bottle as if examining the dregs inside. Then, with a slight, deliberate step unlike her usual twitch, the wren steps, one two, three, straight through Sigurd's eye and into his mind.

Another few minutes and Ida has reached the deepest part of the lake. She lays her oars in the boat and turns to the empty man. She avoids looking again into his face. She takes him under the arms and heaves. Her work is interrupted when something small and fast flies past. She catches only a sense of it as it disappears suddenly into the black air over the water, but it startles her out of all proportion because this dead-of-night stuff is disturbing and she imagines that whatever it was flew right out of Sigurd's head. She gives a great cry and flings herself back into the boat, which rocks dangerously. She clings to the sides panting, staring at the man flopping awkwardly, half in, half out of the boat, his feet weighed down by steel, his head dangling in the water. Impossible! Of course. But even so the impression was so vivid she passes a hand over his face to convince herself there is no hole in it.

My god, it scared her half to death! A moth hiding in the boat. A bat. Gods! Her heart was beating its way out of her chest.

Ida turns on her torch and peers into Sigurd's face. Nothing. Just drool and starlight reflecting against empty eyes. She grunts. That's better. It's not murder when there's no one to kill. Well, it's still dark work but it must be done.

With an effort she pushes the body over the side, picks up the oars, and heads for the shore. She wants her breakfast. Beneath the water Sigurd struggles like a worm in the water, fighting for a life he no longer knows he has. He awakens—at last but so late. All his memories are gone but those that live in the body—even Grimhild can't steal those—and in a flash of dreadful fear, he knows that his life is in danger, that there are things he loves in his blood and his bones, and things he once knew that are worth every struggle and pain. Fight, Sigurd, fight! He kicks his legs: such is his strength, even bound with wire and drained of every thought and feeling, he manages to swim up. His chains tauten on the huge steel weight attached to him, but even that can't stop him. He hauls the weight out of the mud and still he kicks—up, up, up to the air. Two minutes have passed. Slowly, so slowly. Another minute. He is kicking so violently in the water that the body of the lake shakes, and still he goes up—slowly, slowly, a third of a meter up and then a quarter down, a third up, a quarter down. Four minutes. His strength is incredible. And now the impossible happens, and Sigurd's face breaks the surface, his mouth opens—and he sucks in a great lungful of air.

And what good does that do you, Sigurd? Where will you go? To the shore? What will you do when you get there with no memory, no personality, nothing but form and muscle? Sigurd, you are already dead.

There he goes, on the surface of the water, what was Sigurd, kicking, kicking, kicking, breathing, breathing, breathing. It took him nearly five minutes to get to the surface. Ida had beached her boat and was stepping into the house when she heard the splashing in the middle of the lake. Filled with horror, she launches the boat again, rides out with her torch to find what? Sigurd's face, sitting on the surface like a duck, as the lake heaves around him with the violence of his kicks. She is horrified—horrified that he's still alive and horrified at his strength, that he could kick like that and hold a two-hundred-pound weight suspended in midwater.

She lifts her oar high into the air and brings it down with all her violence on the upturned face. The face sinks and then reappears. She lifts again and strikes—again and again, over and over, hard as she can. The face turns red; the water around it turns red. Membranes deep inside burst open. Still he kicks, still he hangs on with his chin to the water's surface, staring at her sideways out of his mindless eyes; and still Ida bangs and bangs and bangs until it seems to her that she's in Hel and this is her punishment—to murder Sigurd forever and ever and ever, amen.

Just before dawn, Sigurd's kicks weakened and he began to sink. Four times he made it back to the air and Ida's waiting oar, before he sank back down, filled up with water and mud, and died. He was just a few months past his sixteenth birthday.

The clone awoke next morning from a deep sleep. He lay for a while gazing up at the ceiling and slowly gathering his thoughts, which seemed to rise up from somewhere deep inside and then gather in front of his eyes like a puzzle solving itself inside him. He was at the Old House. The war was ending. He was making plans; they were almost ready.

He felt deeply rested, as if he'd slept for a lifetime. But odd, very odd. Something was wrong but he had no idea what.

He got up and went to the window and looked out into the cool milky air of the morning. He felt so rested! He had no right to feel so rested after the weeks that had just gone. The call of a curlew came floating across the rough pastures: beautiful. But something was different. There was something on his mind—that wasn't on his mind. Something he had to do. But what on earth was it?

On the other side of the window was a tap, tap, tap. He looked up to see a bird on the other side of the glass. It rapped again, like a scattering of seed flung at the windowpane. A wren! Such shy birds, what was it doing? It was as if the bird wanted to come in. Smiling, he got up, expecting the little thing to fly away, but it just stood there, waiting for him. Around its foot was wrapped a scrap of cloth. A homing bird? A homing wren? He opened the window and the bird flew in so quickly he hardly saw it move. It seemed simply to have changed places instantly and was now sitting on the sill in front of him. It lifted a leg, like a parrot wanting to climb on his finger. He held out his finger and sure enough the bird stepped onto it. The clone smiled in amazement, then reached out and very, very gently unwrapped the little scrap of scorched cloth from around its leg and opened it up.

There were two words written on it, one on each side. LOVE; and WAITING.

What sort of a message was that?

Suddenly the wren, which had seemed so tame, jumped up and fluttered in his face, straight at his eyes. With a cry the clone brushed it away. It darted back at him, struck him on the forehead, and he dashed it away again. With an angry squeak, the little bird fluttered around the room—and then it was gone out of the window and hidden away in the bushes outside. He looked out after it, but there was no sign.

What was that about? A message? From who? Odin, perhaps? "Love" was not a very Odin-like word. Trying to peck your eyes out, that was a bit more in character. Perhaps love was coming his way. Waiting? What did that mean? A warning perhaps, that he was going too fast? It could mean anything. If you didn't know what was going on, you read into things whatever you wanted.

The clone scowled. He wasn't used to mysteries, things were always clear to him. And yet it felt that this was something he should know. Was someone trying to tell him something? Then why didn't they speak clearly?

He put the scrap of cloth in his pocket. In there, to his surprise, he found a number of strange little items; a golden nut from a tiny bolt, a few scraps of material. Meaningless. He threw them in the bin and went down to breakfast.

the clone

I was scared. I'd been scared a lot lately. Scared of turning into a monster, scared of turning into a god. Then it was the war. But that morning I felt empty. I was changing all the time. Was this what the gods felt in the face of the horror of war? Nothing?

Mass murder—that had been our work for weeks. It was difficult to believe that it was nearly over and that a whole nation of murderers would put down their guns, disarm their terrible machines, go back to their families, kiss their mothers, and get back to work. You turn yourself into this great big shit to get it over with. What if you got stuck?

I never saw a dead body during the whole war—that's so sick. I was kept out of the way. I was too valuable to risk. I was saving lives—me, the murderer, the war machine. I started it and I was saving lives so I had to be kept alive and I was the direct cause of thousands of deaths every day. It made me sick. Every time I finished a plan, every time an operation was carried out, I'd start retching like a cat.

But that particularly morning there was no nausea, no fear, nothing. I felt different . . . calm. Maybe I was just so worn out

I'd gone numb at last. I believe that every time you kill someone, you lose a part of your soul. Surely I had none left by this time. And then there was that strange incident with the wren at my window. Such shy little birds and there it was, almost trying to talk to me. That's what it felt like. When it left, I leaned out of the window and there was a honeysuckle growing there. Lovely thing, covered in yellowy pink flowers that smelled of honey. Only the day before, the sight of something like that would have filled my heart to overflowing. Now—well, it was beautiful, I could see it; but I couldn't feel it.

Something was different.

I thought, So soon? I'm only sixteen and I've lost the taste for life already? It made me laugh. At the time I thought it was a part of changing into a god but now I know better. It was something human in me dying. I think I killed too much. I only know that I used to be overflowing with love for the whole world, but that night, something in me died. I dried up.

The numbness didn't surprise me. The war was almost over now, and there'd been no time to mourn before. As soon as you relax, the pain starts. I'd lost my mother and Alf and all the good people I knew back in Wales. Perhaps it was just sinking in.

I got up and went downstairs. Grimhild was away some-where, the staff were all off that morning, I was on my own. I felt lonely. I stopped at the bottom of the stairs to feel—you understand? To feel what I was feeling. And there was nothing there. Nothing. I shook my head. It was as if a plate glass wall had fallen down between me and the world. I remember thinking, This ought to be scaring me. But I had the sense that pretty soon it would.

I had a pee, went into the kitchen to get something to eat. I opened the fridge, took out some milk, had a swig, put it back, turned round—and then it started. The strangest feelings, deep inside. I couldn't place them, I had no idea what they were, but they were moving right down in the deepest part of me, and they were coming closer. I could almost see them swimming up, like monsters rising from the depths.

I stood still and waited for it to go away, but it didn't stop. It just went on and on, it got stronger and stronger. So many feelings, so strong, so confused. Everything was—out of place.

I managed to make myself a cup of coffee and went through to sit on the sofa next door. It felt so big already and it was still getting stronger. Fafnir was nothing compared to this. It's true what they say, the worst monsters are inside you all the time. Stronger and stronger, I'd never felt anything like it. I thought it was the horror of war coming to get me, the weight of all I'd done, all the people I'd helped kill, all the widows and orphans I'd made. The longer it went on, the faster and more powerful it got. There was no end to it. I don't know how long I sat there holding on to the coffee, trying to stop myself going mad, but suddenly the cup fell out of fingers onto my legs, and it was stone cold. I was amazed, I couldn't have had a thought in my head for an hour or more. I knew I was in bad trouble then. It wasn't just feeling bad—I was literally falling to pieces. I was having some sort of a breakdown. I thought, Me? This doesn't happen to me, but having a skin nothing could pierce wasn't going to help me this time. My mind started spinning faster and faster than ever, I was getting giddier and giddier and sicker and sicker, and I was holding on tighter and tighter but there was nothing at the center and pretty soon the whole fucking mess was going to fly off in every direction.

35

gudrun

I was late, we got held up. Troop movements, I can't remember the details but it held me up and I didn't get to the Old House until late afternoon. I was pissed off about it because, yow!—you know, Gunar and Hogni weren't due there until later, Mum was out, so me 'n' Sigurd'd have the place to ourselves. Yeah, yow yow yow I was still hoping—you know? I'd caught his eyes on me a few times. I'd look up and he'd look away. He was so young. Maybe he was shy.

Yeah rrr. There was someone else. I'd have asked about her—the bitch!—but we hadn't time. That month. War! Awful. But even in the middle of all that your feelings for people go on. I was thinking about him all the time. Rrrow. Oh. Poor me. Maybe today I'd find out.

But we had something between us. It was the first time I was going to be on my own with him. So my heart was beating when I came through the door, but what I found I never dreamed of it.

It was a complete shock. I heard it from outside before I went in—this whimpering, like an animal that's been beaten. It didn't sound like a man at all. I pushed the door and went in.

He was curled up into a ball on the sofa clutching this cushion like it was all he had in the world and crying. I was going quietly to surprise him. He didn't see me at first. I just stood there, I was so shocked. I'd started to think of him as almost invulnerable, we all had. So strong! But I realized then— there's a little boy underneath it. Just a kid after all. You could tell by the way he was holding himself that there was something deeply wrong. I thought, Breakdown! At once. I knew something inside him had broken. I was terrified. He was everything to us. But at the same time I was relieved, in a way, because—well, it was like he was human after all.

I called his name and he turned round to look, all crooked. He'd been crying for hours, I think. His face was red and puffy. He looked awful. Not himself anymore.

"Are you all right?" I began, and he started talking—trying to talk, I mean. Odd words and stutters, and phrases, but it wasn't stringing together. I remember frowning and trying to work it out, like I was hearing it wrong or something, but it was just gibberish. He couldn't speak. He held out an arm to me instead and I ran across the room and took him in my arms. It was dreadful, dreadful. Watching something so beautiful and precious and full of love just falling to pieces in front of your eyes. I was so desperate and so scared for him, so scared I was going to lose him. He was the hope of the world, but it wasn't because of that. It was because I loved him. I loved him so much. I know. Everyone loves Sigurd of course, but I loved him like—like a woman loves a man. I'd have done anything to make him mine. I'd fall to pieces myself if anything happened to him—his beautiful body or his beautiful mind or his beautiful spirit.

As soon as I took hold of him, he let go of the cushion that he'd been hanging on to for dear life—it was sodden wet with dribble and tears, and he grabbed hold of me hard, like he was letting go of a beam a thousand feet high in order to reach me.

"Stay here, stay with me, please, I need help . . . stay with me, stay here with me, please . . ." he panted, a long string of words wrapped up in breath and choked in tears.

"Yes, darling, oh yes, yes. Oh, whoh whoh whoh. Okay, okay, I'm here. Don't worry. Don't worry, no no no no, I'm not leaving you. Hang on, hang on, it'll pass," I said, that sort of thing. And all the time he was still saying over and over:

"Please don't go, hold on to me, please don't go, hold on to me, please don't go, please don't go . . ."

It was so awful, it broke my heart. How long had he been there? He held me so tight. I'd been dying for him to hold me tight, but not like this, not like this. I was terrified that he was going to fall to bits on me—you know, just disintegrate and fall totally to pieces in my arms. I didn't know what was going to happen or what to do. I wanted to get up to ring for help, get a doctor or some medication, but I was scared to let him go, he was so desperate for me to be there with him, not to be alone. Every time I made a move he panicked and grabbed hold of me. So I just stayed there, holding on to him, stroking his head, murmuring to him, telling him it was going to be okay.

He stopped crying after a bit and just lay there panting, like a scared animal. I honestly thought he was dying, but he was getting calmer. I kept on stroking his head and waited. I hoped he was going to go to sleep, or pass out or something, and then I could creep to get the phone and ring for help. I was thinking, What are we going to do now? Because one thing was for sure—

if we lost Sigurd, we were going to lose everything. What would the people think if he disappeared?

Gradually he became very still and calm. I kept thinking he was asleep, but every time I moved, he tightened his grip on me. I didn't know if he was gone—do you understand? I mean, his personality. I thought maybe all that was left was something like an animal, nothing but that. And then—it was odd. He was lying across my lap and he started to stiffen up. You know? I could feel it against my stomach.

"Well!" It made me laugh. "You can't be that ill."

Sigurd pulled back and half laughed, wiping his eyes. But he still looked dreadful.

"Okay," he said. He sat up and looked at me, and I looked back at him.

"Are you all right?" I asked, which was stupid because he obviously wasn't.

"No."

"I'm going to ring for a doctor . . ."

"No! Don't go!" He grabbed me again in panic. He pressed me to him. But it was a bit different now. We were front to front.

I didn't know what to do.

"Do you want to come with me to the phone?" I asked.

"Stay here," he said, and he nodded firmly as if that was the right thing to do.

I disentangled myself and we both sat back down. He had one hand on my leg, the other on my shoulder. It was partly like he wasn't going to let me go and partly like he was going to kiss me. "What's all this about, then?" I asked.

He smiled thinly. "I'm going mad." As he spoke, he was

looking closely into my face as if he was seeing me for the first time. "I've been going mad all day. Now I'm . . ."

"What?"

"Now I'm coming back." He scowled. "I don't understand."

"It must be me, I must be completely marvelous, just me being here has made you better," I told him, and we both laughed.

"You are," he said. I smiled at him, but he was quite serious for a moment. Then he smiled back at last, and—yow-yow-yow—my heart began beating like an engine because he'd never looked at me like that before. I mean, he'd looked me over, I knew he fancied me, but I mean—you know what guys are like, they can fancy their own mothers practically if it's just a question of looking. This was different. It felt like—we'd both fallen into the right place.

And you know what that did? It really turned me on. He always made me feel horny, ever since the first time I met him. Suddenly all I wanted to do was grab him and drag him upstairs. In fact I'd have been perfectly happy to shag him on the carpet there and then if I wasn't scared the servants might walk in. I might have done it too, but the poor boy had just had a nervous breakdown. That would be taking advantage. I didn't want to make him do anything he might regret.

We had a cup of tea. We had to go to the kitchen together because he wouldn't be on his own. I made it, he sat at the table and followed me round the room with his eyes. You know? Rrrow. Okay, it was partly because he wanted someone to be there, but all the time it was getting more and more like—Yum! I was suspicious at first. All that weeping and now this. What was going on with him? Another two minutes and he might hate me.

I started to ask him questions, just to get his mind off things. You know, nice day yesterday, did you have a good journey? How's Slipper? When's Mum back, anything like that. He just sat there watching me, and smiling while I talked. It kept making me laugh, and he laughed too. And all the time there was another raft of questions I wanted to ask. Like, What about Hogni, what was that about? He said you had someone hidden away already, what about them? And, How come it's taken you this long to get round to it? I've been practically throwing myself at you. . . .

I sat down to drink my tea with him, and he kept on looking at me until I just couldn't bear it anymore.

"Can I help you?" I said. I felt like I was a waitress with a trolley full of cakes.

"I feel like . . . I just want to . . . it's like I've never seen you before. You really are gorgeous, you know?"

That made me flustered but I tried not to show it. "The important thing is you're feeling better now. We just have to make sure you'd don't get into a state like that again. Let's talk about that. You need a rest. A break of some sort . . ."

He looked at me. "Maybe," he said. "Maybe. But I know what I'd like to do."

And I said, "What?" in a surprised voice, even though I knew the answer. My heart was going like a drum.

"You," he said.

So I had to say, "Well, you can't have me. Sorry." Which wasn't easy! I mean! "You've just had some sort of break-down, Sigurd."

"Yeah, I know. But shall we?"

I said, "No!" in an affronted voice and he nodded. I got up

and dithered about, washing up the teapot. I was so disappointed I was being so sensible. Yes, I know—it was stupid, we'd probably get undressed and he'd change his mind and we'd both be appallingly embarrassed. But still. I wanted to do him so badly. I made another cup of tea and I got as far as pouring it out, when I just couldn't do it anymore. I took him by the hand and said, "Come on."

"What are we doing?"

"We're going to have a shag," I said. "I can't think of anything else. Then we can worry about what happens next."

"Oh. Righto," he said. So we ran upstairs laughing like a pair of kids and went to my bedroom and that's what we did. I kept telling him how stupid we were being and how selfish I was for taking advantage of him, and then we did it again. Then we went to the kitchen and stocked up on snacks, and then we locked the door again and we had the best sex I've ever had in my life. Over and over and over again. In between, we told each other everything—everything we could think of about each other, and what it was going to be like from now on, and what was going to happen and how it was going to happen. Stupid! I asked about the other one—we'd all assumed he had a girl somewhere, he'd told Hogni as much, but he said no, it wasn't true, he'd just said that to get Hogni off his back—so to speak! No—it was me he wanted. It was as simple as that.

I kept drifting off and thinking, But this is mad, he's just had a nervous breakdown, I can't be doing this! He kept saying, But I love you! And then I'd say, No, you don't, you just think you do; and he'd say, No, I'm certain. And in the end I admitted that I loved him, and that I'd loved him since I first clapped eyes on him, right from day one.

I know I shouldn't have. But he seemed all right now. I mean, completely better. I kept thinking, Boy, am I going to regret this! But just then, it was the only thing to do.

And—that was it. Just like that. I kept expecting it to change from minute to minute, then from hour to hour, then from day to day and week to week. But it didn't. It stayed just the same. Isn't that amazing? Isn't that strange? I never heard of anyone falling in the love like that before. He had to go mad before he did it, but once he was there, he stayed there. So explain that to me, please. The strangest thing. It stuck. And it felt so right. He said it was like he had a hole in the middle of his heart, and I'd plugged it. And in a funny way, I knew what he meant because I felt the same way about him.

It's like Gunar said. If it works, don't fix it. Enjoy! And boy, have I!

What a thing a man is! You can make him think anything if you get to him young enough—but to make him *love*? Who can do that?

Clever old Grimhild—but so unwise! She didn't make Sigurd love, she simply removed the memory of who he was in love with. Torn from its structure, its name, and its place, the clone's love existed in a void, a passion with no connections. The most intense of human bonds unbonded, volatile, a free radical ready to attach to anything it came into contact with. That was his madness. There was acid in his soul. Sigurd would have fallen in love with a leg of lamb in the state he was in. All Grimhild had left to do was make sure that her daughter was there at the right time.

She'd withdrawn herself and Ida, given the rest of the

servants the day off, and left Sigurd alone. She didn't want him falling in love with some serving girl or gardener, or some thug from the bodyguard. At one point he'd grabbed hold of the cat and sat clutching that, which had scared her. The way he was hanging on to it—was it possible for him to fall in love with *that*? But then it escaped and he got the cushion instead, thank god. Then Gudrun was delayed and Grimhild was scared that he was staying too long in his broken state. She'd only planned on him being on his own for a couple of hours. By the time the afternoon was over Grimhild was certain that she'd ruined the wonderful boy. But then at last her daughter arrived, and the reaction occurred exactly as predicted.

Clever old bitch! Such precision, such understanding, such insight. Science, magic, and psychology all working in perfect harmony. The woman's a genius.

So Sigurd was killed twice, once by a god and once by an old woman, and brought back to life both times, and both times changed. Well, Grimhild was clever, but no god. Make no mistake: What she has brought back is not Sigurd now. There's a difference between resurrection and cloning, transformation and restructuring. The terrible wound she made has been filled by Gudrun, but this is prosthetic love. This isn't Sigurd anymore. It's just a cheap copy.

But even a cheap copy of Sigurd is worth more than all of us. It was no less than him in depth of heart, loyalty, and conviction. His mind was as quick and sharp as ever. The love between him and Gudrun may have sprung up from another root, but time is a healer; the flesh heals over, the mind and spirit grow.

The next day, by the time Gunar and Hogni arrived, Sigurd

was no longer in any danger of losing his way. He had changed, that much was clear. It seemed to the Niberlins that Sigurd had been something larger than life, something superhuman, but now he was one of them—a human once again. Perhaps he had finished the task the gods intended for him and now they were leaving him to get on with his own life.

If he felt himself to be different—a gap, a falseness, a doubt in himself—he never said anything. He was, he felt, a casualty of war. So many people had lost so much. He had life, he had youth, he had love. Truly, he had so much. And after all, he was human again. There was no god growing inside him now. It may be that Odin himself had given him what he wanted most of all—humanity, with all its faults and weaknesses and failings. He had lost something wonderful but he knew that disappointment is part of the human condition and he accepted that, gratefully and lovingly. He thought to himself that nothing is perfect and that what he was was better than what he'd been turning into.

Sigurd was only sixteen. Such a loss. He was robbed, and so were we all. But perhaps he had already done all he had to do. He had killed the dragon, won the gold and the girl, and saved the country. What was left for him? Growing old? Turning into a tyrant? He was changing so fast—perhaps Odin was scared of what he was becoming. And his legacy remained. England was united. After the destruction, the reconstruction; the nation rebuilt.

But there was something lesser about a world with no Sigurd in it.

36

deep down below

The world moved on. The body of Sigurd rotted in the mud at the bottom of the lake. The worms crept in through his nose and mouth, through the opening of his anus and the soft spot in the middle of his back, and lived inside him. When all the soft body tissue and even the bones had gone, that skin would float again to the surface after a dredging operation three hundred years later, and be displayed in a nearby museum with his name. He was well remembered even then. As for his soul— where was that? Where does such a spirit rest? Part man, part lion, part monster, part god. So many heavens and hells. Who can say?

In the world, the clone took his place entirely, no one suspected it wasn't him. There was no repetition of the breakdown he had that day at the Old House. Sigurd's love cleaved where Grimhild had planted it; he and Gudrun were inseparable. For a time he loved her desperately as well as passionately, but it softened as he grew into his new self. But the god vision had gone. The clone had no ability to see a man's soul, or to watch the dance of the future in a map, and unlike Sigurd, his actions, thoughts, and feelings and the events that befell him were simply his own. His life was not hand in glove with destiny, with the fate of England. He was his own man now, not ours. It was what he would have wanted.

Grimhild saw all this and it pained her. She had not intended to make Sigurd less. But if his life was the working of fate, perhaps his death was too. He was the best of all and he died young, before his star had time to fade.

Meanwhile Crayley was munching its way through deep layers of clay and rock, trying to lift itself closer to the surface. It had creaked on for so long but its functions were failing. It needed more of everything. Fuel! Food! Air—even that. The one entry way to the surface had been made so narrow by the earthquake from Fafnir's arsenal, it could hardly breathe. It was suffocating by degrees. It had been feeding off old landfill sites and low grade ores, its own internal organic systems of bacterial and unicellular plant life and the colonies of breeding creatures it kept in scattered farms, but its reserves were low, getting lower. Such a vast entity needed a great deal to fuel itself. Time was getting short. It was starving to death down there.

Crayley was not stupid. Crawling through the earth hunting for traditional materials to feed on was slow and ponderous. It, too, had listened to the stories Bryony's mother had told her and eavesdropped on the talk between Sigurd and her. As it listened, it learned. A mile above, most of the work had already been done, the food gathered together, the resources harvested. Agriculture and industry, villages and towns. Population! Food and fuel, that's what they meant to Crayley. The ancient factory city didn't care if its prey was single or multicellular, sentient or dumb. Omnivorous, it could utilize anything. Even the soil up there was full of organic material. Underground it was living in a desert, imprisoned in the earth much as Bryony was imprisoned inside it. Up in the sun, that was where the wealth lay. The sun! There was energy in the very air.

The rogue city had to get to the surface. Low though its resources were, it could do that, but it was not able to harvest the wealth that awaited it. Mining, drilling, brewing, manufacture—it could do all that. But it could not redesign itself beyond certain limits. How did you steal and devour a village, a field of cows, a shopping mall, a school full of children? It had not been made to hunt. How did you rob a factory or steal the rays of the sun? Crayley needed to redesign, reinvent, and rebuild itself. Up there it would be like a hungry dog with no teeth in a shop full of tinned meat.

The old woman had helped. If it wasn't for her it would have died already, but she wasn't enough. The city needed a mind of its own. It had been planning to that end ever since it had realized what it had to do. Now those plans were nearing fruition.

These were black times for Bryony. She knew that things had gone wrong the day when, for the first time, Jenny Wren came back with no little gift in her beak or tied to her leg. At once she thought, "He's dead." Sigurd would never forget her, never abandon her. There had been a war. Even the best of us can be overcome.

But there was still hope; there's always hope. She could not be sure he was dead. Jenny might not have been able to find him. He might be imprisoned, trapped, lost in a battle, anything. The days passed. The little bird flew off as usual with her gifts, came back each time still bearing them. But Bryony continued to hope. Those brief months with Sigurd—was that it? Her entire life?

"Not the very first one," her mother used to say, but she'd gone and done it anyway, fallen head over heels in love with the first boy she met. Perhaps he had been the wrong one, how could she tell? What if he was full of lies? Her mother had said boys sometimes told lies.

But she had been so sure! And so had he. Hadn't he?

Days passed, then weeks.

"He might still be trapped," she thought. It was a hope, but a bitter hope, not easy to believe. For now she had to make her own plans. She had her love tokens to remind her: a few scraps of ribbon, a shriveled flower, and, on her finger, a ring. She never took it off. Every day she kissed it. It would never grow cold until her love for Sigurd had grown cold.

Inside her the baby grew. Once started, it was unstoppable. And how she longed for her baby! It was something to care for—another person, another one of her own. Someone to love. She could bear even this lonely drab life, this prison existence, if only she could keep her baby. But the city was waiting too. She could feel its greed. All around her, under her feet, over her head, her enemy, her home, was planning to take her baby away from her.

She made what preparations she could. She built various hides, like a wild animal, and laid in stores of food for each one. As she worked, she talked, sometimes to Sigurd, sometimes to her unborn baby, sometimes to Jenny Wren if she was near, asking their advice, explaining what she was doing. Then she would remember and stop: The city was listening to her all the time. The air she breathed, the food she ate, the ways she walked—the world was all against her.

Crayley began giving her gifts now—pipes of nutrients appearing near her house, a small creature skinned and butchered, lying ready for her when she got up in the morning. At first she never touched them. They could be interfered with in ways she could only imagine. But at the same time the city withdrew what she needed from other sources. The creatures she had hunted disappeared, the water pipes emptied, the nutrient vats turned sour and then dried up. They were only being diverted, removed to a distance from her, but it got harder and harder to travel as she swelled, and in the end she had to give in and eat what was provided for her, like a baby taking food from her mother.

But she had one final, desperate trick up her sleeve. She had seen what Crayley was planning for her baby and she would not allow it to happen. If she had the slightest whiff that it was trying take her baby off her, she would kill it. This much she knew and this much only: Crayley would not have its way. The baby would die.

"Don't think I won't do it," she warned, speaking to the world around her. She was capable of this. Anything rather than let her baby become . . . like that.

Sigurd, where are you? Odin! Anyone! It's almost too late . . . At least she was not entirely alone. Jenny was with her. The little bird had never deserted her, was always there through every crisis and every pleasure. She hunted with her, ate with her, searched with her, inspected prospective birthsites for her. And she was with her, perched on a bucket handle, when the pain began.

The pain shocked Bryony. Agony! She was being torn to pieces! She had to do this on her own? But the waves passed and no damage was done.

"It's time," she told the wren. She packed up her things and made her way to her hideaway, pausing to bend over or sit down when the contractions took over. Jenny piped encouragement and flew on ahead to make sure the way was safe. As she made the journey, Bryony fingered a small bottle she kept on her at all times. This was her final insurance policy: poison. If the city tried to ambush her now and hold her while she gave birth, she would drink it.

"It'll take me less than a second," she said aloud. Crayley was listening, it was always listening. It understood. She made it to the hideaway unharmed.

The place she had chosen was as secure as it was possible to get—a little hole in a solid stone wall, high up out of reach, with plenty of stores, food and water, rags and furs to keep her and her baby warm. She was surrounded on three sides, above and below by solid rock. Below was a vast machine hall, as big as three football pitches, with assemblages of rusting production lines softening under the dust of ages. She could see it all from this eyrie, from rock face to rock face. Nothing could approach her here without her seeing it. It was perfect—as perfect as was possible. But it would not work. Crayley was everywhere, like God. How can you avoid the world you live in?

The birth was more painful than she had ever imagined. Her mother had told her about this, too, but nothing could prepare her for something like that. This was what it was to give life? Impossible—she was dying! But it was not like a wound. It passed without damage as if it had never happened, and then it came again, and again and again. It went on for almost a day, getting more and more frequent, and then the movement began. It began slowly, but then, suddenly, it happened quickly and the baby was there in her arms before she knew it—out of her into the world: into Crayley.

Weeping and gasping, Bryony gathered the little thing up to her. A girl, a baby girl! Her daughter. Sigurd's daughter. He should have been there, it wasn't right that she should go through this all on her own. But the baby was beautiful, even with all the blood and mess and hurt. She held it to her and loved it with all her heart, amazed and delighted that she could still feel like this after all she had gone through. She had a baby. It was hers and Sigurd's. One day she would show it to him.

"Beatrice. That's who you are," she told the baby. Her little girl. She had a name. She was real. She was the most real thing in the world. "With all my heart," she whispered, kissing the little thing on its head. She must have two hearts, she thought, to love this baby with all of one and Sigurd with all of the other.

Now what remained was this: She must never go to sleep again.

"Don't let me sleep, Jenny. We have to stay on guard. Don't we?"

Jenny Wren piped in agreement and looked waspishly about, alert and as full of life as ever. Bryony put the baby to her breast. Warm waves of comfort flooded her as Beatrice began to suck.

Giving birth is the hardest of all work. Bryony was exhausted. Her head nodded a couple of times, but Jenny peeped and her head came back up. She nursed and rested, played games in her head, talked to the wren, to Sigurd, to her baby, sang songs, got up and walked carefully to and fro. But of course it was impossible. She should have known; she did know. If she had been really serious she would have killed the baby there and then, given it poison to sip as soon as it was out of her. But how could she do that? Her own child, and those long years all alone.

Crayley, too, had been about its preparations for a long time. It didn't know whether to believe her when she said she was prepared to kill the baby but it certainly wasn't prepared to take the risk. This could be its last chance to get a decent mind for itself.

It had originally considered flooding the whole area with anaesthetic gas, but dismissed the idea in the end as being too dangerous for the new baby. The little darling must not in any circumstances be hurt. No, the problem called for subtler measures. In the end, after many attempts, it developed a couple of devices that it was sure could steal Beatrice away without harm to either mother or child. Even as Bryony was giving birth, they were creeping across the ceiling and up the walls toward her. Crayley spied on her from a distance, and whenever her eyes closed or she looked away, a hidden device, the color and texture of the rock it sat on, would step like a spider so much the closer.

Once, Crayley had been able to make things no bigger than these that could fly—how handy would that be? But those skills had been lost, the tools corroded, the codes broken and lost. These ones were the size of mice, shaped unsettlingly like giant spiders, but the city had lowered the lighting by degrees during the birth, they were well camouflaged. There was every hope of success.

Progress was slow, but inevitable. Bryony nodded, the spiders ran, Jenny peeped. Occasionally, alarmed by the slight noises, the little wren flew off to investigate and found the devices sitting still as stones on the walls. She inspected them, shrilled at them, scolded them, then flew back. Bryony was concerned—but Jenny Wren had no words, and besides, she was just a wren. What does a wren understand about these things?

The end when it came was sudden. Two of the creatures finally got within three meters of the outside of the cave. Bryony nodded; they dashed. Within the space of a squeak or the blink of an eye, one of them had bitten Bryony on the thigh. She was awake in a second, on her feet, running to the edge—she planned to leap off with her baby in her arms—but the dose was correct. Her legs buckled under her within a step, she sank to the ground, clutching the baby. She tried to crawl along the floor, but within another second her arms became too weak to move. She attempted to roll over, trying to throw the child away, but even that was impossible.

Bryony had been paralyzed but she could still see and hear everything around her. Crayley had borrowed a trick off the solitary wasps who sting their prey with paralysis, and lay their eggs on the living body to be consumed by their grubs still fresh. Like those insect victims, Bryony could not move a muscle, but she could feel, see, and hear everything. So she was able to watch as another device came stepping into the cave. It was made of flesh, carbon fiber and nylon, covered with a living skin, nicely furred to keep the baby happy. Step by step the cyber-mother crept into the cave and lowered itself to the floor where it picked the baby out of its mother's arms. How gently it cradled her! How much it loved her.

It did a few basic health tests and then carried her off to be prepared. Behind it the paralyzed girl watched in silence.

37

consolidation

At the end of the war, old Bill Portland went into captivity as he went into everything else, full of plans. At over three hundred and fifty years old he was used to seeing eras come and go. It was never the end. A big player in business and politics, he had many friends at home and abroad. He negotiated, made plans, and the Niberlins, to his utter amazement and rage, had him quietly shot in the head while he waited for the answer to his latest deal.

Abroad, his friends raged and cursed, the big powers frustrated that their desires were not being taken into account. Sigurd and the Niberlins had gotten rid of one of the ways those powers had of keeping England in its place, but there were many others, including the bomb that had ended Sigmund's reign. Andvari's ring, that device for turning fate sour, lay far below ground, on Bryony's finger. The Niberlins had heard the rumors but no one had any idea of where it was, or what it looked like. A device that bends fate—how does such a thing work? Does it manipulate time to come? Does it reach back to alter the past, and thus the present, and so the future that arises from the present? If so, all the earth, stone and fire that separated it from the world above could do nothing. Time passes in the earth's core the same as in the palm of your hand.

But for now, for the first time in a generation, England was united. The Portland armies had been well equipped with the best advice and foreign weaponry, more than enough to crush any uppity native warlords and terrorists, but Sigurd had out-maneuvred the best military minds from across the world and won the heart of the whole nation to his cause. The remnants of the vanquished Portland forces dissolved rapidly into the surrounding countryside. Small bands of armed monkeys still occasionally opened fire on government troops, or tried to terrorize local people who no longer wanted to support them. They continued to receive money from abroad, but with old Bill and the immediate family gone, there was nothing to hold them together. Troop by troop, the remaining Portlands either emigrated—but they found a poor welcome abroad, where there was still a huge prejudice against halfmen—or settled down quietly to run bars and other small businesses. Business was still their thing, but the family was broken. They formed clubs and associations, affiliated their businesses for mutual benefit, dreamed of regaining the glory days, and rapidly became more or less harmless.

Out of their broken homes the people emerged to search for dead fathers and sons, lost mothers, daughters and wives among the mass graves and scanty records the brief but brutal war had left behind. Rebuilding was going to take a long time. People had for so long been crushed between rival ganglords, funded by this or that foreign power, they had not believed it possible to come together again. But here it was, a power that drew the country into one. The postwar days lengthened into weeks, then months. The only soldiery the people saw were their own, clearing up the mess, leveling the rubble, building roads, schools, and hospitals, laying water pipes and cables. The conflict that had lasted a lifetime was over again. There were quieter days ahead.

This had been the project of the Volsons for three generations: to make a land fit to live in. The Volsons had always represented hope to the people they governed. It was their gift to lift us above the mud, above the poverty and grime and disease, above the wars and the hatred, the vendettas and struggles for power. They were cooperation, they were all-together-now. This they tried to do with the god Odin as their patron—god of war, death, and poetry. What sort of hope was that? Foolish, or just plain false?

Gods—what are we to them? Our lives are just poems, stories that catch them if we tell them well. When the book ends, nothing has happened, no one real has lived or died. Our lives and all our pains and pleasures are images on a page. They shed tears for us, laugh at us, cheer us on, make demands of us, but they don't believe in us any more than a reader believes the pages of a book.

So Sigurd's clone made his story of hope in the family tradition and he told it so well, everyone believed it, man and halfman alike. It had all gone his way, hadn't it? He was the dragon-killer, the crusher of enemies, the bringer of peace and prosperity. With him standing by the throne, nothing could go wrong.

A year passed, then two: the Golden years. The babies were fatter, the births easier, the harvests bigger. Industry flourished and grew. Men and women were easy and kind in each other's company—even the weather was good. In Sigurd's time all this was true. He was like a good-luck charm for his people. There was love in the air. People were looking to the future and thinking at last that this was a place they would like children to grow up in. There was a baby boom; the streets became full of rattling pushchairs and cooing mothers.

And in everyone's eyes were images of Sigurd and Gudrun on TV and in magazines, always together, always touching, holding hands, glancing at each other, smiling at each other. When would they have their first child? Gossip columns and news programs speculated endlessly—it was the most sought-after, eagerly awaited event in the country. The comings and goings of the other Niberlins were front page news as well. Hogni, of course, filled the palace with his boyfriends, who came and went like the seasons, but in a couple of years even he found someone he wanted to stay with, a purebred human, an administrator in the educational service with bright brown eyes and a taste for dangerous sports. Only Gunar was on his own. Women were endlessly proposed, every conversation he had with one was discussed and analyzed in terms of possible romance, but no one special emerged. He seemed out of skew with the times—typical of Gunar, who always had to work so hard to make things happen. He felt this lack himself. He, too, was judging every woman he met, wondering if she might be the one. But all of them had something wrong—too loud, too dull, not his type. So Gunar stayed alone.

And what of Sigurd himself? He loved Gudrun with all of his heart, they were inseparable. He had lost his own family, but with the Niberlins he had gained two brothers as well as a lover. He had a beautiful wife, a beautiful home, he had his work to do. The glory days were gone, but somehow, so was the lust for glory. That was as it should be in a world settling down in comfort with itself. But sometimes there was a nightmare in which he woke up from a deep sleep with the words of an old song in his ears: But this is not my beautiful wife, and this is not my beautiful home. What am I doing here? Then he remembered a time when he was so flooded with love that he could change bad to good—even death into life, with the sheer force of it. Perhaps it was the loss of this precious thing that made him wake up sobbing so desperately.

He spoke to Gudrun about it and she told him that God had lived in him for a while, but that he hadn't been hers then, and she loved him more as he was. He spoke to Gunar about it, and Gunar said that he understood, he felt the same himself from time to time—it was the passing of boyhood, the loss of innocence.

"But I'm only eighteen years old," said Sigurd.

"But you've lived a lot," said Gunar. Sigurd thought of all those lives he had taken. Maybe it was that. He was a casualty of war—and that was just, too, he thought. It wasn't right to come out of such a thing unharmed.

marshall de la la-de-dah de portobello road

Hooo-wha. Yeah, that's right, a scientist. I know it isn't in my name. Well, the *de la* is French. My family began in a French laboratory. The la-de-dah bit came when we came ho-ho-hover here and people thought it was all, you know, all Frenchy, all la-de-dah. The Portobello Road bit was because we spent three generations working on the market. Yes, it does sound a bit like Portland. That's what we scientists call a *coincidence*.

If it makes you happy I'll put the scientist bit in too. Marshall de la la-de-dah de Portobello Road Graphpaper, hey? Nah—that old halfman thing about building up your surname to show your genealogy, it's old hat, man. So what's your name? Charlie Snout-face Muscles-up-my-arse Halfwit Hendersen? Ah! Ouch. Oooh, that hurt. Listen—you guys are going to find out who I am and then it won't be clips round the ear, it'll be Take me to your Leader and yes sir, no sir. Okay? I mean, I fuckin' ran this place. I'm just saying, why not play it a bit cautious until then, okay?

I'm a monkey. The Portlands are Bab*oons*. You know what I mean? Look at the canines on them. And their arses! No trousers, just suit jackets—that's a real baboon thing, they totally communicate with their arses. I'm not even a monkey, I'm a great ape. Bonabo blood flows in my veins. It's kinda like the aristocracy of monkeys, y'know? I dunno, like if your mother was a warthog maybe?

But you know my name. Oh, for the video. Okay, my name's Marshall de la la-de-dah de Portobello Road. Marshall Dee for short. I'm Creative Production Manager at Amicor. We make organic components for industry, from ordinary gene manufacture all the way up to the latest silico-neurological add-ons for the cloning, computing and personal impro-hoo-hoo-hoo-hooovment industries. Lo-tech, hi-tech, that sort of thing. The setup's hi-tech, but after that you just brew 'em up and let 'em grow. You have your basic bacillus going through a series of controlled environments as they develop, so that by the time they come out the other end, you've got these perfect little chips swimming out into the storage vats, cilia waving, circuits pulsing. We've even been working on training them to *swim into place* during manufacture. Yeah!

Hoo. Yes, yes, *if* I was a spy it *would* be a very good position to be in, but fortunately I ain't. So you want the story or not, huh? Okay.

I was ha-ha-hactually glancing out of a window when it happened. Man! The ground just started pouring away like sand going down an hourglass, smooth as you like. Then the corner of the building went—glup! It just turned into sludge and gurgled down the hole. You never saw anything like it. It was making the ground behave like heh, heh, hex-actly like water. I thought, That looks useful; then I ran like shit. Hoo ha ha! The ha ha ha whhee hoo hoo ho! Sorry, it gets me going just thinking about it. Hoo. Yeah, lost a lotta lives, lot of good friends. I got out by watching where it was going—straight for the nutrient vats at the back of the building, the big tanks where we breed the basic bacteria. Man, that was one hungry earthquake, only this earthquake was after *proteins*. I mean! Bad news? Oh, man! It sucked down the whole factory, plastics, nutrients, metals, stone, the lot. Then it headed out to the surrounding countryside. First thing it went for was the fuel station on Lanine Road. Sucked it straight down. Then the village. The school! All melted and gone, kids, bricks, the lot. It gulped up Moremart and then went for the cows in the field. After that it sucked down the fucking earth, man! Whoh! When it had finished it went back to where it started, right where the factory used to be, and pushed out its—well, what would you call it? Its hose, nose? Its mouth, its exhaust? You tell me. And that's where it is now.

Oh yeah? Well, frankly, you sound a bit speciesist to me. Listen, pal, there's two sorts of monkeys—the kind with hairy hands who go on to be top scientists like me, and the other sort who get stuck a tenth of the way up the security services. Look, who do you think designed half of the stuff in there? Yes, that's right, the overhanging brows are there to give me extra brain capacity. Whyn't you go and mention my name to someone who knows about this sort of thing? See, son, you gonna need me.

Some people are just prejudiced. I try to feel sorry for them but it doesn't always work, especially when they're expressing the intention of peeling you like a banana. They actually said that.

"Any more lip out of you, big-ears, and I'm gonna peel you like a fuckin' banana." Everyone looks down on monkeys these days. Not that I approve of prejudice in any of its forms, you understand, but you can see where the humans are coming from. They used to be the One and Only. Wahhhh! They had the place to themselves for about a million years. But *pigs*? I mean. They laugh at us. We get laughed at by *pigs*. And cats and dogs and pretty well everything else, too.

"Monkeys are funny," a friend of mine once told me. That was before the war, mind you. A lot changed during the war. No one finds us so funny now.

So once I convinced those two moving ha-hoo hoo hoo hulks of pig meat that I ha-ha-hactually was in charge of science and engineering at the plant, they took me to see the big boys, and before you know it, I'm briefing Sigurd and Gunar. *Yeah*, that's right. The big man. And yes, I was impressed. In fact I was very impressed. The funny thing about Sigurd was, though, he put you at your ease. You felt like you'd known him for years, you know? Like he was a personal friend of yours. *Nice* guy. It was only when he'd gone and you're on your own, you started thinking, Gods! What was *that*?

Excuse me, I'll just get more comfortable. Yeah. Mmm. Upside down, ahh! Stretches the joints. So. First thing we wanted to know—alive or not? Machine or being? Orgo-mechanical or mechano-organic? The only visible bit of it was that opening, its waste hose-thing. It was maybe twenty-five, thirty meters across. At first glance you'd say it was a trachea or something organic like that, but when we got close, guess what? It was metal. Not manufactured, mind—it was grown. How about that? That thing was *growing* metal.

You know what I mean? I mean, that could be useful.

Then it started breathing.

I was so excited. I thought, Waaaa-ha! Actually it wasn't

obvious at first. Each breath took about ten minutes. You start off thinking it's just a wind or something. But there it was, in and out, in and out—and you know what that meant? That meant it was *alive*. Machines don't breathe.

Wow! Ha? An organism that big, it takes ten minutes to breathe in? What was that about? There were all sorts of theories going around. People remembered Fafnir. Perhaps he had escaped Sigurd after all and he was coming back up, bigger and more dangerous than ever. But I still wasn't convinced. It was so big. And metal growth—nothing alive grows metal. I reckoned it *had* to have inorganic origins. So we did tests and you know what? It wasn't breathing at all. The gases were all wrong. It was oxygen going in but it wasn't carbon dioxide going out. It was sulphur, ammonia, carbon monoxide, that sort of thing. Industrial waste, see? So it had developed from an inorganic base all right. It was just using the same trick as living animals to get oxygen in and waste out of a closed system.

So—we had a closed inorganic system, underground, utilizing metal growth and imitating organic mechanics. That was when I started thinking about Crayley.

You'll have heard about Crayley—the factory city. Great idea—automate all your industry, set it up underground, and then just let it go. And it worked, for a long time it worked really well. It was the primitive mechano-genetic technology that bolloxed it in the end. Once genetic technology really got going, it was obsolete. No one ever worked out how to close it down, so when it was out of date, they just let it go. Think of it—haa! Hoo hoo! Hectares of rogue factory roving about underground. Everyone assumed it would just grind itself to a halt, but there were some theorists who thought that it could just about hang on down there, rambling about underground, surviving off ancient landfill sites, hydrogen and oxygen extraction from water, low-grade organic deposits, that sort of thing.

Pickings were obviously pretty slim down there, so if it was Crayley, it had come to the surface for a very good reason—to feed. And it fed on an industrial scale. Ha! It could eat the whole fucking nation, man. That thing needed terminating for sure. And there was only one buddy who could do that—heh? Yeah, old Sigurd. Bring on the heroes, eh?

But then the priests starting dredging up those old stories about Odin's daughter. You know the one—how the city kidnapped her, carried her off underground years ago? They've been doing the rounds for years. Or she did something to displease him and he locked her down there until someone could come along clever enough to rescue her? Various versions. Yeah, well, listen—I'm a scientist but even I know this much: Stories and destinies, sometimes they're one and the same thing. That's the godworld. It could be true. So who was there you know fit to be Odin's son-in-law? Yeah! But you see, Sigurd was already married.

39

the clone

. . . and I said, "You?"

"You can't do it," said Gudrun. It came out all wrong. Like, poor old Gunar, what are you on about?

"Why not?" he said.

"Because . . . because you're too important, Gunar," she said, and gave him a slightly crooked smile.

"I don't think so."

"It's not your sort of thing, though, is it?"

It didn't make sense. I had words on my lips—"Who do you think you are, Gunar?" But how could I say that, as if I had the only right to great deeds?

"It isn't your thing," repeated Gudrun.

"Don't know if it's my sort of thing or not, how would I, I n-never had a chance to try," he told her.

Gudrun scowled at him. "But this is . . ."

"D-dangerous," said Gunar, half smiling.

"Suicide."

"For me, you mean."

"For anyone! Anyone except Sigurd." She glanced over at me.

"I have the equipment," I said. "My skin. You know?"

"We have Fafnir's skin, I could use that," Gunar leaned forwards and looked at me intently. "I want this," he said. "Listen. D-done my stint. Worked hard all these years. Long hours. It's my turn. W-want to have an adventure."

"Adventures aren't what you think," I told him.

"Admin is," he said. "Admin's always what you think. That's the trouble."

"Death or glory, Gunar?" teased Gudrun.

"Death or glory. Yes," he replied. She looked shocked. They both looked at me. I licked my lips. It was his life, he could lose it if he wanted, none of us could stop him. But this monster under the ground, the girl if she existed . . . these things were for me. That's why I'm here. In a sense, that's why they're there too.

"How can it be yours when you have Gudrun?" asked Gunar, as if he knew what I was thinking.

"Straight to the point." I smiled, but I was blushing.

Gudrun was looking at me, but I found it hard to meet her eye because—well. Life doesn't just happen, it's designed this way. This had my name all over it. There was a girl. What did that mean?

"I w-want this," said Gunar again.

"Is it for you?" I asked. "Do you know? Do you have a sense of it?"

"I don't know until I try."

"If you don't know . . . ," I began.

"If you don't know, it ain't yours," said Gunar for me, and he smiled. "I don't care, Sigurd. It's my *turn*, that's all I know. It's my turn," he repeated, as if that explained it all.

He was my friend. He was my brother. What else could I do?

• • •

Gunar's Big Adventure, Hogni called it. They all teased him about it, but underneath they were scared. Gunar was a good man with many talents, but his gifts sat uneasily with him. He was aware himself that there was something selfish about all this. He had so much. Why was it never enough?

All his life, Gunar had been in preparation, but right at the last moment Sigurd had stepped in and almost overnight given the nation the wealth the Niberlins would have taken lifetimes to build up. Gunar was king only in name, Sigurd was the real power, everyone knew it. As he'd said himself, Gunar was in admin. But inside him there was the sense of something else, something exciting and dangerous, waiting its time. Now was that time, but whether it was his fate to succeed or to fail he did not know.

They set off on the journey all together, Gudrun and Sigurd, Hogni and his partner, Tybolt, and Gunar and Grimhild. It had been a long time since the Niberlins had all traveled together like this. It had been too dangerous, a single assassination attempt could wipe out the whole pack. Now ordinary things were becoming possible again. It was a show of solidarity between governed and governors, as well as a signal that the Niberlins believed Gunar could do this. But it was an anxious party that headed south toward the mouth of Crayley. Only Grimhild seemed unperturbed. Her children thought it was because she had no idea what was going on, but the truth was very different. If her eldest son died, so what? There was another at home just as good to take his place.

• • •

It was autumn, the year turning yellow, the harvest in. Along the road crowds gathered to cheer them on, or just to goggle at the legends. The mood of the people infected them and they became excited themselves. Gods, girls, monsters—fate was at hand. To put yourself in the hand of destiny and face it bravely—what would be better? Crayley had devoured over seven thousand souls when it sucked the village down into the ground and made a desert in the green. It would do it again, getting stronger and bigger and hungrier all the time. Gunar was offering a soldier's sacrifice. If he died, he wouldn't be there to mourn. Death comes to us all: when and how is not important.

But not everyone saw it like that—Gudrun, for example, weeping in her young husband's arms at night; Hogni, shedding his tears when Gunar wasn't there to see them. Were they letting him ride to his death? Sigurd, too, felt helpless. A true pagan, he believed that everything that will happen is already set, but with all his heart he wished he could snatch this adventure from Gunar if he could. He was certain that no good could come of it.

Progress was slow. Some roads had already been remetaled, but most were just muddy tracks. The crowds slowed them too, and it took four days to make the journey. When they got there, they found an area of devastation even worse than the bombed wreck of London.

An area of over five square miles had been utterly destroyed. The rogue city had devoured not only the buildings and all their contents, not only the cows, sheep and grass, the hedges and plants, the people and their pets; even the topsoil and the clay beneath it had been taken down for processing. The site was as bare as a licked plate. Crayley had taken everything.

40

the entrance

How do you destroy a city that lives? As Gunar made his preparations to go down, Marshall Dee was trying to work out how to do just that. He was experimenting with viruses, both organic and inorganic, that would invade and destroy the city's software, hardware, and organic components simultaneously. He had obtained the original blueprints and drawings of the old factory city, but these were of limited value. Crayley had changed out of all proportion, evolved into something dramatically different. Marshall had no idea how this was possible. The city's computing power had been far too restricted to remake itself to anything like this degree.

Sigurd, had he been there, might have told him where that power came from, and known in what way it was related to him. But his clone had no knowledge of anything that appertained so closely to Bryony, including the child he'd had with her.

By the end of a week, Marshall already had some samples, which he released into the mouth of the monster. If that had worked, there would have been no need for anyone to go down there. The girl, if such a girl existed, would have to stay below.

But the viruses all came back out; Crayley was filtering them. However, they came out changed, disarmed in various ways, and this gave the scientist some insight into what might and might not work next time. Working at breakneck speed—they did not know how long the city would remain dormant—he revised his initial models, and within another couple of weeks had a suite of viruses that, he believed, would have some effect at least.

Sonar and magnetic resonance readings had mapped out the size and basic structure of Crayley. The tunnel from the mouth-head slanted down into the earth for a mile before it opened out into the city proper, which was as big as a small town and up to forty stories high.

The maw itself was hard enough to reach. The exhalations and excretions that the city was releasing had built up on the rock bed around it and was over a meter deep in places, full of poisons and acids. The atmosphere was thick with fumes, and the slurry underfoot gave way in places to sudden pits and shafts that led all the way to nowhere. At the mouth-head itself, the heat was enough to melt lead.

Marshall's plan was simple. Gunar was to get as deep inside Crayley as he could and then release his vials of bugs and viruses, as if he was injecting deep inside the body of a living thing. What else he could do would depend on what he found when he was down there. He was taking explosives as well, in the hope that he might find some important areas he could blow up and disable the city still further.

As for the girl, the daughter of Odin, the warrior-maiden . . . well. Everyone knew that in an age when the gods have come back to haunt us, such stories can become the truth; but this was politics, this was life and death and bread and water. Maybe Gunar would find her, but the main thing was Crayley had to die. Other deaths along the way seemed almost inevitable.

That was Gunar's mission. But his careful heart was full of love, ready to burst open—ready to be thrown away. He had dotted the *i*'s and crossed the *t*'s in other people's stories for so long and now he wanted to tell one of his own. He wanted to rescue the girl. What would follow between himself and Odin's daughter—well, who knows?

Gunar and the clone rode together to the maw-head dressed in the dragon skin, inside a little tank, insulated, armored, and carrying all the supplies for the mission. Slipper walked behind. Sigurd had offered him the use of the cyber-horse and Gunar had tried to mount him, but Slipper would operate for no one except his master.

It was a grim scene—a total desert with everything of value to life removed, where a couple of weeks before there had been buildings and workers surrounded by fields of crops and grazing herds. It was a gray morning, spattering rain. The air tasted acidic. Sigurd, who needed no protection, peered in through the visor Gunar wore and grinned at him.

"Good place for a football match," he said. Gunar grinned back with artificial mirth. He had never been more terrified. He felt like a child indulged to the edge of death as Sigurd followed him up to the edge of the mouth.

Sigurd sniffed the air that only he could breathe.

"Bad breath," he said, and stared in a kind of horror as Gunar gave him another thin grin, even worse than the last, a rictus of terror. Why should a man put himself through this? Sigurd wondered—but then he remembered himself at the pit where he had killed Fafnir. Bravery, he thought, was a strange thing, as much stubbornness and cowardice and a fear of failure as sheer guts. In a swelling of love he flung his arms around his friend and squeezed.

"You can do it," he told him, although his heart told him otherwise. Gunar squeezed him back.

"I can d-die, anyway," he whispered. Sigurd drew back his head and looked in through the shaded visor.

"Don't, though," he said, and they smiled at each other, properly this time. They embraced again, then Sigurd climbed out of the tank and onto Slipper's back. He sat and watched as his friend drove forward into Hel.

It was strange for the clone to be a spectator at this sport. He wanted to go forward himself so badly, it felt as if the earth itself was about to carry him down there. Slipper kept dancing on the spot, moving forward and then back, as he picked up on these conflicting messages. The air smelled familiar, and bizarrely, the feelings it carried on it were not those of fear. They were feelings of—of pleasure? Of need? He didn't understand what they were.

"*Déjà vu,*" muttered Sigurd to himself. A memory of a dream of familiarity, without any real connection to anything real. These feelings seemed to be his, but clearly they belonged to someone else. Or perhaps it was a memory from another life?

The clone sighed, closed his eyes, and waited. Behind his lids no pictures formed, no memories rose, no revelations stirred. *I miss you,* said his heart. But miss who? Not Gudrun, he'd seen her only an hour before. Into the false reality of his heart, feelings whirred and spun, sought and failed. The clone was like a man who has had a limb amputated but retains the feeling. Love was in his eyes and ears, his nose and throat, in his heart, in his skin, in his fingers and toes. It was meant to be. To remove the love of Bryony from Sigurd was to remove Sigurd from Sigurd himself.

The dragon-skin suit he had cut out for Gunar puzzled him too. Not so long ago, when he had first met Hogni, he had wanted it. What for? He had told the others it was just a memento of his victory. He knew that was not the truth, but he had no other explanation. It was another mystery inside him, that he had no place for.

The clone leaned forward and stared into the throat of the city, as if he could see through the fire and around corners. Not for the first time, he was overcome with a dreadful feeling that he was already dead, a walking ghost who had lost his soul without even noticing. How many of us are like that? he wondered. Perhaps life itself is a fake and we are all just memories of the real thing.

If he went down there, the clone felt, he would become real again. And he would go down there, he was certain of that. Gunar was going to fail. It was just a question of letting him find out for himself.

And then there it was; the smell of cooking metal, red-hot glass, the acrid stink of chemicals changing, merging, falling apart under intense heat. He didn't wait for the smell of burning flesh, though. There was a moment when he paused—perhaps Gunar would prefer death to ignominious failure. But Gunar was his friend and his brother, and Sigurd had no choice. He pressed his heels lightly against Slipper's sides. The horse reared up and rushed joyfully down into the fires, on Gunar's trail.

The clone was immediately engulfed in blazing pain but he recognized even this with a kind of pleasure. His hair and clothes caught fire, he screamed in agony and rushed on so fast that the fire blew out only to reignite by the second. It was all so familiar. Every moment was an amazement to him, on the brink of a revelation that never came. He was certain that around every corner, through every billow of smoke and fire, he would see something, something beautiful and wonderful, something that he had unaccountably forgotten; something so precious he could not conceive how his heart had lost it.

He did not get far. The ashes of his hair, clothes, and the surface of his skin were still falling from him when he found Gunar's tank. It stood stock still, glowing cherry red with the heat. Its wheels and tracks had jammed solid, first expanding with the heat, then welding together. Now they were starting to melt. Liquids were flowing around it, dripping down onto it. Acids and other reactives were already pitting the surface. Crayley was digesting the tank.

It would take explosives to break open the armored vehicle, or an hour with oxyacetylene equipment while Gunar cooked like a chop inside, but drawing his sword stub the clone simply carved a hole in the side of the machine. So easy. He gloried in this. Inside Gunar was blundering about, blinded. Sigurd reached in, snatched him out, flung him over his shoulder, and leapt aboard Slipper. As they raced to the air, a great tongue of angry fire rushed after them, and a sudden flood of poisons and fluids was released around them. There was a huge bellow, a roar, and clattering from deeper down in the blazing tunnels, as if the city was furious about losing this little morsel—as if it was finding a voice for itself.

They were outside in seconds. Gunar had become very still. Sigurd raced on, across the poisoned sands and rocks of the feed plate, beyond the fumes pouring from the mouth-head. Once he reached the grass, he flung Gunar down and, using his sword stub, cut a hole in the dragon-skin suit. Gunar was blue with lack of air. He was not breathing. Sigurd heaved on the injured man's chest—once, twice, three times, four times—and again and again—until suddenly Gunar took a shuddering breath and turned from blue to mauve. Sigurd waited until he was sure the breathing was regular, before flinging him across Slipper and riding furiously back to headquarters, where his friend could receive some proper treatment.

Gunar was blistered on the outside, but his worst injuries were internal. Crayley had heated his air supply and he had taken several breaths of scalding air before turning it off. He was breathing normally, but his damaged throat and lungs couldn't absorb the oxygen properly once it was inside him. He had burned his vocal cords, too, and could only speak in a soft, painful whisper.

The nature of his injuries made the tanks unsuitable for the time being. He needed to breathe heavy oxy-fluids in there, and the doctors considered his lungs too weak to cope. So he was put instead in an old-fashioned oxygen tent until the internal blisters had begun to heal and he was ready to go in a normal tank.

The family gathered round, although actually Gunar would

have preferred to have been left on his own. He was furious—
with Crayley, with himself, with Sigurd, with everything. The
first time they saw him, he was sitting up in bed in his tent,
panting, his blistered tongue hanging out and looking very
doggy, and his face dark yellow and as long as misery. Hogni
pulled a sympathetic face.

"You look *so* fed up," he said. Gunar pursed his lips but
couldn't smile.

"You tried," pointed out Gudrun.

"I failed," hissed Gunar.

"Was succeeding the point?" she asked. Gunar had always
insisted that he had to try or he'd never know if he could. So
now he knew.

"It beat me so easily," he whispered. "It just cooked me."

"Like a little sausage," said Hogni sadly.

"A st-stupid little sausage," agreed Gunar.

He wasn't allowed to speak much. The doctors wanted to let
his internal burns heal as fast as possible so that they could get
him into the tanks quickly. There were a couple of armchairs in
his room and a basket with a cushion in it put down by the
bedside for Grimhild, although she spent a lot of time lying on
his feet. Ida came and went. Through her servant, Grimhild
was trying to get her son moved home, although of course she
could never say why. Home was where the heart was; and the
replacements. Maybe her damaged son was no longer good
enough. . . .

Now was the time for Sigurd to take over the task of killing
the city, and as soon as possible. As soon as it had finished
dispelling the waste from its first vast feeding binge, Crayley
would withdraw its maw, sink like a whale into the depths, and

go to seek out new feeding areas. No one could say exactly when that would be, but sonar readings showed that the city was already rearranging itself underground, and a move could be imminent. Every day that passed gave Sigurd a narrower window in which to complete the job.

But Sigurd, faithful as ever, would not go without Gunar telling him to. He did not want to steal his glory a second time; Gunar had to give it away, freely. He sat by the sick man's bedside and waited. Gunar watched him from behind the plastic of the oxygen tent. The unspoken question and its inevitable answer remained in the air.

All that first day Sigurd waited, but nothing was said. As the day grew long, he leaned forward at last and spoke.

"Crayley's on the move, Gunar."

Gunar turned and looked at him. "It has to be now," insisted Sigurd. "It has to be me, you can see that, can't you? Unless you know another way."

It was a rhetorical question. Another way than Sigurd? Surely not. But Gunar nodded his head. He moved his lips. Hardly a sound came out but Sigurd knew what he was saying.

"I know a way."

Sigurd nodded. He was strangely unsurprised.

Gunar nodded across to where his mother sat in her basket. She opened her mouth and lopped out her tongue—pah pah pah.

"She showed me how wh-when I was still small," whispered Gunar. Sigurd followed his gaze. Grimhild stared back and panted. Her expression was unreadable.

rescue

Regenerating flesh out of feed and mechanism from industrial waste, Slipper was always young. On his back, the clone felt that he would always be young too. They rode across the uncertain sands of Crayley's feed-bowl as easily as over clay or turf, past the manufactured desert, and into the grown metal maw of the city. Then through the corrosive blast, down the long incline getting steadily steeper, through acids, enzymes, and avalanche, through fires and past obstacles, down the throat and into the body of Crayley. Around him the city crowed and sneered, flung weapons and little armies at him. This was the machine come to life. He'd find no mercy down here.

As he got deeper underground, the heat grew more intense. Slipper was soon without flesh, a titanium skeleton, pure machine now, but still loyal to him, still serving him. But Sigurd himself was untouched by the fires. This time, nothing burned. He was inside one of the dragon suits he had cut out. He was in disguise.

It had been easily done—well within the power of the sorceress Grimhild. It was Gunar who wrote out the runes and prepared the potion; he believed that was all there was to it. But it was she who secretly struck a deal with the god of shapes. A shape is such a thing that can be taken off and put on; nothing else need change. Sigurd kept his skin and his mind, all the effects of the dragon's blood inside him, all of his memories, just as Gunar did. Only their shapes changed. In this way, Gunar the king would achieve his dreams without participation, win the prize in his own absence. He could not have the deed, but he could have the shadow of the deed fall on him. He could achieve it in story at least.

As a favor to a friend the clone went down to Crayley in Gunar's shape. He rode like a fury past tongues of fire and teeth of steel as Gunar, while Gunar himself lay in secret, in his hospital bed, beautiful as he never was in life in the form of Sigurd.

Yes, Gunar was a good man—but he wanted too much. Perhaps his brains had been cooked as well down there. Sigurd, who genuinely did not care for the achievement, only for the doing, gave the glory away without a second's thought, but he would have been a better friend if he had said no. This deed was to carve a wound in many hearts.

He rode through radioactive clouds, past shooting fireworks and blinding gushes of white flame, over puddles of corrosive juices and palpitating, red-hot organs reaching out to devour him. Where was he going? Slipper seemed to know. Deeper and deeper into Hel they rode. He had to get past this heat before releasing his parcel of viruses, or they would be rapidly destroyed. Marshall had reasoned that somewhere there must be layers where the organic and computing networks operated at more comfortable temperatures.

Past metal structures and over stone pathways oozing and puddling in the heat, through walls of fire. Where the way was blocked, Slipper fired a missile or the clone in Gunar's shape simply cut his way through with the sword stub. His power was glorious to him. What could defeat him? Through steel gates, hacked to slices—he could hear the city moan as he did it— past stone walls and organic webs, past tissues that caught and blocked and filtered, like vast membranes, deeper and deeper, to where the heat died down, to where the acids softened, and where at last he saw a strangely familiar creature scuttle with bronzed fur and metallic eyes, but undeniably organic movements.

Then they were riding along an echoing corridor and up to a tangle of sheet steel and furry hides, stuck all around with the dried heads of familiar, unfamiliar creatures. The clone stared in amazement. Why had Slipper led him here? How did he know and not know this place at the same time? There was a doorway, human height, through which he was certain he had passed—but how could he have passed this way and have no memory of it? Why did his heart beat so hard?

He removed the helmet. As he did so, the furs at the entrance parted and a figure came out and stared at him with a look of horror on her face.

The clone stared; she stared, horrified, mesmerized, amazed—as if each expected the other to transform before their eyes into something else. Sigurd reigned in an overpowering desire to jump down and embrace this woman; to his astonishment, tears sprang into his eyes and he had to wipe them away. He wanted to shout, I'm back! But the words had no meaning for him.

"Who are you?" she demanded.

Their eyes had locked together. They were drinking each other through their eyes, trying to understand the force that was between them. How could they know? The one could not remember, the other could not know, but each was looking at the one person they could ever truly love.

Slipper wheeled round; the clone's eyes never left her face. "Gunar, my name is Gunar. I'm the king of everything above here," he said. Never one to boast himself, he only wanted to promote his friend.

Her eyes burned into him. He felt she saw through everything. He could not tear his gaze away. He knew her! But he did not. . . .

"And that horse," she said. These things belonged to someone else! She could not unlock her eyes from his face! Was she falling in love again? Was she someone who could fall helplessly in love with any man she saw—was she doomed to give away her soul every time someone met her? Was she worth so little?

Sigurd's eyes slid sideways deceitfully, but only for a second; then they clamped back onto hers. Bryony smiled grimly. She had resigned herself to life here underground, but the craving for air and all the fullness of real life was still in her. When she heard the clatter of Slipper's hooves on the metal floor, she was certain he had come back at last—her Sigurd, her beloved one, come back to take her away and give her the world! She ran out overflowing with joy, but there was no Sigurd. Instead it was this stranger, who boasted about himself and did not look her in the eye, but stood there in the manner of her beloved. Perhaps he was a murderer. Why else did he have Sigurd's horse?

She was not sure she wanted the world if there was to be no Sigurd in it.

He dismounted and stood in front of her, frowning. It was like a myth; everything had a heightened meaning, but he had no idea why.

"How can Crayley be killed?" he demanded.

The woman, her eyes still fixed into his, smiled grimly. "Murder?" she said. It was on her mind. She'd killed every living thing she had seen for two years. This man was not what she wanted or expected—so why did she want to press herself into him until he became part of her flesh?

"Call it assassination," replied the man. The skeleton horse she knew so well wheeled round like a living thing, and the clone's gaze was torn from her. The bond was broken; they both breathed again. There was a pause while they panted and caught their breath, exhausted by the encounter. Sigurd nodded over his shoulder at the city smoking around them. "Do you know how?" he asked.

Bryony shrugged. Her eyes sought his out and they locked again, like steel clasps on each other's soul. Unwittingly, Bryony's arms rose in the air toward him. She was unaware; her body acted for her. Such love does not need eyes to recognize. And he, seeing her arms rise, smiled joyfully, lifted his own, took a step toward her. . . .

She dropped back and hissed in fear. The clone stepped back too, but their eyes did not part. Their rootless love rendered both speechless. Man and woman gazed into each other's eyes in such a way as if they would harvest the other's soul. A full ten seconds passed before they broke together at the same moment, scared by what they had seen but none the wiser.

For reasons he could not begin to understand, the clone began to sob.

bryony

"Why are you crying?"

He wiped his eyes on his arm. Where was my Sigurd? I wanted to grab him and shake him, as if he had him there with him, somehow hidden. I could feel him, I could taste him. But he wasn't there.

"Where is he?" I hissed.

He looked at me as if I'd asked him for the moon. He shook his head.

"Who?" he demanded. Different face, different eyes. When Sigurd rode through the fire he came to me naked, his bones glowing through his flesh. He was more alive than any other living thing. Now was I falling in love with this pale thing, this look-the-other-way, this cheat-in-the-fire? What manner of a thing was I?

He squinted through his tears. So like Sigurd! But a different man. Were all men like this? He wept such tears, just like Sigurd. It's hard to distrust tears. He was human, another creature. Just to talk to him was like being in love. But this one . . . this one wasn't *mine*.

"Why are you crying?" I asked again.

He shook his head. "It must be shock. I've ridden through fire."

"Are you scared?" I jeered.

"I've come for you," he said. He tried to smile at me but his smile looked terrible. It looked false.

"You've come to kill Crayley," I said. "Do you know how?"

He reached behind and touched Slipper with his hand. "I have viruses," he said. "We don't know if they'll work. You live here. You must know something."

I shrugged. "I know how to kill her. I'm just not sure if I want to."

He started talking about how terrible it was above ground, how all the trees and the beasts and the people and even the ground and the air had been destroyed. I thought to myself, So what? I've never walked on that ground, I've never breathed that air, I've never known those people. All I know is these men with their blood that won't boil who tell ludicrous tales that only a troglodyte like me would ever believe.

All the time he was looking at me as if he wanted to devour me. As if I was his, or as if I'd suffered some terrible disfigurement. Well, I am disfigured. It's called my heart, it's called my soul. I've turned into a monster down here.

"I'm only half alive," I told him.

"You want to escape this, don't you?" he said. "Think about it. The grass, the air, the trees, the people. The world! I've come to bring you the world. I've come for you. I want to give you the world."

"Fuck you!" I screamed. How did he know to say that to me? How did he know I was in love with everything I've never had?

I tried to cover up my confusion. "She is everything to me."

He looked at me curiously. "You call this place *she*?" he asked.

I hunted for Beatrice after it stole her. I thought if I could get to her soon enough maybe she'd be all right. I had her for such a short time, such a short time. It was very hard to know that she would be all alone, just like me. It was very hard to know that she was never going to grow up or smile at me or speak to me.

I went looking without any hope of finding because the only other thing was to kill myself and I wasn't ready to do that. Sigurd might still come back to me. I knew where the place was of course. I thought Crayley would have moved it but I had to fight so hard as I got near, I knew she must be there. It took me weeks—months actually, circling about, trying different directions. I don't know why I bothered, the city kept me at bay so easily. It wants me alive. More babies, more brains. Perhaps that's what this new man is about.

Then one day the ways opened. The weapons in the walls hung their heads, the killer bots sat down and lifted up their arms, the doors unhinged themselves. There was a voice.

"Mother," it said. Mother! How could it? How *dare* it?

I dropped my weapon. I walked past all the deadly things down the corridor and into a room and there she was— Beatrice, my daughter, my baby. Our daughter. She was sitting up in a tank, wired up. So pretty, so pretty. So young. She still had her baby fat. She smiled when she saw me.

"A trick," I said out loud.

"I was inside you. Now you are inside me. What sense does that make?" Her mouth moved in the liquid, her words came out of the air. She laughed, a silver tinkle, a happy sound in that awful place. Such a little girl, and yet she spoke like an adult.

Was she still mine? Was she still even human?

"You can't take me back, Mother. We need me. She is part of us now."

"We?" I sneered.

"You and me, the rats, the machines, the walls, the vats. I am the mother of all. You are the mother of mothers. I love you. We all love you. Everything!"

"What have you done to her?" I wept.

A light came on in her tank. Still so young. A toddler who had never toddled.

"The human brain has seven billion synapses," she said.

"She's so small," I crooned. I went to the tank, I wanted to hold the tank but some creature appeared from behind and held me by my arms.

"Don't touch me!" cried Beatrice.

I held out an arm toward her.

"Perhaps later," said Beatrice.

"Please . . ."

"She's loved. Our mother. I have factories to run and schedules to organize, oil and blood to pump. I have to feed us and grow. I am her, I am us. I am *your* mother now."

I couldn't find words. I collapsed in the creature's arms and wept.

"We will speak to you from time to time, if you wish. You can come and see me."

"I want her back."

"Bryony, she is me now."

"Sigurd," I began.

"Has not come back." There was a note of triumph in her voice. "An absent father. What is he worth? He deserted you, Bryony."

"That's not true!"

"I'm so sorry. So, so sorry."

I put my hand out and this time she let me put it on the tank over her face.

"Why haven't you killed me?"

"Bryony! You are our mother! How could we kill you? How could we?"

I began to cry. It was so unfair! I wept, I begged, I got on my knees. I'd been on my own for so long. And Crayley, oh, Crayley was so understanding, so forgiving, so loving. She sent the machines to stroke me and caress me, she murmured sweet nothings in my ear, she made promises about more babies, more men, a whole population down there to keep me company. I would be the mother of a nation! She would become a real city, a city of living souls. There would be hope, there would be the surface, the world, there would be life. She would get Sigurd back! There would be love.

At the time I let myself believe her. Why shouldn't she get me all these things? Perhaps she was as lonely as I was. She was a city. She needed people too.

Afterward when I could think again I realized what it was about. Backup. Every machine has backup. It's only us poor animals that have just one brain. Yes, there would be another man, because Crayley wanted more babies. She wanted a hundred babies. Why not? What a processor that would be! But there would be no Sigurd. She would never let Sigurd back down here. Sigurd was dangerous.

All lies. Don't you think?

And here he was. Another man.

And that's why I call it her.

"Crayley can be killed," I said. I was thinking, I'll take you to your death, King Gunar. I was part of the system. I will never be part of the system! This man would die, a hundred men would die and so would I, before I would give her another one of my babies.

"Show me."

"And what about me?" I asked. "What's in it for me?"

He licked his lips and glanced away. He smiled cautiously. Again, not like Sigurd, who could hide nothing of himself. "You can come back with me, if you like. Odin's daughter, aren't you?"

"He's not much of a father."

"I'm a king." He nodded. I knew what he meant. Him and me; man and woman.

I just laughed. "What sort of a wife would I make, King Gunar? You don't even know me."

He frowned. "Love is something people can learn." He nodded again. He believed it. Well, who knows? Why shouldn't it be like that?

"If you're willing," he said.

I sighed.

"If you can kill Crayley I'll come to the surface with you. And maybe I'll be yours. We'll see."

He nodded, satisfied.

"We'll go a-hunting then," I said. So that was how it would be; either he would kill Crayley or Crayley would kill him. I never used the word "test"; but I was thinking, If he can do this, then he is as much a man as Sigurd. I have tasted excellence; only excellence will do.

On the other hand, if he dares kill Sigurd's daughter, maybe I will have no taste for him. Perhaps I'll kill him myself after all. . . .

"Take me away from all this," I said. I was as crooked as he was. Kill the city and I'm yours. Kill my daughter and you're dead.

Excellence, yes. And it must be burnished with hate.

43

the hunt

Slipper danced impatiently. The clone reached down and offered Bryony his hand but she drew back. She began to tell him what he should watch out for, what sort of dangers the city had waiting for them.

The clone listened curiously. Every word she told him he already knew, but his mind had no place for any of it. *Déjà vu* at every word; the unfamiliar feeling familiar. He wanted to kiss her, stroke her hair. He wanted to tell her things . . . things he'd never known.

He gestured impatiently for her to climb up behind him.

"I have to tell you how to get there," she complained, but he shook his head.

"Speak as we ride," he growled. He bent down and seized her hand. As he did so, his gaze fixed on a small band shining on her finger.

"Where did you get that?" he demanded.

"It's mine," said Bryony startled, as if he was accusing her of stealing it. She tried to pull her hand back, but he held her in an unflinching grip.

"May I see it? I know that ring. Give it to me. I've come down here to rescue you. A token . . ."

"It's mine, I said it's mine," insisted Bryony. She tugged but his grip was set in stone. The man glanced briefly at her, and then calmly slid it from her finger while holding on to her hand with his implacable grip.

"My ring! Give it back!"

"It's only a little thing. I can give you better jewels by the armful," said the clone. Then he heaved and swung her up into the seat behind him. Bryony was outraged. He had stolen her ring—her only possession, her love-ring from Sigurd. But Sigurd wasn't here. For a second she considered killing this Gunar, if she could. He was even stronger than Sigurd had been. She was squeezed up tight against him on Slipper, she could feel his back against her belly. So close! He turned and their eyes locked again. The eyes, gateway to the soul. So close—just a kiss away. There was another moment of desperate yearning. Do you believe in love at first sight? Perhaps you already met. Perhaps you are two halves of the same thing. They were ignorant, but their hearts knew the truth.

He had stolen her ring. The clone looked away.

"Ha!" he yelled, and Slipper leapt forward, dashing along the corridors and alleyways toward the city's heart. Behind him, a skin's breadth away, Bryony wrapped her arms around his waist and groaned. Rage, yearning, and confusion fought inside her; she hardly knew where she was. A tear squeezed out of her eyelid. If she had been facing him, she would have seen tears in his eyes, too. What manner of a monster was she that she could fall so utterly in love again so soon? As for the clone, he had no idea why he had taken the ring. It was a cruel, petty thing to do, unlike him. He told himself he would give it back to her later, but he never did.

He reached behind and handed her a pair of short, stubby automatic guns.

"Soon," he yelled.

Bryony took the guns and stared at his broad back in amazement. They were going the right way; he even knew what was coming. How did he know so much? From one second to the next, she didn't know whether she wanted to cover him with kisses or throw him off his horse and trample him into the cinders. She grasped his shoulder and felt the muscle and bone. Thin—nothing like her Sigurd.

"Where did you get this beast?" she asked.

The man glanced at her over his shoulder. "Someone loaned it to me," he said.

Bryony's heart jumped. "His name?"

Again the clone glanced back, and licked his lips.

"Sigurd Volson."

Bryony felt as if the hand of death had touched her heart.

"Where is he?" she whispered.

"Waiting for my safe return."

"He told you about me," she whispered.

The rider looked straight on. Slipper was picking up speed, although the obstacles in their way were increasing. He leapt from side to side like a rabbit.

"Sigurd knows nothing of you," he said finally.

"He said nothing?"

"Nothing."

"But I . . ."

"I told you, he knows nothing about you!" Gunar screamed. Bryony shrank back.

"Is everyone like you up there? All men . . . ?" she asked tentatively.

"Not all men are kings," said Gunar eagerly, glancing over at her.

Boasting again; cheap. Sigurd never boasted, he had no need to. Sigurd in Gunar's shape was boasting for his friend, but his hopeless openness made it look foolish. Deceit was one thing he was not good at.

So—Sigurd was still alive. He had lent Gunar Slipper. And, thought Bryony, this Gunar was lying again: Of course Sigurd had mentioned her. In fact he had told him everything—where to go and what to say and how to win her, because if she fell in love with another man he owed her nothing, he was free. He was not dead; he had betrayed her. He had come upon her like a dream, promised her the world, and then betrayed her— handed her on like meat on a plate to another man. She did not yet know what to make of this Gunar, so like and so unlike Sigurd. Maybe she would kill him. Maybe she would never be able to forgive him for not being Sigurd. She vowed this, though: She would never love him, even though her heart yearned for it. Was it possible to murder love? What a self-mutilation that would be!

When you have been so badly hurt for so long, Bryony thought, then hurt becomes your life. Was that all she had? Pain, and the promise of more pain?

And who cared if it was?

So they darted across the halls of fire and rage that protected the brain of Crayley. Now the creatures came—the human-headed rats, the snake people, the suicide mice, the machines. The clone knew how to kill the creatures, each different type; Bryony marveled at how his arm moved like Sigurd's, how his thoughts worked like Sigurd's. It must be a strange world up there where men looked so different but behaved the same, and where knowledge and perhaps even love were things they held in common.

He fought like a demon! Bryony began to believe that they would reach Beatrice and kill her after all.

When the fire grew too hot Bryony had to be stowed away in the hold, wrapped up in the other part of the dragon's skin. The clone put on the unneeded headpiece to his own suit, to maintain the deception. Then he slammed the door on her. Humiliated in the horse's belly she bit her lip and tried not to think about Sigurd, how he was trying to give her away; or how they were riding out to kill her daughter.

On they rode, stopping only to kill. The clone had the sword out now, but Bryony could not see it, trapped in Slipper's hold. Against tanks and fire and viruses, against bombs and soldiers and robots, Crayley could fight, but before Odin's gift, there was no defense. As they got closer, back into the cooler areas it needed for its higher functions, Crayley at last understood that there was real danger inside itself, and it began to beg. The clone heard, but did not understand. Why did the city call out for mother? What mother could give birth to this monster? Why did it weep in the voice of a baby girl?

"Mother—help me, please. Keep him away! Keep him back! Don't hurt us, don't hurt us!"

It struck a feverish shiver in his skull to hear that. The words meant everything—and nothing. Below him, in the hold, Bryony heard it all and began beating with her hands against the sides of the horse, but the clone understood nothing but that this place had to die.

The city howled in terror as they swung a corner close to the room where Beatrice was kept.

"Mother! Please . . ."

"What does it mean?" he screamed, but he could not hear her reply. He goaded Slipper forward into the quiet place at the center of things, where Crayley kept its consciousness.

There was a moment of stillness. Slipper's belly opened and Bryony tumbled out into the neon-lit room. She got to her feet and in the pale blue light saw her daughter again. She was sitting up now, under the crystal clear liquid, her hair floating like weed. She seemed to have grown gills, feathery blood vessels on the sides of her neck. Her legs were out straight in front of her, and she was twisting to one side to watch them.

She had his face.

"Mother!" begged the child. "Mother—what does he want?" The child—she was still just a baby—looked at her fearfully. Under the liquid, her mouth moved but her voice came out of speakers on the tank. Bryony turned to the clone and gave him a terrible grin. How much of this was her daughter, how much was it Crayley playing tricks? Even if it was nothing more than a box of tricks, an illusionist's play, it was better than no daughter at all.

"She's . . ."

"Don't let him hurt me, Mummy," pleaded the child, and sobbed.

Bryony looked at the clone, who stared at the strange girl

with . . . what was that expression? Disgust? Tenderness?

"Your daughter," he said. His face trembled.

"Mummy!"

"She's been turned into a fucking component! She's just . . ." The clone was lost for words in rage, humiliation, grief that he had no place for. He stepped forward and raised the sword. With a cry, Bryony cast herself at him and tried to pull him away, but he held her back with one hand while she clung like a monkey to his back, screaming and shouting, fighting and begging him to leave her baby be. The strength in him was terrible. He raised the sword. The strange child with his face looked up into his eyes and recognized him.

"You!" she hissed. Then, in a quieter voice, "Father!"

The clone stood with his sword raised, and trembled from head to foot.

"I know you, Volson," said the child. "Listen—it's not too late. Impregnate the girl and go back where you came from. Do as I say. You can keep your secret. Neither of you will come to any harm. Father? Daddy? Please?"

The clone glanced behind him. Bryony was fighting his back, her screams drowning the voice; she had heard nothing. He wasted no more time. Violently, he brought the sword down through the tank and across the child's head. The head divided in a clash of glass, poured bright red into the wave of fluid that crashed down upon them. Then, one two, one two, he diced her up like a slice of liver. Bryony screamed in horror. The city shrieked and burbled. The clone pushed her off his back.

"I had to do it, it was eating the world," he screamed. "It's done now," he added quietly. He looked at the mess at his feet, and gagged at the sight of his work.

Bryony lifted her own gun and fired at the clone's head, but he was unharmed. She flung the gun down. She was unable even to aim straight in this man's presence.

"Murderer!" she screamed. "Murderer!" She took a step forward to the ruin before her, but there was nothing to nurse or hold or even stroke in that pile of offal that was her daughter.

"I had to!" sobbed the clone. "If you saw what she'd done you'd know. Do you think that was me doing that? Do you think I wanted to? It had . . ."

The man—part Sigurd, part clone, pretending to be Gunar—choked on his words. He was losing all sense of who he was or what he was for. He was about to say that the child had his face, but he had his deception to play.

"It had . . . his face," he gasped.

"Yes, his face. Sigurd's daughter. Do you think a man like that will forgive you for killing his child? Do you expect me to?" screamed Bryony.

"Him—me—here?" demanded the clone. So close! So close to being Sigurd! Just a memory away. Surely it will happen—the memories will burst out of Bryony and pour into him like blood.

"No! I've, he's . . . we've never been here! You took us here. We knew . . ." The clone floundered for words. His child? He had killed his own child? Impossible! "You . . . you understood. You took me here. You knew this had to be done. You killed her as surely as I did!"

Bryony flung herself at him, striking him violently in the face. In a fury the clone raised the bloody sword. Bryony lifted her face to it. Yes! Death was all she had now. But the blow never came. Instead he turned and looked at the slaughtered child.

"How much of it was her?" he whispered.

"We'll never know, King Gunar, because you were angry and killed too fast. Sigurd would have rescued her."

The clone could only stare. Was that true? It felt like the truth. How far had he fallen beneath his own star?

On the banks of computers and panels around them the lights had begun to flash on and off. Outside violent bangs and explosions were pounding the walls. There was a low, shuddering moan. Far off they could hear pumping, like a giant heart beating fit to burst.

"The city's dying. Quick!" gasped the clone. He lifted Bryony up and flung her like a doll into the hold, yelling at her to keep wrapped up in Fafnir's skin. He seized from his pack a bundle— the package of viruses Marshall had prepared, and jumped aboard. The horse reared up. The clone flung the package down on the floor where it broke into fragments. The viruses were airborne; it was done, it was all done. Slipper wheeled round and made a dash for the door. It was the last run, up to the surface. Gunar had fulfilled his mission in front of the girl's eyes. The clone had served his friend well, but he was never so close to being his true self as now, at the heart of deception. He understood nothing of the passion and rage in his heart, or any of the things he had seen and done, but life still beckoned. The woman trapped beneath him in the hold stirred such terrible feelings in him. He didn't know if he wanted to make love to her or murder her. Maybe in this case they were the same thing.

Slipper rushed away, past the bellowing fires that were now devouring the city itself, past trembling metal organs, rupturing vessels and failing machines, past the screaming creatures running for their lives, back up to the world where life went on.

44

daylight

What had happened? Meanings down there were broken before they even formed. It had been so charged and yet there was no place in him for any of it.

As the clone rode Slipper across the poisonous wastes surrounding the maw, he felt that he was emerging from a nightmare, but it was worse than that. It was real; he had been to Hel and back. He remembered the old stories. The place of shadows, ruled over by Hel herself, Loki's daughter, half living, half dead. What had the girl told him?

"I'm only half alive."

The clone shuddered. Was that it? He had her with him now, then—Hel herself, Princess of death. Not Odin's daughter at all: Loki's. But she had seemed so alive, she had such sweet flesh. He had longed for her as if he was in love. How could that be? Perhaps half dead was not what the story meant. What if her soul rotted inside her living body? Half dead. Or her mind. Can the mind rot? Then only her flesh was alive.

He had brought Hel up into the world, and death is always jealous of life. And yet he loved her! Oh, yes, he loved her. Was that how it was with her? Would everyone who met her love her—love death? If that was so, the slaughter would be endless.

They were not yet out of the feed bowl when under Slipper's feet there was a tremor; then the rock underfoot shook like a struck table. Deep underground, Crayley was going through its death throes. Behind them at the maw, a deep, dull whistle sounded and grew rapidly louder. The massive explosions now taking place deep underground were producing billions of cubic meters of burning gases. Much was escaping into fissures in the rocks, but a great deal was finding its way out of the dying city's mouth parts, forcing this terrifying whistle from the earth. The noise grew from a piercing screech, to a howling bellow, to a bawling of the earth, shaking the world.

The clone geed Slipper up and galloped off into the green. He fled, tearing across the pastures, leaving the exploding rock behind him, dodging flying boulders and stones until the noise became a dull moan in the distance.

It was a wet day, late morning. A tower of gas rose high into the air behind them, stirring the mist and shaking the trees even at that distance. The wet pasture heaved around Slipper's legs. There were cows watching, there were trees, hedgerows of twisted hawthorns.

Gradually the roaring died down, the wind dropped, and the day returned slowly to its original stillness. The cows dropped their heads again to the grass, the birds began singing in the hawthorns. The clone took a deep breath. How sweet, how fresh, how full of life the wind was after the thick, smoggy air below ground. And now at last, there was a memory, something perhaps that Grimhild had missed.

He had ridden before through fire and out of the ground. He

had come out into a wet day just like this one. On that occasion he had not been surrounded by pasture and trees, but by bare and broken rock.

He had been to Crayley before. But he had no memory of it, only of his escape.

The clone dismounted. He had no idea where he was, he knew they had moved HQ away from the maw in case of such explosions, but Gunar would be able to track him down soon enough. He did not have much time alone.

He stood by the side of the horse and drew his sword.

It would be easy. He could plunge the sword stub into Slipper's side and through her. Slipper would be unharmed. She would never even know.

The clone stared intently at the side of the horse, once again burned clean of all flesh. Slipper stamped and snorted, but did not move even though he knew his master planned to stab him. The clone could sense exactly where she was, as if his senses were attuned to hers. There, she crouched just there, he could almost see her image. One stab, one thrust, it would all be over. But she was so sweet, so delicious—not like death at all. And her fierce spirit, the way she moved and thought and felt. She was his! But what possible good could come of bringing her up here?

Unwilling to finish his task, the clone crouched down and put his ear to Slipper's side where he knew the girl to be. Without thinking, he spread his arms and embraced the side of the horse as if he could touch her. Inside, Bryony, who had felt the journey end, and was listening intently to see what would happen to her next, did the same thing. Open armed, cheek to cheek, chest to chest, separated only by a titanium skin and a few inches of insulation, they unknowingly embraced. Two pairs of hands clenched as if they could hold hands. Two pairs of arms pressed, as if they could embrace, two faces pressed together. Love and loss, love and loss. They were tearing themselves in two. No one ever loved like these two. They could give their hearts away a hundred times, they could betray and even forget, but theirs was a love that could not end.

Bryony wept. The lost lover, the dead child. Loss, loss, loss. The clone wept. The child with his face! He did not even know what his losses were.

Filled for the first time in his life with a conviction he was unable to carry out, Sigurd's knelt in the grass and sobbed. That was how he was when Gunar found him, so lost to his unhappiness that he did not hear him come, and started round at a hand on his shoulder, to see himself.

How to explain Bryony's feelings when the hold opened and she tumbled out into the damp air, the smells of earth and vegetation, cows and rain. There was the grass at last. A hand touched her shoulder but she shrugged it off angrily. The light blinded her at first and she had to lie with her hands over her face for a long time before she could bear to look. Gradually she took them away, taking little peeps before she could open her eyes fully—and there it all was: the world. The enormous sky, the trees hissing softly in the rain, and green, green, green as far as she could see. Gunar stood nearby, smiling anxiously at her. She gestured with her hand—it was too much.

"Has it been w-worth it?" he asked. Bryony had no answer. It was enormous and endless, it was everything she ever wanted but there were ashes in her heart now and the terrifying feeling, something she had never dreamed would happen to her, that the world was not enough.

From the hedgerow, a tiny dot dashed rapidly across and landed on Bryony's hair. She put up her hand and Jenny Wren stepped onto her finger. The little bird had hidden back in Crayley while the clone had been around. Bryony hadn't even thought of her since but now she was delighted.

"You got out!" She raised her to her lips and kissed her tiny head. "She was my only friend," she told Gunar. Gunar nodded anxiously. Sigurd had not mentioned a tame wren.

In her beak, Jenny had a tiny bunch of pretty red berries. Bryony took them and smiled.

"Still making presents," she said.

"Over there," said Gunar. He pointed across to where an old hawthorn tree grew by a ditch. It was a gnarled old thing, but it stood draped in berries from head to toe, hundreds of thousands, millions of them, a hopeless abundance. Bryony looked from her little gift to the fountain of berries. She began to cry. For Jenny's sake she thanked her, kissed her beak, and tucked the gift in her hair, brushing away the tears. She had gained everything she wanted and lost everything she had. What worth has the sun and the sky, the world and all its wonders, without love?

At the same time, in a room not far off, Sigurd was trying to explain himself to Gudrun. He sat by the window twiddling with the ring on his finger that he had stolen from Bryony.

This ring. The child with his face. Slipper knowing the way through the fire. Those feelings of the familiar, of knowing when he did not know, of sorrow and loss and love. The memory of arriving on the surface when he had never been underground before. What did it all mean?

But he said nothing to Gudrun about how he had felt for Bryony.

"If it was Hel, you've destroyed it now," she said.

"A Hel made by man," said Sigurd.

"Why not? People say the gods are man-made too. What does it matter?"

"Maybe." The clone chewed his nail, trying to work it out. "What if there's more than one of me?" he demanded suddenly.

"More than one of you? God help us!" said Gudrun, rolling her eyes, trying to make a joke of it. She hadn't seen Sigurd like this since his breakdown.

"How do I know things I never knew? Do you think that when I died, maybe Odin made another one of me?"

Gudrun stood up. "This is nonsense, Sigurd. You've been through a lot. You need to look after yourself, that's all. Rest. Think about it—if there was another Sigurd we would have heard about it—everyone would have heard about it. Look at you!"

Sigurd was wonderful, his golden tawny hair flowing round his wide face and down his shoulders and back. Beautiful! But it scared her. She was so scared of losing him—to madness, to another woman, to life.

"I don't know myself anymore. I feel . . . like there's another life somehow, that I haven't even lived."

Gudrun laughed nervously. "Sigurd! If you could hear yourself . . ." She went to take his hand and saw, there on his finger, a band of gold.

"That's pretty," she said. "Where did you get it?"

Sigurd glanced down at the ring. He meant to give it to Gunar to give back to Bryony.

"Bryony gave it to me when I was in Gunar's shape," he said, and wondered even as the words left his lips why he lied.

"Give it to me." Gudrun smiled at him, watching his reaction.

Sigurd frowned. "It's hers. I should give it to Gunar. He can decide what to do with it."

"No, give it to me. You can tell him the ring was lost on the journey back up. It could easily happen."

"Why should you have it? It's not mine to give."

She pulled a face. "I'm a jealous bird. If she gave it to you and you love me, it should be mine now, by rights."

The clone let her ease it off his finger. "That's better," she said. "You can't wear any ring but one I give you," she scolded.

"If you want it," he said, although he didn't want her to have it. "But you can't wear it. If Bryony ever sees it, god knows."

Gudrun put it on her finger. "It's still warm," she said. She rubbed it against her lips. "I'll put it away somewhere safe."

The clone went to the window to look out. Somewhere out there, Gunar and Bryony were walking together. He was showing her all the good things of the world.

It should be me with her, he thought, then shook his head. Why was he troubled by such thoughts? He had Gudrun; he loved her with all his heart. But he was aware that the world used to be more wonderful for him than it now was and it seemed to him that somehow he could regain his love for it by showing it to Bryony himself.

"She should die. We should kill her," he called over his

shoulder to Gudrun. "What have I done? What have I brought back?"

Gudrun paused. "I'll speak to Gunar, see what he thinks of her. Don't worry. You've been under a strain, that's all. This deception—it's not you, Sigurd. You should never have agreed to it." She left the room and stood awhile in thought. She needed to talk to someone about this. What was it about this girl? Was he right about her, or was he on the edge of another breakdown?

45

meeting

It happened like that. Don't ask to understand why it was so cruel. There are events so wedded to the shape of time that nothing else can happen. It was cruel in this way, as gravity flies away from the sky. There was God in these things unfolding.

The clone had done for his friend Gunar what was alien to his nature, something he could never do on his own behalf: an act of betrayal. Just as everyone had to live in the truths Sigurd made, now they had to live in his lie. At last, he was hunted by that enemy of life, regret—a snake that threatens and never will bite, but always has bitten. We remember, we look into the future uncertainly, and we feel the poison working.

The clone had done what he set out to do. He had killed Crayley and won a bride for Gunar. He had given him someone to love. Such a gift! Gudrun told him to be happy with that. But far from making him happy, strange thoughts gnawed at his insides. Yes, he was happy for Gunar, but why did a part of his heart rage against him? Jealousy, envy, was that it? He had never been prey to such feelings before. Why now? And how could the thought of Bryony shine around him like a light when he loved Gudrun so much? Grimhild's trick had worked and worked well, but even she could not change the shape of things. The love between Sigurd and Bryony was something in the architecture of time. They would have missed each other even if they'd never met.

Bryony did not meet the other Niberlins straight away. Hoping to put off the day when she had to meet Sigurd, she told Gunar she wanted to see something of the world they lived in first so that she would at least have that in common with them. They spent a couple of weeks alone at the Old House on their own before leaving to explore the country.

Before they left, the clone had to debrief Gunar about the time he had spent with Bryony in Crayley. They'd had an hour together when he first came back, talking in the grass while she waited in the hold, wondering what was going on, but Gunar wanted to be certain that he had memorized every second of their time together and made it his own.

There was a dispute about Bryony's ring. Gunar wanted it back but Gudrun refused to let it go. It was uncharacteristic of her and she did not understand it herself, but she felt that somehow, since her man had courted Bryony for her brother, something was owed her. If there were any love tokens in this strange affair, they were going to be hers. Gunar was angry; he expected her to respect his feelings in this. But Gudrun was unmovable and so he'd had to explain to Bryony that he had lost her ring somewhere on the journey back up. He apologized for taking it off her, explaining that he thought it had been given her by another man and was jealous. It rankled with Bryony, but too much was happening for her to think too hard about it yet.

Then they went away. So much to see! Gunar wanted to show her everything. It was a holiday, an exploration, an education—a lifetime to fit in. And perhaps, it would be a honeymoon, too. Both of them wanted love. If you yearn for it and reach for it, surely you can make it yours. Six weeks, a couple of months—they would know by then. Does it matter so much that they began their courtship before love was there? They looked for love and perhaps, in those first few weeks, they found it. It was the same adventure of body and soul; two people together. They became lovers after the first week. It made Gunar so happy that Bryony couldn't help but feel that something special was happening. She wondered if it was enough that he loved her, that she might learn to love him in the light of his love. He wanted to nurture her, and she could not help but respond.

The trees and hedgerows, the clouds. Towns. There were houses and shops and a sickening whirl of people. It was endless. The cinema, rivers, sports, the ocean, insects, birds, airplanes. Bryony was intoxicated, fascinated, terrified of missing anything or everything. The act of betrayal was always there, but the world was hers now. She refused to let anything spoil that for her. At the back of her mind she supposed there would be a reckoning, an explanation that might or might not seem adequate. Perhaps love itself was shallow, a trick of nature. Perhaps the worms are as intense swallowing the earth underneath us as a lover is. What did she know about the value of feelings? In that first riot of her senses, she hoped that they were small change.

Her moods swung so violently from passion to rage that sometimes Gunar felt that she was swinging him around her head like a weight on the end of a piece of string. But this was what he had wanted, wasn't it? Passion, brightness; an adventure. Bryony was the real thing. Who could imagine what it was like to see all this after a lifetime under the ground? Of course she was tired, upset, depressed, happy, angry—whatever she said. Gunar was exhausted, but delighted. After just a few weeks, he was already telling her that he was in love.

By the time they were due to go home and meet the family, Bryony had decided too. She could promise nothing—it was too early to speak of love. But Gunar was a good man, she liked him and she wanted to learn how to love him, if he was willing to take the risk.

Gunar kissed her fingers and smiled. "That's all I could ever ask," he said, and she was amazed at how happy this seemed to make him.

They arrived back at the Old House a few days before the others. It was a chance to relax and settle down after the whirl of the previous weeks, before day-to-day life began. That evening and the following day the rest of the family arrived one by one. Bryony met them as they came, kissed, embraced, was made welcome. When Gudrun came she felt nothing. That surprised her. Perhaps it was going to be all right. Maybe it was only broken memories stirring up inside her when she thought of Sigurd making love to this woman.

As the evening meal approached, Sigurd had still not arrived. Upstairs in her room, Bryony stared into the mirror as she did her face. It was wonderful what this paint did but she wasn't sure that she liked it. On her shoulder Jenny Wren piped and bent down to peer in the mirror.

"Pretty, aren't I, Jenny?" Bryony asked. The wren stared back at with her bright black eyes.

"Maybe I'm another person now," said Bryony. She stared hard at her face as if it would suddenly twist into a new set of features to suit her new self. "I'll know when I see him, won't I?" she begged the wren suddenly and hid her face in her hands. This had to end. She had forgotten in the glory of the world but she knew now: It was not possible to live like this. She had locked him away somewhere deep inside, emasculated, love in chains, but now she was going to have to meet him and she felt as unequal before her feelings as a child under the treads of a tank.

The clone was frightened too. When he had gone down to Crayley disguised as Gunar, it had been more to fool the spectators—playing politics to show them that the king was able to do the hero job as well as Sigurd. But the deception had taken root in their lives. The clone had convinced himself that this was why he felt so uncomfortable about meeting Bryony. Away from her, he had been able to forget the hold she had over him and dismiss the confused feelings he'd had down in Crayley—the passion, the desire, the need, the sense of loss. No doubt Crayley had developed the same sort of machines that Fafnir once had. Some version of Fear had been at work. It was over now. But as soon as he got near to her again, the fear began again. He had no idea what would happen when he saw her, but he wished with all his heart that he'd left her underground where he found her.

As the Niberlins gathered for the evening meal, the tension grew. Everyone except Bryony knew about the deception they were perpetrating on her. Nobody liked it, but nobody stopped it. Somehow, they hoped, it would come out all right. Bryony would be told one day after she had grown to love Gunar and was able to forgive him.

Gunar came to take her for a walk in the garden at dusk before they ate, but the rain had started and they had to go inside to the conservatory where the table was laid out and waiting for them. Grimhild was there in her dog basket. Her tongue lolled out and she stared steadily into Bryony's eyes as Gunar rubbed her ears. It was quiet; rain pattered on the glass above their heads. There was a vine spreading under the roof, where Jenny had hidden herself away. Bryony was looking up to see if she could spot her when the clone walked in.

Her eyes caught him. He was prepared and smiled encouragingly at her, but inside his heart cracked. He did not understand how he could keep his face so still. Gudrun had advised him that it would be all right once he had begun the lie. Once he got used to it, she said, it would become a kind of truth of its own.

" . . . and this big boy is Sigurd," said Gunar. Bryony, who had averted her face for fear of showing how much she felt, turned and looked coolly at him; but she had to grip her sleeve to stop her hand from shaking. She would show him nothing, not even that she recognized him, until he acknowledged her.

The clone smiled his pleasant smile and bent to kiss her cheek. As he did so, there was a movement in the vine above. A tiny head looked out from Bryony's breast.

"Oh!" exclaimed the clone. "Jenny Wren!" As he spoke the name he looked at her in wonder that he knew it.

"Jenny Wren," said Bryony bitterly, at what to her was an acknowledgement that they'd known each other before.

The little bird piped a high, loud note. The clone was staring at her, a half smile still stranded on his face. Suddenly Jenny left her hiding place and flew straight for his face. With a cry, he lifted his hand, but the tiny bird was already perched on the edge of his eye socket. He felt her sharp claws pricking. She squeaked, flicked her tail, and stepped in through his eye.

The clone staggered back as if he'd been struck a blow. Forgetting everything for the love of him, Bryony took two steps forward and held on to him as if she'd never let him go again.

"No," said Gudrun in a flat tone, as if she understood that everything was about to change. The clone's eye had turned into a dark pool that seemed to have no surface. Bryony reached up to touch his face, and as she did so, the wren flew out of his eye like a rocket, straight over her head, out of the window, and was gone. He raised his hand and looked at Bryony. . . .

And the clone remembered. In that second he made the journey from death to life once more; he became Sigurd. Jesus did it, Odin did it; but only he ever made the impossible journey twice—a third awakening. And during death the great soul of Sigurd was kept safe—in the tiny heart of a wren.

As his soul slotted into place within him, a pulse of energy left him. Gunar, Hogni, and Gudrun fell back before it, then were scooped up again toward him by a second pulse of pure love. But Bryony stepped through it and into his arms. Sigurd was love. He seemed to be clothed in light. Each of the others, unconscious of anything else, lifted a hand toward him but they didn't dare touch.

Sigurd threw back his head and screamed in pain.

Memories! Bryony, Crayley, Jenny Wren. Love! Falling in love, making love, being in love. Every second of it with all this heart. And more. His dying struggle in the lake, fighting for air while Ida beat at his face. Yes, Jenny had seen all this too and given it to him as well.

As he gazed into Bryony's eyes, she saw it all—the light dawning, the understanding, the love, like a flash of color. She cried out, "Sigurd!" He was hers still! She smiled joyfully and reached up to take his bowed head in her arms. They were in each other's hearts forever. But Sigurd wept—for her, for him, for everything they had missed and lost.

Sigurd remembered more; not only his memories, but the memories of the clone, lived by him as surely as if he had been there. Love! Doubleness. Love in lies, betrayal, treachery. There was Gudrun, whom he loved. And Gunar, to whom he had given a gift that no one had the right to give. He hadn't known—but the gift had been given. What greater betrayal to yourself or another can there be than to give love away? How could such a crime ever be undone?

He held Bryony tenderly in his arms for a moment longer, then he groaned and turned away. Bryony froze. Had she made a mistake? How could there be a mistake?

"Sigurd? What is it?" Suddenly he turned and stumbled out of the room. As he went he cast a haunted glance behind him. The world was not back together at all. On the contrary, in the face of love everything had been made more crooked than ever.

Bryony took a step forward, but before she could run after him, Gudrun pushed her to one side.

"Sigurd! Sigurd! Come back!"

From where she stood, Bryony could see him through the

window running like a deer across the wet grass, his form blurred by rain. Trailing behind him onto the lawn was Gudrun. She called his name but he was already jumping over the hedge at the end. She screamed, "Sigurd! Sigurd!" again and they caught a brief glimpse of his face turning to look back; then he was gone.

Soaked with rain, Gudrun stood and stared. She rubbed her face in her hands as if she couldn't believe what she'd just seen, then turned and trudged back toward the house. As she approached the conservatory, she caught sight of Bryony's face staring at her through the window and cast her a look of pure hatred.

46

sigurd

Sigurd could have run for the rest of his life—he had the strength to do it. But he knew there were things that could never be left behind. After a few miles he followed a valley down to a small stream flowing through rough pasture and lay down among the watercress and fallen leaves in the muddy margins.

It was pitch-black here, away from the roads and towns, but at that moment he was aware of all life, from the microscopic animals living in the water and mud around him, to the trees shedding their leaves crowding on the slope above, to the planet itself and the vast stars themselves, bending time and space to look down on him.

He wriggled himself deeper down among the crushed plants and mud as if this was a warm bed and let the memories in.

Memories, yes! Memories are holy, Bryony had told him that. Our record of our contact with the world, the glory of our lives. He had been kept from them, but now he could give them their proper place, surround them, engulf them, make them his. Falling in love with Gudrun; dying, forgetting, fearing, losing, being weak; living out of step, out of place with the world.

Every second of every hour of every day of his life as the clone, he made his.

Sigurd lay in the mud and felt the rain wash him. Around him, he could feel a thousand tiny wrigglings as little fish, water shrimps, snails, and other creatures gathered round him. A deer came to lick the salt sweat off his arm. Above, small birds gathered in the branches, all to be near him. He was the perfect one, made to love all and lead all and do everything right; but he had been tricked into betrayal, and betrayal was the one gift he didn't have. His fears had come true after all. He wasn't human; he never had been. He was a monster all the time—a monster of love. To be truly human you need to be able to betray. Perfection has no place in this world. He lay there, loving everything, but unable to lift a finger to stop anything, save anything, change anything—not himself, not Bryony, nothing.

Up at the Old House he could feel the people moving in their lives. To be a person—what could be more lovely? But the poisons were at work now—jealousy, frustration, rage, failure, betrayal. Nothing could be changed. The grip of fate was irresistible. Then, death. How was it possible to face this, the loss of all hope, and still remain yourself?

Sigurd sat up in his watery bed. Around him the animals started in alarm.

"Is that possible?" he whispered. "Is it possible to love death? Is it possible to love hate itself?"

And if it was, how stupid is that!

Then he went back; but first he made a prayer to all the gods—to Odin and Jesus and Allah and any one of them who might be listening. Thank you, Father, he said, but you don't know what you do.

47

gudrun

It rained during the whole of July, but then in the second half of August we had two weeks of sun. Yow—blazing hot! You couldn't move. Everything was exhausting. It was the real damp heat, you know; you can't breathe, you can't sleep, you can't do anything. The cats spent all day sleeping inside, the dogs were lying on their sides with their tongues hanging out panting away. So were we. Our family's funny in the sun. Suddenly we're walking round with our tongues out going, heh heh heh. We couldn't help it. When the three of us got together, we looked hilarious.

Not that we were spending much time together these days. Rrrr. I don't think we've spent more than a few weeks together all year. We used to be together all the time. That was before the Shit Queen came along.

Yeah. It's this gift she has. She's a shit machine. She turned me into shit, she turned Sigurd into shit. We used to be in love. Grrha ha ha, remember that? No, nothing happened down there in Crayley, of course it didn't. It was entirely innocent. Then why does he turn to shit every time she looks at him? Because she has shit-ray eyes? And she's turned Gunar into shit, he goes around looking like shit all the time, that's shit. Our family's shit, the country she happens to be queen of is shit. See? The Shit Queen. She's only been here under a year, that's all it took—one year to turn the whole world to shit.

Gunar and Hogni were out boating. Away, away, everyone wants to get away. Yow. Sigurd was away. I hardly saw him. I missed him like Hel and then when he was here it was awful. Hogni spent some time with me but I wasn't seeing much of Gunar. Things were pretty difficult between us since his wife was so obviously in love with my husband.

Rrow. It's all Gunar's fault in the first place. He should never have asked Sigurd to go down there in his place and Sigurd should never have agreed. Bloody Gunar—he has everything, a kingdom of his own, and is it good enough? No; he has to be Sigurd, too. So there she is trapped down there and this man turns up; she's never even seen one before and she falls in love with him. Well—yes. What else is going to happen? She must have thought it was Christmas. And then, of course, she gets up here and lo and behold, the man suddenly has a completely different personality. Well, you have to feel sorry for her—what's that going to do to your head? And then, oh look! Here's another man, an utterly gorgeous, *delicious* man, much nicer than the one she's got, who just happens to have the same personality as hers did when she fell in love with him in the first place.

Rrr. Pah! She's not stupid. She knows something's going on. I don't blame her. It was a stupid trick to play on her, but now it's gone wrong and here we all are suffering from Gunar's greed and Sigurd's naïveté. And her shit.

So, Gunar and Hogni were away having a good time leaving

me in the shit on my own to cope with the Shit Queen. I'd been working—a new initiative for hospitals. Hospitals are a problem. With so many different body types you need your doctors trained in about ten ways for even the most basic treatments. But it was just so hot. I'd had it. I had a cold drink and went outside to see if it was any cooler out than in, and there was Bryony reading on the sun lounger.

Oooh, Miss Shit has come outside. We're honored. She doesn't work. She doesn't do anything except sit around emanating shit waves. But, then . . .

Like I say, I do feel sorry for her. She looked so pretty, lying there with her toes bare and her dress off her shoulder, reading her book. Butter wouldn't melt. Yow. She kept looking across at the cat lying under the plum tree, flicking his tail and watching the birds at the feeder. You get all sorts at the feeders—there was a woodpecker that summer, beautiful black and white and red thing. Yes, a beautiful day, just so swelteringly hot. I thought, She's the one who's been used. At least we all know what's going on. She was trapped down there on her own all that time, all she wants is to come up here and have the same things everyone else has—ordinary things—and then when she gets here, it's all fucked up for her.

You have to try, don't you? So I asked her if she wanted to come for a swim.

The river's half a mile away, it's a job to get there on a day like this with the heat baking down on you, but it's great when you get there. We hadn't been down there for ages. Granddad had a dam put across the river and it makes a great swimming hole. There's still the rope up where we used to swing as children. We should have been there, having a laugh in the river, with a picnic and a bottle of wine, instead of sitting about sweating in the sun. But the others were away, it was just her and me, and so I asked her. But I was surprised when she said yes.

"Oh, great," I said. She always says no to everything. I thought, There, you keep trying, you get somewhere. I smiled at her. She couldn't quite manage to smile back.

"I'll get some swimming things," she said, but I just laughed and shook my head.

"There's no one there. You can keep your knickers on if you want, I won't look." She smiled back then. So I thought she was happy for once.

I went inside and got some towels and a bag, a couple of bottles of wine, some bits of cake and crisps and things, and we set off across the fields. It's a pretty walk, you get nice views from the top of the hill. I tried to talk but she just nodded and smiled so I stopped bothering. It was uncomfortable, but what do you expect, we'd hardly been talking for months. Actually, it took all your breath just plodding along in the heat, so I thought, well, maybe she was happy just to be out walking and going for a swim, maybe it was just me babbling away like a big twat that was making things feel funny.

When we got there, Bryony went straight to the beachy bit—muddy bit, really, but we call it the beachy bit. She stood on the water's edge squidging the mud between her toes. It was nice. Silly, the sort of thing you do when you're little. I came and did the same thing. It made me laugh.

"It tickles!" I said, giggling, and she looked at me and smiled again. I was—well, I wasn't exactly happy, but I thought for the first time in over a year that maybe it was possible to be happy. I don't ask for much, do I? Just a smile now and then. "Come on," I told her, "let's get our things off." I was getting excited—going swimming in the nuddy. Naughty girls! I went back to where it was dry and stripped off, but by the time I got down to my bra and knickers I was feeling uncomfortable again, because she was still just standing there in the mud. She was looking at me when I glanced across. She nodded across the water. "I think I saw a kingfisher," she said. I looked up but I missed that lovely flash of blue.

"Come on," I said.

"You go, I'm just getting my toes wet."

I paused. I didn't want to have nothing on anymore, not with her just standing there fully dressed. But then I thought, What the Hel, just do it, fuck her, and I took them off. I could see her glancing at me. You'd have thought even she'd have the sense not to stand there sneaking a look at my tits the way things were between us. But I tried to make light of it. I put my hands in the air and wriggled.

"Da-dah!" I said, and she laughed.

I felt so bare. I wished I had more doggy hair, like Hogni, to cover me up.

I walked down a few meters upstream to her and went slowly into the water. It was almost warm. I wanted to rush in and splash and scream but it was a bit hard with her standing there watching. I got deep enough to get my bum wet and then I just stood there wondering what to do next. And you know what she does? She turns away from the water, walks along the bank. I was thinking, At last, she's going to strip off and get in too, but all she did was walk a few meters past me upstream. It was a bit of a drop into the water from where she was and she stood there for a second before lifting up her skirt and stepping clumsily down again into the river.

So what was wrong with the place she'd started at? It was really awkward where she was.

"Aren't you going in?" I asked.

She didn't look at me. She kept her face the other way.

"Maybe in a bit," she said.

I stood there a second longer, feeling pretty cross by that time. I'd made the effort, hadn't I?

"So, Bryony," I said. "Why didn't you stay down there? That bit's all awkward."

She turned to look straight at me and she said, "Because I didn't care to stand in water that had gone past you."

I didn't think I'd heard her right at first. I said, "What?" And she repeated it, nice and clearly in case I'd been too stupid to understand.

"I don't want to have water that touched you touch me."

There was this terrible pause while it sank in how foul she was being. It was so deliberate, like she'd come all this way just to humiliate me. I blushed all over my body, I could feel it. You think you only blush with your face, but you don't. I could feel my whole body blushing. I put my arm across my chest. She was watching me to see what I'd do, like I was some sort of experiment. I didn't know what to do, it was out of the blue, I hadn't expected it.

I turned and splashed back to the bank. Stark naked—it just made me feel so stupid, so pathetic. I'm not the world's most gorgeous nude, I must have looked ridiculous. I was trying not to cry. I'd made an effort, hadn't I? I'd put myself out—it wasn't as though I *wanted* to go swimming with the miserable bitch. I was doing it for her, for us, and she just used it as a chance to humiliate me. I was in such a hurry to get out of the river I was slipping and stumbling. I fell over on the bank and hurt my foot, got covered in mud. She didn't come to help or anything. She just stood and watched me, her nasty little face taking it all in. I pulled on my top and my skirt, and turned to look at her. She'd turned away again. She was standing there gazing out across the water as if nothing had happened.

"So you think you're so much better than me, is that it?" I demanded. I wanted to go up and thump her one, but there was no way. She was strong, Bryony. She'd have killed me.

She cleared her throat.

"I am better than you," she said.

"Oh, why's that? Because you sit around all day doing nothing except sulking and pissing everyone off? Thanks, I don't see what's so great about being you. Your life looks pretty shit to me, lady. The only problem is, you make everyone else's life shit, too."

She was pretending to be calm but she'd turned red. "Maybe it is," she said in a shaky voice, and I knew how angry she was then. "But I'm still better than you, Gudrun." And she turned away as if that was that.

I just wanted to shout, "Fuck you!" and run away. I wish I had. It would have happened sooner or later, though. I wanted to hurt her, I suppose, and I knew how to do it, too.

"I have Sigurd, and you don't," I said. "That's what this is all about, isn't it? Gunar's not good enough. The whole world isn't good enough for you. It has to be every bloody thing you want and you want Sigurd. Well, you'll never have him, darling. He's mine. So you can sulk all you like."

I was still fighting back the tears but I felt better after that. There, I thought, it's out in the open now. Maybe she'll just fuck off and leave us in peace now. I snatched at my bits and pieces that were lying in the grass. I was out of there. Let her think on that!

"Sigurd's not half the man Gunar is," she said. I just laughed! Who did she think she was fooling? Herself? Not me, that's for sure. I just looked at her and shook my head. "Yeah, Gunar makes you so happy, doesn't he?" I told her. I waved my knickers at her and stalked off. You could hear it in her voice. I'd hit the nail right on the head.

But she hadn't finished yet. "Gunar came down into Crayley while Sigurd waited up here where it was safe. Odin would never let any but the best of all come down and get me."

Well, I could have told her a thing or two, but why bother? It was so pathetic! You don't love someone because they're better than anyone else. You love them because you love them. Because you love them and they love you back.

"Gunar'll be back soon, why don't you run home and jump into bed with him, if he's so fantastic?" I said. I knew perfectly well they hadn't been sleeping together. "If you love him so much," I said. It was a bit wet, but I couldn't say what I wanted to say. She was coming out of the water now. She was losing her calm face.

"I don't sleep with him, that's true. But at least it's my choice," she said.

"What's that supposed to mean?"

"It's not your choice that you don't sleep with Sigurd. You don't sleep with him because he doesn't want to. That's how much he loves you. No, Gudrun—you don't have anything I want, believe me."

I stood there feeling the blood drain out of me. How dare she! How dare she! And how dare he tell her that!

She looked at me with that nasty, crooked little smile on her face. "You've seen the way he looks at me, Gudrun," she said. "You know who Sigurd loves, I think."

I started to nod. "Oh, so that's it." I was shaking. So they'd been sleeping together—is that what she meant? I didn't dare ask. "No one loves you, Bryony, not even Sigurd. I don't know what happened between you two when he was down there, but I can tell you, you don't make him happy. So he loves you, does he? Yes, I've seen him look at you. If that's your idea of love, you can keep it. He loves me. And if you could see him when you're not there, you'd know it."

My heart was going like a drum. I thought, Oh, no, she's going to tell me, she's going to tell me that they're having an affair. I didn't want to hear that, but I couldn't tear myself away, I had to wait and hear it. It had been so long. . . .

I hadn't even realized I'd let the cat out of the bag.

She was looking at me like a hawk. She started to come toward me. I glanced over toward the house. Suddenly I felt very unsafe.

"What do you mean?" she demanded. "What do you mean about when he was down there with me? You know that? What has he told you?"

"About what?" But even as I spoke, I realized what I'd said. She didn't know that he'd been down there with her; she thought it was Gunar. It was a misunderstanding, you see. I didn't do it on purpose. I was so hurt, so angry. Even then it wasn't too late, but I didn't know the full story either. I only learned he'd been down there before much later on. I didn't know that we weren't talking about the same time.

"I . . . didn't know you knew about it," I said. Just for a moment I felt sorry for her again. So she knew! For how long? No wonder. I held out my arms. "Bryony, I'm so sorry."

"How do you mean? What do you mean?" She was right up to me. Suddenly she leaned forward and seized me by the arm. "Tell me what's happening!" she hissed. I was so scared. You should have seen her face. I thought she was going to kill me. That's why I told her—only because I thought she'd kill me. It wasn't what I wanted.

"But don't you know? You said . . ."

"Never mind what I said." She was grinding her teeth. Her face—I never saw anything like it. She'd been so dull for so long. Suddenly she looked like the devil. "Tell me," she hissed. "Tell me what you mean or I will kill you here, Gudrun. I'll pull you to pieces with my bare hands."

She meant it. I understood that. And she could do it, too. Her grip was like a dog's jaws on my arm. "That . . . that Sigurd changed shapes with Gunar. Bryony, it wasn't Gunar who came down to Crayley. It was Sigurd in Gunar's shape."

I felt sorry for her even as I was saying it. She loved Sigurd, that much was clear, but at least she'd thought Gunar had been brave enough to go down and fetch her out. Now she didn't even have that.

"It wasn't Gunar. It was Sigurd," I repeated. "Gunar could never do it. He tried and failed." I put my chin up and looked her in the eye. "Only Sigurd could go down there."

She'd turned as pale as ash. She was looking like murder; I

thought I was going to die. She let go of my arm, gripped my shoulder, and forced me to my knees. She stood bent over me, all twisted up and bent like an old woman, but an old woman with the strength of a machine. I thought she'd pierce my bones with her grip.

"Please don't hurt me, Bryony, it's not my fault, I didn't do anything," I begged, writhing under her hand. I wanted to ask her what she knew, because she knew something I didn't, that much was clear. But I was so confused and scared I didn't dare.

She looked down at me, then she put out an arm and helped me up. "No. You didn't do anything. Or maybe you did." She looked curiously into my face. "But tell me, Gudrun; why should I believe you? You know Sigurd loves me, you want me out of the way. Perhaps you're lying to me because you want to hurt me."

I was scared, you see. And maybe I did want to hurt her. I wasn't thinking straight. But once you start, you can't stop.

"He gave me your ring," I said. "I have it at home."

It was the worst thing I could have told her. I was cursing myself even while it came out of my lips. She literally sagged. I didn't think she could have gone paler than she was, but she did. Then she shook herself up and drew me to my feet. "Show me," she demanded.

"Bryony, I can't. Sigurd made me promise."

"Do you think I care about his promises? Show me. I have to know if this is true. Show me. Now!"

What could I do? She was a warrior, she could have killed me—I think she would have been glad to. I led her up the hill. There wasn't a word said. She marched me back, pushing me firmly in the back when I was slacking, like a parent encouraging a slow child. Grimhild met us in the passage and yapped something. Neither of us replied, but she knew something was going on because she stood at the bottom of the stairs while I led Bryony up to my room and took out my jewelry box. I hadn't looked at it for ages. That ring was a beautiful thing, not valuable in any way, but she had given it to Sigurd down there, and I guess it meant everything to her. Heaven alone knows why I didn't let him give it back to her.

She took it in her hand and nodded.

"Bryony . . ."

She took no notice of me, she might not have even heard. She held the ring in the palm of her hand and stared at it. It must have been the last straw. What had she got left now? She glanced briefly at me, dropped the ring on the carpet, turned, and walked out. I waited until she was halfway down the corridor and then ran to the door. I was afraid she might go out to look for Gunar and kill him, or that she would try to kill herself, but she was turning into her room. I waited for her door to close and then ran out to call Gunar and Hogni back. It was at a head now. Nothing was going to be the same. It was out of our hands.

48

betrayal

Bryony could have ended it then. She knew how strong she was, she could have held her breath until she died just lying there if her traitorous body wouldn't snatch at the air as soon as she lost consciousness. Her spirit was so heavy she couldn't haul herself out of bed, but she felt, building up inside her, the power to destroy everything.

She lay raging silently at her fate for a long while, until she fell into a black unconsciousness. When she woke, Gunar was standing over her.

"Gudrun told me," he said. He looked down at her, licked his lips nervously. "You shouldn't have hurt my sister," he began. But Bryony's eyes flashed.

"Gunar," she said. "Get out of here or I'll kill you."

"You?" he said, trying to laugh.

"Just go."

Gunar hesitated. He knew some of her strength, only some of it. She'd lived her life as a hunter, fighting for her life, but she had never shown him what she was really like. For the past months she had been depressed, weak. He thought of her like that still. He reached out to take her hand, but in a second

Bryony was out of the bed. He went flying backward and slammed into the wall ten feet away.

"Go," she repeated. He got to his feet, his breath rasping in pain and fear, stared at her in amazement, and left the room hurriedly.

Yes, she could do it now, easily. But there was unfinished business. Sigurd would come to her at last. Nothing would happen until then.

At some time during that day, a servant poked her head round the door with a tray. Bryony sat up and blazed silently at the woman, who quailed and left without a second's more fuss. Later still Gudrun opened it and looked in. Bryony got out of the bed and walked toward her; Gudrun saw what was coming and fled. Bryony could hear her feet on the stairs, making it to safety. But there would be no safety anywhere for any of them once she decided to act. Perhaps they would kill her first. They wanted to by this time, she was sure of that. But first, Sigurd. They would let him try first. He would be on his way already. She'd wait that long; so would they.

The secret was a year old. In keeping it from Bryony, they had suppressed their own thoughts, too. They had gagged it, smothered it, suffocated it; now the gag was off and suddenly there were words everywhere. Gunar and Gudrun, talking, talking, talking. Hogni was there too, arguing for Sigurd's good faith, but his words sounded hollow in his own ears. He knew the Sigurd before Crayley and the one after; he knew the difference between a closed heart and an open one. What had happened down there? Why was Sigurd so different since he came back? Theirs was not the only secret, that much was clear. Deals had been struck, plans had been made, understandings reached behind their backs. Now was the accounting hour. They had come clean; it was time for Sigurd to tell his story too. Each one of them in their hearts felt that somehow he had betrayed them.

But Gudrun did not want to lose her man, and Gunar did not want to lose his wife. He'd had a month with Bryony before she met Sigurd. It seemed to him that she had loved him then. He wanted her to love him again.

Gudrun was onto Sigurd as soon as he arrived. They took a walk in the garden, where she made her accusations. Sigurd denied nothing but admitted nothing, and she left him more frustrated than ever. Then it was Gunar's turn. He bit back his angry words; he had a favor to ask. He wanted Sigurd to talk to Bryony, to try and bring her round.

"I got her for you, do you want me to keep her for you as well?" asked Sigurd, half joking but with a flash of anger.

Gunar hated him for that remark, but he swallowed his pride and begged.

"I need you again, yes, to keep her for me," he said. Sigurd dropped his eyes.

"She knows now," he said. "Do you think I can do any good? It was me who betrayed her."

"Not betrayed, not her, Sigurd," said Gunar. Sigurd understood what he meant—that it was Gunar he had deceived. He looked at his old friend closely, then nodded.

"I'll go and speak to her, for your sake, Gunar," he said. "But no good'll come of it."

He turned to go, but Gunar took his arm, thinking that Sigurd meant some kind of threat.

"Don't let me down, Sigurd," he begged.

Sigurd looked him in the eye. "I'll never betray you, Gunar," he said. Gunar smiled grimly, thinking that he already had. Sigurd left him and went upstairs.

Sigurd knocked, waited for a moment, then opened the door and went in. She was sitting up in bed. Their eyes met for the first time in months and bound them like one flesh. He closed the door and went to sit on the bed by her side.

"Won't you come out, Bryony?" he asked. "The rain's been and gone. It's washed clean outside. The wind. The clouds," he said, and he smiled slightly.

Bryony looked at him in amazement. Even now he could keep up this game! "Have you come to torment me?" she said bitterly. "I know what happened. You made me love you, you promised me this world, and then you gave me away like a scrap. You betrayed me! All this time. Who has ever been betrayed like that—to come to me in the shape of another man and give me to him?"

"It wasn't me who did it, Bryony," he said quietly. And then he told her the story—the whole thing, from the day he left her in Crayley to get the dragon skin. Of the war, of his plans to get her out. How he woke up with no memory of her and everything that had happened since; of Grimhild the witch. The whole story—the theft of his memories by the bitch and her servant, of the door in the ruined outbuilding, the slogans on the wall; of his death in the lake, kicking for air while Ida beat at his face for hour after hour. Of his falling in love with Gudrun, and the miracle of his memory coming back that day he saw her in the conservatory.

"It was Jenny," he said. "Remember? She flew through my eye."

Bryony scowled. She had seen it; and then Jenny had left her forever. "But how did you forget? How is such a thing possible?" She sat up in bed and stared him in the face, as if she was trying to see the truth. Then, carefully, unsure of what she was doing but hoping that this could all be made right again, she put her arms around him and hugged him, gently at first, but then harder as he hugged her back. For so long the ice had held their hearts; now it melted. They ran their hands over each other, through their hair, felt each other's faces, and kissed and breathed and wept in the other's scent. All this time they had both been wanting this, every day of their lives, every time they saw each other, every time they thought of each other, at every scent and sight and sound of each other. It was like water to their parched hearts. And so they were reunited at last, felt their hearts beating against each other, and became themselves again.

"I love you," she whispered.

"And I love you, and always have!" he whispered back fervently.

She let him go to look at his face. "But you waited all this time? You never said! Why didn't you say?"

Sigurd smiled sadly—this wasn't over yet—and shrugged. "I'm two men in one body," he whispered. He was telling her something dreadful, but she didn't realize yet what had happened to him.

But Bryony was hardly listening. She let him go and jumped out of bed. She ran to her cupboard and began scooping up a few handfuls of clothes.

"Now we go," she said. She turned to him, her face blazing fiercely. She didn't understand, that would come later. But it was unthinkable that this should go on. "It wasn't you, I understand. That little bitch did this to us. But now we're together again. Sigurd, get ready. We're going to drive out of here and never come back. I love you—I love you so much! Now we're together again." She gazed triumphantly at him. "Even this didn't part us!"

But Sigurd sat still and stared at the floor.

"What are you doing? Let's go! Sigurd?"

"Bryony." How could he explain the impossible? "I can't do anything anymore."

"Then don't resist me!"

"I love her, too. You see? I've given her my heart."

Bryony tried to laugh. "No one can have two hearts, Sigurd."

"Monsters do," he said, and smiled weakly at her.

"And Sigurd, which of us . . . which of us do you love the best?"

Sigurd lifted his head, glad of a simple truth. "You were my first love, Bryony. I was Sigurd when I fell in love with you; I love you more than anything. But I can't betray her. I can't betray anyone. Not you, not Gudrun, not even Gunar."

"That slug, that shit? You put him on the same level as me? And then you say you can't betray?"

"I never betrayed you. It was . . . someone else. You see?" he begged. But true though this was, it meant nothing to her, or, indeed, to him. He had been tricked, interfered with in a way that should never have been possible; but it was still him who had done it.

Bryony said, "Yes, you were tricked. But this is you, now. This is your decision. Her or me. Now you can decide. This life or life with me. You're yourself now, Sigurd. What happened was done to you as well as to me. Now you choose. Who do you love more?"

"I love you more, you know that. But I can't leave. There's nothing else to be done. We just have to live this life, do you see? And make the best of it. People do, don't they, Bryony? They make the best of things. That's what we have to do."

"You'll let that little bitch conquer us and get her way? After all the things you've done? You choose *that*?"

"I can't . . . I can't choose. I don't . . . I don't do that, any more. Bryony," he begged. "I can't *move*. I can't move," he whispered.

"You want me to live like this? This half life? In another prison? You want me to watch you cooing with Gudrun? You want me sleeping with Gunar, you want me to have his babies? Sigurd, you must be mad! Do as I say!" she commanded. "You will leave her. You *will* come with me!"

"No," he said flatly.

She thought she'd kill him then. She let out a terrible, strangled cry and rushed at him, but he caught her in his arms and hugged her hard, while she flailed and struck at him uselessly. Then he whispered in her ear.

"Bryony, Bryony. I'm going mad."

She stopped struggling and stood still, listening.

"I have too many lives in me. It's killing me. I've been too many people, I've died too often." How could anyone understand? No one had ever suffered the injury done to Sigurd. If they had, no one would ever have won their memory back. Jenny Wren had killed him all over again.

"I'm not anyone anymore. I've become no one."

"That's just confusion, Sigurd," she said calmly.

"No, it's true. The dragon, the clone. Odin. My father! They've all claimed a part of me. Bryony, I'm lost, I'm lost in here. You must help me before I destroy everything."

She pushed his arms away and looked at him sitting there like a little child on the chair, his head low, trying to watch her. "What do you want me to do?"

"I don't know. I've had too many lives. I'm so, so lost." He buried his face in his hands and wept.

She stared at him for a while. "We should be in love. Everything is as simple as that." She shook her head. "We should have stayed in Hel."

Sigurd nodded. "We'll love again, in Hel," he agreed. He began to sob, his face dissolving in tears and snot. She sat there watching him, part of her in pity, part of her in love, part of her in disgust. How had she ever fallen for this weak thing? She had an inkling, just an inkling of what had been done to him, how he had been ruined. He had not an ounce of betrayal in him, but he had been made to betray. Two lives, each in opposition to the other. In the gap in between those two lives, Sigurd could not move, could not choose, could not act. He above all people was for the one vision, the one life. Without that he was nothing.

"You're not who you were," she said at last. "You've been beaten by that sad old bitch. All big bones and shit. Go on— fuck off. Take your miserable tears with you."

Sigurd stood up, looked at her with a dreadful expression that broke her heart all over again. He left the room. As he reached the door, she called softly, "But I love you forever, my darling." He paused, then left. She never knew if he'd heard. It was the last time she ever spoke to him.

Bryony sat still a long time, thinking. She thought to herself, Let Gudrun have what was left of him, let her remember every day how her family had ruined something that was once so splendid. But Sigurd was still Sigurd; she still loved him with all her heart and soul and he loved her back. There was still one way for them to be together. He had said it himself: They would love again in Hel.

It was time to die.

49

truth and lies

Death is not unexplored. Jesus went there and back, so did Odin. Sigurd made the journey at least twice. But where did they go? In those places, can lovers be united? Yes, surely you can love—Bryony was the proof of that. Death is a place where more than one can be and now it was time for her to go home, and to take her Sigurd with her.

Bryony lay in her room for the rest of the day and all that night, but she did not sleep. As soon as the light was in the sky, she called for Gunar.

He came up soon enough. He'd been waiting for me. He still wanted me. Imagine! You steal something, you destroy it, and then you want it back whole. What kind of man is that?

He didn't come near me though, and he was armed. He had nothing to fear, although he didn't know it. He was staying behind.

He peered at me anxiously. Poor, dishonest Gunar!

"Sit down, Gunar, and listen," I said.

He sat, never taking his eyes off me. He loves me and fears that I am his death. No death for you, Gunar! You're just the messenger.

I began by telling him true things. True things make the best lies—the lie is in what is left out. How Sigurd had ridden down into Crayley before he knew him. How we'd been lovers. How we'd sworn to belong to each other forever. We were children in love. He believed me. Of course. It made sense. He'd seen us together. He knew how Sigurd once was and what he'd turned into. The truth—it's irresistible.

Then I moved on to lies born out of the truth. How Sigurd and I made our plans, dreamed our dreams. How we planned to emerge and take over the world—to conquer the country! Our ambition knew no bounds. Unite the country! Make it whole under us. The whole world would share our love!

Gunar frowned, but didn't argue. Then back to the truth; how Sigurd had gone back up to fetch the dragon skin to rescue me.

"It's true," said Gunar. "He was looking for the skin, he told us that." I could see him thinking, that clever man Gunar! He *wanted* to believe. You see, Sigurd was in his way. Sigurd had always been in his way. But Gunar was a good man. You understand? He could not act unfairly, he had to *believe* that what he did was right. And that he did easily, politician that he was. He believed that sending Sigurd down in his shape to get me was right. He believed that taking a woman who had fallen in love with another man, against her will, without her even knowing, was right. Yes, Gunar, you're gullible enough when it comes to fooling yourself for the sake of yourself. You even want to feel righteous about your wickedness. An overdose of sincerity—how good that makes him feel!

"And yet Sigurd married Gudrun," he pondered.

"Politics, Gunar! He came up here and what did he find?

You were in the way. He wanted your organization, your government. He knows a good job when he sees it. He did what he had to do. You see him with Gudrun almost every day. Do you think he loves her?"

"He did once."

"He grows tired of the deceit," I said.

He shook his head. It did seem to him that Sigurd had once loved Gudrun.

"He loved me once, but he forgot me quickly enough. He loves easily; he forgets easily. Now he has forgotten her."

He half nodded. Yes, that could be true. Sigurd had loved me, he had forgotten me. He had loved her; now he did not love her. At least not with a love Gunar could understand.

I shrugged, as if to say, The mind of Sigurd! Who knows the nature of his deceit, it comes in many layers. Gunar nodded. Whatever the explanation, he could see that there was deceit in Sigurd.

Then I began the real lies, the big lies. How when Sigurd came down a second time in Gunar's shape, he'd told me at once who he was. At first I didn't believe, I had no idea such things were possible, I'd lived away from the world, I knew so little of it. But Sigurd knew things about me, about us. He soon convinced me.

"Why?" Gunar could not understand. Why had his friend appeared to deceive me, and yet deceived him?

"Gunar—we were lovers. We are lovers." Ah, poor Gunar— see him turn pale at that! "He said there was a kingdom. It was in the way. I would be queen, he would be king. Don't you see how he's changed, even you must be able to see that? He's tired of this game. A man like that—do you think he'd be content to be anything but the highest and most powerful of all? That's what he was made for, that's what he is. He's conquered everyone else. There is only one man left in the way, Gunar. You."

And Gunar began to nod. Yes, he could see it. "His time is over, you see," I said. The truth again. "The time for heroes and monster killers and generals is gone. It's your time now, Gunar—the time of politicians and lawmakers. He wants what you have."

And Gunar, poor weak Gunar, who wanted so very much to have what Sigurd had, found it so, so easy to believe that Sigurd wanted what he had.

"He wants to rule," he said. He was amazed that he hadn't seen it before.

"He's fooled us all, Gunar. Do you think he can't fool you, as well? His ambition never stops. He gave his wife my ring—*my* ring!" I never needed to act out anger. "He swore to me he'd stop sleeping with her to get me back on his side and broke his promise the night he came back up and handed me over to you. It made me feel dirty, Gunar, to marry you just because Sigurd had ordered it. I knew nothing of these things. Every promise he ever made he broke. He has all the charm and the good words, but we are little things to him. His heart is full of lies."

Gunar, poor weak Gunar, thought hard about it. But you see how much sense it made? He had no idea about Grimhild and her tricks but he knew that Sigurd had once been open and free, and that now he'd become withdrawn and secretive. Why else? He had secrets, that much was clear. What other secrets could there be but these ones, which made so much sense? These were the secrets that offered Gunar what he wanted: Sigurd out of the way. They offered him his dreams come true.

"I can't believe it," he said. But he already did.

"What can we do about it?" he asked. But he already knew.

Before he left, Bryony told him one more secret, just in case he needed to know. In between Sigurd's shoulder blades was a spot the dragon's blood had not touched. There and there only could Sigurd be pierced.

Gunar's eyes flashed. She knew that? That was the final proof; they had been intimate. Everything else followed from that.

50

cleansing

With Gunar gone, Bryony lay back on her bed. Outside the sun was only just beginning to warm the air. She had nothing more to do until darkness.

So sorry, Bryony! Sorry, Sigurd! Sorry, Gunar and Gudrun. Things haven't worked out the way they should. You're all people of goodwill—how has it gone so far? Bryony lies still and stares at the ceiling. The heat is rising. Wet fingers of it creep into her, under her clothes, behind her eyes. Good weather for a murder. She takes off her top, but she's still melting. She strips and lies there naked while the sweat pools between her breasts. So beautiful, Bryony. So ill-used, so deadly. A creature of vision and imagination, she needed to be handled with care—more care than Gunar knew how to provide.

Gunar and Hogni sit hunched together in a far part of the grounds, arguing and agreeing, agreeing and then arguing again, unable to believe where they are headed but unable to turn away. In turn they try new lines of thought, new explanations, but all lead to the same place. Sigurd is lying, Sigurd has his own agenda. After each excursion they look into each other's eyes and see the same thing: death. They wonder that such a thing is possible. But it is not merely possible. It is the only thing that can happen.

Sigurd himself sits alone by the lake, remembering. Down there he lies—he can see the spot. He winces as he recalls the oar beating down over and over again onto his naked face. Generous Jenny Wren gave him everything from that night.

He is at his lowest ebb, but even now he is not defeated. He could stand up if he wished, lift the world on his fingertip, and send it hurtling in another direction. If Andvari's ring is the twister, he is the straightener, and he is the stronger of the two. And yet he has chosen submission. Is the world not good enough for him? Surely he can't be hoping to wash away our sins with his blood—the guilt he would leave behind is a sin in itself. No. The truth is Sigurd is falling in love again. He can't help it. And this time, it's total. Now he loves everything—not just his lovers and his friends, not just mankind or nature, but everything: the dirt, the shit, the depression. He loves murder and hatred and death. His spirit had been crushed by the betrayal of having lived two lives and he loves even that. Sigurd was finally falling in love with all of creation. He has seen the future and he is not in it. He goes forward toward it as he must, glad or not glad, but with an open heart.

As night became deep, like the vampire, Bryony rose. She knew what to do. Sigurd had told her everything. Now she went to see for herself.

Grimhild did not know how, but she understood well enough that somehow Sigurd had recaptured his stolen memories. He'd told her—taken her on his knee, held her tight in one hand, and explained to her. She had licked away his tears and pretended not to understand, but her little doggy heart has not been still since that day. She has experience of how such discoveries tend to pan out. On the day Bryony found out about her betrayal, Grimhild had peeped in through the door and seen terrible danger in the white face staring back at her. She had taken to sleeping in the bluebell woods lately. Her house was no longer safe.

She was rusty now, with lack of exercise; but when she saw Bryony coming through the woods in the dead of night, far beyond the house where no one could watch, she turned and ran, but felt in no immediate danger. She was a match for most things on two legs. To her surprise and horror there were feet behind her tail in moments, and, though she put on a burst of speed, she was swept up into the arms of her enemy in a moment.

She turned and snapped, but Bryony dealt her a blow to the muzzle of such violence that she lost two of her remaining teeth, felt the bones in her neck open and close, and her eyes pop in her head.

"I eat bitches like you for breakfast," Bryony told her.

She carried the trembling little dog to the folly. Grimhild tried to bark; Bryony snapped her forearm just above the wrist and held her muzzle tight while she cried.

"No," she said. "You've lost everything. If you want to live, if you want your children to live, call your servant."

Grimhild had no choice; but there was hope. Bryony was surely no match for Ida, who had been improved long ago. She had the power of a bear in her fat red arms. Grimhild regretted now not changing herself; she'd been thinking of it lately. Her children needed her, and she was getting old. Perhaps a more youthful clone . . . ? Ten or twenty years off, a nip and a tuck, some extra muscle hidden away, why not? Her children, too. They had become . . . well, a little too complicated, perhaps? Maybe it would be better to wipe the slate clean and start again, with a Gudrun who didn't love Sigurd, and a Gunar who hadn't fallen so foolishly in love with this disastrous young woman?

She called Ida up with three short barks. They had planned for such an emergency as this. Bryony did not know, but of course she guessed. She could have no way of knowing how powerful Ida was—but Ida had no way of knowing how powerful she was. She was the true beast, daughter of Odin, born in Hel. When Ida came storming out of the lift with an ax in her hands, her flat mouth set in a hard straight line, her neck bulging with fury, her face and arms red with angry blood, Bryony stepped neatly behind her, slipped a cord around her neck, kicked the ax out of her hands, and strangled her quickly and quietly, holding Grimhild the while between her knees, where she squeezed just tight enough to crack the old dog's jaw. Don't doubt it; Bryony had no pity left.

Down they go, the girl and the bitch, into the magic space hidden inside the door—and there it all is. If Bryony had any doubt of Sigurd's words, it is dispelled now. Rows of Gunars, Hognis, and Gudruns, all waiting to be sparked by their mistress. By their sides, the banks of equipment with their latest memories stored. Little Grimhild whimpers as Bryony's finger strays toward the plugs. She turns her pleading doggy eyes up to her captor: Spare my babies! But Bryony has already moved on. The murder of futures is not yet begun. She turns a corner—and there they are, the Sigurds, eight of them, all perfect, all beautiful, even with their pruney underwater skins.

Ahhh . . . here's a thought. Was she tempted? Grimhild yaps and nods. There's enough for everyone! One for Gudrun, one for Bryony—two, if she wants. Why not? He is the best after all. Doesn't every woman deserve the best? You could start an industry! Grow your own! Roll up! Built like a stallion, moves like a panther, loves like a hero.

Bryony stares in disgust. Sigurd after Sigurd, mindless, unloved, unloving; not Sigurd at all, but robots of flesh, ghosts with trick blood. It is with this kind of clumsiness that Grimhild has ruined everything.

She ties the little dog up in a corner, binds her mouth with tape. Grimhild has a bit of a cold, the sniffles. She chokes for breath and has to curl her lips up at the front to get a wisp of air; maybe she'll suffocate. Who cares? Not Bryony. She is only concerned not to be disturbed while she works.

DNA is fragile enough, but a copy is kept in every single cell. Bryony has her work cut out if she wants to make sure that Sigurd is not only dead, but stays dead. Murder is not enough. She could chop him up and dice him to a pulp and it would do no good. Molecular destruction is what Bryony is after—every cell of him must go, every molecule must be broken up. She intends to reduce Sigurd and all his copies to their very atoms. Her method? Fire, of course, the gift of Loki, god of lies. Fire, a lie so complete it renders the truth unrecoverable. It is the only thing that will unwrap Sigurd so totally that no future can ever know him again.

But where is this fire? She could call to Loki himself—he'd give her a light for a trick like this one, surely? But no need—Bryony knows where the house armoory is. There are flamethrowers there. A long job, of course—but there's not even the need for that. As she walks past the warm tanks she sees Grimhild's newest installation: an incinerator. How thoughtful! Puzzled by how Sigurd had recovered his memory and knowing nothing of Jenny Wren, she had nevertheless come to the conclusion that someone, somehow, had stolen the memories that she had left in that empty bottle eighteen months ago. Ida had communicated to her how unpleasant the business of bashing the corpse down underwater had been. An incinerator was the obvious answer. Ashes remember nothing.

In vain does Grimhild whimper and beg. If only she could speak, she would make her promises, offer her deals. She could recover the old Sigurd, put him back in the past before all this happened, wipe Gudrun out of his mind, and give him back to Bryony as he once was. Too late! Bryony is beyond trust now, there will be no deals, only an end to things. Grimhild watches. Murder! She tries to shout, but all that comes out is a strangled whimper. Ah, Grimhild, those who tell no secrets say no truths. You should have written *that* up on your wall as well. All she can do is watch as Bryony carefully empties the tanks and with an air of careful concentration incinerates the silent Sigurds one by one. When each one is done burning, she rakes over the ashes to make sure nothing too big remains. Only when they are turned to powder is she happy with her work and moves on to the next.

Four hours later, the job done, Bryony turns her attention to the machinery that houses his memories. Turn them off? Not good enough; there will certainly be batteries. Once again she has no need to visit the armory. Grimhild's laboratory is armed well enough, and a brief search soon reveals the weaponry. Thoughtfully, Bryony takes her pick. It's confined down here, she doesn't want to die just yet—she has to make sure her love is going with her first. She chooses a shotgun with explosive shells. One after the other, she pops off the machines. They bleed, they fizz, they cough up their guts, they sparkle and burst into flames, but not one of them cries out or begs for mercy. They have no mouths. When she is certain they are all dead and broken, she rakes through the wreckage, looking for hard drives, brain matter, or nervous tissue that might somehow have escaped the carnage. Anything suspicious goes into the furnace. She is thorough, is Bryony. She has learned that there is no such thing as a second chance.

But the other clones, of Gudrun, Gunar, and Hogni, those she does not touch. See, Grimhild, there is hope—not all is lost. She does not want to take anything of them with her. Even the spirits of those silent ghosts Bryony will not tolerate in Hel.

Outside the day is already warming up when she comes back to where her captive lies and looks down at her. Grimhild whines and cringes. Is this it? The end? No. Bryony has no desire to pollute the loving place where she and Sigurd are about to journey with the likes of her. She takes Grimhild up to the surface, tiptoes up to her room, sliding quietly past the kitchen where the Niberlins are already at breakfast. Carefully she ties the little dog up with parcel tape—mouth, legs, and over the eyes.

"Don't worry, I'm not going to kill them. I've had enough of them in life," Bryony promises. She locks her captive in the wardrobe and holds a finger to her mouth. "So long as you stay quiet."

The job done, she goes to stand at the window. She is tired, she could sleep for a thousand years, but she has sworn that her next sleep will be the one that never ends.

51

3rd death

They came upon him in the garden, Gunar, Hogni, and a loyal guard. The brothers did not want his blood on their hands. Sigurd was sitting on a low wall to one side of the pond. It was teeming with tadpoles and water insects, newts hanging in the water like miniature submarines, thick with weeds and flowering rushes. Sigurd stared into its depths. It was lovely.

They did not try to hide how serious this was.

"Sigurd," said Hogni. "We need to talk."

He turned with a little sigh. He felt hopeful. Perhaps they were going to tease his troubles out of him, break his secrets free. Things had changed, now they were changing again. He needed to talk. He nodded. Hogni turned and led the way down the garden along the stream that led from the lake down to the river. The water chatted and giggled over the stones. Behind Sigurd's back, the guard lifted his weapon silently to his shoulder and took aim.

"We've been speaking to Bryony," said Hogni. Sigurd nodded, his eyes to the ground, the water in his ears.

"She told you?" said Sigurd.

"Told us what?"

The guard opened fire at twenty rounds a second. He hit Sigurd exactly between the shoulder blades. A plume of blood spurted into the air, bright with life. Sigurd fell; the assassin followed him down with the gun—twenty rounds a second, the appalling clatter of gunfire echoing off the walls of the house. As he fell, Sigurd twisted round so that the guard had to walk sideways to follow through into the wound. As his hand touched the ground, Sigurd found a small branch lying in the grass. He flicked his wrist, sent it spinning through the air so fast it was a blur. It struck the guard directly in his eye, pierced it, smashed the socket, passed through the brain, and thudded on the back of the skull, denting it from the inside. The man fell to the ground, dead before he hit it.

Sigurd lay there, half twisted round on his front with one arm underneath him. The blood had stopped pumping and was barely oozing now in a darkening pool around him. Gunar looked over to Hogni, who stared appalled at what they had done.

At their feet Sigurd squirmed. In a sluggish movement he put his hands on either side of his body as if he would push himself up. Gunar and Hogni looked on in horror. It was so unreasonable, so sickening that he was still alive. This was just a final reaction of the nerves, surely? They wanted this to stop, now, for it to be over. They were good, they wanted no pain, no knowledge for him of what they'd done. Please, god, let it be quick! But Sigurd began slowly to climb to his feet. His movements were already speeding up.

Neither man was armed. The dead guard's gun lay two meters from Gunar.

Sigurd laughed weakly. He put his hands on his knees and bent over, supporting himself as he regained his strength.

"Two hearts!" shouted Gunar. "Like the dragon—he has two hearts."

Sigurd wheezed and shook his head. "I don't need a heart, Gunar," he said. He laughed. "Look, Hogni, look, Gunar! You thought you could kill me, but I don't even need to breathe!" He shook his head weakly from side to side and laughed. Gunar and Hogni stared, terrified. What was he? Nothing human, surely. Quickly, without thinking, they followed the training they'd had since childhood and separated, one on each side of him, to get him surrounded.

Sigurd hiccuped. He raised his head, smiled, and nodded, then turned to face Hogni.

"You first?" he said. And he opened his arms as if to embrace him. Hogni took a small step back, but Sigurd took a step after him, so quick, so vital and responsive, that Hogni knew he could never escape. Against his will, his eyes drifted behind Sigurd, to where Gunar was crouching down, silently lifting the gun with shaking fingers. He was no soldier, it was obvious to anyone what he was doing, but Sigurd did not turn. He smiled at Hogni and shook his head as if to say, Whatever next!

He knows, thought Hogni. Maybe he'd known all along. His eyes filled with tears. It was too late now.

"Don't cry, Hogni," said Sigurd gently. "Don't do this and then cry."

Behind him Gunar lifted the weapon. Sigurd's head twitched slightly to the side.

"Oh, Gunar, this was badly done," he said. Gunar fired. Down went Sigurd. Gunar did as the guard had done, followed him to the ground, but his aim was poor and half the bullets ricocheted off Sigurd's skin. Hogni ran across and seized the gun off him. He went to the fallen man and, kneeling over him, forced the muzzle into the wound in his back. He held the trigger steadily down and fired, twenty rounds a second, twisting the barrel this way and that, from side to side and up and down. Sigurd jerked and twisted. The bullets were passing through his flesh and striking his skin—you could see them battering it from the inside. Sigurd's face began to lose its features, his limbs their structure as the body filled with a pulp of bones, blood and flesh.

When Hogni had done, he dropped the gun and fumbled in his pocket. He took out a small device, no bigger than a large marble. Bending over the body, his face a pale sheet, still unable to believe that they could get away with this, he put the device through the hole in Sigurd's back. With the barrel of the gun he pushed it as far he could, deep into the body. Then he and Gunar ran fast into the house.

Meanwhile the gun's voice had been heard. Gudrun, who knew nothing of this plot, had been locked in her room, but had managed to climb out. As they went in, she ran past them. They had to turn and catch her, drag her inside between them, screaming and kicking, begging and weeping, striking out at them. She wriggled free; they doubled back, caught hold of her, dived through a doorway.

Sigurd exploded. The contents of his skin erupted out of the hole in his back ten meters into the air, a red plume of blood. The skin vanished from the grass. In the dying rumble of sound that followed, drifting into quietness, it reappeared above them, drifting to the ground through the disturbed air. Then, as silence fell, the air began to turn pink. It was a rain of tiny droplets, a mist of blood falling from the sky. Shaking her captors free, Gudrun ran out into the open, held out her hands, raised her face, and stood there, letting him soak into her. Slowly she turned red with blood.

The mist fell, all that was left of Sigurd. He was eighteen years old.

Out of the house now stepped Bryony. The plot was almost worked through. Before any of them could move she joined Gudrun in the blood-mist and opened her coat. Around her waist she had strapped explosives.

"It's what you think," she assured them. "If you want to live, run."

She gave them time to seize Gudrun and disappear behind the first trees before she pressed the transmitter on her wrist and went to join her lover forever.

Here's a peek at *Sara's Face*
A timely new tale by Melvin Burgess

Just about everyone knows the story of Jonathon Heat and Sara Carter. It's common currency, revealed to us through a thousand newspaper headlines, magazine articles, news bulletins, TV shows, and an endless commentary on the radio. Heat's sheer celebrity is one factor that made the story of such universal interest; while he still had one, his was perhaps the most famous face on the planet. We've been hearing about him for years but the strange nature of his crimes and his terrible fate have made this particular story his most lasting legacy to us.

Sara is different. She comes down to us as a mystery, a figure without explanation. Her refusal or inability to speak have led to endless speculation about her, but the story of her hopes and dreams and her role in the terrible way they were fulfilled, remains elusive. How much did she plan? Was she in control the whole time, or was she just the innocent victim of Heat and his surgeon, Wayland Kaye? It's the purpose of this book to try and cast some light on the girl herself.

As someone used to trying to create an impression of truth, investigating actual truth has proved to be a tricky affair. Both Heat and Sara seem to have been master dissemblers themselves, with only very shaky ideas of who they really were or what they wanted to become. Heat, of course, is in prison. Sara's fate is more open to speculation. Since her failure to come and give evidence in court, rumors have circulated widely; madness or death, or the terrible nature of her injuries seem to be the most likely options, but to this day, no one is really sure. I'm a novelist doing a journalist's job, and my brief has been to get at what people thought and felt, and what their motivations were, as much as simply to describe the unfolding of events. What goes on in people's hearts is a notoriously tricky thing to know. I've done my best to understand rather than speculate, but frankly I've been amazed at how little positive truth you come across after even the most thorough investigation. Everything that happens is filtered through opinion and memory, and of course by how much other people want you to know. No two people remember anything in exactly the same way. I've done my best to verify everything before I came to write it. Most of all, I've done my best to be true to Sara.

I've been able to speak to almost all the people involved in the events that took place in Cheshire in 2005, except of course the two main protagonists. Even with all the contacts in my hand, Sara has proved to be incredibly elusive. She told so many different versions of what was going on to so many different people, it's as if she has done her best to extinguish her real self in favor of her own legend. Perhaps that's the nature of her tragedy. Like a religious figure or a character from myth, it's nothing she ever said or did but her story itself that forces her on our attention and inspires our imagination. In that sense, she more than achieved her ambition of making fame itself a work of art.

• • •

Sara seems to have been a very popular girl while she was at primary school and stayed that way for the first couple of years at high school. After that her popularity wavered. Some people thought she was just plain weird, others that her behavior was put on for effect. Either way, she was too strong a taste for many of her contemporaries, but those who did love her loved her dearly and were loved in return. Even when she rose above them, she never forgot who her friends were, or what friendship meant to her.

Sara and Janet Calley met each other in their first year at high school and that was it—they were friends for life. For a couple of years they did everything together, ran around the corridors giggling at the same jokes, read the same books, sometimes even wore the same clothes. Anyone who saw them would have thought of them as two peas in a pod, but Janet already knew that Sara was altogether different. When, in Year 9, Sara suddenly turned into a different person, Janet wasn't in the least bit surprised.

Sara shot up. In a few months she put on over thirty centimeters. Her figure, which seemed to have been holding puberty at bay so far, suddenly bloomed. After a brief spell of acne her face healed in a few weeks into the clearest skin, without blemish and so finely grained that not a pore was visible to the naked eye. Her flawless skin was one of the things that attracted the attention of Jonathon Heat, who had always had an open complexion.

At the same time she developed a scent all of her own.

"I noticed it on her one day," said Janet, "and I asked her what she was wearing."

"Can you smell it too?" she asked. "It's not anything. I didn't even wash this morning."

They were both astonished by this trick of nature and went to lock themselves in the toilet so they could smell the skin on her arms, her legs, on her back and shoulder, and verify that it was her skin all over. It was true. She smelled all over of salted almonds and musk.

"She never had to wear deodorant all day after a shower," said Janet, shaking her head in amazement. "I never came across anything like it. Her own perfume! She used to say she was fed up with it, she'd like to smell of something else, but really, she was very proud to be her own perfume. They could have made a fortune if they ever put it in a bottle."

As a result of her height and her looks, Sara suddenly began to attract a great deal of attention from boys, which she suffered with a kind of bemused tolerance, always keeping them at arm's length. Later, when her face was known across the world, the newspapers tried to make out that she'd slept with a great many of those boys—that she was a sex maniac, almost. Janet always maintained that it wasn't true.

"She wasn't like that at all. In fact she used to have this joke about how she was going to be the last virgin on earth, because she was still holding out when all the rest of us were already at it. But I suppose it's her own fault. She liked it that people thought that about her. I had to promise not to tell anyone she was a virgin, although actually she was very proud and wanted only to do it with someone special."

"It'd be bad for my image if people knew," she said. In fact Sara was a virgin right up until she met Mark, a little after her seventeenth birthday and, as far as Janet's aware, she never slept with anyone else.

When the sexual attention got out of hand, Sara put a stop to it in a way that won a great deal of disapproval from her classmates. It happened like this.

It had started as a game of chase years before at primary school. The old story—the boys chase the girls and rough them up or put their hands under their clothes. The game had died down at high school, when people didn't know each other so well, but a small group of boys and girls had started it up again sometime in Year 8. They were good friends, all five of them, and spent time together out of school as well as in it. The three boys would pounce on one of the girls, drag her into the boys' cloakroom, and have a quick grope with much shrieking and howls of laughter.

The girls enjoyed it as much as the boys; but there's a fine line between rough play and bullying, and another again between bullying and sexual assault. It wasn't quite childish anymore and it wasn't just chase. Once or twice the boys tried it on someone else and just about got away with it. Their fatal mistake was trying it with Sara.

Sara was friendly with these boys—not close, just friendly. She was the most desirable girl in the school and it's a sign that more than fun or curiosity was involved that they tried it on with her. One day, as she was walking with her past the cloakrooms, they pounced, dragged her off out of sight, and rummaged inside her clothes.

Janet was standing outside with another girl when it happened. She stood and listened to the boys grunting with laughter and Sara's shrieks of indignity, her heart beating furiously. It wasn't Sara she was worried about. The boys were going places they weren't welcome but Sara was in no danger—it wasn't real violence.

"They didn't ought to be doing that," said the girl next to her. Janet remembers thinking how right she was.

It was over in a few seconds. The boys came running out, giggling and smirking, and Sara came staggering after them tucking her shirt in. She walked up to Janet, whipped out her mobile phone, and dialed. She stared straight at them as she spoke.

"Police."

The corridor, which had been abuzz a moment before, suddenly froze.

"I've just been sexually assaulted in the boys' toilets at Stanford High School by a group of three boys. My name's Sara Carter, I have the boys here. I'm with some friends so it's safe. There are witnesses. Please send a squad car round as soon as possible."

She stabbed the phone and started another call.

"It was just a laugh," said one of them.

"You can't do that," said another.

"She wasn't even dialing," said the third.

She didn't answer them. "Hello. Can I have the news desk? My name is Sara Carter and I've just been sexually assaulted at Stanford High School. The police are on their way. Three boys. Yes. I'm only fourteen years old."

"Bollocks," said Barry. They were all looking really scared.

"It's a game, right?" said Joey.

Then she rang the Head. He was in a meeting at the time, so she spoke to his secretary. "Tell him to get his arse over here, the boys' toilets near the math block. This is Sara Carter and I've just been molested by some pupils from this school. The police and the press are already on their way."

She turned off her phone and stared at the boys.

"Watch me," she said. She crumpled up her face and began to cry.

"Oh my God," said Barry Jones. By the time the Head came running down the corridor with members of staff around him like a herd of rhinos, they knew it was real.

"It's them," said Sara. "They nearly raped me," she said—which wasn't true. "They touched me," she said, which was. Then she burst into tears. Above the shouting and cries of complaint, they could hear the squad car howling in through the school gates.

And all hell broke loose. The school, the press, the police, everything. The drama was played out in full public view, like so much of her life to come. The boys were arrested as the press cameras flashed; the Head granted a desperate interview while the police overacted for the film crew. The story, as Sara had realized at once, was a beauty. It hit the local TV news that evening and was all over the papers the next day: Gang of teenage boys attempt rape of girl, fourteen, in school toilets. Fabulous!

Sara split the school neatly in half. Some thought the boys had it coming, they'd practically committed assault. Others thought she was using the situation. The papers were all over the place; the school was obviously a pit of sexual perversity and abuse, as if that sort of thing and worse had been going on for ages and no one had done anything about it. It was an object lesson on the nature of press truth.

Gradually, however, the hysteria died down; a consensus emerged. The boys were simply very immature. They needed to be taught a lesson, but a court case wasn't really it. Pressure built up on Sara. A number of people tried to get her to drop charges, including Teresa Dickinson, one of the original two girls who were friends with the boys.

"They were just mucking around, you know that," she said.

"I turned a bunch of potential rapists into decent citizens, that's all I know," replied Sara. "No one gets to touch me unless I want them to—so tell that to your friends. And I've got plenty more where that came from."

In the end, though, she did drop the charges. There was talk of expulsion, but the boys got away with a suspension for the rest of the term. Just as Sara said, they never did anything like that again. And they weren't the only ones. The school did actually have a problem—not quite as abusive as the press made out, but there was bullying going on. It was big against little, strong against weak, the tough against the delicate in that place, and had been for ages. The staff had turned a blind eye to a lot of it—some of them joined in—but now, with the world's eyes on them and their mistakes and failings reported in a suspicious press, they did something about it. They had no choice. Unfair she had been maybe, but Sara put an end to a lot of tears and fears by her action.

That was her. Whatever she did, she did it full on and only started thinking about it afterward.

As Sara grew older, she developed fabulous ambitions. Janet had no doubt that Sara would follow her star and that she, Janet, could never go with her to such distant places. But although the two girls were developing in different directions, they somehow never grew apart. Right up to the end, they loved one another like sisters.

Sara had been taking lessons at the Stagecoach performance school for years, but by the age of twelve she was already saying that she was going to become famous for being herself rather than for any skills she might cultivate. At the same time, the question of exactly *who* she was became an issue. As a child, Sara had always enjoyed games of pretense, role plays, that sort of thing. But as she got older, instead of dropping them as most people do, she incorporated them more and more into her daily behavior, to the point where it became difficult to separate what was real from what was make-believe.

It began with accents. She'd pick up on an accent and speak it for days on end. She'd turn up on Monday morning in Irish, or Scots or with a faint Japanese accent, and that was her for the week. But it was more than that; the voices developed lives of their own. They became new people. Often they would have completely different tastes from Sara herself. Janet recalls characters who loved things Sara always hated, like red meat stewed in red wine, scraps with her fish and chips, or T-shirts that hung down to her hips.

Janet found it bewildering. Sometimes she didn't like the new girls, but mostly she fell head over heels in love with them, just as she had with Sara herself. Then—pop!—she'd wake up one morning and they'd be gone. It used to spook her out.

Once, Sara was a Filipino girl for three weeks nonstop. Her name was Maria and she was twenty years old. She'd joined a marriage club back in the Philippines to find a western husband, and her parents had got her to marry an older man who'd brought her back to live in England. Now she had to get a job and send back money and support the whole family; but she wanted to get some education first. Her husband was forty-five years old, and because he was a big cheese in the civil service he was able to pull a few strings. That's how her passport said she was a fifteen-year-old English girl who was entitled to a free education instead of a twenty-year-old Filippino girl who wasn't. Maria was having to pretend all the time that she was English. She swore Janet to secrecy. She was prepared to do anything to get an education and look after her family. She said her husband was really kinky, hinting mysteriously at any number of weird sexual things she had to do, without ever specifying them. She told Janet and her other friends that they were never to go with an older man because they were all pervs. But they all thought, because Maria was so innocent, it was probably something actually really rather normal; but no one ever liked to ask.

Maria stayed for three weeks and then disappeared, like all the others before her. Janet was mortified. She swore that while she was being Maria, Sara actually started to look Filipino.

"She had Filipino eyes, I swear it," said Janet. "It killed me. I really missed her. I couldn't believe I was so upset, but that's how I felt. I made her do Maria one more time so she could say good-bye to me—I couldn't bear it that she'd just gone. We even worked out a happy ending for her, where she left her husband and found a lovely Filipino boy who took her away to live in America and really respected her."

As well as becoming other people, Sara, at the age of

fourteen, began to have visions. Ghosts, apparitions, voices. She never said much about that, even to Janet, and Janet was never sure how real they were either. Sara once claimed that she had seen Maria walking around her bedroom packing up her clothes.

"Freaky!" said Janet. "What was that about? Seeing your own inventions as ghosts after you've just killed them off!"

There are one or two other characteristics of Sara's that must be mentioned here, since they have an important bearing on what happened later on. One is Sara's reputed anorexia. Anorexia is a word much bandied about these days, in an age where thinness and beauty are more or less the same thing. Sara was never a lollipop-girl, never in any danger of starving herself to death, but she did feel fat—always, throughout her life, no matter how slim she really was. She was permanently several kilos overweight, no matter what her weight actually was, permanently on a diet that she was never able to stick to, and permanently disgusted with her own perceived weakness—in short, she felt permanently ugly. The briefest glance at any photograph would tell anyone else that none of this was true.

At the same time that this incipient anorexia became apparent, her desire for cosmetic surgery developed as well. It would seem that both urges had the same psychological root. As, perhaps, did one other characteristic.

It's this: Sara had accidents. That would come as a surprise to many people who knew her, since she had tremendous grace and precision in her movements. People describe her as moving like a dancer just when making a cup of tea or leaning across to listen to someone speak. But she had accidents—not with things, but with herself. She spilled hot drinks down her front on several occasions, and had to be treated for burns. By the time she was seventeen, she had broken her arms and legs no less than four times, each time by falling down the stairs. Another time, she dropped a brick on her foot the day before she was due to enter the final of a dance competition, and spent the next two months in a cast, hobbling round on crutches.

These accidents have come under much suspicion. The suggestion is that Sara engineered them herself; in other words, that she was self-harming. It is a charge that she always denied, but as many people have pointed out, Sara saying that something was true or false doesn't always mean much at all.

It was one such accident, incurred just after she split up with Mark, that took her into the hospital where she first met Jonathon Heat.

about the author

Melvin Burgess is justly regarded as the godfather of young adult fiction in the UK. Since winning the Carnegie Medal for *Junk*, the seminal teen drugs and love novel, he has produced a body of work both challenging and thrilling. His books have been adapted for stage, television, and cinema and are widely translated. Most recently *Lady: My Life as a Bitch* and *Doing It* have put him in the public eye, but *Bloodtide* is considered by many to be his masterpiece. *Bloodsong*, which stands as a bold and brilliant novel in its own right, is a worthy successor.

FIND YOUR EDGE WITH THESE STARTLING AND STRIKING BOOKS—ALL FROM FIRST-TIME NOVELISTS.

JASON MYERS

AMANDA MARRONE

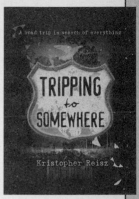

KRISTOPHER REISZ

Gritty. Electrifying. Real.

ALLISON VAN DIEPEN

KRISTEN TRACY

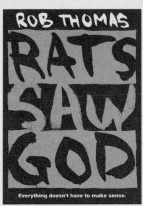

UGLIES
SCOTT WESTERFELD

Everybody gets to be supermodel gorgeous. What could be wrong with that?

In this futuristic world, all children are born "uglies," or freaks. But on their sixteenth birthdays they are given extreme makeovers and turned "pretty." Then their whole lives change. . .

PRAISE FOR *UGLIES*:

★ "An exciting series. . . . The awesome ending thrills with potential." —*Kirkus Reviews*

★ "Ingenious . . . high-concept YA fiction that has wide appeal." —*Booklist*

★ "Highly readable with a convincing plot that incorporates futuristic technologies and a disturbing commentary on our current public policies. Fortunately, the cliff-hanger ending promises a sequel." —*School Library Journal*

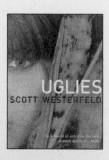

PUBLISHED BY SIMON PULSE